FATAL REACTION

TOM ALLAN
FATAL
REACTION

NORTH OF SCOTLAND
NEWSPAPERS
Wick, Caithness, Scotland

NORTH OF SCOTLAND
NEWSPAPERS
42 Union Street, Wick, Caithness, Scotland.

Published by
NORTH OF SCOTLAND
NEWSPAPERS

ISBN I 871704 14 6

Typeset in 10½/12 New Century Schoolbook by
North of Scotland Newspapers, Wick,
Caithness, Scotland.

Cover Illustration – Chris Ryley

ACKNOWLEDGMENTS

I wish to record my thanks to those of my friends who contributed specialist knowledge in areas where my own was sadly lacking. I am also indebted to staff at Glasgow Airport, Highland Regional Council Archaeology, Wick Airport and Wick Library for their expertise and willingness to share it.

Over the years I have drawn on a wide range of monographs and reference books for technical information, and from numerous articles published in New Scientist, Atom and Janes. The UKAEA's own excellent publicity materials have been most informative. In no way can I attribute factual inaccuracies in the text to any of these sources. The rest is pure fiction.

With special thanks to John Ritchie, Jean MacLennan and, above all, Mary Fisher for her invaluable assistance with the manuscript in its final stages.

Tom Allan was born in Glasgow in 1945 and educated at Aberdeen University. After spells of working in Alberta, Dumfries and Fraserburgh, he moved to Caithness in 1974. He hopes to be able to remain there! He is a member of the Society of Authors, with some previously published educational materials; and is currently working on a historical novel set in the Viking period.

To the finest friends a man has ever been blessed with.
Thanks for your sustenance over the years.

Contents

Part One

1

Lest Thou Be Consumed

THE driver of the silver grey Bentley cursed his way through the mid-morning mayhem of Mayfair.

'Should've stayed in Aberdeen, Davie. None of this fuckin' hassle,' he snarled at the shoal of cars inching their way along the narrow stream which flowed out from Berkeley Square towards Chesterfield Hill.

'Aye, man. Union Street's a dawdle compared to this right enough, Sander. Mind you, even it took a bit of getting used to after the Broch, did it no'?'

Alexander Buchan mellowed towards the minnows flitting around him in the narrow maze of streets as he thought of their lowly origins as redundant 'Toolies', as the natives of the Aberdeenshire fishing port of Fraserburgh affectionately, if rather disparagingly, referred to the employees of the local Toolworks Company. Like many a provincial enterprise with a limited UK market for their products, the Fraserburgh pneumatic compressor manufacturers had never recovered from the disastrous three-day week in 1971-72 as the Tory Premier Edward Heath had struggled against a crippling miners' strike which was destined to bring down Heath, his party and damn near the whole country with them. The Toolies had avoided going to the wall completely; but it had been forced to shed around half its workforce.

The publicans had had a field day as dozens of men with never a hope of another day's work in their lives squandered their severance payments in a massive, short-sighted binge which did nothing to brighten their prospects for the future, let alone soften the starkness of the present.

But not so Buchan and his mate Dave Stronach.

The Tuesday after they had been paid off, they went down to the Football Social Club as usual for a couple of pints and a few games of pool, a throw at the arrows, and a 50 pence syndicated assault on the bandit.

'Typical. Not even a hold, man.'

'The way our luck's been going lately you surely don't expect to win the jackpot, do you Sander?' asked Dave as the machine gobbled up their last tenpence piece. A melon, a grape, a cherry and a laughing dog clicked into place to the accompaniment of an infuriating synthesised leitmotif.

'Too true, Davie. Too true, Davie.' Alexander mimicked the gaming machine's metallic melody and slowly shook his head as he placed his pint on the beermat which offered him a free holiday in Sweden.

'Might've fuckin' known,' he muttered as he turned over the piece of cardboard. The closing date for the competition was just over three years ago.

'One thing's for sure, though, Davie. There's no way I'm going under to Joe Gormless or Ted Teeth the way those silly buggers are over there.' Sander nodded towards a few of their former workmates who were slobbering all over each other as the drink they had been guzzling since 4.30 in the afternoon was beginning to make a mockery of them. 'No way.'

'I'd like to think that about myself as well, Sander; but I'm not so sure. There are no other light engineering jobs around here to turn to. Everyone from the ropeworks to the ice factory are cuttin' back. Even the two fish factories are payin' folk off now that the boats can't afford the diesel to put out to sea.'

'Aye, and even if they could, those continental cunts from the Common Market are taking all our fish from right under our noses,' added Sander.

'So what's left for us then, Sander?'

'Oil, man. Oil.'

'Oil?' Dave was incredulous. 'We couldn't even break into the castor oil business with our miserable thousand quid each.'

'Don't be daft. I'm not talking about going prospecting, building rigs or setting up in the helicopter charter business.'

'What are you thinkin' of then, pal?'

'Oh, something much more modest, Davie, something much more modest.'

'Like what then?'

'I've been thinking this over for a few months now, Davie. With the discoveries of so much oil in the North Sea this whole north-eastern area of Scotland is going to be booming into the '90s.'

'There's not much sign of it here in the Broch, Sander.'

'Admittedly. That's because of our position facing north into the Moray Firth. But look what's happening already in Peterhead. It's only eighteen miles away, but it's facing straight out into the open sea. It's in an ideal position to become a major supply base for the rigs. And there's talk of starting a refinery once work is finished on the natural gas plant at St. Fergus.

'Anyway,' Sander continued, 'that's not what I'm interested in. I'm looking to Aberdeen for the future.'

'Aberdeen? I thought you were plannin' something modest. Aberdeen?' He shook his head.

'Uh huh. Aberdeen. There are signs already that it'll rival Dallas in a few years time. Didn't you read the latest planning applications in the P & J last week?'

'Who reads the Press and Journal, Sander? Unless you want a cheap car.'

'Away with ye, man. There's nothing wrong with it. It's a grand provincial paper.'

'Provincial? You mean parochial, don't you?'

'Aw, come on. You're not going to mention the bloody Titanic again, are you?'

'And why not? They say it's a true story: North-East Man Lost At Sea!'

'Och aye. But it's come a long way since then, Davie. I tell you, it's a damn sight better than yon rag of a thing you read anyway. Or goggle at, I should say.'

'Aye. Did you see that cracker on page three today? What a

pair of . . . .'

'You say that every day. But are you not interested in my proposition?'

'Hell, man. What's the hurry? It's not as if we have to get up for work in the mornin'. More's the pity,' Dave added with a gloomy sigh.

'But we could have to, David. If we wanted to.'

'Oh aye. I'd forgotten. Aberdeen. Wait till I get another couple of pints.'

'Not for me, Davie. I've had enough.'

'Well, you'll take a dram then?'

'I could be persuaded. Aye. A dram. Make it an Old Pulteney,' Sander grinned. 'But just a wee droppie of water in it, mind.'

'Right on, skipper. Whatever you say.'

When Dave returned with the pint and nip, Sander wasted no time in airing his scheme.

'Like I was saying, Davie. There are a dozen firms lining up to come into Aberdeen.'

'No doubt, Alexander. But they'll either be looking for highly skilled blokes or pen-pushers for the office. We come into neither category.'

'Granted. But hear me out, for godsake, man.'

'OK, OK. On ye go.'

'There's one thing they'll all have in common.'

'Aye!' Dave butted in again with a grin. 'Company houses with bits of skirt in them at Bucksburn.'

'Be serious. Apart from that.' Sander chuckled too. 'They'll all have offices or factories.'

'God. You should be Brain of Britain old son. Offices and factories,' he sang mockingly. 'Who would have guessed? And what fucking good is that going to do us?'

'A lot of fucking good if we're prepared to take a risk with our redundancy payments. Listen, Davie.' Sander leaned over the table and whispered conspiratorially, 'I'm really on to something.' He gripped his mate's forearm. 'There's builders, and suppliers and job agencies galore in Aberdeen. But there's a gap waiting to be filled. All of these premises are going to need cleaners when they're constructed, equipped and staffed. That's where we come in, Davie.'

'Cleaners?' Dave nearly exploded. 'There's cleaners galore in Aberdeen, man. Anyway there's no way I'm going to work as a cleaner. I'd rather stay on the dole.'

'Who's talking about being a cleaner? Though there's nothing wrong with that,' Sander added, mindful of the fact that his mother worked a couple of mornings a week for one of the local doctors. 'I'm talking about employing cleaners. Setting up an agency.'

'But like I said, Sander. There's hundreds of cleaners in a city the size of Aberdeen. There's no room for any more.'

'I never said there was, Davie. But there's no organisation. I tell you. I've checked it out. None of the employment agencies have any cleaners on their books.'

Sander shook his friend's arm vigorously.

'There's an opportunity here for us, Davie. All we need is an old minibus and some headed paper. We contact the new firms as they get set up. Quote them for the job. They'll be delighted not having to bother arranging such a menial matter. We'll do it all for them. Right down to supplying the buckets, mops and Handy Andy. We get a few women together. Bus them from site to site. Offer them regular jobs instead of the usual hour or so a day. It's bound to catch on.'

And catch on it did. To an extent neither of them dreamed was possible. The only hiccup had been in their first year of business. Dave still had six months of a drink-driving ban to serve and Sander had to do all the driving around in their old fifteen-seater Ford Transit, which they had conned from a pompous local headmaster. Sander, however, had let the MOT expire by a couple of months. The two bald tyres, leaking exhaust and spongy brakes had been enough to land him in court facing a possible ban after he had been caught belting down North Anderson Drive at 55mph to drop off a squad of chattering chars. A ban would have killed their enterprise stone dead right there and then. Sander had gone before the sheriff and literally cried. Tears had streamed down his cheeks as he pleaded his own case and pointed out how many poor families depended on his giving employment to their mothers. It was a touching performance. And it worked. An endorsement and a £150 fine.

Within seven years Sander and Dave were well on the way to

a million. A pleasant office overlooked Golden Square just off Union Street. They commuted in from Banchory on Royal Deeside in their BMW and Lotus. Their cleaners were ferried around the 270 businesses on their books by a strictly timetabled trio of brand new Transits. The two boys from the Broch began living the good life. Travelling to all of Aberdeen's many away games on the continent. Golfing at Gleneagles and Muirfield in the summer and in the Algarve in winter.

'And we had to give up all that and come down to this fucking madhouse,' said Sander as he turned onto Chesterfield Hill and pulled up without signalling outside No. 172. 'We must be crazy.'

'Once we've made another million we can go into semi-retirement up north again,' laughed Dave. 'Though it's not going to be easy with all the competition down here.'

'Too true. And it looks as if we might be losing another contract,' Sander nodded up towards the wide open windows four storeys above.

'Probably. It must be bad for Elsie and her squad to have downed tools till we came over ourselves. There's not much can put that bunch off their stride.'

But put off their stride they certainly had been.

'Look 'ere, matey. 'Ere's no way me and the girls can sort out this ol' mess. No way.'

One glance around verified Elsie's conclusion for Sander and Dave.

'Fuckin' hell!' Sander exhaled, sotto voce. 'This is no' real, Davie. Did you ever see the likes in your life?'

Dave hadn't. Despite the through draft from the open door and windows, the sweet smell of marijuana and opium lingered still. Dave inhaled deeply with some satisfaction and appreciation.

'Good stuff! There's been one helluva do in here alright, Sander.' Dave shook his head; but couldn't suppress a grin of admiration for the perpetrators of such conspicuous hedonism.

'It's no laughing matter, mate,' said Elsie. 'You're not the buggers as 'as to clean this little lot up. There's no way, I tell you. Look at this,' she dragged Dave by the sleeve through the mass of empty bottles and cans. 'This carpet's had it with booze and puke. It's stinking. And some dirty dog's pissed in

14

the corner here – look at the wallpaper peeling off! Pigs.'

It really was a scene of devastation. Piles of ash were everywhere. There were burn marks in the carpet and curtains where joints had been stubbed out. An expensive velvet sofa was sodden with still sticky semen where one of the revellers, high on hash and Pernod, had given herself to every man in the room who had been interested. Her tally for the night would have made the infamous Messalina herself sick with envy.

'Listen, my loves,' said Sander, shrugging his shoulders, 'we've just got to make some sort of effort. Do your best anyway,' he trailed off.

'OK, guv. We will,' nodded Elsie. 'But I'd love to get me 'ands on the pig wot was responsible for this.'

2

And Abraham Begat

ELSIE the char's wish was not to be granted.

The object of her fury was putting twenty-three miles per minute between himself and the scene of his final thrash, reclining in pseudo-oriental splendour aboard Concorde en route for Bahrain. He washed down the last of the smoked quail with a long draught of the superb 1976 Château Gruaud-Larose Bordeaux, declined the cheeses and savoured a fresh salad based on his favourite kiwi fruit.

This is the way to travel, reflected Taherali el-Fazzah. Whispering through the deep purple stratosphere at Mach 2 on the very edge of space; the curve of the earth's surface eleven miles below as surreal as the superbly shaped aerodynamic wing of the plane itself.

It was the first time, despite the massive wealth at his disposal, that Taherali had flown Concorde. When he had enrolled at the London School of Economics four years previously British Airways had been undergoing a difficult phase in their managerial and operational structure.

Savage staffing cutbacks – shedding the fat, as their leading independent rival, British Caledonian, had put it – combined with aggresive marketing and advertising involving such gimmicks as putting Concorde onto the London-Glasgow shuttle, and giving free travel to top names in the world of showbusiness, had worked wonders for the state-owned corporation. British Airways had emerged as the most profitable of all the international carriers affiliated to IATA, the governing body of the world's airlines, and the Thatcher government could proceed with its plans for privatisation on the basis of this prosperity.

The main bonus of this new-found vigour and efficiency as far as Taherali was concerned was the restoration of the Gulf route which had been withdrawn for four or five years in an effort to concentrate Concorde on the more lucrative North American market.

Like the other sixty-seven passengers on board that day, Taherali was totally unaware that he was flying in a machine which had not only lain idle for five years, but which had been used as a sort of vital organ bank for spare part surgery for the other six fully operational aircraft in the Concorde fleet. Not that there was any cause for concern. Over £3m had been spent on refurbishing this most complex of all passenger aircraft; and, like all Concordes, it was only allowed into the air for each flight after the most rigorous checks and maintenance routines imaginable from a team of dedicated engineers, technicians and flight crew stretching over a period of fifteen hours before take-off. Despite its incredible intricacy, from its massive Rolls-Royce Olympus 612 turbo jet engines and its computerised systems and navigational controls, to a body which has to withstand temperatures of 119 degrees Celsius and expansion of 8 to 10 inches, it was probably the safest machine ever to take to the skies. Even the final check list occupied the Captain, his First Officer and Flight Engineer for a full hour and a half immediately prior to flight clearance.

'I shouldn't really,' protested Taherali, half-heartedly raising his hand and shaking his head towards the smiling stewardess with the box of cigars and bottle of port.

'Oh, but they are much too good to miss, sir,' he was told in a throaty voice redolent with more than a hint of western promise.

And they were. The port was a superb Graham's and the cigars amongst the finest that Cuba produced.

Ah well, thought Taherali, this will be the last temptation I can give in to for quite some time.

'Very well, then, I shall. But just a drop of port, if you please.'

'Is that enough, sir?' The inflection and smile were both veneers, Taherali decided: the products of training school rather than of an innate warmth. Still, he would have invited her to his welcome party had the plane been flying in the opposite direction.

'Ample. Thank you very much.'

It was only just over half a normal measure, but Taherali was correct. It was sufficient, given the amount of alcohol still in his bloodstream from the revelries of the previous evening – his legal drinking party as he had wryly referred to it when doling out invitations to the many friends he had made in his four years at the London School of Economics studying for his master's degree in business management. Released from the restraints of even an enlightened Muslim upbringing, the youthful Taher, as his London friends knew him, had gorged himself on many of the forbidden fruits of his faith which were freely on offer in the most cosmopolitan capital city in the world. Even now, as Concorde idled through Egyptian airspace at the speed of a .303 bullet to avoid creating a sonic boom over the Pyramids before the massive Rolls-Royce engines doubled their output to streak down the Red Sea and over the Arabian Desert, tantalising images floated through Taherali's mind. There was no doubt about it: he had had himself a ball. And what a final thrash to end it all last night! At one point there must have been well over a hundred people in the small Mayfair flat.

Taherali hoped they had not done anything to endanger the lease on the property which he intended to maintain indefinitely. And, if they had, there was no real problem. He would just buy a flat instead. As the only son of the vastly wealthy Hanif el-Fazzah he could have bought the best in Belgravia had he so desired.

Forty minutes out of Bahrain Captain Jim Barnett began his steady descent and deceleration in preparation for landing. The curve of the Persian Gulf was just coming into view for the three man crew on the rather cramped flight deck.

'Re-heat off, sir,' announced Flight Engineer Frank Church,

flipping the appropriate switches before the plane resumed sub-sonic flight.

'What a sight, lads. Pity I was too old to be a cosmonaut.' Barnett nodded over towards the Gulf and the now clear outline of the Trucial States, as he still called them.

As Church retracted the transparent heatshield which was used to dissipate the searing heat in front of the cockpit at supersonic speeds Barnett handed over control of the plane to his First Officer.

'She's all yours now, Bill. Take good care of her,' he said, parodying the BA advertising motto.

Ex-Wing Commander William R S Mortimer heard this joke each and every time he was given the controls.

'Aye, aye, sir,' he chuckled back as he had done dozens of times before. Now in command of the most sophisticated civil aeroplane in the world Mortimer was glad that he had not gone back into the RAF. Bored with the administrative nature of the duties associated with the rank of Wing Commander he had been equally disenchanted with the endless shuttles between London and Glasgow on the Airbuses.

Then had come the opportunity to train for Concorde. He had almost packed that in when he was put back on the flight to Scotland, but fortunately BA did not maintain this particular charade for long. Then the Middle East route had been re-opened. He had found his niche.

Taherali could now see the Gulf of Oman and his home state of Dhubat from his window seat towards the back of the plane. The last wistful thoughts of London evaporated with the reality of returning home. Not that the reality was in any way undesirable. The el-Fazzahs had as much wealth as many a small nation at their personal disposal, and the connections which invariably accompany that kind of money. Taherali did not need to work, but his father had nevertheless obtained a top administrative post for him in his country's nuclear power station, the only one of its kind anywhere in the Arabian sub-continent. The younger el-Fazzah had gratefully accepted this opportunity to attain his own status rather than bask in the reflected glory of his father's. The job would certainly offer him prestige, if not power. Taherali only sought the attainable. He knew that real, unadulterated power – the raw power which only politics could provide – would never be his. A long-standing feud between his family and that of the Emir Hussan Rampuri would see to that.

Still, he reflected, a man could not have everything. And London was never more than four hours away.

Bill Mortimer effortlessly eased the Concorde down from its soaring heights far above the weather. The colours of the surrounding sky and the perspectives of the ground beneath gradually assumed those obtaining from a normal aircraft. Twenty minutes later Frank Church carried out the pilot's orders to lower the nose section of the plane as the airspeed dropped under 250 knots to aid visibility for landing. Concorde's shape and angle of final approach greatly increased drag as its speed fell. Because of this, automatic throttle was always held down to forty feet above the ground. Bill gently touched the rear wheels of the 177 ton superplane onto the runway at exactly 157 knots. A further 17 feet descent brought the nose section down.

The bedlam of Bahrain was swallowed in the 138 decibel roar of 240,000 brake horsepower thrown into reverse. As with every Concorde take-off and landing anywhere in the world the most blasé of airport personnel stopped and took notice in wonderment.

Taherali el-Fazzah breathed his customary sigh of relief as the plane did not catapult, explode and burst into flames.

Hanif el-Fazzah was a proud man; and justly so. It was this pride – not to be confused with conceit – which made him personally supervise the tricky process of manoeuvering his 168 foot luxury yacht through the maze of sand bars which had been built up over the centuries at the entrance to the only harbour of any significance on the coast of Dhubat. His professional crew was more than capable of carrying out the operation, especially as the Elvira was equipped with the most up-to-date electronic navigational systems which money could buy. El-Fazzah in no way lacked confidence in his hand-picked crew, all of whom had trained for years with the British and

Australians and were amongst the best in their field. He simply liked, as many successful elderly men do, to show his men that he knew the ropes as well as they did. He enjoyed being in command. As a boy and young man his shallow-draughted dhow had hardly given the sandbars a second's thought, even with the heaviest possible haul of oysters or mullet. Now in his early sixties, and with around $20m invested in one pleasure craft, he was not about to strand himself while still in sight of home. He concentrated all of his considerable skills and local knowledge on the task in hand.

Twenty minutes later the Elvira, back in the hands of Captain Youmah, was set on a course almost due north which would take her parallel to, but a safe distance from, the coast of Oman, hence through the Strait of Hormuz into the Persian Gulf to arrive in Bahrain some twenty hours later. That would mean a wait of no more than four hours before his son's arrival from London – ample time to take care of the other matter which had brought el-Fazzah in person from his luxurious fastness in Dhubat.

El-Fazzah was glad of this time at sea. Time for calm reflection and reassurance. Allah knew how tense he was. The strain of the past few months would have shown on a man half his age. And the effect of the next few weeks were incalculable. So many questions nagged away at him. His immediate family he could trust with his life. But who else? Could there be a traitor amongst them whose betrayal would not only cause them to forfeit that which they now possessed, but would also cost them their lives? Would all continue to go well? Or would there be some crucial oversight in his faction's plans to infiltrate the Palace Guard, the army and security forces, and the top echelons of the civil service? He desperately needed to share the burden of his thoughts with someone; but how much of all this should be revealed to his son, Taherali, who was dearer to him than all he already possessed or hoped to achieve? It is always difficult for fathers to really know their sons at the best of times. Where would the young man's sympathies lie? To what extent would he share his father's concerns and condone his actions? Or had his four years in London, with only the occasional visit home, changed him beyond measure?

The warm fecund waters of the Persian Gulf had always been good to Hanif. In his youth, when the land was barren and worthless, its shallow coastal waters had prospered him with pearls, whilst its deeper reaches had filled his nets to bursting with shard, seer, mullet, sardines and dozens of other varieties of fish for him to dry and sell in the local markets. In time immemorial it had laid down the primitive life forms which were to become the basis of his present wealth in oil. And now its deep azure surface, broken only by the bubbly champagne wake of the Elvira, seemed to reflect the serenity of the Only One, and gave the old man the answers he was looking for. By the time Manama came into sight the following morning el-Fazzah was utterly refreshed and at peace with himself. He was looking forward eagerly to the reunion with his son; but, before that, he had a matter of business to attend to.

Any directory of the world's richest people would have to include Hanif el-Fazzah in its top dozen or so. The oil revenues which had catapulted him into riches beyond comprehension almost overnight had not transformed him into one of the world's idle rich. For a man of lesser character the temptation to luxuriate in his good fortune would have been irresistible. The work ethic, however, is not the preserve of puritanical protestantism, as some tunnel-visioned historians would have us believe. El-Fazzah had always used the time and energies he believed God had given him to the best of his ability. He had taken the oil bonanza entirely in his stride as a not entirely un-deserved gift and blessing from on high, and had immediately put it to work for himself. Within a few years he had concluded deals in the major stock exchanges in Europe, America and the Far East, building up a diversified base in property, commodities and service industries which would secure his family's fortune well beyond the day when the wells ran dry.

El-Fazzah had worked tirelessly in the midde years of his life, rising above severe personal and political difficulties to his present status. As he became older, and his family grew up, his mind turned increasingly to politics, and to the problems facing his country.

He did not neglect his business interests; but simply spent less of his time in quotidien concerns and delegated increasingly to people he could trust. He had accrued sufficient acumen over the years and possessed the natural abilities to lead and command respect, that he could afford to do this with confidence, secure in his own judgements and the loyalties of those nearest him. On no-one did he depend more than on his niece Shamin. He was looking forward, as always, to meeting her in Bahrain that morning.

Shamin el-Fazzah was the brightest jewel in her uncle Hanif's sparkling dynasty. He was inordinately fond and indulgent with his son Taherali; but for the only daughter of his revered elder brother, he felt something special. It was not so much her striking resemblance to his wife, who, despite the finest of care in London's Harley Street, had died giving birth to their son, that endeared Shamin to him. No-one could ever replace his beloved Ayosha. He quite simply adored his niece for being herself, and not for being the daughter he would have given anything to have had. Shamin had only been six years of age when her parents had been murdered – beaten to death by a group of thugs armed with bamboo staves on the orders of the Emir Hussan Rampuri. She was taken into the household of her uncle Hanif, the oldest of the three remaining brothers, and by custom, indeed by law, now the head of the family. He and Ayosha, who had been childless in eight years of marriage, had almost smothered little Shamin with their love, so eager were they to compensate for the terrible tragedy in her young life. It was easier for the adults to cope with their grief – they could, after a while, articulate their feelings and so comfort each other. But what of the poor little one, they often thought. What does she feel?

They worried that she never even spoke of her mother and father. What confusion and anguish was she bottling up inside? They looked anxiously for signs of alienation, withdrawal, or other disturbed behaviour from the little girl; and to their amazement found none. In her childish way, and in a manner beyond the realms of adult comprehension, the six-year-old had accepted her changed circumstances and was quietly getting on with her life. Her pre-conceptual mind did not question the will of Allah, did not hark back to happier times or dwell depressingly on what might have been, nor did it take any thought for the morrow.

The sheikhdoms of the Persian Gulf, the Islamic monarchies of Saudi Arabia and, until the republican revolution of 1962, Yemen, had been steeped for centuries in the repressive sway of the Koran and age-old desert tradition. Nowhere were the twin influences more insidious and reactionary than in their teachings on the status of women. The scriptures wrote that women should not participate in education, civic or professional affairs; that they should live in seclusion, their faces hidden under veils; that the will of Allah, the only true God, ordained them to household duties, childbearing and subservience to their husbands. 'No man is less than any woman' is one of the most used Arab proverbs.

The rigours of Bedouin nomadism, where the very existence of a people was dependent on how successful a response they made each day to the cruel challenges of their harsh environment, with its rigid authoritarianism, summary forms of justice and retribution and unquestioning fatalism, imposed further restrictions on the female chattels. The teachings of the Prophet Mohammed were thus welcomed as the embodiment of their everyday austerity. Submission to the will of God came naturally and easily to people who for thousands of years had been forced to submit to the will of nature in order to survive in one of the most inhospitable regions on earth.

As the centuries advanced and the militancy of Islam spread into a vast empire brilliantly chronicled by the great medieval Maghrebi historian Ibn Khaldun, the fusion of church and state into the theocracies of the Arabian sub-continent became complete. With the advent of the rabid puritanism of the 18th century Wahabi sect, which pronounced all music, imagery, tobacco and alcohol anathema, and which preached the virtual imprisonment of women, female subjugation was total. Unwavering codes of moral, social, religious and political conduct were mercilessly enacted by a judiciary composed exclusively of the Moslem hierarchy. While Britain swung through the 1960s, with mini-skirts, marijuana, pop music and promiscuity, members of the Society for the Promotion of Virtue and Prevention of Evil patrolled the streets of Arabian cities beating up unveiled women with their barbaric bamboo staves, knocking cigarettes out of the mouths of foreigners, thrashing little boys for whistling and smashing transistor radios. And woe betide any woman taken in adultery, or whose reputation was even sullied by local gossip. Ritual stonings, beatings and drownings were – and still are in some remote fastnesses – everyday occurrences; as often as not carried out by members of the unfortunate girls' own families.

Fortunately for the young Shamin, and others, the tail of the wind of change, which the British Prime Minister Harold MacMillan had spoken of as blowing over the African continent in the late 1950s and early '60s, created a slight turbulence over Arabia. In 1963, Prince Faisal ordered the building of Saudi Arabia's first-ever girls school in the remote desert town of Buraida. It opened after much protest, persuasion and, ultimately, the use of troops to enforce the Prince's wishes. From then on, girls who could read and write were no longer regarded as outcasts and, with the process of liberalisation which is the natural concomitant of education, many of the old barriers to women's liberation were being gradually dismantled throughout the sub-continent.

Dhubat was no exception; although progress took some bizarre forms. An adulteress who in years gone by would have been stoned to death by a jeering, self-righteous mob, as often as not containing the very men who had taken advantage of her, was now buried to her head in a pit to await the Mercedes tipper truck unloading its couple of tons of rocks onto her. Thieves could now choose to have their hands surgically removed rather than chopped off with a rusty old blade – an agonising decision to take, as a painless anaesthetised operation is irreversible, whereas a barbaric hacking holds out the remote hope of micro-surgery repair by the self-same surgeons wearing their Hippocratic hats.

Fortunately, also, for Shamin, her uncle Hanif was amongst the less reactionary members of his generation. He was a devout man, but sufficiently rational and liberal to realise that the Holy Scriptures could not have foreseen everything and did not have to be taken literally. A man of high principles himself, he nevertheless possessed enough tolerance to allow others, within reason, to arrive at their own value judgements as long as these did not degenerate into the permissiveness and decadence of the West, and as long as the precepts of the Koran were adhered to. He genuinely welcomed the progress his country was making in living standards, and determined that his own family, which had always enjoyed prestige, would now benefit from their new-found wealth in oil. With the death of his wife, Ayosha, two years after the little Shamin had been taken into their home, and the birth of his son, Taherali, Hanif el-Fazzah spared nothing in terms of time and money to ensure the welfare of his son and niece. They received the finest of elementary education from private Scottish tutors; the best boarding school provision in England; and their pick of British and American Universities.

Shamin had chosen Cambridge University for her higher education. Unlike some members of the British Royal family she more than met the academic entry requirements. Study came easily to her; but she had difficulty in making up her mind what to specialise in. As a result, though she was capable of much more, she graduated with a very average ordinary class degree which contained elements of the biological sciences which had appealed to her in the first year of her course, but was mainly made up of units in Moral Philosophy and Ancient History, subjects into which she had matured as she became more aware of herself as a person. Like her cousin Taherali, she enjoyed these formative years of study and play in England. She also made many contacts which were to prove invaluable over the years ahead.

With no thoughts of her own of an early marriage, and with Hanif in his wisdom not pressurising her into an unwanted arrangement, the world was at Shamin's feet. She could have lived and worked anywhere. But it pleased her, after a year's course in business management in Basel, to join her uncle's organisation. And Hanif was immensely gratified when

Shamin asked to be taken into the management of his affairs.

In the course of fifteen months of frenetic activity, spending weeks on end being briefed by the top management personnel throughout the world-wide tentacles of the business, Shamin absorbed a vast store of knowledge about Consolidated Holdings Inc., the name through which her uncle operated from his near anonymity in Dhubat. Her particular forte, it had quickly become apparent, was in what was euphemistically called data gathering and analysis, and she became Hanif's chief executive in charge of this division six months after she finished training. Not to put too fine a point on it, she was her uncle's top industrial spy.

In this respect, el-Fazzah's financial empire was no different from any other in whatever part of the world. Industrial espionage is as essential to the continued wellbeing of the multinational corporation as its more sinister and infinitely more glamorous counterpart is to the nation-state. Without it there would be millions lost in blind alleys of research; potential markets would never be tapped because competitors had monopolised them through the world's patent systems; and investments in ailing sectors would be continued beyond the point where profits were maximised and diminishing returns set in. Currency speculation, in which all of the big companies indulged, would not pay such handsome dividends without advance warnings of governments' intentions from politicians and civil servants. The would-be apologist could write a treatise on its advantages and importance.

There is also more than motivation in common between industrial espionage and its more publicised counterpart. Both forms of spying employ the same methods of gaining their information: a few highly specialised operatives who bribe, blackmail, or even lovingly cajole those with something to gain or hide into helping them. They utilise similar devices where necessary: micro-photography, electronic surveillance, computer tapping, and whatever raw or subtle violence is called for in the circumstances. And they share similar rewards for success: mainly in the form of currency deposits in numbered accounts in Switzerland, Luxembourg, Cayman, or any other country which has abdicated its moral and ethical conscience to grow fat behind a veneer of fiscal respectability on the largely illicit proceeds of the world's profiteers. And they pay the same penalties for failure: heavy fines or compensation orders in the courts; prosecution and lengthy jail sentences, under the Official Secrets Act or its equivalent if government departments are involved; or retribution of a more swift and summary nature at the hands of the opposition before the processes of law are involved.

A spy is a spy is a spy.

Shamin was a spy.

The latest information she passed on to el-Fazzah on the morning of his arrival in Bahrain reassured him that his cause was not only just, but absolutely essential to the wellbeing of his country. He must see it through whatever the cost.

That evening Shamin dined and stayed aboard her uncle's yacht.

3

The Promised Land

THE family chauffeur was most apologetic as he ushered Taherali into the capacious rear seat of the hired Mercury Monarch. Not quite up to the thoroughbreds he was used to handling in Dhubat. Still, it whisked them in most people's idea of luxury the eleven or so kilometres from the airport to the marina where the Elvira was moored.

Normally the Elvira took pride of place wherever she was moored. But not today. Magnificent though she was, her former owner's latest $115 million extravaganza most definitely overshadowed her on this occasion. It was without doubt the largest, most sophisticated and most ostentatiously vulgar private yacht to be found anywhere in the world. Satellite communication, surface-to-air missiles, underwater video scanners, helicopter landing pads, right down to the 24-carat solid gold fitments in every part of the ship exuded the enormous wealth and paranoid preoccupation with security of Hassan Shakhbut, the wealthiest man on the planet.

Taherali never even glanced at it.

'It is a joy to see you again, your Excellency,' he was told by the Elvira's master.

'Thank you, Captain Youmah. It is good to be back.' Taherali decided to put London behind him and adopt an entirely positive attitude towards his homecoming.

'And my father? He is well?'

'As you will soon see, sir. His Excellency should be aboard very shortly.'

'My father is here in Bahrain?' Taherali was genuinely surprised and somewhat flattered. His father was no longer young and had much to see to in Dhubat. It was indeed an honour that he should take time off and make such a welcoming journey in person.

'But that is excellent news, Captain.'

'Meanwhile, you would like some refreshment, sir, after your journey?'

Taherali instantly reverted to the Islamic tradition.

'Some iced mint tea would be most welcome, Captain. You will join me, of course?'

Several hours out of Dhubat the younger el-Fazzah gradually became aware of the rhythmic drumming of water against the ship's hull as the Elvira scythed through the slight swell. Even at close on full throttle making around twenty-seven knots into the faint breeze, the silky turbo-charged engines were effectively silenced by the extensive sound dampening carefully designed into the yacht.

'A refreshing sleep?' His father's slightly sarcastic tone brought him round.

'Indeed, father. I am sorry to have been such a bore on this journey.'

Hanif could not suppress a grin.

'When I was your age, my son, I could not go out to sea often enough. I loved it, and still do. It was my life then. How times have changed.'

Taherali felt rather embarrassed about his earlier bout of seasickness shortly after the Elvira had left the sheltered waters of Bahrain. His father's chiding reminder about the relative capacities for endurance between the two generations did nothing to help.

'I was fine during the flight; it's just that I have not been on board a ship for some years now,' Taherali began defensively.

'Come, come, Taherali. It is of no concern. Have you not noticed how your father never travels by air?'

Taherali had; but the strongly inculcated Islamic respect for one's parents had prevented him from mentioning it.

'Now, why not come on deck for a while? You will find it most invigorating.'

Their conversation on the previous evening at the berth in Manama had been confined to personal and general topics with Shamin present. It had been over a year since all three had been together. There was much catching up to do; and all had been in an expansive mood. They had talked late into the night before Shamin, who was leaving early in the morning for Teheran, decided to turn in.

Now, however, as the Elvira veered slightly to the south-east, causing the coast of Qatar to vanish in the heat haze, Hanif el-Fazzah judged the moment had arrived to turn their conversation to more serious matters. The past twenty-four hours had removed his few remaining reservations: he would not waver in the weeks ahead. And, if his son was going to fulfil the key role which he envisaged for him, now was the time to take him fully into his confidence.

'The Elvira is quite something, father. You have come a long way from the dhows of your youth. Amazing craft. Unchanged for centuries, eh?'

'I cannot remember that far back, Taherali.' His father was pleased with this rare flash of humour. 'But, yes, the dhow is a rather special craft. Unfortunately,' he sighed, 'our country is not so unchanging.'

'But surely that cannot be a bad thing?' Taherali was prompted to say in deference to his fairly liberal upbringing.

'In many ways you are right, my son. Our country has prospered. Our babies no longer die unattended in infancy. Our elders no longer surrender to the sands in their old age. All this is to be rejoiced at. My unhappiness, however, is with more recent events.'

'You surprise me, father. Only last year when I was home on vacation everything seemed to be going so well. Our currency reserves were at an all-time high. We were the envy of the Middle East with our newly operational nuclear power station. Even the old feud between yourself and the Emir was virtually over.'

'I agreed we had prospered,' his father interrupted. 'But prosperity of the sort we have experienced in recent years must be tempered with firmness of leadership and government if moral degeneracy is to be avoided. Alas, Hussan Rampuri does not hold his people tightly enough in rein. Standards are falling. Crime, immorality, disrespect are all increasing. Prosperity, my son, has hastened the process of decay in our land.'

'If the history of past civilisations is anything to go by you have a point there, father.' Taherali recalled a quotation which he had memorised for a term examination from Gibbon, the chronicler of the decline and fall of the Roman Empire, who had declared that prosperity ripened the principle of decay.

'I am glad you agree, Taherali. Although, as you will see, even this prosperity itself is currently being endangered. Shamin confirmed yesterday morning when I met her in Bahrain. . . .'

So that is why you came in person, thought Taherali, uncharitably.

'. . . . that Rampuri is fully intent on a unilateral reduction of 50 per cent in oil prices in the near future if other members of OPEC do not cooperate with him in a general phased reduction in prices.'

'Are you certain?' Taherali asked incredulously.

'Absolutely. Shamin's sources within the cartel are impeccable.'

'But that is madness! Why would he do that?'

'He is worried about losing out to the European Community fields in the North Sea, and to the North Americans in Alaska and Alberta. Not to mention the future development of Antarctica. Our sales are declining. The fool thinks we can reverse the trend this way.'

'I do not believe it. He must have taken leave of his senses. I know that our proverb says that a sparrow in the mouth is better than a goose in the sleeve, but this is sheer folly. Does he not know that their resources are as limited as ours? Ultimately the West will still have to buy all the oil we can supply. So why give it away now?'

'Precisely, Taherali. Hussan Rampuri is panicking. He is a shadow of his former self. Moreover, the Emir who wants to throw away our prosperity tomorrow is throwing away our prestige and self-respect today. Border raids by our dogs of neighbours go unanswered. Our leader is afraid of further reprisals escalating into war and threatening his beloved atomic installation. The surrounding Emirates know this, and are playing on Rampuri's cowardice. It is sickening to behold.'

'But surely people are not acquiescing in all this? The Army, the industrialists, the financiers . . .?'

'I am gratified that your studies have not been in vain. There are certain elements within Dhubat who would like to see a change of government.'

'And yourself, father?' Taherali thought that he already knew the answer.

He did; and he felt an undeniable sense of pride in his father's resolve, and elation at his willingness to confide in his son.

'But what about the Emirates? Will they not assist a counter-revolution to ensure Dhubat's continued effeteness?' he asked his father.

'It is most likely; but any such reprisals would take time to prepare. Time which we would not be wasting!'

He then explained his son's crucial contribution to the audacious plot he had been working on for the past six months.

An hour and many questions later the familiar pearl-fishing dhows of Dhubat heralded the approaching coastline. Taherali had completely forgotten the fleshpots of London. His home-coming was going to be incredibly more exciting than he had thought.

By comparison the feast given for the return of the Prodigal Son was like a Gulag goulash. While the welcoming banquet for Taherali's final homecoming was not quite on the extravagant scale of Trimalchio's legendary dinner parties in the heydey of the Roman Empire it was still a spectacular affair. Arab sheikhs have always been rightly famed for their hospitality.

'Thou shalt not turn away a guest' was the code of the Bedouin. Hanif el-Fazzah had never been stinting in the past. Now he excelled himself.

For over three hours the guests were festooned with the finest food on offer in the Middle East, with each man being served, in ancient Bedouin fashion, according to the position he occupied in relation to the host. The myth that the Arabian desert is one gigantic barren wasteland was exploded in a riot of colour and flavours, as dish after dish was placed before the discerning and appreciative guests. Pomegranates, figs, dates, plums, grapes and lemons; nuts and honey of every description; pickled olives served with a traditional sauce of figs, raisins, dates and vinegar; cucumbers, onions, leeks, beans in oil, stuffed vine leaves, and leaves of lettuce dressed in the potent araq liquor; oysters, mullet, turbot and swordfish; gazelle, hare, hedgehog, goat, mutton, camel and chicken: stewed or roasted and exquisitely flavoured with dill, cummin, coriander, sesame, mint, rue and mustard; even locusts, roasted on the fire before having their heads broken off. Lastly, mint tea, or coffee flavoured with cloves or cinnamon and served as always in the most beautiful, highly-polished ornate utensils which were prized and passed on within households from one generation to the next.

About an hour after the banquet was over and the poets, singers, musicians and dancers had finished, the guests began to depart. There was not a Mercury Monarch to be seen. Instead, a fleet of Rolls-Royces, Mercedes, Lamborghinis, even the occasional connoisseur's Lagonda, whispered their chauffeur-driven charges into the stillness of the desert night.

A few privileged houseguests remained behind. Their names were virtually unknown beyond the boundaries of Dhubat that night: four weeks later, if all went well, they would be broadcast to the world as the new Cabinet of Emir Hanif el-Fazzah.

'Gentlemen,' began el-Fazzah once absolute privacy had been guaranteed, 'the news I bring from Bahrain confirms our worst suspicions on the economic front. Rampuri is privately trying to gain support for his schemes of tariff reform within OPEC. He is not meeting with much enthusiasm and is making no secret of the fact that he will go it alone if necessary. Our oil prices could be halved within six weeks, in a disastrous bid to halt falling sales now that the North Sea and Alaska are nearing peak production. Our major asset is a dwindling resource. To accelerate the inevitable drying-up of our wells in this way is the utmost folly.'

'Indeed, el-Fazzah. We are all in agreement,' said Ibrahim Aziz, President of the Bank of Dhubat. 'There would be, of course, a short-term improvement in our balance of payments – hardly necessary, as you all know!' he added with a smug grin. 'But the loss of real income in the long term would be disastrous for the continued diversification of our economy.'

'It is eminently clear, then, that we must press on with the utmost haste in our plans. The future well-being of our children and our security as a state are in jeopardy,' said the sheikh. 'And now, gentlemen, to details.'

As their progress reports unfolded and further points were thrashed out over the next few hours Taherali had to admire the thoroughness of their preparations. Revolutionary movements had been a module in a Political Economy course taken by him at the LSE in his second year. What he now heard from these middle-aged plotters in his father's study sounded like a revision seminar on certain aspects of the works of Lenin, Trotsky, Mao, Fannon and Jackson. Taherali had never imagined as a young student that these ideas would ever take on more than a theoretical significance for him. His father's faction certainly meant business.

A fortnight after his homecoming Taherali smiled as he drove to work for the first time. Not with self-satisfaction, as he barrelled along the magnificent new highway in his Ferrari Quattrovalvole. He was too sophisticated for that. Nor was it a nervous smile at the thought of starting his first real job. He was too self-assured for that. No. It was the irony of it all that amused him.

The scene flashed before him. A cold November morning in London four years previously. Why was it that students at the London School of Economics were always the first to protest about any controversial issue? Were their lecturers more politically motivated, or their student bodies more effectively infiltrated by Marxist agitators than in other institutions, as the right-wing press often alleged? Or perhaps they were simply more aware about the issues of the day than the mass of conservatively minded middle-class students? Taherali would never know; nor did it matter. The fact remained that, only four weeks after his course had started, there he was: out on the streets of London with a placard in his hand denouncing the latest proposed sale of a nuclear plant to an Arab state!

The more he thought about it now the more ludicrous it became. At the time he had not exactly been sure why he was marching. He had been swept along by the enthusiasm of Christine, the petite, fragile beauty from Godalming at whose flat he had spent the two previous nights. She was a bit of a whole-food freak and member of, what had it been called? 'Friends of the Earth'. At any rate she had dragged him along, without too much protest on his part, until he had found himself waving that damned slogan in the air. He was protesting then, all right, for the first and only time in his life. He had just hoped that no recognisable photographs of himself would appear in any of the major papers.

He need not have worried about that. By far the vast majority of photographs that day were not taken by pressmen but by Special Branch agents under the guise of safeguarding public order. The resulting mug-shots would not be for publication.

That night Taherali had invited Christine and a few of her fellow-protestors back to his flat for a drink.

'I'd like you to meet some of my Friends, Taherali.' Christine beamed as she introduced Annabel, Tim, Will and his new acquaintance Michael, whom she had only just met herself.

'Of the Earth, of course?' Her pun was not lost on Taherali.

'What else, mate?' Tim Craig almost fused Taherali's fingers together with the vigour of his handshake.

A few beers later the conversation was beginning to get a bit animated for Taherali's liking.

'It's not as if there are no alternatives,' exploded Christine, all of her fragility gone as her features took on a passionate intensity which Taherali had not seen before. 'Wind, waves, solar energy are all perfectly feasible sources of energy.'

'And at a fraction of the investment costs,' added Will Oliver, a second year student reading for BSc Economics.

'Not only that, but they all avoid the possibility of total destruction for mankind.'

'You bet!' The speaker was Timothy Craig, one of the most active anti-nuclear campaigners in the UK. 'What really worries me is the rate of proliferation of these plants throughout the world. With all due respect to our Dhubati host,' he added deferentially to Taherali.

'But you are all missing the point!' Taherali felt, rightly, that he was being got at as a result of his country's recent agreement with a Franco-German consortium to build a pressurised water reactor for an undisclosed sum reputed to be around $1,200,000,000.

The debate had raged on television, in the international press, and in the European parliament for months; but the industrial lobbies had met with their predictable success.

'These plants do not pose a threat to the environment. They are perfectly safe. Nor can they be subverted for offensive purposes.'

'You're wrong on both counts, mate.' Taherali wondered if he would ever get used to this form of address as Tim waded into him. For the first time in his education Taherali was being exposed at university to direct contact with working class intellectuals. 'Admittedly a lot of care does go into the design of reactors. And their safety record to date is reasonable. But it is a syllogism to conclude that they are failsafe. There have been God knows how many incidents already within the UK alone. It is statistically probable, and indeed likely given human error, that a major accident will occur sooner rather than later. When that happens the consequences will be disastrous.

'Anyway,' Tim had continued, 'your second assumption is even wider of the mark.'

'I'm afraid it is, Taherali.' Annabel Jones was slightly older and infinitely more mellow than the others. Her tenderness of tone more than compensated for Tim's abrasiveness. Taherali sensed immediately that she was the most compassionate of the four. He could not imagine her surviving long the callous world of publishing which she had just entered. Had he been able to see a decade ahead he would have revised his opinion. Allied to these warm human qualities Annabel had been blessed with an ultra-sharp brain, steely resolve, and that undefinable 'feel' for quality. She was destined to become one of London's most respected publishers.

'Look what happened in India. In 1974, within two years of their Canadian-designed reactor becoming fully operational, they had carried out an underground nuclear explosion in Hyderabad. This despite all prior assurances and arguments to the contrary. And now there are rumours that Pakistan is planning a joint underground explosion with Libya of all people!'

Taherali had not known that.

'Libya?' He was genuinely shocked. 'But that is irresponsible.'

'Damned right and it is,' said Will. 'These are the dirty bastards who filled rockets with stolen, heavily-contaminated radio-active isotopes and virulent chemicals only three years ago.'

'Mind you, Will, the silly buggers killed off more of their own workers in the process than any potential enemies,' Tim reminded him.

'Not the point, Tim,' Annabel chided him. 'Taherali and Will are correct. It is Libya's intentions that are the worry. Only fifteen months ago they annexed large areas of Chad which are believed to be rich in uranium. Where will it all end?'

'I just hope you Dhubatis will be less reckless.'

'That was quite unnecessary, Tim.' Christine could see that Taherali was becoming a bit rattled.

'Yes; let's change the subject and stop boring our host with our preoccupations,' said Annabel.

The only person who had not contributed to the discussion was Will's friend. The dour provincial peasant had sat supping his bottles of Beamish in silence. What was his name? Taherali could not immediately recall.

Now there was not a single protestor in sight as the shimmering sci-fi mirage resolved into reality in the desert valley ahead of him. None could have survived the desert heat. None could have evaded the intense security surrounding the plant, from the surface-to-air missiles on the sheltering cliffs to the fiercely-armed motorised patrols.

Little wonder Taherali was smiling.

4

They Make A Covenant

STUDENTS of the violent revolutionary coup have long since
refined the theory down to a checklist of a dozen or so main
items. Lenin and Trotsky, Hitler and Goering, Castro, Che
Guevara, Huey P Newton and the Black Panthers: all had
known precisely what to do, though not all had met with the
same degree of success. Given the right permutation between
the faction's resources and the strength of the opposition, a
coup d'état can be a surprisingly easy operation to carry out:
although, as Lenin knew in the abortive July days in 1917 in
Petrograd, seizing power and holding on to power are two
different things.

El-Fazzah had no major worries. His own group was strong
and resourceful. The leaders he had hand-picked himself to
form a small, ruthless core bound together with a near-
fanatical right-wing ideology, a common purpose, and fear of
the consequences of failure. Their preparations had been
thorough. The government of Hussan Rampuri, on the other
hand, was more benign than oppressive. It displayed a laxity
and permissiveness uncharacteristic of the surrounding
Emirates, and had created widespread disaffection within
Dhubat. The balance of probability as to the likely outcome of
the coup was heavily weighted in favour of el-Fazzah.

Nevertheless, he naturally harboured a few nagging doubts up to the very last minute.

The disquiet in the ranks of the armed forces, police and civil service had been exploited from the start by the rebels. Their higher echelons especially had been easy to infiltrate. El-Fazzah knew from his business dealings that for most people the big question was not whether they were willing to transfer their allegiance, but what was it going to cost? Still, he never ceased to be amazed at how readily a man could be bought. The promise of a quick or long-overdue promotion; the chance to settle an old score; petty inter-departmental rivalries; personal weaknesses for gambling, drugs, women or young boys; or simply straight forward financial gain. All could be turned to advantage. It could not be ruled out that some people were even prepared to act out of idealism or moral rectitude; but such were few and far between. Human nature was base indeed.

On the stroke of 11.00 hours on the morning of 3 September, Lt-Colonel Abdu Chakir promoted himself to full Colonel. He did so over the dead body of Colonel Mummad, his Commanding Officer of twenty seconds earlier. He had shot Mummad from point-blank range precisely in the centre of the black patch which he had affectedly worn over his perfectly good left eye since Moshe Dayan's leap to worldwide prominence in 1967. Chakir had acted without the slightest twinge of remorse. Not only had Mummad been incompetent and corrupt, but, as the son-in-law of the Emir Hussan Rampuri, he had resisted all pressures from his closest colleagues to call for firmer action against the bordering Omalis who had been raiding with impunity for years.

Chakir had arranged for all members of the General Staff to be present at Army HQ this morning. A few seconds after he had radioed el-Fazzah's residence he summoned the other officers into their new CO's presence.

'Gentlemen,' he proceeded calmly, 'in precisely fifty-eight minutes from now a new Government will be announced in the State of Dhubat with Emir Hanif el-Fazzah at its head. I need not remind you as officers in the army that your allegiance is to the State and not to any one ruler or form of government. Colonel Mummad,' he indicated the corpse, still hideously oozing blood, with the barrel of his gun, 'Colonel Mummad did not quite see things this way. I trust, gentlemen, that your loyalty to the new regime is not in doubt.'

It was not a question. Chakir knew already that he could count on three of the five officers present, and the key divisions they commanded. He was prepared to shoot the other two if necessary, as he had personally dispatched Mummad, and two lesser officials for their indiscretions a week previously.

He did not have to use his Walther again.

'Lt-Colonel Fadhl.' Now that his leadership was confirmed Chakir rattled out instructions.

'You will be responsible for all border posts, ports of entry, and the civil and military airports. I need not remind you of the possibility of an immediate attack from Omali or Qasar. Such an opportunistic offensive will be repulsed with maximum force.' Ex-Major Fadhl was delighted with his orders, which he considered long overdue. His new promotion did not immediately dawn on him.

'Major Hamid, I want you and your motorised infantry detachments to go immediately to the Presidential Palace. The Palace Guard is split. Some are loyal to our cause, but there will be some resistance. It must be crushed. On no account must anything happen to the person of Rampuri. I hold you personally responsible for this.' Hamid did not need to have the consequences spelled out. 'Act with all possible speed.'

'Captain Ahmad.' Chakir addressed the only remaining member of the conspiracy. 'All public buildings, financial institutions and newspaper offices. Put double guards on all offices of overseas banks and the Bank of Dhubat. Allow no transactions to take place. The Head Post Office must be sealed off and a total telecommunications blackout imposed until further orders. The Broadcasting Corporation is your personal responsibility, Captain. It is imperative that we retain exclusive access to all radio and television networks.

You will receive further orders here in just over one hour from now.'

'Sir!' Ahmad, like Hamid and Fadhl before him, saluted his new Commanding Officer with pride, nodded full comprehension of his pre-arranged instructions, and left immediately.

'Major Kaled, Major Hamoud.' Chakir addressed the two whose allegiance had just been declared minutes earlier. 'You will remain with me at Headquarters. At 12.30 hours you will rejoin your respective divisions which are confined to barracks meantime. A purely precautionary measure, you will understand, gentlemen.'

The revolt at police headquarters was even easier to execute. Almost to a man the force was longing for a return to a more severe code of discipline in their small, once strict, community. The old standards of law and order as detailed in the Koran – the Shari'a, or 'road to a watering place' – were harsh, unequivocal, easy to enforce, and, above all, highly effective. All that a law enforcement officer could wish for.

Captain Mahadi paraded all of his men at 11.00 hours, and announced the new regime.

'Our orders are quite straightforward. Colonel Chakir, the new Commanding Officer of the Army of Dhubat, directs us to assist the army over the next few days in the enforcement of law and order. In addition to our normal duties we will have specific functions to carry out at the port and the civil airport until the excise officers have been purged. The Shari'a is to be strictly imposed.'

Mahadi detailed his men methodically. There were no dissenters.

The Presidential Palace was situated well out from the centre of the New Town of Dhubat on the landward side,

43

sanitized from the odours of the fishmarkets along the quay and the bustle of the crowded, noisy town centre. It was well screened from the exclusive surrounding area by a deep, expensively cultivated ring of tall flowering shrubs and trees. At 11.00 on this September morning all was normal. A handful of hopeful petitioners were approaching the two sentries on duty at the main gate. Several members of the Secretariat were deep in conversation crossing the outer courtyard in the blistering heat on their way to a briefing session for heads of departments which had been unexpectedly scheduled for 11.20 that morning. Two visiting Ministers from Kuwait and Abu Dhabi were waiting for their audience with the Emir Hussan Rampuri to begin. They were not too hopeful that their pleas for a moratorium on oil prices for the next six months were going to meet with much success.

By 11.10 Major Hamid's troops were converging on the Palace. At 11.12 one frantic phonecall got through to the Emir's Private Secretary from the first occupied building in the town before Captain Ahmad's men had seized full control of the Post Office Exchange. It was too late to alter the course of events. Major Hamid was personally leading one hundred and fifty of his crack troops at the double across the outer courtyard. They were quickly in control of the wings accessible to the public.

Resistance within the inner sanctum of the Palace was much stronger than had been anticipated. El-Fazzah's faction had only been able to infiltrate the lower echelons of the Palace Guard, people not in a position of command. They had not dared to approach any high-ranking officers for fear of immediate exposure.

Chakir and Hamid had known from the start that this would be the most difficult part of the entire take over. They had worked out the operation meticulously using detailed drawings of the layout of every part of the building. Hamid deployed his men exactly as planned.

Even so, it was touch and go at some points.

Loudspeakers broadcast to the Palace Guard that the coup had already been successful and that they alone were holding out. Further resistance could in no way alter the outcome. An amnesty was offered to all members of the Guard. At this, eighteen of the Guard accepted. Only four made it to safety as they were gunned down from behind by those who were prepared to die on their personal oath of loyalty to Hussan Rampuri.

The ensuing battle was brief and bloody, and raged throughout the grounds and buildings of the Emir's private quarters.

Despite an agreement with Chakir to minimise damage to property Hamid had no option but to allow his men free use of mortars, grenades and incendiaries to gain entry. Once in the actual corridors there was bitter hand-to-hand fighting before Rampuri personally ordered the twenty-five or so remaining members of his force to surrender in return for guarantees of their and his safety.

Hamid himself held Rampuri under close arrest.

The remnant of the once-proud Palace Guard was taken to a desert outpost and machine-gunned.

'A purely precautionary measure,' Chakir later explained to the new Emir.

At 12.20 all radio and television channels in Dhubat began broadcasting the same message. 'There follows an announcement of national importance from the Emir, Hanif el-Fazzah.'

'I am speaking to you as Head of the Government of Dhubat and your new Emir,' began the unfamiliar voice in a sonorous tone devoid of any trace of a nervous tremor. 'The effete, spineless government of Hussan Rampuri has been overthrown in a bloodless coup. The armed forces, police and civil service are entirely loyal to myself. The new Cabinet will meet this afternoon. May our country continue to prosper and defend itself.'

The message was repeated continuously for the remainder of

the day.

At 12.30 Major Kaled and Major Hamoud were escorted back to their regiments. All of their officers had been dispersed and transferred to other divisions, and their places taken by men known to be loyal to Fadhl, Hamid and Ahmad.

The new Emir called his first press conference at 15.00 hours on the day of the coup.

It was not entirely coincidental that representatives from several leading international agencies and newspapers in the USA and Europe had arrived in Dhubat the previous day for a fact-finding tour of the country's new nuclear plant.

The conference was therefore much better attended than could have been expected otherwise.

El-Fazzah read out a brief statement on the reasons for the coup and what his faction hoped to achieve now that they were indisputably in power. He then indicated that he would be prepared to answer a few questions only, as he had a Cabinet meeting in half-an-hour's time.

'Ed Dayton. Reuter. Your Excellency, what is to be the fate of Hussan Rampuri?'

'The ex-Emir is currently under close house arrest in the Palace. He is completely unharmed, and arrangements are well in hand to provide him with safe passage to any country of his choice.'

'And his assets, Excellency?'

'He will be allowed to retain his overseas holdings.'

'Should just about be able to survive on that,' Dayton whispered sarcastically to Tom Winters sitting beside him.

'Winters, Excellency. Press International. Many American companies have substantial investments in Dhubat. What assurances can you give that these investments will be safe-guarded under the new regime?'

'Your countrymen can be assured, Mr Winters, that their investments are as secure in Dhubat as I trust ours are in the USA.'

Winters grinned and sat down.

'You mentioned your faction's. . . . . er, your Government's concern about violations of your frontier.' Paul Renée of Paris Soir had forgotten to introduce himself. 'Can we assume from that there will be an upswing in arms sales to Dhubat?'

'Trust the Froggies.' Dayton again. 'You'd think they had sold enough damned Exocets to the Argies and Iraqis,' he whispered to Winters.

'You cannot assume anything.' El-Fazzah had recognised the French accent and knew perfectly well what was behind the rather transparent question. 'The armed forces of Dhubat have always been able to defend themselves. It was the will that was missing under Rampuri. That has now changed. We will view any infringements of our national boundaries most seriously, and will take whatever steps necessary to protect them.'

'Walter Tyson, The Times, Your Excellency.' Despite all of the troubles it had gone through with takeovers, unions, strikes and circulation problems, The Times was still 'THE' Times. There was, as yet, no need to prefix it with London. 'It seems to me that your desire to improve public order by returning to the old-fashioned law of the Koran is somewhat misplaced in this day and age.'

'I must remind you, Mr Tyson, that what you refer to as "old-fashioned law" is, in fact, the "sacred law". Muslims believe that the Shari'a is the very path of God. Its reprovals and exhortations, instructions and comments are there to guide every aspect of our lives. It follows that it must be applied as the Prophet taught.'

'But is this not going to discourage Europeans and North Americans from living and working in Dhubat, Excellency?'

'Not at all. Why should it? The Shari'a will only be applied to the faithful. Others,' the Emir was far too cultured to say infidels, 'will be governed by a new codification which my new government will produce as soon as possible. They will have nothing to fear.'

'Thank you, Excellency.' Tyson sat down for the third time.

'I was very impressed, Your Excellency, as I'm sure we all were,' the next speaker looked around the audience for confirmation, 'with our tour round your recently operational nuclear plant yesterday afternoon. Oh, sorry, Nick Hauser, Chicago Tribune,' he belatedly introduced himself. 'Do you envisage any major change of policy vis-à-vis nuclear energy now that the nature of your government seems to have changed somewhat?' He had wanted to say 'shifted to the right', but had caught himself just in time.

'I'm afraid I do not quite get the drift of your question, Mr Hauser.'

'Like hell he doesn't,' Dayton nudged Winters.

'As you probably know, the acquisition of nuclear technology for our future electricity needs was eagerly sought by all responsible Dhubatis. It was, in fact, the main reason why the ex-Emir and myself had resolved our long-standing feud. So that we could work together for the wellbeing of our country.'

'But not for the wellbeing of Mr Rampuri, eh Tom?'

El-Fazzah glowered at Dayton. He was beginning to resent the barely audible, but still distracting, asides.

'Your Excellency, if I may.' The Emir had no difficulty in recognising the editor of the local Dhubat News, whose office was still, and would remain for some time, under guard.

'Could you enlighten us as to the position of the Palace Guard?'

'The ex-Palace Guard,' the Emir reminded the hapless reporter. 'Those who accepted our amnesty are free at this very moment,' el-Fazzah lied. In fact they would be held in custody until Rampuri was well clear of the country. 'The survivors who surrendered are under temporary arrest at Army Headquarters.' Their carcasses were, at that very moment, being torn to pieces by desert jackals as vultures and lesser carrion-eaters waited patiently nearby.

'And now, gentlemen, I must adjourn this conference and meet with my Cabinet.'

El-Fazzah acknowledged his personal aide, who had been flapping about at the side of the room, with a reassuring nod. There was a flurry of applause as the new ruler of Dhubat left.

5

To Buy Corn

ON the afternoon following her uncle's successful coup Shamin felt sufficiently secure to leave the closely guarded confines of her new home in the Presidential Palace. The new Emir had no fears for the safety of his niece. There had been no need to revise and codify the laws, establish a new judiciary, or give the police sweeping new powers as was the norm after a violent seizure of power. On his Cabinet's insistence, albeit slightly against his own grain, just one simple pronouncement which had been instantly understood and accepted by all – 'The Laws of the Koran will be observed and enforced from today onwards.' It would have been impossible for a Marxist revolutionary like Lenin or Castro to have made a similar statement with such immediate and profound effect. There would be no need in Dhubat to slowly and systematically introduce state terror leading to the setting up of a Gulag Archipelago. Divine terror is a far more effective weapon amongst a superstitious and believing population.

Shamin's chauffeured Mercedes sped along the marvellously smooth road from the Palace towards the Old City. She was growing more excited by the minute at the imminent prospect of travelling some ten to twelve centuries back in time.

Unlike many a person who spent much of their working life travelling the world, Shamin always looked forward to a journey. The fascination of seeing new places – and no matter how often she returned to certain locations there was always something new to take in – was in her blood. Nothing delighted her more, however, than being able to delve into the past. She was straining her eyes in the harsh desert light for the first signs of the approaching medieval town. It was hard to tell the city from the sand, forged as they were from the same stone. The only hope was to delineate the marbled mosques and minarets from the background browns of the interior mountains.

After a few minutes Shamin saw the city shimmering out of the surrounding wasteland. She sent the car back to the Palace with instructions to return for her in two hours' time. As she went through the Bab al-Dhubat, the main gate in the formidable walls which had once withstood a Portuguese siege, her body reeled from the suddenness of the attack on her senses. After being abroad for perhaps a year at a time, the old city always affected Shamin like this. She drank in every sensation.

Unlike the surrounding desert, which was colourless and silent, Old Dhubat was vibrant and raucous.

Over the centuries all but the poorest mud-brick and sandstone houses had been plastered over and painted. Where the whitewash was still intact the six-storey walls reflected the colours and multiplied the sounds from the masses of people packed into the maze of narrow alleys below. The veils on the women offered tantalising glimpses of rainbow-hued faces which, with few refinements, could have been lifted from a 'Vogue' cosmetic fantasy: yellows, greens, reds, blues from turmeric, henna, antimony. Drovers of donkeys and camels permanently encrusted in desert dust. Market stalls ablaze with fruit, vegetables and spices of every shade in the spectrum. Even the ubiquitous flies, thought Shamin, dazzled with their beauty.

Above all was the fantastic noise. Merchants shouting each other down. Beggars, fewer than in the past, pleading for alms. Street musicians performing on wind, reed and percussion. Elderly devotees of the Prophet reciting the Koran from memory while the next generation could be heard chanting verses from the open courtyard of the madrassa. Hawkers and housewives haggling at the stalls and workshops scattered throughout the souk. The endless chatter of the harem women coming down from the wooden balconies floating magically above.

Shamin loved it!

Suddenly, for the third time that day, the call of the muezzins – 'Allahu Akbar, Allahu Akbar' – came floating down from the tops of the minarets, calling the faithful to prayer. Shamin, who had long since renounced the strict Muslim ways, nevertheless went through the motions with the rest of the throng.

Devotion over, bedlam returned, and Shamin continued her inspection of the craftwork on display. Suddenly, there was near silence, broken only by the wails of a blind beggar. A small procession appeared in the centre of the market place, led by a colonel of the new Palace Guard, and flanked by members of the police force.

A murmur started from the crowd as they slowly realised what was about to happen.

A young couple were led forward to the colonel, who began cataloguing their misdemeanours to the people. The girl was the daughter of a wealthy trader – her crime had been to marry in secret the man she loved. Under the precepts of the Koran you did not marry the person you loved. You loved the person you married – and always by parental arrangement. Shamin pressed forwards, curious, despite herself, to see what form the chastisement was to take. By the gleeful expressions on some of the older faces they were in no doubt. The sight of the police captain's drawn pistol, and the huge sword held loosely in the hands of one of the guardsmen, rooted Shamin to the spot. Her finer feelings urged her to get away as quickly as possible. But, and this she did not want to believe and indeed denied to herself afterwards, she felt a gut compulsion to stay and watch. The haunting visions which plagued her for months to come made her wish she had obeyed her better instincts.

The girl was shot five or six times from point-blank range. Her body had barely stopped convulsing when her husband was forced to his knees.

The crowd jostled furiously, each trying to get a better view. The murmur rose into a shout as the swordsman lifted his weapon. Shamin, this beautiful, cultured woman of twenty-nine was mesmerised. Her eyes, like everyone's, followed the dull glint of the blade as it smashed into the back of the man's neck. As the rusty old piece of iron fell again and again and again the horror she experienced was mingled with a warm spreading glow deep inside her. With each blow the faithful clapped and cheered and danced, until the pulverised neck was finally severed.

'Allahu Akbar,' chanted the crowd. 'God is Greatest.'

Shamin was thankful for the loosely fitting cotton djellabah she wore that day. She was not the only woman whose fingers were at work beneath the many folds of their garments.

She made back for the Bab al-Dhubat gate and her air-conditioned limousine, disgusted with the sexual arousal she had not been able to control, and with the sight of spurting blood and the sounds of splintering bones indelibly imprinted inside her skull.

For the rest of her days she would keep the promise never to witness the laws of the Koran being carried out again.

Hopefully the intense activities of the next few weeks as she set about her key role in her uncle Hanif's audacious plans would lessen, if not altogether expunge, the horror.

'Taxi, ma'am?'

'No thank you,' the commissionaire at the entrance of the Hilton was politely told.

Ignoring the fleet of Mercs and Cadillacs, Shamin headed instead for the old part of Bahrain about half a mile away. The flash cars quickly gave way to antiquated rickshaws pulled by a strange assortment of men, donkeys, bicycles and motor scooters. She settled back quite comfortably into one harnessed to a placid, well-nourished donkey and instructed the owner, a wondrous cross-mingling of Arab and Oriental features, to head for the ancient ruins on the southern outskirts of the city.

Just over a month previously, when she had had more leisure time at her disposal, she had been privileged to have the company and expert guidance of Professor Muhsin Jaidah, the foremost authority on the area which was one of the finest archaeological gems in the entire Near East. Excavations on the site of the sixteenth century Portuguese port had revealed, some twenty feet down into the ground and 3,900 years into the past, a prehistoric harbour site of considerable proportions easily capable of taking reed boats with cargoes of thirty tons and more. Piecing together evidence from microscopic particles of copper, stories from ancient legends, and the present-day existence of reed boats built on the same superb construction as depicted in drawings in the early cities of Ur and Uruk in Mesopotamia, it was clear that this area so beloved to Shamin was none other than the Dilmun of Sumerian legend.

Professor Jaidah had explained all this to Shamin as they had explored the extensive site. She had enthused about the temple remains with its beautifully cut, finely jointed stonework: further evidence of the skill and industry of those earlier times. Shamin could only marvel at the initiative, organisation and status of a people who were able to import large quantities of a stone found many miles away to the northwest on the island of Jiddah.

The only area of the remains, she recalled, which she had found slightly disconcerting had been the group of some 100,000 burial mounds, varying in height from six to over forty feet, and perfectly rounded, which stretched for several miles in each direction. This largest of all prehistoric cemeteries anywhere in the world confirmed the importance of Dilmun over four millenia previously.

Today, however, Shamin only had a couple of hours available before her meeting with Matsumi Mishu in which to indulge her passion for nostalgia and archaeology. With the early October temperature now past its mid-day peak of 95 degrees, but still in the high eighties, Shamin was grateful for the generous calico canopy over her head as the rickshaw took her past the busy harbour area with its tall cranes and stark concrete block warehouses. Its brilliantly lit waters supported an enormous fleet of ugly container ships.

The modern marina nearby was a more welcome sight; but Bahrain, she reflected, could not in any way be classed as one of the more photogenic harbours in the world. Shamin closed her eyes and drifted back to her first visit to the Hawaiian Islands three years previously. She would never forget that initial breathtaking sight of Lahaina on the island of Maui. Its gorgeous golden beach lapped with the deep blue waters of the Pacific; its old-world whaling sea front; its mounds of pink coral walls; the colourful vegetation and lush mountain backdrop: now there was a harbour! Bahrain lacked all of these attributes; but it did have one quality of its own. The piercing blue of the sky and the vibrant yellow of the desert had been mixed on Pan's palette to produce the most sparkling green water to be found anywhere in the world. Had her own eyes not been their velvet, beckoning brown Shamin could have wished for no other colour than the waters of Bahrain.

Shamin's plodding, traditional mode of transport eventually deposited her beside the large sand-coloured, roughly-hewn blocks which seemed to have been scattered in a random pattern like some petulant giant child's discarded Lego. They were by no means spectacular – nothing like the highly sophisticated remains of ancient Corinth – but perhaps it was this very lack of refinement, whether by design or as a result of weathering she knew not, which so endeared them to Shamin. Perhaps, simply, it was because they represented one of the few lasting remains of the remote civilisation from which she was descended. At any rate she was content to stroll and weave her way through the maze, completely relaxed and at ease with herself, slowly absorbing more of the ethos of that long-lost epoch.

The arrival of the middle-aged Japanese business executive in the rented air-conditioned Lincoln, which he had been advised to drive himself, was an unwelcome intrusion into Shamin's reveries. Not that she showed any resentment for an instant to the profusely perspiring, rather overweight and slightly incongruous gentleman in the blue pin-stripe suit who stumbled towards her through the dust.

'I trust I have not kept you waiting by my late arrival?'

Mishu's English was faultless as he approached Shamin in the glaring sun.

'No, no. You are actually a little early yourself,' Shamin smiled. 'I came a bit in advance on purpose to give myself some time amongst the ruins,' she gestured round about.

Mishu glanced around quizzically.

Not only is there nothing here, he thought, but in this temperature!

However, he was forced to admit that the young lady did not look at all unbalanced. On the contrary; but in this heat he could think of one thing only.

'Perhaps,' Shamin rescued his obvious discomfiture, 'we could return to your car and discuss business as we drive back to town?'

'I would be pleased to do that.' Mishu was genuinely relieved at this proposal. He was much too cultivated to ask why they had not met there in the first place.

As the Director of Marketing Research for Mitsushima Industries Inc. of Tokyo, Mishu had come to Bahrain for the second time in a month a worried man. The company for which he worked, and would, incidentally, have died for if so ordered, was part of one of Japan's 'Big Five' cartels. Protected by favourable government fiscal policies and by an impenetrable maze of import regulations designed to deny foreign competitors access to Japan's lucrative home markets, these once modest family concerns had managed to achieve by trade what Japan's militaristic rulers of the 1930s and '40s had failed to achieve by aggression – penetration, then dominance, not only of Far East but of world markets. Mishu's prime function, like Shamin's, was to travel the world and personally gather information from the many sources which would enhance his company's ability to compete effectively in its continuously on-going quest for an even greater share of the world's prosperity.

One of the prime areas of growth opportunities in recent years had been the Middle East. The oil-glutted governments of the Arabian Gulf were in the process of altering the economic bases of their states. Diversification was the key word – develop a whole range of secondary industries with the wealth gained from the primary one of oil; and at the same time spend lavishly on social and welfare services to further benefit the populaces. This general strategy was welcomed by the Japanese and others. Mishu's own company had not been slow to capitalise on the first round of orders thrown out by the sheikhdoms.

However, things were changing. Contracts were being more closely contended, tenders more carefully scrutinised. Japanese concerns, including Mitsushima Industries, had just lost major contracts to equip, man and service three new hospitals, worth around $1000m over the next five years. The so-called weakness of the British pound in late 1984 and early 1985, which had thrown the British Chancellor of the Exchequer into a frenzy of indecision over interest rates and support for the pound, had enabled British companies to seize the initiative in this and other overseas markets. Mishu knew that Dhubat and Omali both planned similar building programmes in the immediate future. He did not want his company's tenders turned down again.

Mishu had been contacted personally by Shamin, in what he had known intuitively at the time was not a chance encounter, on an earlier occasion in Bahrain after she had learned from her own sources of Mitsushima's failure in Abu Dhabi, Kuwait and Saudi Arabia. She made it quite clear to Mishu that his company's tenders for Dhubat's new general hospital would be most favourably considered if certain other pieces of information were forthcoming. Mishu could well understand her country's concern over the vulnerability of its nuclear power station in the event of a counter-revolution or invasion by a hostile neighbour. He had agreed with her that the Sellafield complex in the United Kingdom was a model for the world as far as security was concerned, and assured her that his undisclosed source high up in the management structure of the Nuclear Fuel Development Corporation of Japan would be able to supply the necessary guidance for Dhubat.

When the Windscale nuclear reprocessing plant had finally gone into production its managers had heaved an enormous collective sigh of relief. Only after a full-scale public enquiry costing the British taxpayer £2m had the government finally given it the go-ahead. Hundreds of individuals and organisations had given evidence; eminent overseas scientists had reported their findings; even the President of the USA had tried to pressurize the government against the scheme – though not out of concern for the British environment.

The findings of the public enquiry, however, while admitting that there was a certain amount of risk, were confident that the proposed safeguards would ensure against any unacceptable degree of danger.

One of the main fears expressed by some had been the possibility of international terrorist action. It was anticipated that many overseas contracts would be taken, and it was feared that these would be much more open to risk than internal movements of fuel. The proponents had convinced the enquiry that the risks were minimal. Without going into detail, there would be adequate precautions taken. 'Impregnable' was the favourite description of the security arrangements.

As the first main overseas customer to use the Windscale facility Japan had required similar guarantees on the security aspects. Unlike mere Members of Parliament or the general public in Britain, however, the Japanese were privy to official and classified sources of information to convince them that their hundreds of millions of pounds worth of orders each year would be adequately protected. Mishu had obtained access to this information for Shamin.

'Impregnable' was the correct word to use. The Sellafield complex, as it had been re-christened in a futile attempt to improve its image, was in a wild and remote part of the country. The immediate area around it was under constant surveillance by British intelligence. Armed guards, reinforced by specially trained commando units when a foreign shipment was leaving or entering, were fully equipped to meet any projected threat. The cargo loading area and specially constructed harbour were guarded round the clock, even between shipments. The narrow entrance to the docking area was ceaselessly covered by a sonic scanner so refined that a solitary sardine could be identified.

Not only was Sellafield more impregnable than Fort Knox, Shamin was informed, even had terrorists been able to penetrate to the dockside there was no way they could have seized a shipment of plutonium. The cargo was entirely handled by remote-control. No scientists or administrators were present. Even the high-ranking ships' officers never left their sealed-off bridges. No-one whose life was worth saving could be used as a bargaining pawn. The security men and commandos were fully aware of this, and had incontrovertible orders to kill any unauthorised intruders without regard to hostages.

Mishu's worst fears were allayed the moment he conveyed his findings to Shamin. She assured him that his company would have the order for the hospital, and that his Contract Director, the second son of Yakumo Matsushima, the President of the corporation, would be officially informed within the week. Mishu was elated. Because he had no family relationship he knew that he could never aspire to the presidency of his firm; but he knew that his services in obtaining a contract like this would never be forgotten in the intensely loyal hierarchy of Matsushima Industries Incorporated.

For her part Shamin knew she had paid a small price for the information so invaluable to her uncle's cause. Like Mishu, she left Bahrain that evening well content with the bargain they had struck.

6

A Ladder To Heaven

THE time was now ripe for Hanif el-Fazzah to disclose his
plan to his Cabinet. With his son Taherali, niece Shamin, and
closest personal adviser the Mulla Abdel Hakim, he had been
secretly plotting for months since the coup. Indeed, the
concept of what he was about to announce had been in his own
mind for some time even before he had organised the
overthrow of Hussan Rampuri, and had started working out
the fine details with the only people he could trust. Now that
the feasibility of his ideas had been shown, he needed to take
his government along with him before putting them into
action.

He called the emergency session of the Cabinet to order at
15.30 on the afternoon of 9 June.

'Gentlemen, I have the gravest matter to discuss with you
this afternoon. Our country is on the verge of war. I have
called you here so that we can have the fullest and frankest
possible discussion of the situation.' Without further ceremony
he introduced the commanding officer of the army of Dhubat.

Abdu Chakir had been seated beside a large-scale map of the
Arabian Gulf countries. He stood, in true military style, to
address the Cabinet.

'Our country, as you well know,' he nodded respectfully to

several renowned former desert fighters in the Cabinet, 'has always been extremely vulnerable to attack from without.'

He pointed to the surrounding Emirates and the state of Qasar.

'The sporadic border raids which took place in the week after the coup to test the loyalty of our troops to the new government were successfully repulsed, with relative ease, I might add. Our enemies were surprised at the ferocity of our containment.

'However,' Chakir continued, 'we are receiving continuous intelligence reports of a concerted effort on the part of our enemies. Our agents are certain that a major offensive is being planned to take place within the year. It will, I am afraid, involve a simultaneous attack on two fronts.'

'The situation is serious, my friends,' the Emir came in. 'Thank you, Colonel.'

The Minister of Finance, Ibrahim Aziz, was the first to speak above the general hubbub.

'I could have understood this conspiracy theory had it materialised a few months ago immediately after the revolution. But why now? We have shown ourselves to be financially responsible, politically sound and militarily strong. Why now?' Aziz trailed off.

'Hussan Rampuri, who took refuge in Iraq after being deposed here, has been reported in Qum, the capital of Omali, and in Jaddah, the capital of Qasar,' said Chakir, indicating the immediate neighbours to the north and south. 'His presence there is not coincidental.'

'That makes sense,' said Salaam Kaddous, the Minister of the Interior. 'Given that there is a complete dearth of support for him within our state,' Kaddous continued, failing to mention his own rigorous liquidation of the remnants of whatever support there had been, 'it is natural that the traitor will try to stir up trouble from without. We should have shot him after the coup,' he added with regret.

'That would have lost us much credibility in the eyes of the world,' chided Yusif Karim Kassem, the Minister of Foreign Affairs.

'In your opinion, Kassem, will Rampuri have much success in gaining allies?' asked Ibrahim Aziz.

'Who knows, my friend. The Koran says that all the treasures of the earth could not have united the Arab peoples: I do not quarrel with that. However, a cause will always find rebels, as my ancestors used to say. You know the history of our relations with our neighbours. For centuries they have tried, whenever an opportunity has presented itself, to enslave us. Why should they change their spots overnight? Indeed, with our prestige as the only Gulf state which has been able to afford the West's most expensive piece of technology, there is now all the more reason for them to try again.'

'But we have only recently repulsed them,' interjected Kaddous. 'Surely they will not want their noses bloodied again? What do you think, Colonel? How well equipped and prepared are we to face such an attack if it were to come?'

'Not if it comes; but when it comes. It pains me to say so, gentlemen, but we would be over-run within 48 hours.'

Chakir's statement brought cries of disbelief from the Cabinet.

'Impossible,' said Aziz. 'That has never happened to us before.'

'May I remind you that we are talking about an entirely new situation,' continued the Colonel. 'What we are contemplating is not a series of disjointed, sporadic raids. Those we can easily handle, as our record shows. No. We are talking about a fully co-ordinated attack. A war on two fronts, with the distinct possibility that our neighbours will be reinforced with Iraqi troops. We are simply not equipped to contain such an eventuality.'

'And what would it take to so equip us, Colonel?' asked Aziz.

'Given time and money, and a crash programme of conscription and intensive training, we might manage to hold out for a few weeks in about a year from now. The odds, I am afraid, are simply too great. No matter what strides we were to make, they would be matched, indeed bettered, by our enemies in the same timescale. They are equally well supplied with British and French equipment, and any requests for more will be met with the usual alacrity on the part of the arms salesmen.'

'Then perhaps we should be looking for allies ourselves in order to counter this threat,' said Kaddous. 'If the discredited

Rampuri can be successful in drawing people to his hopeless cause, then surely we could counter in the same way.'

'We could, of course, try,' agreed Kassem, 'but I can assure you we would not be successful. Not, that is, in the sense that we could rally useful allies into our camp – allies whose presence would deter an attack on us. To the immediate north of Omali lie states with the closest of family ties. There is no way they would join with us. South of Qasar the only two states with a useful military establishment, Riyah and Yameni, are torn with internal factions. Under more stable regimes they might have been of use; but, for the present, any agreement which could be reached would be a liability to us. Beyond these states we need not look. The major oil cartels to the far north are too preoccupied with the retrenchment in their share of world markets, and are too resentful of our acquisition of the nuclear reactor to intercede on our behalf in the present dispute.'

'I see,' said Kaddous with an air of fatality. 'I had not realised our position vis-à-vis our neighbours was quite so bad.'

Which is why you are not in charge of Foreign Affairs, you jackass, thought Kassem.

'We should have shot Rampuri when we had the chance,' Kaddous repeated.

'And what is to stop us doing it now?' The matter-of-fact voice belonged to Aziz, the Minister of Finance, and was all the more chilling because of that. Aziz, although he had willingly taken part in the recent coup, had played a mainly administrative part in it. His family background had been remarkably free of the internecine intrigue which the popular myth quite accurately ascribed to most successful Arab families.

'Are you really serious, Ibrahim?' The Emir came into the general discussion for the first time.

'Your Excellency, I am,' replied Aziz. 'Such an event is not without precedent in the world of international finance, let alone the realm of politics.'

'Come, come, Aziz,' said Kaddous scornfully. 'What would you know about anything like that?' Kaddous, like so many men who thought and acted on a purely physical level, regarded cerebral types like Aziz as unworthy of serious attention.

'My friend, you would be surprised,' said Aziz. 'I have, as you know, always managed my personal affairs peacefully. But please do not infer that the absence of violent tactics is synonymous with a lack of knowledge of violence and its various applications. The circles in which I move are absolutely riddled with intrigue, scandal and, at times, violence. When vast sums of money are being moved around the world, as often as not in currency manipulations and speculative deals, and when a large volume of this, er, trade, is of an illicit nature, then violence often ensues.'

'But surely you do not employ Mafiosi hit men to assassinate prominent people as we are contemplating here, Aziz?' Aziz was beginning to rise somewhat in the estimation of Kaddous.

'Not I personally, of course; but it has been done. You must have heard the reports of the Italian banker, Roberto Calvi, who was found hanging under Blackfriars Bridge in London in 1982. Far from being the suicide which the coroner's inquest ruled it to be at the time, I can tell you quite categorically that Calvi was taken out, as they say, on account of the mounting scandal in his bank which was involving the Vatican and leading figures in the Italian political, military and business worlds. To preserve the secrecy of their dealings with Calvi he was, quite simply, murdered. By Mafia-style hit men, as you say, Kaddous. But, I digress. To return to the matter in hand – perhaps we should contemplate an assassination attempt on Rampuri, given the seriousness of the situation we find ourselves in thanks to him.'

'And how exactly would we go about this?' asked Kaddous, fascinated now to see just what Aziz did know.

'My dear friend,' said Aziz with a mocking grin. 'I am flattered that you are asking me how to plot an assassination. I should have thought you had little to learn on that score. But, since you do ask, there are basically three options open to us.'

Aziz was somewhat put off by the deep frown surfacing on the wrinkled face of el-Fazzah, but he continued.

'First, we send in some of our own men. I take it, Colonel, that we have some sufficiently skilled to carry out such an operation?'

'It would present no difficulties, Minister. We have desert

patrols capable of the most clandestine activities. I think I can assure you that, given such a mission, we could carry it out successfully.'

'The only trouble with that,' said Kassem, ever mindful of the diplomatic ramifications of failure, 'is if anything goes wrong and our soldiers are clearly implicated. The ensuing scandal would only add to the likelihood of war and would lend an enormous amount of international credibility to Rampuri's cause.'

Aziz glowered at Kassem.

'I am merely going over the various possibilities,' he said acidly. 'If I may continue?'

'But of course,' soothed Kassem. 'I only thought it best to discuss each option as you presented it.'

'Our second option is to enlist the support of one of the disaffected groups within Omali or Qasar.'

The mutterings around the table left Aziz with little doubt about what his colleagues thought of this scenario.

'As I thought,' he continued, 'you can foresee as many problems as I can. There are no end of factions to choose from in both countries. But can we trust any of them? You all know the answer to that question,' he smiled.

'And your third option, Aziz?' Kaddous was beginning to revert to his former opinion of the Minister of Finance.

'We hire some soldiers of fortune.'

'How original,' scoffed Kaddous. 'And where do you propose to get them? Cuba? North Korea?' he added with a sneer.

'It might not be all that difficult to arrange.' The Foreign Minister came to the rescue of Aziz. 'You may not all be aware,' he looked directly at Kaddous, 'but when the British left Aden after the bloody victory of the National Liberation Front over its rival group of terrorists known as the Front for the Liberation of Occupied South Yemen, all was not peace in that unenviable area. Although FLOSY had lost its support from Egypt after the Six Day War of June 1967, and many of its members had perished in the ferocious fighting in Aden in November of the same year, a nucleus of its fanatics continued operations from their bases in the wild Radfan mountains in the interior. They have survived there for over a decade now, disrupting the workings of the government with their incessant guerilla tactics. Even the best of the British mercenaries who remained in Aden and sold their services to the NLF have been unable to flush them out. Not only have they terrorised their own country of South Yemen, but they have become a base and a training ground for communist terrorists operating into the Yemen and Saudi Arabia.'

'And they would be prepared to carry out a little assignment for us?' Aziz asked hopefully.

'Given time to establish the proper contacts, and given the right price, I am certain they would cooperate,' replied Kassem. 'My latest information is that they are desperately short of funds now that the Libyans have ended their token support in the vacuum left by Eygpt.'

'Given time. That would seem to be the nub of the matter. Time which we may not have. But must we sit back and wait for such an attack against us?' The quiet, rhetorical question came from el-Fazzah's Minister of Education and Culture, the ultra-conservative Mahadi el Sabah. This retiring, highly motivated man, whose noble and religious family had instilled in him the unwavering faith and high moral principles of the Wahabis – who were to Islam what the Puritans were to Christianity – and who had earned himself a double first at Oxford, was always listened to with the utmost respect.

'When it comes to deterring would-be aggressors we could learn from the Americans and the Israelis: from the sins of omission of the former, and the sins of commission of the latter.'

There were audible sighs of relief from several of the ministers present, as it was obvious now that el Sabah was not going to make a conciliatory speech on behalf of Yankee imperialism or Jewish nationalism, both of which were anathema throughout the entire Arab world.

'When the United States were threatened by the Soviet attempt to build missile bases in Cuba in 1962, the military in America were in no doubt about what should be done. However, the Kennedy brothers, John, the President, and Robert, the Attorney General, carried the day with their wishy-washy liberalism and refused permission to remove Cuba from the map. The result? Czechoslovakia 1968; Afghanistan 1979; Poland 1982 – two decades of barely restrained Soviet imperialism, and a continued decline in America's influence.

'Contrast the Israelis,' el Sabah continued. 'Like all of you I detest their presence in the midst of our people and lands. But how prosperous and secure they have become! In 1967 when Nasser called for a new holy war to drive the Israelis into the sea once and for all, and when Syria, Iraq and Jordan rallied to his crusading call, a full-scale invasion of Israel looked imminent. What did the Israelis do? Sit around and wait in fear and trembling for the Day of Judgement? Try to invoke an alliance with God-knows-who? Plot assassinations? Discuss economic sanctions? No, my friends. They launched, under the persuasion and guidance of General Moshe Dayan, the Six Day War: the most efficient and ruthless blitzkrieg ever. In less than a week the Egyptian airforce had been destroyed before they could scramble a single plane, and its army humiliated and swept out of Sinai to the west bank of Suez; the Jordanians had lost Jerusalem and the west bank of the river Jordan; and the Syrian artillery had been dislodged for ever from the Golan Heights.

'The pre-emptive strike, your Eminence, is what we should be going for,' he concluded, addressing el-Fazzah directly. The round of applause for this speech indicated the Cabinet's approval of el Sabah's plan.

'You seem, my friend, to have won wide support for your thesis,' the Emir nodded sagely. 'Alas, for once it is not as simple as you make out. Our neighbours are infinitely better prepared to cope with such a surprise attack than were the Egyptians and Syrians in 1967. Our boundaries are under constant radar scan. Mobile anti-aircraft missile batteries are operating along corridors designed to intercept any attacks on the main civilian and military targets which we, or anyone else, could launch. The Omalis have just taken delivery of twenty Russian MiG-25 Foxbat supersonic interceptors. Qasar has a potent force of French Mirage III-E Dagger jets and Super Etendards – I need not remind you of the havoc they created against the British in the Falklands a few years ago.'

Chakir'was amazed at el-Fazzah's grasp of detail. Even he had been unaware of the number of Russian fighters so recently supplied to Omali. But then Shamin was not on his staff.

'No, Mahadi, it is not often we are in disagreement, but I must rule out your suggestion, as you and the others have ruled out every other idea put forward this afternoon.'

'Then it would seem to me that we have no option but to discuss terms with Rampuri,' the Minister of Foreign Affairs made a despairing gesture around the Cabinet table, knowing full well that many of their heads would roll if this were to happen.

'Not quite, Yusif Karim.' The Emir had decided that now was the time to reveal all.

'We could', he continued, looking hard at everyone present and daring them to disagree with him, 'develop a nuclear offensive capability which would deter even the most fanatical.'

There was, as el-Fazzah had anticipated, a totally stunned silence. It was followed a few moments later with utter bedlam.

'Impossible,' cried Kaddous. 'Technologically impossible.'

'It would be too immoral.' Kassem shook his head gravely. 'The conditions of sale expressly forbade any attempt to establish a weapons' capability. Moreover, as you all know, we also signed the Non-Proliferation Treaty which is internationally binding.'

'We signed it, Yusif, but we did not ratify it,' reminded the Emir.

'Bah. Words. There is principle at stake. I could never be party to this,' Kassem said emphatically. He blanched at the prospect of a nuclear holocaust.

'Terms. Agreements. Meaningless!' Colonel Chakir looked around menacingly. 'There is only one question to be answered, Excellency. Could it be done, and within the time-scale at our disposal?'

'The short answer, Colonel, is yes to both parts of your question. But the matter is of such importance that I would like the Cabinet to be fully briefed before arriving at a decision. We have already had an arduous three hours debating the various options this afternoon. I propose we break for an hour just now. When we reconvene my son, Taherali, will deliver a paper to you. We can then proceed to have an informed discussion on the matter.'

El-Fazzah dismissed his colleagues with a curt nod, and led the way out to the dining room which had been prepared for a substantial meal in anticipation of a lengthy evening session.

Taherali el-Fazzah was remarkably cool and composed as he stood to address the Cabinet. Generations of aristocratic breeding, a lifetime of opulence and years of socialising amongst the intelligent and the chic had combined to produce an air of assurance and urbanity far in advance of his twenty-five years. There was no doubt in his mind, nor in the minds of anyone present after he had finished, that he was the next ruler of Dhubat.

'Gentlemen, I shall be as brief and direct as possible in outlining our thinking on this matter. It would be most fruitful if I were to present a summary of the entire question to begin with, and to take up specific points in more detail with you in our ensuing discussion.

'While Kuwait decided back in 1978 to cancel its plans for a small training reactor, and while the Saudis were dithering with proposals to set up an Atomic Energy Commission and to establish small-scale nuclear desalination plants on the Red Sea coast, we, alone amongst the Gulf nations, forged ahead with a full-scale commercial programme. We were scorned at the time by our neighbours. We did not have the density of population nor the heavy concentration of industry to avoid rendering such a technology superfluous, they told us. We would be driven to the verge of bankruptcy by the soaring costs of such a programme. Admittedly, we have a current overcapacity in our 600 megawatt reactor – but this will disappear once we have completed our electricity supply grid system in about eighteen months from now. And, let us be honest, gentlemen, costs have soared from the original $1,250 million to around $4,000 million as construction delays, inflation, fuel supplies and consultancy fees have been added – but we are far from bankruptcy, as I'm certain Mr Aziz will confirm,' he grinned in the direction of the Minister of Finance, who nodded his agreement.

'What we now have is an energy base for the future industrial expansion and diversification of our economy for the years beyond the oil boom. Our neighbours will increasingly regret their parsimony and lack of vision on this issue.

'Moreover, gentlemen, what we also have is the foundation of our inviolate national security. There is no doubt in my mind that the acquisition of nuclear generating equipment is the most direct and most assured way of establishing a nuclear weapons' capability. This, of course, was not uppermost in the minds of the previous regime who negotiated the purchase of our reactor; but it is the most vital consideration forced upon us now by the crisis and threat facing our country. You have already discussed the conventional solutions to our dilemma, and have found them all wanting. We must now consider in detail the only option left open to us, leaving aside the morality,' he stared directly at Kassem, thereby acknowledging that he had been permitted to eavesdrop electronically on the afternoon's session of the Cabinet, 'and concentrating on the realities of the world in which we live.

'In order to build nuclear weapons we require two basic ingredients – fuel and expertise. To be frank, gentlemen, we have problems in both areas which will take great ingenuity to solve.

'First, fuel. As you are aware, we were not permitted to buy a heavy-water reactor which would have enabled us to become virtually independent of the main supplier countries in terms of our continuing fuel needs. The Saudis had already established, with the help of French and American exploration companies, that our part of the world has a considerable potential for natural uranium extraction, and supplies are readily available from countries like Nigeria, Libya and Algeria. However, our light water reactor requires slightly enriched uranium, for which we are currently dependent on France, Germany and the USA; although we have already started open negotiations with Brazil and Spain, and clandestine talks with Italy and Portugal, in an attempt to become less dependent on the political whims of any one group of supplier countries. But, in order to build an explosive device we require highly refined fissionable materials, either extremely enriched uranium or, preferably, plutonium. These weapons-grade materials are exceedingly difficult to produce or acquire.

'As far as the production side is concerned there are basically two approaches which can be adopted. The first is to concentrate on enriched uranium. As I have said, it is relatively easy, though time-consuming because of the detailed negotiations to be made, to acquire supplies from outside. Iran, before the Ayatollah Khomeini cancelled its nuclear programme and began converting already completed cooling towers into the biggest grain silos ever envisaged, had bought itself a ten per cent share in the multinational uranium enrichment plant run by Eurodif at Tricastin in the south of France.

'Iraq bought in enriched uranium from France, Brazil and Portugal in unspecified amounts and degrees of enrichment. Despite the fact that further enrichment to weapons-grade was necessary, the Iraqis had, by the end of 1980, certainly the know-how, if not an actual stockpile of sufficiently fissionable materials, to make several atomic bombs. It was for this reason, even more than the fact that the Mossad attempt to sabotage Iraq's nuclear reactors when they were under construction by the French in Toulon in 1977 had been less effective than planned, that the self-righteous Israelis launched their irresponsible bomber attack on the Iraqi nuclear stations in June 1981.

'The drawback, of course, with buying in supplies from abroad is that the degree of fuel-enrichment is strictly controlled by the supplier nations and by the International Atomic Energy Agency which has wide-ranging rights of inspection even in the purchasing nations. This means that any would-be maker of nuclear weapons has to develop the capacity to further upgrade these supplies to weapons-grade uranium.

'This upgrading can be done officially or unofficially, indeed illicitly. Let us take the case of Pakistan. In 1975, after years of negotiation with France and the IAEA, it was agreed that Pakistan could purchase a complete commercial-size reprocessing factory from the French. The Americans, however, who had blackmailed their economic puppet,

Canada, to break off all nuclear connections with Pakistan in 1976, now applied the same degree of pressure on France. In consequence, the French reneged on their commitment to Pakistan in 1979. However, the Pakistanis contrived to purchase independently, and through dubious channels, from a number of French and Canadian companies, the necessary components to enable it to build its own gas centrifuge uranium enrichment plant to the south of Islamabad without any further outside help. By such means, Pakistan had, by early 1984, sufficient supplies of bomb-grade uranium to begin the manufacture of weapons.

'Even before 1984, however, Pakistan had clearly demonstrated the second way to manufacture weapons-grade materials, through the enrichment of plutonium. While international attention was focused, or should I say directed, on to the wranglings over the uranium plant at Kahuta, forty kilometres south of Islamabad, a small plutonium reprocessing plant was being built in utter secrecy near Rawalpindi. Before the Canadians had been forced out of the Pakistan market they had sold and built a heavy-water reactor at Karachi, which had gone fully operational in 1972. This type of reactor produces plutonium as a spent fuel. It is normally stored on site pending the future development of reprocessing or storage of high-level radioactive wastes in stable forms. Part of this pool – sufficient for about three or four bombs – was reprocessed and enriched at their clandestine plant by the Pakistanis and led to their test explosion, courtesy of the Chinese, in 1983.

'Given sufficient time we could develop a programme along one or other of the avenues mentioned. However, that is the one commodity we do not have in the present crisis. Iraq had been planning its programme since 1956 when it established an Atomic Energy Commission; Pakistan has admitted wanting to develop a bomb since the 1960s; but we are newcomers in the field since 1976.

'Even if we did have another ten years' grace in which to build our own reprocessing plant such a scheme would always be vulnerable from outside attack. I have already mentioned the arrogant Israeli attack on Iraq in 1981 when the Jews poured scorn on the Iraqis as being too stupid to require such a nuclear research programme as they were establishing. The only thing that saved Pakistan from a similar attack on their installations was the fact that 2,500 kilometres, and the considerable might of Pakistan's air force, stood in Israel's way. I am not suggesting that Israel would attack us – although they would not be slow, like Hitler against Poland in 1939, in inventing a reason if they felt it necessary. But if Rampuri continues his so far successful wooing of Iraq we could be under threat from that direction, especially now that Sadaam Hussein is coming to the fore.

'No, gentlemen. We cannot produce our own fuel; nor can we buy it, legitimately or otherwise, from abroad. We must, therefore, help ourselves to some.'

At this seemingly preposterous suggestion, the Cabinet, which had hung on Taherali's every word up until then as the plan and its implications had been gradually unfolded, started buzzing.

'Before you all start telling me how crazy I am, let me tell you that what I propose has been thoroughly researched by us over the past few months. It is not without precedent, and we are now at the stage in our planning that it could be put into effect almost immediately if you approve.

'If the Israelis could hijack fuel back in 1968 after France had cut off their supplies and before their own uranium extraction from Dead Sea phosphates was fully under way, then I believe that we could do the same now. Admittedly our task would be greater, as we must obtain high grade uranium or plutonium which could only come from a country such as the United Kingdom. The Israelis simply had to board a Panamanian cargo boat and steal a consignment of natural uranium in transit from Nigeria to India and not, therefore, subject to very tight security. Nevertheless, it could be done.

'Although I cannot go into exact detail with you at present' – he turned to his father, who nodded his approval – 'I cannot expect you to agree to give us carte blanche. What we propose is roughly as follows.

'Our target is British plutonium. Ideally, we would like to acquire bomb-grade plutonium which would require a minimal amount of effort on our part to turn into weapons. However, at no stage in the process would it be possible for

72

anything other than several Red Army divisions to do this. Security within Sellafield in the north-west of England is unbreachable. Transportation from there to the Royal Ordnance Factory at Burghfield near Reading is entrusted to the British Army. Burghfield, where the nuclear warheads are actually built, is the single most secure government site anywhere in the UK. To the outsider or CND protester it is guarded only by high fences and armed Defence Ministry police with Alsatian dogs; but we know better. Crack members of the famous Red Berets, the British paratroopers, are there to take whatever action would be necessary against attack from any source. With all due respect, Colonel Chakir, we do not want to get involved in a suicidal shoot-out with these highly trained and barely restrained thugs.

'There is, of course the nearby Atomic Weapons Research Establishment at Aldermaston. It is a much easier, but much less fruitful, target, as the work done there is essentially theoretical involving much analytical computer work in the fields of mathematics, physics and electronics. It is not our intention to out-think the Soviets in highly sophisticated weapons technology. We simply want a few kilos of fuel,' said Taherali with a rare hint of humour which was lost in the intense atmosphere of the Cabinet room, 'and so shall have to look elsewhere.

'Reactor-grade plutonium, which has a lower explosive yield due to the large element of plutonium-240 it contains, has already been tested and has produced a very satisfactory explosion. Really, this only leaves the fast reactor site at Dounreay in the far north of Scotland. This fast reactor, or breeder reactor as it is sometimes known, uses plutonium-239, which is the fissionable isotope we need, enriched to twenty per cent in the form of ceramic fuel rods mixed with uranium oxide. This fuel is actually made at Sellafield, or Windscale as most people still call it, and transported to Dounreay in a variety of ways by road, sea and, in the near future, air. Once the fuel has been partially burnt in the reactor it is reprocessed on site, along with the plutonium which has been 'bred' during the fission process, and the plutonium is recovered in a nitrate liquid form. It is then sent by sea to Sellafield where the nitrate is converted back into oxide form.

And so the cycle continues.

'Our problem has been to decide at which part of the cycle to intervene. Obviously we can only consider obtaining the plutonium when it is in a stable state for transportation; and this further narrows our options to one of two points. We either attempt our seizure when the fuel is en route from Dounreay to Windscale, or vice-versa, as we have clearly established that security within the Windscale plant is watertight.

'There are advantages in both propositions. On the face of it, the easier option would be the sea journey from Caithness to Cumbria. Security during the loading operation at Dounreay is risible, and the cargo boat then proceeds entirely without escort. However, for two reasons we have rejected this.

'First, our experience of this type of operation is nil. We would be working in a totally alien environment at sea in the British Navy's own paddling pond. The weather is notoriously unpredictable in those seas; the operation would be difficult to time and coordinate; and there would be a lack of the one element which virtually guarantees the success of this sort of terrorist activity – the proximity of innocent people who can be threatened or held hostage. And, I must be honest, gentlemen, we have been unable to ascertain exactly what the ships' captains have been instructed to do in the event of an imminent boarding of a plutonium carrying vessel. The British are very much aware of the possibility of such an attempt – possibly from a source like the Irish Republican Army – and as well as probable rapid air support from one of the mainland bases, the ship's captain may well have orders to scuttle the entire cargo to the bottom of the Atlantic.

'Second, even if we were to overcome the difficulties just mentioned, we would have to face up to the fact that the plutonium in this liquid nitrate form is not nearly as useful to us as the actual fuel rods. The process to isolate the plutonium-239 from the nitrate solution would, quite frankly, be beyond our resources. However, we could quite readily adapt the ceramic fuel rods which come from Sellafield.

'Consequently, we must go for the seizure of a shipment en route from Windscale to Dounreay. It will be difficult, but not impossible. All I can say about this for the present is that we are confident of evolving a scheme which will be workable.

'If I can deal quickly with our other basic requirement – expertise. Please do not get me wrong, gentlemen. I am in no way implying that our present nuclear establishment is in any way defective. We have recruited the best in their fields from the top nuclear countries in Europe and the Americas at no inconsiderable cost; and we currently have a rigorous training scheme under way for our young people here in Dhubat as well as about thirty studying at universities in Britain and the United States. No, our personnel are not defective; merely deficient in certain key areas of training and experience – deficiencies which would take about a decade to overcome if we were to depend on a recruiting and training drive of our own. It is ten months we have, not ten years. To get straight to the point, we need people who are expert in working with plutonium and the handling of highly fissile materials in the construction of atomic weapons. I have in mind a variation of the British nineteenth century press gang. At this very moment in time dossiers are being compiled on half-a-dozen key personnel who would fit the bill.

'In conclusion, gentlemen, what we are proposing is not without risk; it is a bold, daring and imaginative response to the challenge facing us. We are confident it can succeed. We ask for your loyal support in turning our ploughshares back into swords.'

Twenty minutes after he had started speaking, Taherali sat down, unaware that his closing Judaic allusion had been lost on all save el Sabah. His speech had not been the brief introduction to the debate he had promised the Cabinet. Like all experienced public speakers who have to win support for a controversial plan he had gone into considerable convincing detail and had in fact pre-empted every conceivable question, or had invoked security reasons for disallowing debate.

His father thanked him curtly.

The ensuing discussion lasted a mere ten minutes, and ended with a near-unanimous verdict in favour of the plan.

'It grieves me, your Excellency, but I cannot go along with this madness,' said Yusif Karim Kassem. 'I . . . . .'

'Very well, my friend,' the Emir cut him off with a conciliatory and understanding gesture. He then closed the meeting after swearing all present to the utmost secrecy.

Three kilometres outside the town, Kassem's chauffeured Cadillac was purring along the highway en route for his palatial residence when the time switch clicked quietly and ignited the briefcase bomb which the Minister of the Interior had been ordered to place in the boot. There were no remains left of Kassem to place under house arrest the following morning.

At 12 noon on the next day the sudden death from heart failure of Yusif Karim Kassem was announced to the world along with the appointment of Taherali el-Fazzah as the new Foreign Minister for Dhubat.

Part Two

7

The Counsels Of The Wise

EVEN in the liberal days of the Shah, the city of Teheran had
not exactly been the fun capital of the Middle East. Not that
Alister Graham was aware of this, as he was on his first, and
he fervently hoped last, trip to Iran. Now, under the rabid
right-wing leadership of the Muslim fanatic, the Ayatollah
Khomeini, it had even less to offer than Stornoway, the capital
of his birthplace Lewis in the Outer Hebrides.

Much of the modern part of the city had still to be rebuilt
after the recent bitter fighting of the civil war. What was left –
apart from the splendid conference centre at the university
which had somehow escaped damage – was dull and
unattractive in the extreme. The new government had issued
orders closing down every establishment in the sprawling city
which had catered for the vices of the Christians, as the
Ayatollah liked to put it. As a result, not only were there no
nightclubs or brothels – indeed it later emerged that all
known prostitutes had been shot in the streets – even the
cinemas and discos had been boarded up. It was, as Alister
said to himself, a right asshole of a place. At least you could
get a good drink in Stornoway – not to mention a good bit of
the other, as he smilingly recalled.

Fortunately he did not intend to stay too long. The

conference he was due to address on the subject of fast breeder nuclear reactors would be over in three days time. His part, in fact, would be over after the following afternoon's session, but protocol dictated that he stay to the end. Not that he always followed the dictate of convention. In fact, he recollected, most of his sightseeing had been done whilst truanting from boring sessions in lovely cities.

He had read recently that the 21.00 hours curfew had been lifted as a sign of a return to normality.

Christ, he thought, they could have brought it bloody forward to seven o'clock, and it still wouldn't make any difference.

Thankfully, his flight in had been in the late afternoon. He did not have too much time to kill. There was nothing for it but to return to his hotel room. Cursing his lack of forethought in not bringing in a bottle of Scotch through customs – although it was not worth risking a public flogging for – he settled down on top of his bed and switched on the wall-mounted radio. All five click stops gave the same sound – nothing.

Jesus; he must have banned music as well, muttered Alister, as he complimented himself for at least remembering to bring along a couple of his favourite types of books, picked up from the W H Smith stall at Heathrow. Like many an intellectual with a scientific training, Alister could not abide fiction – with two exceptions. He loved a good thriller in the Frederick Forsyth or Jack Higgins mould; and he was hopelessly addicted to pornography. Knowing that he'd probably get a finger, if not something infinitely worse, chopped off if caught with the latter entering this most recent, and therefore most extreme, Muslim republic, he had picked up a title about Tsarist gold and the Germans in World War Two, and a tale of CIA intrigue in South America. As he would be meeting some old colleagues from the States on the following day he chose the one about the CIA. It would give him some more ammo with which to bug his over-serious American friends.

The conference got off to a livelier start than usual. The first speaker, Soviet academician Alexei Suvarov, had as his theme state control of nuclear development. His remarks about security and safety procedures, in the course of which he castigated the record of the USA as compared to the USSR, brought about a highly volatile exchange – most out of character for such a forum – during question time. Suvarov accused the USA of gross negligence in its management of the nuclear industry, well-armed with numerous specific details which the Americans had been forced to make public under their Freedom of Information Act. He delivered a devastating polemic on the western members of the Nuclear Suppliers Group for their indiscriminate and irresponsible sales push of the 1960s in the course of which nuclear knowledge had proliferated around the world, making the later upsurge of nuclear weapons inevitable. The Americans' attempts to exercise controls over particular systems in the late 1970s, when they had forced developing countries to purchase light-water reactors instead of the cheaper and relatively less-complicated heavy-water reactors, were dismissed by Suvarov during question time as further examples of Yankee economic imperialism.

'The only reason,' he told his furious American questioners, 'your country belatedly tried to exercise some degree of licencing responsibility was to ensure the dependency of developing nations on the west for supplies of enriched uranium needed for light-water reactors. The activities of the Middle Eastern oil cartel OPEC in the 1970s will seem like kindergarten games compared to the pressures you will be in a position to exert in the 1990s,' he added, petulantly and almost wistfully, as he began to drift away from the main line of his theme.

The session broke up in near pandemonium as the chairman, Professor Kurt Bradheimer of the UN's International Atomic Energy Agency in Vienna, vainly tried to restore order from his podium.

Graham had arranged lunch with two long-standing

American acquaintances. Harvey Lubeck was Director of the Atomic Data Bank attached to the Massachusetts Institute of Technology, and as such was responsible for servicing virtually the whole range of the sciences. He was one of that tiny number of people who, having specialised deeply, could turn their minds with equal aptitude to whatever problem faced them. His working knowledge of a dozen different scientific disciplines was nothing short of genius. Alister and he had collaborated on a number of projects over the years. Gary Wasylciw, whom Alister had known since their doctoral research days together at Oxford, had for years held a senior administrative post in the Nuclear Regulatory Commission, the bureaucratic organisation charged with controlling the nuclear industry in the USA. He had resigned from this prestigious and highly lucrative post in the middle of 1979 in the wake of a number of revelations which had exposed the NRC as a body much more concerned with protecting the industry than the American public. There had even been widespread calls for the scrapping of this supposedly independent body in favour of a permanent branch of the Federal government. Realising the validity of the criticisms, though there had been no complicity in the cover-ups on his part, Wasylciw had resigned. Not only that, he had immediately joined the Union of Concerned Scientists based in Cambridge, Massachusetts, a self-appointed commission to regulate the regulators.

Alister was itching to get at both of them.

'Hi Harve, Gary,' he affected an exaggerated Southern drawl as he shook hands enthusiastically with them. 'You guys sure got one hell of a roasting this morning.'

'Great to see you, Al,' grinned Wasylciw, patting him on the back. 'But we gave as good as we got to that ol' sonofabitch. Right, buddy?' he looked at Lubeck for reassurance.

'Sure we did,' agreed Harvey. 'And you know that for damn sure, Ally.'

'OK, OK. You should know by this time not to take

everything I say seriously,' laughed Alister, whose laugh changed to a scowl as he eyed the suspicious fluid which the waiter was placing before them.

'Speciality of Iran, lads,' grinned Alister. 'Camel piss soup. Always serve this for starters over here. Tastes like what it is, but at least it's sterile. Which is more than can be said for what's to follow,' he winked across at the next table, who were one course ahead of them. The Americans, who had known him for years, were still not accustomed to his couthy and often caustic Scots humour.

'Seriously though, Harve, the Russkies do have a point when they talk about safety controls and procedures. You people had a hell of a near thing in '79 when the Three Mile Island plant at Harrisburg, Pennsylvania, had a partial core melt-down.'

'Yeah. Agreed. Although had they been following the procedures laid down by the NRC . . . .'

'But that's the point. Suvarov was pretty near the mark talking about monopoly capitalists cutting any kind of corner which would increase their profitability. The procedures weren't properly laid down for fear of offending big business.'

'Come on, Ally, that's a gross distortion of the truth. You know as well as we do that Three Mile wasn't like that. The NRC enquiry, backed up by President Carter's special commission headed by Johnny Kennedy, showed that it was largely due to human error. After the pump failure in the secondary cooling system the auxiliary feedwater pumps couldn't deliver their coolant because some stupid cunt had left the discharge valves closed during an earlier maintenance drill. And when it came to using the emergency core cooling systems the dumdums didn't know what the fuck to do. On, off, on, off, ...'

'More times than a whore's knickers,' Alister finished the sentence with a grin. 'That was at the point when the reactor core temperature went off the scale and you had a melt-down of some of the fuel rods around 3600°F. You were lucky the whole lot didn't go right there and then.'

'Yeah. But stick to the point, Ally. It didn't happen because we were cutting corners like you and Suvarov were saying.'

'Like hell it didn't, Harve. Good God, man, your own enquiries were severely critical of the training of plant operators. Half of them wouldn't even get to do a craft apprenticeship in Europe. And, anyway, our state-controlled plants rely on automation and electronics to a far greater extent than yours. But all of these cost money, and tend to reduce profitability. Your totally independent companies just won't spend the cash on such refinements.'

Wasylciw, who had kept out of the conversation up to this point, now came in.

'I hate to admit it, Harve, but, being perfectly honest, Al is right in a sense when he speaks about cost-consciousness and profitability.'

'Cost-cutting and profitability,' corrected Alister.

'OK. Cost-cutting. There were numerous faults connected with the Babcock and Wilcox cooling systems. Jammed valves; pump failures in the primary and auxiliary coolant systems; faulty pressure gauges. I'm not saying these were as a result of a deliberate attempt to cut corners; but the NRC knew about them at least six months before Three Mile after a series of similar failures at the same company's reactor outside Sacramento, California. The Commission turned down its own inspector's report which advocated a detailed investigation of the company's plans. In fact, this put the final nail in the Commission's coffin as far as I, and a number of others, was concerned – especially in the wake of the revelations of the Nugget File.'

'Yes. I was going to ask you about that, Gary,' said Alister. 'I can just about believe the reports of incidents where workers left tools, pieces of plywood, and even welding kits inside reactor cooling systems after they had carried out repairs. But the one about the basketball must surely be apocryphal?'

'Wish to hell it had been, Al.' Gary shook his head resignedly. 'It's hard to believe that anyone would be so dumb as to plug a hole in a reactor coolant conduit with a basketball, covered in tape to add on a few centimetres in circumference, then walk away and start the whole system up. But that's exactly what the stupid bastards did. As soon as the pressure built up thousands of gallons of radioactive water spilled out.'

'Fucking incredible,' Alister couldn't suppress a grin, though he knew full well it was no laughing matter. 'What have you got to say to all that, Harvey?'

'Not a lot. There have been a few regrettable incidents. But you can't put them down to defects in our economic system.'

'A few regrettable incidents?' mimicked Alister. 'Jesus Christ, man. Venting of radioactive steam and gas over Harrisburg; discharges of contaminated waste into the Susquehanna river endangering the drinking water of 100,000 people in down-river Lancaster; a potentially explosive build-up of hydrogen in the reactor dome; partial core melt-down; evacuation of nearby residents and civil defence plans to evacuate a ten-mile radius? And you call that a "regrettable incident"? And what about the basic arithmetical mistakes which caused the temporary closedown of five reactors in 1979 because their cooling systems would not have withstood the stress of even a minor earthquake?'

'OK, OK. You've scored your debating points, Ally. Anyway, before you cast any more stones, as the good Lord said, you English aren't without sin in this respect either.'

'English?' bellowed Alister, not failing to rise to the bait. 'Did you say English, Kraut? Bloody British, if you please.'

'Fine. You British, then,' continued Lubeck, delighted with himself for needling Alister, and eager to launch a counter-attack of his own. 'You've had a few gems of your own.'

'Very droll,' nodded Alister, appreciating the metaphor. 'But at least we don't have enough to publish an entire File.'

'Like hell you don't, fella.' Lubeck was rising to the task. 'You could fill a book on Windscale alone. Over three hundred reported accidents, leakages and emergencies!'

Alister knew what was coming, but there was no way he could avoid the roasting he was about to receive.

'You've polluted the air, the sea and the land over a vast area around the Cumbrian coast, and done untold damage to the ecosystem. You've killed God knows how many people already, including a dozen or so kids. You've contaminated hundreds of workers and thousands of local inhabitants. Christ, man; don't get me started.'

'Oh, come on now, Harvey. It's not that bad,' Alister interjected lamely.

'Isn't it, buddy? What about the fire at Number One Pile in 1957, then?'

'1957? That was almost before I was born, Harve. We've come

a long way since then,' said Alister, vainly trying to sidestep the issue.

'Oh no and you don't,' scoffed Lubeck. 'That argument won't wash. Your own National Radiological Protection Board eventually admitted – after a quarter of a century of denials from the authorities – that thirty-two deaths were directly attributable to the '57 fire, when vast quantities of cancer inducing polonium polluted the atmosphere. Young girls in Ireland who were exposed to this fallout in heavy rain later gave birth to deformed children. And God knows how many other genetic problems have still to come to light.

'More recently the blow-back incident in the Head End Plant in 1973 filled a whole fucking building with highly radioactive ruthenium gas and contaminated thirty-five men – one of them so badly that his whole body became radioactive. Yet you still disclaimed any responsibility for his premature death at the age of fifty. And there have been repeated releases of radioactive gases, mainly iodine, into the atmosphere around the plant, contaminating fields and livestock. For Christ's sake, man; one farmer alone has reported forty unusual deaths amongst his cattle. And what about all the ones slaughtered before any symptoms showed? Pity the poor buggers who have had a Sunday joint from one of them.'

'Yes. But we haven't been complacent about it. The management of the plant have been censured for their lack of judgement and safety consciousness in a government report which said quite clearly that they had broken the law.'

'Come on, Ally. And why weren't they prosecuted? I'll tell you. Because BNFL is 100 per cent owned by the Government. They are not going to cut off their nose to spite their face.'

'You're being unfair now, Harve. BNFL have voluntarily cut down the amount of effluent discharged into the sea as new evidence of contamination has been accurately evaluated and verified.'

'I was coming to that, boy. Don't worry. The mothers have been dumping one million gallons of waste, containing over thirty different radioactive elements including plutonium and americium into the Irish Sea every day for nearly thirty years now! An amount equal to the total marine discharges of every other country in the world together! A quarter of a ton of plutonium alone – and it is going to remain active for 100,000 years. Shit, man; the Irish Sea is the most radioactive in the world. Some fish samples are five thousand times more radioactive than fish caught off Iceland.'

'Granted. I can't dispute that. But the Authority has admitted that some locals have already consumed more than the recommended lifetime doses of certain elements. They've been quite open about it.'

'Big deal! They've been as open as my arse, Ally.'

'Now, now. Restrain yourself, Gary. He doesn't really mean it!' Alister brought a vivid blush to Wasylciw's face.

'You know as well as I do,' Lubeck continued, 'that independent research has reported contamination levels double those conceded by the government. It's reached the level now where anyone who regularly eats fish from the area around Windscale is quite significantly at risk. In fact, at least thirty, and perhaps as many as one hundred and fifty deaths are statistically probable from the dumping of wastes into the Irish Sea. It's the last place on earth where you would want to be on a sea-food diet.'

Not that Alister had to be told this. For years now, and long before Peter Taylor's figures to which Lubeck was referring had been published, he had been aware of the hazards of even so-called low-level effluents. Many of his friends in the North of Scotland would not touch lobster or crab caught between Strathy Point and Holborn Head, and even outwith this ten-mile radius of Dounreay were wary.

'That's why I didn't have the lobster salad for starters,' said Alister. And he was not jesting either. 'I won't eat crustaceans unless I know for sure they were caught nowhere near a nuclear factory.'

'Precisely. I had the soup too.' Harvey grimaced at the recollection. Then, just as Alister was beginning to think that he was being let off the hook, Lubeck resumed his tirade.

'But it doesn't stop there, Ally. The plutonium which was supposed to lie dormant on the sea-bed is, in fact, moving. It's getting washed ashore. The beaches and estuaries of Cumbria and south-west Scotland are full of it. Ten times natural background radiation levels are considered mild in those areas. Hell, the salt marsh fields on the edge of the

Ravenglass estuary have levels 100 times greater. It's a hazard to even walk on them. Yet sheep are allowed to graze there. Thousands of unsuspecting liver eaters up and down the country are having their body cells assaulted and deformed as a result at this very moment. There's gonna be a helluva crop of cancers in the late '90s.

'And even that's not the end of the story.' Lubeck was driving for the touch-line now. 'As the silt dries, airborne particles of plutonium, americium, caesium and God knows what else are being carried inland and deposited inside people's houses and bodies. Little wonder that cancer rates amongst adults in rural Cumbria have risen by forty per cent in the last decade. But far and away worst of all is the way the children have suffered because of their enormously greater vulnerability to plutonium. Stomach, kidney, bone, brain, lymphatic and, above all, blood cancers have incidence rates varying between six and sixty times the statistical national averages. And it does not happen by chance, despite what the BNFL health and safety experts would have us believe.'

Alister was relieved that the memorandum sent to the government in 1958 by John Dunster, Windscale's then health and safety manager, was still on the secrets list. God knows what his American friends were going to say when it became known that radioactive discharges were deliberately high as part of a callous scientific experiment on the local populace.

'And what does your government do about all this, Ally?'

'Wel.......'

'I'll tell you. It sets up more commissions of enquiry, and pays out the odd few thousands in compensation here and there. But can your unions get radiation exposure recognised as an industrial disease? Like shit they can. No more than ours in the States. Your nationalised nuclear industry is no more willing to pick up the compensation tab than our private enterprise ones are. And your government has consistently ignored every international entreaty to stop dumping nuclear waste into the sea. Why? Because it's conveniently cheap for it to continue so doing, and it doesn't place the lucrative four billion dollars worth of business it gets from Japan and half of Europe in jeopardy.

'No sir, Alister. Don't run away with the idea that we Yanks are the only ones who have cut any corners.'

He was just about to regale Alister further about the unquantifiable damage to the ecosystem around Sellafield with the continued seepage of thousands of gallons of highly toxic waste from the Magnox Waste Silo through its nine foot thick concrete and steel walls into the earth when Wasylciw mercifully cut in.

'Come on now, you guys,' he said. 'We shouldn't be sniping at each other's programs like this. Know what pisses me off the most? The way the Soviets still won't admit to having caused the biggest nuclear disaster of all times in the Urals in the winter of 1957-58, probably killing hundreds. And at the same time levelling off at everyone else for their lack of safety and security. That guy Medulov . . . . . . '

'Medvedev,' corrected Alister.

'Yeah, Al; Medvedev. He spilled the whole beans in 1978 when he was expelled to the West. Not that there hadn't been an inkling of it before then. Several Russian Jews who had been repatriated to Israel in the early '70s had brought out some whispers of something having happened. But Medvedev painted the whole picture.'

'Yes, I've read his book, *Nuclear Disaster in the Urals*, said Alister. 'What a sorry catalogue.'

'And confirmed by our Oak Ridge National Laboratory team,' added Lubeck.

'Yeah. There's never been anything like it,' continued Wasylciw. 'Dozens of townships have been removed from the map in the southern Urals between Sverdlovsk and Chelyabinsk. Freshwater lakes over an area of one thousand square kilometres have never been stocked with fish while all those round about have been. An entire river system has had to be diverted to lessen the risks of water-borne contamination being spread outwith the devastated area. We can even tell from the Russians' own radiological studies, which they readily make available to us, almost exactly how the disaster happened. They stopped short in their whole waste disposal process and stored large quantities of virtually untreated wastes which contained high levels of ammonium nitrate. It would only take a failure in one of their storage tanks' cooling systems for the whole damned lot to go sky-high. Capitalism cutting corners? Jesus. The commies could sure show us a thing or two about that. State safety my ass.'

'Agreed, Gary. And as you say, still the bastards won't own up,' said Alister. 'But you must admit they have us whacked on the security angle, eh, Harvey?'

'Granted, Ally. But we live in a free society. So free that, under our Freedom of Information Act, you can get answers to just about anything from any branch of the government or industry. Congress and the general public wouldn't tolerate the military guarding every nuclear installation in the States. We've almost ninety reactors on the go, and at least three times that number of plants handling sensitive materials. The security Suvarov is advocating is only possible in a totalitarian regime where everyone is too shit-scared to protest anyway.'

'There's already a reaction setting in against the so-called nuclear state,' confirmed Wasylciw. 'People are voicing fears that we've already passed the point of compatibility with civil liberties. We three have all been positively vetted,' he continued. 'But nuclear industry workers are now being psychologically tested; people are being sacked if they dare to question company policy; there have been cases of phone-tapping; hell, one or two people like Karen Silkwood have even disappeared or been murdered in the States and in Italy. We can't go any further along this particular line.'

'Don't get so worked up lads,' said Alister. 'But I know exactly what you mean. We're not into it in such a big way as you folks, but we couldn't even begin to look at the safeguards Suvarov is suggesting. Not until there's a National Front government at any rate. Although that mightn't be too far away.' Alister was genuinely alarmed at the prospect. 'Still,' he added, 'by that time Scotland will have its independence, and there's no chance of us ever being anything other than a socialist country with our traditions. In the meantime, however, I must admit our plants, all of them, are pretty vulnerable to terrorist attack or sabotage; with the possible exception of the new reprocessing plant at Windscale. To satisfy the public enquiry and all our foreign customers we had to make that establishment absolutely failsafe.'

The lunchtime conversation had got a lot deeper than any of

them would have wanted. But, as Alister remarked, it had sure kept their minds off the crap they were being forced to eat.

It was now time to return to the conference hall. Alister would have to bug his friends about the CIA activities over dinner. He looked forward to that. The novel had given him enough angles to last for several dinners. And maybe after he'd read *Kolchak's Gold* this evening he would be able to bug Suvarov next. Not that he could have got anywhere near the esteemed academician. State security and all that, he thought.

'Shee'it, fellas. Time for y'all to learn all you ever wanted to know about us fast breeders, but were afraid to ask. Just keep the questions clean. We don't want to contaminate any more minds,' grinned Alister, as he dug his right index finger into Gary's ribs.

Gary felt the temperature rise as his neck, ears, face and glinting cranium all glowed a bright red. He could feel the tiny droplets of perspiration standing out on his scalp and hoped to hell that no-one else could see them. They could. Jesus, what an affliction to go through life with, he cursed to himself. His strict Lutheran upbringing in the tiny hamlet of Hines Creek, Illinois, had mentally scarred him for life. He felt as guilty as hell about anything with the remotest sexual connotation, even although he lived a life of relative innocence himself. He bitterly envied Alister Graham's liberal Roman Catholic upbringing in the Western Isles. Ready access to the confessional, with its on-the-spot dispensation and easy penance, made for well-balanced adults with consciences remarkably free from the guilt which plagued so many fundamentalist protestants.

Alister Graham was not the only delegate disgruntled with Teheran. Not that it came as any surprise to her, as Shamin el-Fazzah had been there more times than she would have wished. No-one in their right senses ever went to Teheran on a pleasure trip, but, as Shamin well knew, it was excellent for conducting business. Or, rather, it had been at one time. A crossroads of culture and trade in centuries past, it was still on every major international jet operator's list of stopovers from Europe to the Far East. Shamin had interests in both directions from Teheran.

On this occasion, however, she was hoping to combine more than a little pleasure with her business, if the background information she already had on Alister Graham was as accurate as her sources normally were. She was desperately in need of something pleasant to erase the horrendous memories of the public execution she had witnessed two weeks earlier. She was not to be disappointed in one sense; but she would find the vivid imagery was too deeply engraved to be erased in one night of ecstasy.

This was going to be a longer visit to Teheran than her usual one-night stopovers. One of the things Shamin could not tolerate was the pseudo-luxury of modern plastic and glass hotels. So she had broken with two of her basic codes of practice for this trip. First, instead of using the anonymity of a commercial airline, she had arrived direct from Dhubat in the family Lockheed executive jet. Second, she was staying at a friendly diplomat's luxury villa set in spectacular scenery high up in the foothills of the Elburz mountains near the town of Demavend, some forty miles to the north-east of Teheran. It had come through the recent revolution unscathed. Indeed, many of its inhabitants had been unaware of any momentous changes taking place at all. Cooled by the downward sweep of the north-easterly winds from the high Elburz, it was a perfect retreat from the blistering heat and dust of the high plateau around the capital city.

Shamin eagerly looked forward to returning there in the evening after the conference's first day.

Nuclear technology fascinated Shamin, although she had not specialised in the physical sciences at Cambridge. Not only had she taken a keen interest in her country's purchase of European technology in 1977, but she had played a not inconsiderable role in persuading certain top officials in the EEC, and at Euratom, to agree to the controversial sale by the Franco-German consortium. The politics of locating nuclear energy in the Middle East had been explosive, especially in the wake of Kissinger's failure to negotiate a stable peace between Sadat and Meir. Differing factions had found themselves in violent opposition, she could remember. In the end a few well-placed, highly lucrative business contracts to diversify other exports to Dhubat had placated the politicians and industrial lobbies, if not the general public. A couple of dozen deposits in the Luxembourg banks had also helped.

Shamin, therefore, actually enjoyed the first morning session of the conference. Many of the issues raised had been stirred up by the European press as arguments against the Dhubatis in 1977. She was sympathetic to the obviously hurt feelings of the American delegation.

She lunched alone, but sufficiently close to observe Alister Graham's table without being noticed herself.

As Alister rose to go, Shamin left her table also and timed her arrival at the exit to coincide with his. She was in no way offended by the obvious interest in the Scotsman's eyes as he made way for her. Perfect timing, Alister mistakenly complimented himself.

As the spokesman for the country which had led the world in fast-breeder reactor development – although it had long since lost that lead due to the dithering and lack of commitment of successive governments – Alister Graham was accorded an almost rare degree of respect by the other delegates. No-one present had to be convinced of the desirability of such a programme; nor did Alister assume that any one of the one hundred and twenty delegates needing converting. Each of the delegate nations, apart from the Soviet Union, had been subjected to pressure – some would say threats – from the Carter administration on the availability of high-grade plutonium supplies in the future and of America's aid. True, Carter had been less than subtle in trying to shape the future world-wide spread of nuclear technology by resorting to threats, veiled or otherwise, as in the suspension of massive aid to Pakistan in 1978. But no-one dared make the assumption that the USA would not enforce selective embargoes at some time in the future. Only those few countries possessing fast-breeder technology, with its unique ability to constantly produce more fuel than it actually consumed as an almost incidental by-product, were immune to such intimidation. Instead, Graham confined his talk – indeed he had been so requested by the International Commission on Atomic Development – to a résumé of the practical problems experienced by the UKAEA in their pioneering work.

In just under an hour, Graham sketched in considerable detail what to many non-scientists would appear to have been a catalogue of monstrous errors, but to the initiated were a fascinating and inevitable part of the empirical process. Cracks in the reactor core; unreliability of the sodium-to-water heat exchangers due to thermal corrosion, fatigue, vibration, fouling, maldistribution and flow and half-a-dozen other factors; over-heating of plutonium rods; accidental damage to marine life from low-grade effluent – all received the undivided attention of the delegates. In fact, Alister told little that was not already known to those with sufficient interest in the matter. The international scientific press – not to mention the local John O'Groat Journal, whose then editor had been openly anti-nuclear – had made no secret of the teething troubles. One of the few encouraging signs of a more responsible approach to international relations over the last decade or so had been an ever increasing openness about scientific matters, to which all nations – including the communist bloc – subscribed.

At the same time, Graham was not at liberty to divulge any information which might have been damaging to the security of the United Kingdom; and he was too seasoned a campaigner to let any slip. It would have been futile for anyone to attempt to elicit more details than had already been given: Graham was thus given an easy time during the open session following his talk.

Predictably, thought Alister, the Japanese delegates asked one or two general questions about the delicate balance of marine ecology surrounding such a plant. Ever since the famous press conference in Tokyo in 1954, following the American H-bomb test at Bikini Atoll in the central Pacific, where several of the fishermen who had been severely burned by radio-active ash were put on display by doctors, and when it was revealed that their catch had also been badly contaminated – though some of it had been sold before this was discovered – the Japanese fishing industry had put up a constant environmentalist lobby to their government.

Alister had been warned by the Foreign Office people who had been involved in screening his speech to expect something along this line. Not that Alister or anyone else present would have been lacking in understanding or sympathy for the Japanese position. As the only people on the planet who had ever experienced the full horror of the military applications of the awesome power which was under discussion released on them by a war machine which had been only too keen to see just exactly what their new weapon could do on a civilian target, they could be readily forgiven a pre-occupation with matters of such concern.

Alister assured the delegates that exhaustive tests had been carried out, at the instigation of the Atomic Energy Authority, to ascertain the effects of low-grade effluent. He was sufficiently candid to admit that in the early days some short-term damage had been done to plankton and had consequently worked its way up through the biological chain to affect some of the crustaceans. He did not tell the conference about the lobster fisherman's family from the local village of Reay who had been taken to the Bignold hospital in nearby Wick suffering from 'food poisoning', and who had been diagnosed, though not informed, to be suffering from mild radiation sickness by the young house doctor who had left her highly paid job at Harwell to return to hospital work only the year before. Her alert to the Authority had triggered off their investigation. What Dr Sim had really wanted to do was to make the matter public through the local press; but as yet she had not been able to shake herself free of the classified chrysalis in which she had been enmeshed at Harwell; nor did she know anyone locally sufficiently well, as yet, to trust with this sort of information.

At any rate, the problems had soon been resolved, said Alister, by further diluting the effluent before it was released, and by piping it beyond the confines of the sheltered bay and discharging it directly into the deeper waters of the Pentland Firth where the vicious tides and contradictory currents soon dispersed it with absolutely no damage to the environment.

The Japanese and other delegates seemed entirely satisfied with this explanation. Had Graham been absolutely candid with them he would not have been let off so lightly. Discharges of radioactive wastes are monitored on a quarterly basis at Dounreay. It was not unknown for those responsible for the accountancy procedures to release large quantities of waste at the one time as the end of a three month period approached, simply to use up the permitted quota. Actions like this probably explained the cases where radioactive spots had been found washed up on local beaches.

Alister instantly recognised the next questioner as the cracker he had just managed to restrain himself from bumping into at lunchtime. Her voice matched her eyes — alluring, confident, unafraid.

Christ, Alister, concentrate on what she's saying, he reminded himself.

'Dr Graham, I was very interested in the section of your talk which dealt with the frequently recurring problems connected with leakages in the sodium cooling system. Could you perhaps give us some account of what, in your opinion, has been the single most difficult problem to deal with in this sphere?'

Not that Shamin was unaware of the answer. The matter had been well-documented in the scientific and industry press at the time. What she wanted was a name.

'Without a doubt, I'd say it was back in 1972. The whole reactor was closed down for eleven months while a team of four hundred worked on the problem of finding a tiny hole only centimetres from the core. There was no danger of contamination from the leak,' Alister added, not for the scientists, but for the press, 'as the reactor is surrounded by stainless steel and concrete specifically designed to contain any leaks. These, however, made our normal methods of locating and repairing such leakages inoperative. Part of the trouble was that the leakage, as you will appreciate, all but disappeared once the reactor had been closed down. Remember, we are talking of trying to find a hole measuring only 0.038 of a centimetre across amongst a vast area of pipework. It took five months of the most rigorous computer-assisted analysis to pin-point the exact spot.

'Simultaneously, the problem of entering the radioactive area and of cutting and welding by remote control was being tackled by a team of engineers from Dounreay and from the Risley Fast Reactor Design Office. The breakthrough came from a brilliant young Cambridge man who had actually moved from Risley to Dounreay two years previously. The special cutting and welding equipment he designed was so successful that the repair was carried out only forty-three centimetres from the reactor's core.

'The originality of the design and development work for this task stretched our men, and our ladies,' added Alister with a smile in the direction of the questioner, 'to the limit.'

Shamin nodded and smiled her thanks back to Alister. No name, it was true; but enough extra detail, missing from the UKAEA publication in which she had first come across this incident, to enable the engineer in question to be identified.

Alister, meantime, had decided that it was time for his own welding gear to be put into action before it became rusty. Not that the crack in this little reactor is going to be so fucking difficult to find, he mused. With this highly unprincipled thought, one of Britain's leading experts in nuclear fission left the podium to enthusiastic applause.

In his earlier days Alister would have spent the rest of the conference wishfully thinking how nice it would be to encounter the young lady again by chance. And would have gone home thinking, 'what a pity ....' Now, as he stepped down from the dais, he made a bee-line straight for her.

'Most impressive, Dr. Graham,' she beamed, and was in no hurry to take her proffered hand away as Alister gently and almost imperceptibly caressed his thumb across the back of her hand.

'Thank you, er......' he mock-bowed.

'Sorry, I should have introduced myself first.'

Christ, what a smile, he thought.

'Shamin el-Fazzah, delegate from Dhubat on the ....'

'Persian Gulf?' finished Alister.

'Close. Actually, it's just round the other side of the Strait of Hormuz on the Gulf of Oman,' Shamin gently corrected him.

Not that Alister was very much the wiser. His interest in travel seldom extended beyond that which came free with his job. As the Arab world had few nuclear plants and had not, to date, played host to a major conference as Teheran was now doing, he had never been in that part of the world. To him, Qum and Qatar were two fluids manufactured in his body; the first expelled at the climax of sexual activity, the second only when he had a chesty cough. Shamin, mercifully, had no inkling of the eminent scientist's thought patterns at exactly that moment.

Alister and Shamin small-talked their way out of the conference room and headed by mutual tacit consent for the lounge area. Shamin, in particular, had no time to waste. This was purely business – although by now she was certain it was going to be mixed with more than a little pleasure; such was the immediately favourable impression Alister Graham had made on her. As a result, several yards before they arrived at the rather tawdry vinyl seating area, where Alister could already see Harvey and Gary grinning a welcome, they had decided – how Alister would love recounting to his Yankee pals at some future date – to head for the hills.

Or, to be more precise, the Elburz mountains.

Once the pleasantries had been exchanged, Shamin and Alister left.

'Trust that Scottish bastard,' muttered Gary, gazing enviously at Shamin's shapely back being ushered through a door by Alister's solicitous hand.

As Shamin released the central locking system in the dust-covered Range Rover which had been specially customized for wealthy overseas owners, a blast of searing stale air swept past her. Despite the shaded parking spot and the light creamy-coloured paintwork, the temperature inside the car had built up to about 140 degrees in the course of the day. There was no way they could go in. Shamin reached over the suede driver's seat, taking care not to touch it, and punched in the code to the electronically computed ignition. She gingerly started the motor, pressed another couple of buttons, then stood back beside Alister and closed the door.

Two minutes later they both stepped into what at first seemed to be a desperately cold 75 degrees compared with the 110 degrees they had been standing in, but which instantly relaxed and refreshed them. Alister had been in 'refrigerated' cars before in the States, but this was something else, especially as there was hardly a drone to be heard.

Shamin was to curse herself later for her stupidity, but fortunately Alister never noticed the only slip-up she was ever to make in all the time they were to know each other. Without asking where he was staying, she drove straight to his hotel.

In the depressing little room Alister began to look out one or two essentials for his overnight stay.

'Fuck this,' he muttered. 'She's not going to send me packing after only one night. Not after she gets a taste of this,' grabbing his genitals and grimacing like a gorilla into the only mirror in the room. He packed the lot, only discarding the CIA exposé of the night before. Like many scientists he had little use for novels other than the momentary pleasure gained in reading them. He would no more place a piece of fiction on his shelves after having read it than he would throw away a reference book.

As they moved out of the immediate city centre where the only rebuilding had taken place since the revolution, the signs of the conflict became increasingly obvious. Cosmetic facelifts soon gave way to sporadic repairs, which in turn were all too quickly replaced with ramshackle slums, then by whole areas of utter ruin – evidence of the fierce passions which had surrounded the Shah's overthrow.

'Thank God we've left that behind,' said Shamin, as the last clawing remains of the sprawling city appeared in her rear-view mirror.

'Yes. Mind you, this isn't all that better,' Alister indicated the searing steppe dotted with dirty brown villages on all sides with a nod and a sweep of his hand.

'Come, come, Dr. Graham. These are the traditional settlements of the Iranians. They were living like this centuries before mesolithic man stumbled ashore on your deserted homeland.'

Bloody looks like it too, muttered Alister to himself, as the Range Rover crawled over the rutted track through an ancient village.

At least they could only see occasional testaments to the recent turmoil scattered here and there; even then, they had to look hard, as they were virtually indistinguishable from the centuries of dry, dusty decay which surrounded them.

As they approached the town of Demavend they met with a similar tapestry to Teheran; except that this time there had been no attempt by the Ayatollah's administration to cover up the signs of conflict. Obviously, thought Alister, most of the fighting between the Muslim fanatics and the royalist supporters had centred on the towns, with the greater part of the countryside unscathed. A view immediately confirmed as they began climbing out of Demavend into the steeply rising lower slopes of the Elburz.

'At least the peasants managed to come off lightly in the fighting,' commented Alister. 'Probably too apathetic to get involved.' A statement which he immediately regretted, even before his delightful chauffeuse corrected him.

'Apathetic? To government, perhaps; and who could blame them? Shah or Ayatollah? Tsar or Stalin? As the French say, plus ça change, plus c'est la même chose.'

'You're right, of course.' Alister was determined to salvage his position. The last thing he wanted to do with a woman like Shamin was to appear politically naive. He recalled the scene in the movie *Catch-22* when the old man in the Roman brothel reduced the teenaged American GI to a state of despairing confusion over the morality and principle of warfare. He decided to quote the old rascal verbatim.

'It's better to live on one's knees than die on one's feet, I suppose.'

'Exactly,' echoed Shamin, much to Alister's relief as he suddenly realised he had got the quotation wrong. The old boy had been joyously proclaiming the virtues of living on his feet, not dying on his knees. Shamin, however, had not noticed his gaffe.

'There is nothing immoral or unprincipled about caring for your own and your family's existence,' she continued. 'These people have been living their lives for millenia now. They have been conquered by goodness knows how many Tartar, not to mention imperialistic, hordes,' she pretended to glower sideways at Alister. 'They have been trampled and trodden on by foreigner and countrymen alike. What should they care if two rival oppressors want to fight out a civil war? Governments come and go. But these people, like the very steppe they struggle with daily, go on for ever, involved only with themselves and the natural elements around them.'

Shamin had by now left behind any pretence of a road. The Range Rover was being eased towards an isolated structure of mud-brick building blocks, softened only by the odd archway and curve in the roofline. What made the building so spectacular was not the front it put on to the outside world; but its setting. Shamin had been too tired to fully appreciate it on her arrival the previous day; but now, refreshed and totally aware, she drank it in. The house had a truly magnificent position, high up on the hillside on a rocky promontory giving marvellous vistas over the foothills and the steppe land to the south-west towards Teheran. Backed by the now close peaks of the Elburz, towering to over 18,600 feet, the house, with its simple geometry, blended into its surroundings and allowed the landscape to dominate. Now that she thought of it, she wondered whether the designer of Princess Margaret's house on the tiny Caribbean island of Mustique, at which she had once been a house-guest with her father and which, indeed, her father had seriously contemplated buying when the Princess moved to Saint Lucia, had had a hand in this one also. As they crossed the paved courtyard and looked through the arched gateway which perfectly framed Mount Demavend in the distance to the north, the conviction grew that Oliver Messel had been involved.

The main living area, close to being stark in its design, subtly caught the eye from almost any point in the room and directed it with an almost mathematical certainty towards the enormous windows. Facing north, which was the only direction in these latitudes to ease the harshness of daylight, the view was breathtaking. Especially at twilight with the mountain heights bathed in the blood red of the rapidly setting sun. A lilac haze enveloped the now shaded foothills, while the lower plains of the steppe were deepest purple. Yes, her father's friends knew where to build their holiday homes.

Even Alister, who could scarcely be described as an aesthete, was suitably, and quite genuinely impressed. As the light faded by the second, the Bakhtiari serving-girl lit a few well-placed oil lamps. Within minutes the room was bathed in a sepia glow. The curves in the roof appeared as through a graduated tobacco-coloured filter depending on the angle the light touched them.

An hour later Alister and Shamin had showered and changed and were enjoying a light supper of traditional local delicacies prepared for them by Sairozha the young mountain girl. Alister heartily sampled everything on the long deeply carved table, as Shamin complimented Sairozha on her efforts.

'It's amazing how quickly young people adjust,' said Shamin, indicating the girl. 'Just a year ago she was living a harsh and primitive life in the high mountains to the east, near the border with Afghanistan, with her people. Each spring the entire tribe left the sheltered valley and trecked with their goats and sheep over the highest peaks, many considered well-nigh inaccessible by less hardy tribesfolk, to reach their summer pastures.'

'They must be one of the last remaining nomadic tribes in this part of the world,' said Alister. 'Why did Sairozha leave?'

'Yes; but like young people everywhere, no matter how hard the elders try to maintain the old standards, many of them rebel. Its easier for them nowadays – at least it used to be under the Shah – to break away. In fact the government, as it became increasingly aware of its welfare role, actively encouraged these nomads to settle. Especially as many of their leaders held high office under the Shah.'

'But from what you've been telling me these Dromedaries, oops, Bakhtrians,' Alister could never resist a pun no matter in how bad taste, 'are almost totally isolated. They could surely be left to get on with things undisturbed.'

'Bakhtiari,' Shamin corrected him. 'We....ll, I'm not so sure. Although the Ayatollah Khomeini seems to agree with you. In fact, if his administration wasn't even more chaotic than the Shah's, then youngsters like Sairozha would be rounded up and herded back, like so many of their goats, to their own communities. Unlike the 1920s when the then Shah tried to enforce a policy of settlement rather like Stalin was to do in Soviet Central Asia a few years later.'

God. I must read up on some world politics before I meet this cookie again, thought Alister.

Gradually the conversation became less formal. Alister declined the opportunity to listen to some traditional Iranian music as background; but Shamin was unwilling to compromise totally, absorbed as she was with her surroundings. Anyway, the house's absentee owner did not have any of the Sandie Shaw or Dusty Springfield albums which Alister requested. Shamin chose, instead, a seminal recording made by Ravi Shankar and Yehudi Menuhin, entitled *West meets East*, and settled down on the soft sofa beside her guest. As the sitar droned and sobbed and insinuated itself into their every level of awareness, a trance-like mood came over them. They were mesmerised as an insistent, though to Alister unfamiliar, rhythmic drumming on the tabla joined in. Even before the music started Alister and Shamin were well on the road to a high on the best grass either of them had ever smoked, courtesy of one of the Bakhtiari girl's kinsfolk who kept her regularly supplied. Now, as the incense burner mingled with the marijuana's own sweet aroma, and Menuhin's searing, soaring violin conversed with the sitar in an evening raga, Shamin and Alister melted into each other in what they would both remember as their most totally sensuous experience to date.

It would be difficult for them to delineate the separate elements of that night. Neither had taken nor given; conquered nor submitted. Their senses of sound and sight and smell and touch were utterly sated. They did not so much fall asleep towards dawn as sink into a state of sublime well-being and oblivion.

During the remaining two days of the conference the new lovers had to force themselves to attend and feign interest in the proceedings. Shamin, it is true, was her own mistress and was free to come and go as she pleased. Alister, however, had superiors to answer to and could not, much as he desired to, cut more than one or two of the sessions. In actual fact, having left their mountain nest for the day, there was no real point in not attending. There was little for them to do in Teheran apart from talk; and there was plenty of time for that later. Not that they wasted much time in conversation with so many other things to occupy them. And it was much too dangerous for them to contemplate using Alister's room in the hotel. So, they attended the majority of the lectures, most of which they both found genuinely interesting. Alister even had time and sufficient largesse to give Harve and Gary a proper sniff at Shamin, as he was to remind them in Sam Wo's vastly over-rated restaurant in San Francisco's Chinatown the following month.

The couple, however, did not have their minds on the proceedings. Every contact of their bodies – and there were plenty – sent their minds racing backwards in time to the night before, or forwards in anticipation to the night to come. Both were surprised at themselves and what they felt. Alister was not old enough to merit being called a roué; but he had been around a bit. When asked, he always retorted diffidently that he could count his lovers on one hand: ten, twenty, thirty......, as he held up one finger after the other. Shamin had once been browsing through a copy of *Cosmopolitan* during a flight to London from Tokyo and had come across a survey on the sexual habits of the magazine's readership. Without hesitation she had placed herself in the group who numbered their lovers in the twenty-plus bracket. Yet, now, in Teheran of all places, they found themselves acting like a pair of silly young things – nudging, touching, caressing, looking, whispering.

It was with genuine regret that they said goodbye at the end of the conference. Shamin, however had the edge over Alister. She knew they would meet again in the not too distant future.

Three days later Dr Alan Cameron's name had been added to Shamin's shopping list.

8

Thee Would I Kiss

HIS journey had really only just begun, but already Alan Cameron was wondering what in hell had induced him to leave his beloved Audi Quattro at home in the tiny village of Sandside near Reay. The ancient diesel engine crawling over the woefully substandard track which twisted tortuously along the course of the river Helmsdale, favourite salmon beat of the Prince of Wales, was not his idea of what travelling was all about. He had driven the Audi down the single-track road through the Strath of Kildonan, deserted by the Clearances in the 19th century, on many an occasion, laughing scornfully as he screamed past the train heading at a snail's pace in the same direction. Now, he looked out wistfully at the battered old Morris Marina which seemed to be surging past the train on which he was presently a passenger.

Imagine envying the driver of that old heap, he thought. The two young kids waved gleefully from behind their father and ya-hooed their fingers and faces at Alan and the train, secure in the knowledge that their dad would not have swapped them and the old tub for anything.

Regretfully he manoeuvred himself back rather gingerly into the dusty, badly sprung and much stained piece of upholstery which British Rail had the nerve to call a seat. He was not really an over-fastidious sort of person, but he had no intention of allowing his freshly washed hair, or what was left of it after the ravages of five years of premature male pattern baldness, to come in contact with the greasy fabric which formed the headrest. He had to struggle to repress thoughts of the luxurious leather upholstery in which he could have been cosseted had he not allowed Linda to talk him into going all the way to Paris by train. Still, at these prices he couldn't really complain. And with the massive repayments on the Audi – more than double his mortgage – he could not really afford to go more upmarket. Maybe the next time.....

'It's such a marvellous bargain,' Linda had enthused at the Field Club's annual cheese and wine evening the previous weekend. 'Five days in Paris for only £96, with free rail travel from Thurso to London and back. Don't know how they do it.'

The kindly middle-aged editor of the club's bi-annual bulletin had prattled on about her recent holiday with Paris Travel Service so much that it was that rather than the paper on Scandinavian place-names in Caithness and Sutherland which remained for Alan the predominant impression of the evening.

And he did need a break. In fact, he had just been ordered by his GP to take one. Severe headaches, near insomnia, and one bad dizzy spell at work merely confirmed that Cameron was working under the most acute stress. His duties at Dounreay were of the most demanding type imaginable. He was, without doubt, an engineering prodigy, having arrived at Dounreay from the Risley Fast Reactor Design Office where he had rapidly exceeded all of the expectations with which his Cambridge tutors had endowed him. He diffidently referred to himself as a coolant engineer, which, in a sense, he was. However, the particular cooling plant with which he worked day in and day out was at the very heart of the fast breeder reactor. The technicalities and practicalities of working centimetres away from the very core of the reactor by remote control methods which he had played an indispensable part in developing, and in which he and his team were pushing to and beyond the absolute frontiers of technology, amounted to a fearful responsibility. The disaster most feared at a nuclear power station was a melt-down of the core, the so-called China

Syndrome, caused by the reactor going uncontrollably critical. Such a disaster, though remote, would not create a thermonuclear explosion; but it would release untold quantities of highly radioactive materials and cause massive loss of life and ineradicable long-term damage to the environment. It was Cameron's job to prevent this unthinkable disaster from ever happening. He had succeeded brilliantly to date; but at times like the present the strain showed through.

The Monday after the cheese and wine, Cameron found himself in Alpha Travel Services as Carol phoned London for confirmation of a late booking for him. Three days later saw him southbound. By the time the train had got to Inverness Alan had resigned himself to a long drawn out ordeal of discomfort and tedium. He was not, therefore, surprised that the sleeper he had booked as an optional extra did not solve his recent insomnia. He noticed the name of every station passed through between Inverness and London, and was quite worn out when he arrived in Euston at 06.15.

A breakfast of greasy tea, stodgy white toast and a barely-dead sausage, did little to cheer him up. He crossed London to Charing Cross in irritable mood, compounded by a fifteen minute breakdown in the underground between Tottenham Court Road and Leicester Square.

The remaining train and hovercraft journey saw him arrive in Paris shattered. He collapsed into a brown Peugeot taxi and asked the driver for the Hotel du Sud. Never again, he vowed, would he repeat a journey like that.

Alan had never been much interested in travelling. As a student he had had the usual opportunities for cheap travel during vacations, but had never made use of them. Apart from two or three long weekends hillwalking in the Pennines he had spent most of his time studying; and once he had started work he became so engrossed that it had become his consuming passion with no time out for holidays. True, there was the field club once he moved up north, which he thoroughly enjoyed; but like his earlier hillwalking excursions he rationed himself to only three or four outings a year, promising himself more in the future as work eased off.

Now, he found himself in Paris for the first time in his life.

He crashed out onto the bed in the spacious first-floor room without as much as noticing the reclining whore dressed only in a cotton wrap on the balcony a few feet away across the narrow street. He slept deeply until 10.00 the following morning.

Once he had got over the journey he was amazed at the sense of excitement he felt at being in this most seductively sleazy and splendid of all capital cities. The moment he stepped out of the rather shabby, though atmospheric, little hotel into the seedy side street in the 10th Arrondissement he felt captivated, as generations of travellers had before him. Tiny Citroens and Fiats were almost piled on top of each other on both sides of the road and, indeed, on the pavements. Piles of refuse and empty cartons awaiting collection, which would have been offensive in any British town, somehow managed to add to the character of the street. Sun-faded awnings sheltered the fruits of the provinces in one shop, and the quite amazing range of pastries and confectionery in the next. A group of old-timers, puffing contentedly on the most foul-smelling Turkish weed, sat round a table in the first pavement cafe he passed, their sanguine nods and grunts and shrugs indicating that a matter of the utmost gravity was under discussion. Squat bull-necked men unloaded barrels of wine as if they were empty and rolled them into the little bistro which would later dole out the contents in house carafes for next to nothing to their regular clients with their meals. Similarly built people, though wearing headscarves, black dresses and thick woollen stockings, were gradually filling large baskets with provisions as they prowled purposefully from shop to shop. It was all so typically French he could hardly believe it.

When he reached the junction with the Boulevard St.-Denis, Cameron glanced at his street map and turned to the right intending to follow the easier route into the city centre. Each pavement now was wider than the entire street he had just walked down; though this particular section of the 'Grands Boulevards' as they were known was not the most fashionable. There were few shops as yet, and the garish advertising pillars seemed to outnumber the trees bordering the road. Suggestive stills and posters pointed the way in to cinemas advertising blatantly pornographic movies. Outside, even at this early hour of the day, equally suggestive ladies only a little less blatantly advertised themselves to passing males, the mayor's attempt to brick up their studios and drive them out of business having failed miserably. Alan couldn't believe it.

In the distance, the boulevards undulated gently as they slowly curved towards the Place de L'Opéra at the heart of the city. Leaving the obvious route, and risking every bone in his body, he bounded across the road and began zig-zagging down the side streets again in a generally southerly direction which he hoped would bring him down to the Seine close to the Louvre, the first of all the main attractions he wanted to see.

That evening, and the next, Cameron returned to his hotel reeling with the impact of the many wonders of the city and absolutely exhausted by the sheer physical effort of doing the tourist round. He trudged the corridors of the Louvre; climbed wearily to be amongst the gargoyles on the roof of Notre-Dame; refreshed himself in the coolness of the Roman Crypt; sweated profusely inside a perspex enclosed 'bateau mouche' which didn't quite realise the promise of the old song Under the Bridges; and queued for hours to get to the top of the Eiffel Tower. He even managed an afternoon tour to Versailles, although he didn't have time to visit its most enchanting part, the Hameau of Marie-Antoinette.

On both evenings he disdained the pleasures of Parisian night life – though he was now fully aware of the intriguing young lady in the bathrobe virtually within reach just outside his shuttered window. He ignored the noise of chatter and clinking bottles which rose merrily from the cellar bistro next door, and instead yawned his way into the two best nights' sleep he could recall in years.

For his last full day in Paris, Alan reckoned he would take things at a more leisurely pace – if only to fortify him against the horrors of the return rail journey. He had only one goal that day, and it stemmed from a programme he had seen on BBC a few years previously about the life and work of the sculptor Rodin. He had marvelled at the excesses of the man's way of life, vividly portrayed by a BBC team determined to prove that Mary Whitehouse was not their 'Auntie'. And he had marvelled even more at the work the master had produced. A quiet day's reflection in the Hôtel Biron which housed the finest of Rodin's masterpieces, followed by an evening recital of Baroque harpsichord and woodwind music which he had seen advertised in the stupendous church of La Sainte-Chapelle, would set the seal on this far too brief introduction to Paris.

Alan, who by now was quite at home on the Paris metro, easily made his way from Bonne Nouvelle to Invalides. He wasn't in the slightest tempted to revisit the vulgar, ostentatious tomb of Napoleon in the Dome church, and within five minutes of surfacing into the already warm morning air he was strolling along the Rue de Varenne towards the museum. He was in no hurry that morning, and wandered around the lovely gardens for about half an hour, then spent another twenty minutes or so marvelling at the beautiful bronze cast of *The Thinker*, which was much grander than he had imagined, even allowing for its position atop a massive stone plinth which symbolically echoed over the centuries the elevated position given to the philosopher by the Ancient Greeks. Inside, in common with all but the most affectedly nonchalant visitor, he made straight for *The Kiss* the most famous of Rodin's works. He had heard and read of its sensuous allure, its deftness of form, and smoothness of touch; but nothing had prepared him for its utter tenderness. That a robust roué like Rodin could so endow a massive chunk of mortuary marble with such warmth and delicacy and feeling was beyond the comprehension of his finely tuned scientific mind. The lightness of hand resting on hip, of foot upon foot, of lip on lip, astonished him. He had never, not even in the Louvre, seen the like of it, and he doubted if he ever would. He looked at the sculpture from every angle, distance and perspective which its surroundings allowed. He touched it, and almost recoiled in amazement at its creamy unctuousness and warmth, which he could not decide came from the sun's rays which poured through the massive arched windows, or from some spirit of love trapped within the stone and burning as constant as the Eternal Flame itself. He could well understand the charge levelled at Rodin by some of his envious contemporaries that he had moulded onto the actual bodies of his models.

For what seemed like a few minutes, but was in fact nearer half-an-hour, Cameron quietly, reverently and, to his eternal credit, unwittingly broke the second Commandment. Indeed, had Aaron shown Moses *The Kiss* instead of the Golden Calf it is just possible that Moses would have had to believe him when he denied having made it himself and had tried to tell Moses it just came out of the fire looking like that, the product of some supernatural entity.

Alan wandered out onto one of the balconies overlooking the rose gardens and the thickly-treed boundaries of the grounds and silently thanked the citizens of Paris for having preserved the works of the artist in their place of origin, especially as it was sufficiently off the tourist path to avoid an endless stream of giggling gawpers and children with sticky fingers ready to clamp all over the exhibits. There were only a handful of afficionados there, even at this late hour of the morning in the height of the tourist season, each one respectful of the other's right to contemplate without disturbance. There was, he thought, more of a truly spiritual atmosphere here than in any of the major churches he had visited, the only possible exception being La Sainte-Chapelle with its magnifcent woodwork and stained glass to which he would be returning that evening to listen to the group of young musicians from the Paris Conservatoire.

Ignoring Rodin's personal collection of late and post-Impressionist originals which dotted the walls, Alan continued on his rounds, although he knew that he had already seen the essential pieces, and could quite happily have left at any time. Ten minutes later he was glad he had stayed.

It happened in the large room housing *The Hand of God,* and while he was studying the highly erotic, though more contrived piece portraying the two kneeling lovers, *The Eternal Idol.* As he focussed on the enormous mirror which covered the wall behind the statue, and which allowed the viewer to contemplate both sides of the composition at once, his eyes locked onto the loveliest woman he had ever seen. The sunlight from the window cascaded onto her long chestnut coloured hair, spotlighting the top of her head and rimlighting the edges. Her verdant green eyes calmly accepted his transfixed gaze, which she returned with a modest smile and slightly quizzical, though expectant, tilt of her head. Her figure was clearly, pleasingly and unselfconsciously outlined underneath the lightweight top and skirt around and through which the warm rays glowed, giving her a translucent, ethereal quality. It was as if the perfectly formed marble lover had broken off her kiss next door, barely covered her nakedness, and gone for a stroll through the gallery to ease muscles tired by holding a pose for too long.

'Je . . . Je t'en prie . . .' Alan started muttering an apology for his gaucheness in stumbling French, unaware of his wishful use of the familiar form of address.

'Its alright,' she replied in English tinged with a slight Scandinavian accent. Her warm reply and continued smile set him instantly at ease.

'It must be the surroundings,' he grinned, shrugging his shoulders and indicating the walls with a sweep of his hands.

'Yes,' she almost whispered, 'it is quite overwhelming. Especially if it is your first visit.'

'Well, it is. What about yourself?'

The girl laughed.

'Not exactly. I have been here just about every day for the past week now.'

'I see. I take it that you have a special interest in Rodin then?' asked Alan.

'You could say that. In actual fact I came to Paris a month ago to continue my studies in Fine Arts in general. It was not until last week that I got around to this place in particular – and now it has me under its spell. It is like a narcotic drug to me. Having once experienced it I need ever increasing doses to keep me satisfied.'

'I think I know what you mean. Unfortunately for me I am going to have severe withdrawal symptoms from tomorrow, as I must leave Paris for home.'

'But you will come back?' It was more a statement than a question.

He nodded. 'Most assuredly.'

Fearing that their brief encounter was drawing to a premature close, and sensing that such boldness would not be rebuffed by so sensitive a soul in this of all places, Alan impulsively made the quickest move of his life.

'Having been here so often, you must know if there's somewhere handy where we could perhaps lunch?' The hope in his voice was undisguisable.

'Actually, no,' she replied. 'This is not really a residential area; and most people who work in the neighbourhood are employed by one government agency or another, each with its own refectory. I have tried in vain to find somewhere all week.'

His face fell a mile.

'However,' the girl continued in faultless English, 'we could buy some things in the little grocer's just around the corner and have a picnic in the Champ de Mars. It's only ten minutes from here.'

Alan was overjoyed and made no attempt to hide it. His reaction pleased Karyn immensely.

'Oh; Alan Cameron,' he said, breaking protocol by extending his hand to her.

'Karyn. Karyn Bertilsson,' she smiled as their hands clasped.

Twenty minutes later they were sitting dangling their legs into the large fountain pool which lay between the École Militaire and the park leading up to the Eiffel Tower.

'Sitting' is the wrong word. The marbled stone surround of the pond was so steep and slippery that they were bracing themselves to prevent a sliding, bottom-first, entry into the water. Karyn's sky-blue skirt was hitched well up over her slim bronzed thighs. Alan had rolled his similarly coloured trousers up as far as they would go over his dissimilarly coloured legs which, though pale white, were at least hairy and muscular. Their bottles of red vin de table and still mineral water were cooling slowly at the bottom of the pond. Despairing of preventing themselves from falling in they stood upright and began walking towards the fountain. The bottom was unbelievably slippery and after a couple of steps they naturally and involuntarily took hands to help steady each other. Despite a temperature of over 90 their hands were cool and pleasing. As Karyn slipped their grip tightened. They smiled warmly at each other.

'Feeling thirsty yet Karyn?'

'You bet.' Alan marvelled at her command of even American colloquialisms. 'The bottles should have cooled down by now, Alan. Let's go and see.'

Just then a piercing whistle blew and a uniformed park attendant gesticulated with typical Gallic fervour, leaving them in no doubt that they were violating some bye-law and that they should leave the water immediately on pain of death. They collected their bottles, food and sandals and headed for the nearest shady tree. No doubt in breach of some other bye-law, but at any rate unnoticed by any of the attendants, they enjoyed a refreshing lunch of bread, Roquefort, grapes and peaches, washed down with a 50:50 mixture of wine and mineral water.

Afterwards, Alan glanced towards the pond again.

'Pity the little general is still there,' he said, pointing at the attendant. 'I'd have loved another paddle.'

'Why don't we go for a swim, then?' said Karyn.

'That would be fantastic. But there's probably nowhere for miles around. And anyway I don't have any gear with me.'

'No problem,' answered Karyn. 'There's a lovely open-air pool on the banks of the Seine not too far from here. You could hire trunks at the pool.'

'And what about you? I suppose you've got a costume and towel in your shopping bag?' he grinned towards Karyn's large hand bag.

'As a matter of fact, yes,' she laughed, pulling out a tiny piece of cotton and waving it tantalisingly in front of Alan's face. 'Towels we do not require with the heat in this sun.'

'Right, you're on.' Alan jumped to his feet, wondering if Karyn had forgotten to take out the top half of her costume from her bag, or whether that was all.

Within forty minutes, after a leisurely stroll along the embankment, his conjectures were answered.

He pulled on the briefest pair of trunks he had ever worn,

carefully arranging himself to present the most flattering profile. Like many men over six feet tall Alan had a slight inferiority complex about the size of his equipment in the dormant state. In fact his misgivings, which were occasioned by the downwards viewing angle from his height, were needless as he was perfectly well proportioned when viewed from the front and side from a lower angle. He stepped out into the glaring sunlight, terribly self-conscious of his white body amongst the bronze and black ones round about, and began scanning for Karyn. He gasped as she came towards him out of the sun, shimmering and naked. She waved and smiled and walked confidently towards him. As she came close he noticed the tiny flesh-coloured cache-sexe she was enforced to wear in public. Her body was equally tanned all over; her breasts, which he had earlier seen outlined under her clothes, were exquisitely shaped and uplifted; her waist appeared even more slender as the harsh sunlight tended to bleach out the contours of her figure. He had never seen or imagined anything so perfect.

Karyn, for her part, was slightly taken aback at the paleness of Alan's skin; but he hoped she would notice his well-muscled arms, which were deliberately folded and flexed across his hairy chest. He was proud of these arms, which he had carefully built up over the years with his Bullworker; and pleased that nature had compensated for his premature baldness by simultaneously, and in direct proportion, increasing the growth of his body hair. Had he known more about the female sexual psyche, however, he need not have bothered trying to impress in this way. His honest, pale blue eyes and friendly disposition had already passed muster; as had his sense of humour, his unassuming nature and strong but gentle touch. Mind you, had there been no bulge in his trunks Karyn would have been off like a shot!

Karyn began to run towards him, then suddenly wheeled to the side and did a perfect swallow dive into the water, cutting the surface so cleanly that she barely made a splash. Alan recalled his last disastrous belly-flop, and sat down on the edge of the pool. He couldn't take his eyes off Karyn's naked back and buttocks as she neared the surface in the middle of the pool.

'God, she is beautiful,' he informed the people round about him.

'Come on,' beckoned Karyn, turning onto her back and heading down the pool in an easy, but deceptively fast, backstroke.

He plunged in, spluttered to the surface and, fighting to keep his face out of the water, started after her using the only stroke he could. Fortunately he had once been shown the proper technique for the breast stroke, and, despite his fear of getting water over his head, was able to make a fair pace using short, powerful arm movements. Even so, he was nowhere near catching up on Karyn when she suddenly stopped and began floating lazily as if she had no idea that she was outstripping him. Her hair drifted languidly around her head and shoulders; her breasts were only half-submerged, with nipples taut and prominent in the coolness of the water. Alan reached her side and began treading water – not just because he couldn't float, but because he wanted to continue looking at Karyn.

Without warning, Karyn turned onto her side and ducked his head under the water. He instinctively grabbed her by the hips but could not hold onto her well-oiled body. He threshed his way to the surface, squeezed the water from his eyes, and made a playful lunge for Karyn. As she deftly twisted away his hand brushed against her breast and down onto her thigh. She laughed and ducked him again as he was off balance. When he surfaced this time and was able to see, Karyn's fast crawl had taken her almost to the far end of the pool. There was no way he could compete.

A few lengths later Alan hauled himself out of the water onto the poolside. Karyn immediately headed for him and held up her arm to be pulled out. As she got both feet onto the tiles she stumbled forward and pressed against him, her cheek resting on his shoulder. Alan held her briefly then led her by the hand towards a relatively uncrowded part of the terrace.

Outside the enormous 18th century, black-gilded, wrought-iron gates which guarded the entrance to the Palais de Justice, Alan glanced at his watch.

7.30 pm, he thought. I should have asked Karyn to meet me a bit earlier. People were streaming past and round to the entrance to the church, even though the concert did not start till 8.00. He just had not thought it would be such a popular event. Most folk were dressed quite informally; though the odd couple with perhaps more of a sense of occasion, or more of a sense of their own importance, appeared as if they they had intended going to the Opéra instead. Within a few minutes, during which he gazed up through the gold filigree of the gates to the beautiful spire of La Sainte-Chapelle, Karyn had arrived looking cool and casually elegant in a multi-speckled black skirt which fell from her waist in countless small pleats parting as she moved to reveal the shape of her legs, topped with a stone coloured blouse of fine silk. She carried a lace shawl folded over her arm.

'I hope I am not too late, Alan,' she said rather breathlessly. 'I had a nasty experience on the metro on my way back to the flat from the swimming pool, and I missed my stop. I should have taken a taxi back, but I decided to walk and got lost. I am sorry,' she trailed off.

'Not at all, Karyn. I'm just here myself. What happened to you on the metro?'

'Oh, it was nothing really, but I got a bit uptight at the time. Anyway, I'd rather not talk about it just now. It looks as if we had better go in and see if there are any seats left.'

They walked round to the church entrance, which was down a little side street, and joined the queue moving slowly through the doorway. By the time they had crossed the threshold the last of the seats had been taken. All that was left was the stone bench which ran round the inside walls of the church. Fortunately they were ushered to the side opposite the high gothic windows which were the church's main attraction. The sun was very low now, pouring in through the smaller windows at the west end of the building, imparting a glorious hue to the ancient woodwork and throwing the most magnificent colour casts onto the surrounding stone and into the church. The flatter north lighting on the main windows was colder, but this was more than compensated for by the quality and intensity of colour in the windows themselves. They were justly the most famous examples of their art in the whole of France and, consequently, the world. The wondrously intricate circular window set into the east wall still was sufficiently well lit to give more than a hint of its grandeur. The overall effect was a feast for the eyes.

Shortly, the ears were to receive their treat, as the sound of Telemann's Oboe Concerto in F minor burst forth into the ancient building. After a few moments break, during which the musicians slightly rearranged themselves to put more separation between the oboe and the violins, it was the turn of Albinoni's B flat Oboe Concerto. Without doubt its gorgeous adagio was the highlight of the performance. With the last triumphal bars of Handel's Concerto No. 3 in G minor the recital closed at 9.15, too short if anything, but carefully calculated to leave the audience longing for more rather than wishing for it to end. Certainly for those like Karyn and Alan seated on stone which was growing harder and colder by the minute, any longer would have become a test of endurance.

The audience gave the students, most of whom were in their final year of study at the Conservatoire and were destined for sparkling international careers, a rapturous round of applause which seemed to shake the lofty arched ceiling towering above their heads.

One advantage of having been amongst the last to enter the recital was that Alan and Karyn were the first to leave. The air outside was still very warm, warmer indeed than the interior of the church, but much fresher. They both breathed deeply.

'That was wonderful, Alan. Thank you for asking me along,' said Karyn. 'I really love woodwind music. And to think that I didn't even know the recital was on.'

'Well, you've only been here a month. It's just as well you bumped into someone who really knows Paris.'

She poked him in the ribs.

'What do suggest now, Karyn?'

'Oh, there's no end to the possibilities. Montparnasse. Marais. Montmartre ......'

'Mmmmmm. Montmartre? Montmartre,' he nodded

approvingly. 'You wouldn't let me leave Paris without seeing Montmartre, would you?'

'We could do much worse,' agreed Karyn. 'Do you really mean to say you haven't been there yet?'

'Honestly, no. It was either that or a quick tour out to Versailles. I chose the latter.'

'What a fortunate choice, Dr Cameron,' laughed Karyn. 'Versailles is closed this evening, but I don't think Montmartre will be.'

'That's settled then.' Alan was delighted at the prospect.

He knew it was too far to walk, and began steering Karyn towards the Cité metro station.

'Wait a minute, Karyn.' He stopped dead. 'Maybe you'd prefer a taxi?' He recalled her remark about her metro ride that afternoon.

'No, no. The metro will be fine.' Karyn was touched by his sensitivity.

It hadn't happened to her before, although several of her friends had experienced the same discomfort. Young women on their own are a prey for all the dirty, frustrated perverts, old and young, who frequent the Paris underground at peak periods for the sole reason of playing out their erotic fantasies. Their most frequent ploy is to prowl in pairs, sandwiching their victim between them, racing to see whether she felt the hard-on in her buttocks or her belly first; all the time whispering obscenities in her ears and discharging hot, foul garlicky breath on her neck. Like Italians, who are always careful never to pester their own women, these loathsome creatures always go for foreigners who would be incapable of making a scene. That afternoon Karyn had been dry-raped by a Tunisian and a Turk working in tandem. She had rushed in panic back to her hotel, blundering along through unfamiliar streets beyond her usual station. She literally tore off her clothes of the day and then spent half an hour under a piping hot shower scrubbing the imagined filth from her body.

None of this she wanted to tell Alan.

This time the carriage they entered together was almost empty. They sat close together, holding hands, not even trying to compete with the noise of the train in conversation. Alan, by the time a few stops had gone by, had managed to decipher the sign above his head sufficiently to know that if a blind or infirm person, a mother with child, or, above all, an injured war veteran should require his seat he was to vacate it immediately. The demise of the French in Indo-China and Algeria had done nothing to diminish their respect for the 'mutilé de guerre'. Alan chuckled at the extravagance of the language. Not for the French 'injured' or 'wounded' or 'veteran'. Nothing less than 'mutilated' would do for them. The spirit of Charles de Gaulle was obviously still alive and well in socialist France.

They left the carriage at Barbès-Rochechouart and Alan began leading Karyn towards the exit.

'We would actually be better changing lines and going to Place de Clichy, Alan. It is a much more interesting walk if we start there and go through Pigalle to Montmartre rather than the reverse. And, besides, there are more restaurants down at that end!'

Alan, now that he thought of it, was ravenously hungry, and annoyed that he hadn't been the one to suggest they eat before doing anything else.

'That's a much better idea,' he said, as Karyn expertly led them through the interchange to Line No. 2, direction Pte. Dauphine.

Four short stops later they got out at one of Paris's major interchanges. The Place de Clichy is an enormous junction with at least seven main streets intersecting at it, and numerous minor streets having junctions within sight. Alan thought they would never get across to the south side where Karyn was pointing out several restaurants side by side; but having negotiated several pedestrian barriers, broken two red stop signs and brought at least one Simca to a screaming halt, they finally made it. One look at the menu and the rows of ready made-up plates in the first self-service joint was enough for both of them. The second restaurant was infinitely more enticing, with deeply recessed entrance foyer, beautiful decor, and coat-tailed waiters flitting past spaces in the heavy lace curtains. It specialised in sea foods, and tanks filled with live specimens could be seen along the walls. The menu was incredible. Alan had read about the famed French dish 'Homard à l'armoricaine' – diced lobster flambéed in brandy –

and it was one of the first dishes he recognised on the pages of menu encased behind heavily-leaded glass. He could not believe how cheap it was.

'That's what we want, Karyn,' he enthused. 'Have you ever tried it before?'

'I can't say I have, although its fame has reached Sweden. But it is fantastically expensive.'

'No, no!' Alan was getting excited at the prospect of such a gourmet treat. 'It's only 45F. You'd pay that for fish and chips in London.'

'45F........ per 100 grammes!' said Karyn, pointing to the small print underneath.

'You're joking, Karyn.'

'No, look. Read it for yourself.' She directed him to the appropriate tiny letters.

'Jesu,' cried Alan. 'Do they know what a lobster weighs?' he asked incredulously. 'Of course, Karyn, that price will be for the dressed meat. They couldn't possibly charge that for all the shell and pincers?' There was no conviction behind the last rhetorical question.

'Maybe. But I would not chance it,' said Karyn. 'There is nothing on the menu to that effect.'

'If that's the case then I bet we wouldn't be the first customers to end up at the 'préfecture de police', laughed Alan.

'Nor the last,' added Karyn, nodding in the direction of the Welsh voices which had just come into the entrance.

As they left the foyer Alan noticed a sign to the left, a couple of turns off the roundabout in the opposite direction to the one they should have been taking. They crossed over the Rue de Clichy and the Rue d'Amsterdam to the restaurant, which advertised 'Italienne', on the corner of the Rue de Leningrad. A quick check at the externally displayed menu which all French restaurateurs had to show by law indicated there would be no problem paying the bill, so they entered. Alan managed to ask for a table for two in fairly passable schoolboy French. Either that, he mused, or the waiter, without crediting him with too much sense, saw that there was just the two of them and shepherded them to such a table with the comment, 'Certainly, Sir' delivered in perfect English.

Alan, with more than a little assistance from Karyn, whose French, though not quite up to her English, was excellent, ordered two glasses of cassis while they studied the menu together. It was strange, but they both arrived at the same choice of starter and main course quite independently: mussels in butter sauce; followed by trout grilled with almonds. They settled on house white, a Chenin Blanc, and ordered a little carafe for starters.

The mussels were quite superb. Their texture and taste made it obvious that they had not come from the malignantly polluted waters of the Mediterranean, but more likely from the Atlantic coast of South Brittany or Finisterre. They went down a treat with the white wine, which was perhaps insufficiently dry to accompany seafood. It was not Sancerre, but it more than did the job.

By the time they had reduced the enormous platters of trout to a few skeletal remains neither felt like any more to eat. Alan, quite pleased with himself, asked the waitress for some 'cure-dents' and 'l'addition, s'il vous plaît'. He wondered why more British restaurants didn't stock a supply of toothpicks as all French ones did. Then again, British motorists didn't believe in pissing at the roadside, he mused wickedly, as he carried out his oral hygiene in front of the unconcerned Karyn.

The bill, when it came, was ludicrously modest. All in, for food, drinks and service, it only came to just over £30 for them both. So much for the myth, perpetrated out of mischief by the London-based British travel fraternity, that Paris was an impossibly expensive place to holiday in. There was nowhere in London where such a meal could have been bought for anything like the price.

Outside the restaurant Karyn took Alan's arm in a quaintly endearing old-fashioned sort of way. No-one had actually ever taken his arm before. It was nice to feel her nestling in so close as they walked slowly along towards Pigalle.

The only Paris guide book in the Thurso public library had described Pigalle as a seedy version of Soho. Good God, he had thought. What in hell must it be like?

The Moulin Rouge, the first real sign that they had entered the iniquitous area, was disgustingly respectable. It liked to cultivate an air of decadence, but most of the middle-aged tourists trooping in from glass-domed sightseeing coaches would have been equally titillated at the Beach Pavilion in Southport for a fraction of the cost, albeit in not quite the same style.

Further along the boulevard the crowds thickened and the neon signs mushroomed. Well-dressed touts beckoned people to watch live sex shows, many specialising in lesbian or homosexual fare. Sex shops were packed with videos, films, magazines and appliances of every description, being drooled over or laughed at by the hungry masses.

On the corner of Place Blanche the most blatant prostitute Alan had ever imagined lounged against the wall wearing nothing but a pair of black leather boots and a black leather sheath which started just below her nipples and ended just below her pudenda. Karyn laughingly pulled him along past.

They entered a tiny bar, deserted apart from the patron, his wife and the inevitable large Alsatian guard dog. The patron poured them fairly generous measures of Cointreau as his wife looked on frostily. At the first opportunity she banished him to a back room, took up her rightful stance at the head of the gantry, and began chattering pleasantly to them. Before an hour had passed she had revealed herself as quite a character and regaled them with her views on politicians, trade unions, the unemployed, the church, and the Boche. She positively spat venom when recounting her experiences of the German occupation of Paris in World War Two.

Alan was pleasantly surprised to find out that, once he had got used to the sound of the language, he was able to follow a large part of the conversation, although there were obviously a number of times when he had to turn to Karyn for help.

One thing madame could do supremely well – among others, that is, she told them with a sly wink – was to pour liquor. With not a pewter measure in sight she unerringly poured shot after shot to within a drop of the rim when she placed the small brandy-type glasses on edge and rolled them back and forth across the top of the bar. Little wonder she had scorned her husband's lack of expertise earlier on; not to mention his profligacy with the profits. At 11.30 Alan asked for the bill as he and Karyn bid the lady, who had proudly recounted her rise from a poor working girl in a porcelain factory in Limoges, goodnight. A scrap of paper was produced from under the small cupboard where she kept the mixers and passed over the counter. It asked for 480F, just over £45. Alan was astounded, and queried it at once. His attention was drawn to the tiny notice on the wall which intimated that all drinks doubled in price after 22.00. Little wonder the lady had risen so rapidly above her station, he thought.

'But the drinks are much cheaper in St. Denis.'

'Aha, my boy, that is so; but there you do not have the ambience. This,' she swept her arms proudly through the air, 'this is Pigalle.'

It could have been Piaf herself talking.

What the hell, he thought, this is Pigalle, and paid gladly, thanking the lady and her husband for 'l'ambiance' as they departed.

They quickly left the main boulevard and began zig-zagging up the ever rising side streets towards Sacré-Cœur. Alan was content to drift along at a snail's pace, but Karyn pressed on, almost dragging him up the slope, determined that he should see the famous church in all its floodlit glory.

Suddenly, he stopped and spun Karyn around into his arms. He brushed her hair back from her face, caressing her as he did so, then kissed her for the first time. Karyn's lips lightly returned his kiss. She felt his tongue probing gently at her teeth and parted them slightly to let their tips meet. Alan's large hand cradled the entire side of her finely shaped face; his index finger stroking her earlobe while his thumb traced her eyebrow and his pinkie gently caressed from the nape of her neck to her throat. His right hand lay lightly on her hip. There was no need for him to hold her tight as she willingly leant against him down the slope. Alan could feel every contour of her body as they continued to kiss and they both became aware of him beginning to harden.

Such was the atmosphere on this terrace on Montmartre that none of the passers-by minded in the least the sight of this couple embracing. At last they broke off their tender Rodinesque kiss and continued on up the cobbled slope. After their kiss Karyn was more content to linger slowly, but, his courage amply rewarded, Alan was now the one to be striding on ahead. Even so, the magnificent domes of the church had only just come into view, scarcely registering on his consciousness, when the lights were extinguished.

Seconds earlier the steps beneath the church were thronged with young people of all ages singing John Lennon peace songs. In the gardens below, the glow of phosphorescent headbands and beads amidst the shadows of the terraces and bushes indicated where people were strolling aimlessly. Now all hell broke loose. Bottles smashed on the steps as the Paris bovver boys moved in to stake their claim over the dark hours. Two rival gangs went careening down the terrace not caring who they felled in the process. Terrified screams for help came from the bottom end of the gardens as the chase spilled over into the cobbled streets below. It was not a pretty scene.

All the while Alan held Karyn close, his body tense and ready to defend her against anyone. He had sensed a similar need as they jostled through the crowds of Pigalle earlier that evening. Now it was for real.

'I........ I had not meant it to be like this,' Karyn, clearly shaken by the mêlée, began to apologise.

'It's hardly your fault that such people exist,' Alan began to comfort her as he led her up towards the church where a few people, mostly stoned out of their minds, had sat on unconcerned with the disturbance all around.

They moved past them with a few mutters of 'Peace' and 'Hi' and made their way round to the Place du Tertre which was still packed with folk enjoying the warm summer evening at the many outdoor cafés. They wandered through the noisy square where artists were still at work making a handsome killing from their charcoal sketches of tourists. None of this postcard Paris appealed to Karyn and she was relieved to follow Alan through the throng rather than become part of it.

On the far side, and just off to the right of the main square, a small bar opened directly on to the pavement. It was just as busy as any of the open-air cafés they had passed; but it was entirely different in character. The noise of cutlery amidst bottles and glasses, of laughter and guitar music and quiet singing and humming, indicated a hostelry devoted to the French themselves and not a cafe pandering to the preconceptions of tourists. They mounted the two stone steps and Alan bowed his head through the low doorway into the air-laden smoke.

Several Cointreaus and ice later they managed to get a seat beside an elderly man and his vivacious middle-aged wife who had just finished eating and were about to start on their third bottle of wine, a magnificent tawny house Merlot which almost everyone was drinking. The benign old boy was beginning to nod off in the corner. He was humming an old Piaf melody which was just recognisable as La Vie en Rose. Unfortunately, the guitarist was singing Plaisir d'Amour, accompanied by a couple of dozen customers. Not that it mattered.

The lady, however, was obviously one of those fortunates who came alive with alcohol and was eager for company. They chatted away in English, which she spoke with a thick eastern Mediterranean accent. For convenience, and not a little mischief, Alan told her that he and Karyn had just got engaged and had come to Paris to celebrate. Karyn nipped him under the table, but she seemed as pleased with the tale as he was in the telling of it.

The old fellow came awake with a start. Tenderly, his wife stroked his head and shooed him back over again. She had no intentions of leaving yet.

'My son,' she continued with a look of immense pride and affection. 'You should see my son. My beeg, beautiful son. He is a doctor. Alas I do not see him often enough,' she sighed. 'He lives in our house in Athens; and when he is not there he is usually with friends in London. My beeg, beautiful son.'

Eventually it was not only time for her to take her husband home, but for the bar to close as well.

'But it is only half-past two,' someone complained good-naturedly to the patron.

'And the prefect of police says I should close at two, my friend,' the patron gave a mock growl. 'You would not want to see me closed down, now, eh?'

The possibility was unimaginable; but everyone was in too good a humour to argue.

The night air was magnificent as Karyn and Alan strolled down the ancient Butte past the Lapin Agile, whose cabaret was frequented by countless artists and writers in its heyday, and the many bistros and other artistic haunts of the turn of the century. Van Gogh, Renoir, Picasso, Berlioz, Jacob – what names had gone before them.

As Montmartre emptied, so Pigalle filled. Indeed, taxis were arriving in Pigalle from all parts of Paris. It was much busier now than a few hours earlier, despite the absence of the tourist coaches. Hordes of rough-looking characters of all nationalities were loud-mouthing their ways up and down the streets. Alan felt the old tension returning.

Just let one bastard touch her, he muttered to himself as his arms cosseted Karyn from the crowds.

It was also much dirtier than it had been. Papers, cans and the remains of Chinese carryouts were everywhere. The traffic noise, the blaring discos, all seemed magnified. The contrast with Montmartre was glaring.

Alan's hand flew out. Karyn shuddered, then relaxed as she saw the black Citroen taxi pulling to a halt.

'Place de la Concorde.' Alan's French accent had become much more authentic with alcohol and hours of tuning in. Karyn, unlike Lot's wife, did not look back. Her eyes changed with the neon reflections, then returned to their natural green as they left the lights behind.

Ten minutes later they got out at the Obelisk and cut across to the other side of the square. In the distance the bulk of the Arc de Triomphe loomed over the Champs-Elysées. On an impulse, they headed for the river and went down the steps onto the deserted quay. Several bridges later, just within sight of the Eiffel Tower, they surfaced and made for where they imagined the Arc de Triomphe to be.

It took an hour of meandering, with many a comforting caress on the pavement; but at last they were there. They had been crazy going down onto the lower embankment at that time of the night in this the most crime-ridden city of Europe. It was the haunt of all sorts of weirdos, often in groups, invariably hyped up and totally irresponsible. Fortune had favoured them and they had not met a soul; but they had stayed on the river's edge for too great a distance and had actually begun to curve away from their intended direction.

The Etoile when they got there was deserted, apart from a couple of gendarmes. They crossed over and sat on one of the stone benches at the base of the massive arch looking down the wide avenue. The police left them undisturbed.

'Why do you look so sad, my Alan?' Karyn kissed him on the temple and stroked his hand.

'Oh,' he shrugged. 'Just thinking how futile it all is.'

'But we have had the most wonderful evening?' There was a slight trace of doubt in her voice, as if she thought he was displeased with her in some way.

'Of course, Karyn,' he replied with conviction. 'I can't remember a night like it.' He wanted to add 'my love', but didn't dare. 'It's just, well....... I mean look at this.' He indicated the thousands of tons of stonework towering over them. 'All those names inscribed on the columns. The ghosts of past armies marching down the Avenue. Those tattered banners in the Invalides church. That poor bastard lying beneath the Eternal Flame. Curses on Napoleon and Hitler and all those other warmongerers who glorified in the carnage.'

'I know, my love,' said Karyn. 'I understand.'

'And now we must part.' Alan was almost tearful. 'What time is it, Karyn?'

'It's 4.30. Time to go to bed,' she whispered in his ear.

A fortnight after he had returned from Paris Alan Cameron was still obsessed with the memories of that one night with Karyn. Fortunately the immediate pressure of his work had eased off. In fact, like many fellow employees, he had so much time on his hands during some shifts that he was in danger of becoming bored. However, in many ways, this was what he needed. While colleagues did Open University work, or diverted themselves with crosswords or chess problems, Alan found himself moping. He took out a few sheets of paper and began several letters to Karyn. They all ended in the waste-paper bin.

Then he began to scribble down some lines of verse. He had never written any poetry before, and was pleasantly surprised how easily the simple rhymes came. They should probably have followed the letters into the bucket; but, because of their novelty, he decided to keep them and work on them. By the end of his shift he had finished one:

L'Arc de Triomphe

Triumphal Arch or Bridge of Sighs,
Which would you rather be;
Standing there so proud, so vain
O'er the Champs-Elysées?

Napoleon built you, he'd no doubts:
A monument you'd be
To all his battles great and small
Each one a victory

If not for France then for mankind,
Whose greatest end, it seems:
To fight, to wound, to maim, to kill;
To shatter innocent dreams.

In contrast to your transient stone
The Flame Eternal glows;
The Unknown Soldier wasting there
Unlike Napoleon knows

How futile all this carnage is
How senseless is this strife
That lost him all his dearest ones,
Deprived him of his life.

What sombre thoughts at four a.m.
Seated there with you –
In contrast to the joys I felt
In Montmartre at two.

What caused this change of mood in me?
What brought this air of gloom?
Words; talk; analysis:
A sense of hopeless doom

That you and I would have to part,
And from this cold stone rise:
No Arch of Triumph to span life's stream –
Just a Bridge of Sighs.

He dithered over sending it to Karyn at her flat overlooking
the Parc Monceau in Paris.

Two days later he got a simple postcard:–

Dear Alan,
Arrive Thurso 11.15, 23 July.
Love, Karyn.

He couldn't believe it. Karyn coming to Caithness as she had
promised! And arriving on his birthday!

This, he knew, was going to be a summer to remember.

9

Pieces of Silver

MICHAEL Booth heaved a long, contented sigh as the 08.00 train pulled out of Kings Cross for Edinburgh.

'Good riddance,' he bade London farewell. God, but he hated the place. A Yorkshire lad by birth, he had moved south with his parents just after his fourteenth birthday. It was the complete antithesis of all he enjoyed as a boy. Gone forever was his long-eared spaniel gundog, Toby, and the Chinchilla rabbits he so expertly reared. Gone were the wood-pigeons and trout he and the other lads in the clay-mining village of Dungworth poached regularly from the nearby forest and dam. Gone was his sole ambition to be taken on as a gamekeeper's assistant at any of the three big estates down in the valley over in the Bradfield direction. And there was nothing, not a sodding thing, he had been able to do about it. They were moving; and that was that.

His only reason for staying on in London beyond the age of consent had been his smouldering ambition. Ambition to avoid the sort of dead-end job which his father had been, in a sense, fortunate enough to find in a Stepney warehouse after the accident in the clay pit which had forced them to leave. Ambition to do well at school after a shaky start. Ambition, above all, to control his own destiny rather than continue as the pawn of forces he as then barely understood.

Up to the present time in his life he had received one lucky break only. As a village lad from a poor background, and with no parental encouragement to do better, he had found himself attending a rural secondary modern school where standards and expectations were low. He seemed likely to follow his dad into the clay pits, despite his own wish for a cleaner, healthier life in the open air. On coming up to London, however, he was compelled to enrol at a bewilderingly large comprehensive school run by the Inner London Education Authority. His life was a misery at first, but Michael was exposed to genuine educational opportunity for the first time. It could not have come at a more expedient moment. Comprehensive education was tailor-made for him. A bit of a late developer, he was able to find his own feet and work at his own level in a range of subjects. As a result, he took five mediocre O-levels before surprising himself, but not his teachers, and delighting his parents by securing three good A-levels and a place at the London School of Economics to study Political Economy.

Actually, he reflected as the train gathered speed going out through the north-west of London, there had been more than one set of fortuitous circumstances in his life after all. Take the job he was on his way to start at this very moment. He still squirmed uncomfortably at the recollection of the interview three months before. Bunch of bloody stuffed shirts! Obvious from the start they had not approved of his South Yorkshire accent, background or schooling. Though they couldn't argue with his upper second BSc (Econ) degree, of which his father, in particular, was inordinately proud. God knows what the bloody Foreign Office must be like. Booth would not, of course, have got anywhere near an interview with the FO. No; the upper crust southern twits had decided he was not quite the type they were looking for to work in personnel. But they had offered him a job in security at the fast breeder reactor site at Dounreay in the north of Scotland. He had accepted immediately.

Fortune had not really been too unkind to Mr Booth.

Can count myself bloody lucky to have got a job at all, what with four million out of work, he told himself as the train reached the relatively open spaces of the Hertfordshire conurbation. Not that these Tory bastards out there would know anything about unemployment, he nodded towards the endless rows of neat little houses in Welwyn Garden City.

Upper class twits Booth's interrogators may have been, but the chaps at the Atomic Energy Authority did know how to interview and assess character. Two things in particular had struck them about Booth. First, the fierce drive and ambition which obviously raged beneath his grim, hard-done-to manner. Second – and Booth had been amazed that they knew, as he had not thought it relevant to mention on the application form – they had been impressed by his distinction as a member of the university's rifle club, and the single-mindedness which had made this his only known social activity at the LSE.

Booth settled back comfortably in his wide reclining seat. It was the first time he had ever travelled First class. One of the perks of the job, he reflected as the first hour slipped past. Only another fourteen to go to the UK's most northerly mainland town and rail terminal, Thurso, seven hundred miles away. It was going to be a long journey.

The hostel accommodation was excellent. The Authority had gone out of its way to provide congenial living quarters for the many young bachelors it recruited to Caithness each year. And at only £28.50 a week, all found, it was definitely another of the perks of the job for young Booth. Nor was that all; although he had no intention of taking advantage of the two return air tickets to London which were his for the asking each year.

Six weeks after his arrival Booth's attention was taken by a small classified advertisement in the local Caithness Courier. It offered a small croft for rent at a very reasonable rate. Memories of his childhood dream of working on the land were stirred. A careful calculation taking into account every penny of likely expenditure on food, fuel and extra transport cost down to the road-end where the free company bus would pick him up, convinced the tight Yorkshireman that he would not be too much out of pocket. He made the move after another fortnight's deliberations. 'Moostn't roosh int'it things,' he told his confidant, the hostel warden, whose opinion he had endlessly sought on all matters local.

The croft was about four miles west of Thurso and six miles inland. Not the most hospitable of locations, yet it suited Booth. There were, indeed, many similarities to the Yorkshire of his youth; especially to the bleak moors of Midhope and Bradfield. Except that Caithness was even bleaker, as he would find out in the coming sub-polar winter. It suited him very much, he decided. There was excellent shooting with the first brand-new 12-bore he had been able to afford in his life. There weren't many parts of the country where he could have gone out at will and be guaranteed to return with a brace of pheasant or grouse. All that remained was for him to save enough to buy one of the trained pointers which would be ready in about three month's time out at Melvich.

Added to this, there was a wide variety of loch and river fishing in the county with an abundance of trout and salmon. It was a sportsman's paradise. Booth had no regrets about coming north.

The isolated croft did not do much for his social life, however. In the hostel he had already made a few casual acquaintances; but out here his nearest neighbours were over a mile away. This, too, suited Booth. He had never been one for socialising. Even in London he could only recall one or two occasions when he had been in company other than that of the rifle club, and invariably he had sat in a corner saying nothing the whole night long, content to sup his favourite Beamish and let the rest worry about the bomb or whatever.

The Authority knew, of course, that not all of their recruits would be loners like Booth. For those who wanted them, Dounreay had some of the finest social and recreational facilities to be found anywhere in the UK. Rather like the oil companies in Alaska, the London government had been concerned about staff morale when remote Caithness had 'won' the right to play nursemaid to the world's most potentially dangerous experiment in nuclear physics. A generous allocation had been made to the designers for staff amenities. This, of course, had all been explained to Booth on his arrival at Dounreay by Roger Brookes the Principal

Personnel Officer. Booth's only question had been to ascertain when and where the rifle club met.

Iain Wallace had no time for Brookes. Not that he had ever tried it on with Wallace. No way. The ex-Glasgow cop and airport security man would have hit him with his truncheon. 'Though maybe jolly old Roger would find that a pleasant change from a handbag!' Wallace used to howl at his mates in the local, blowing froth from his Tartan Special in the process as he said this. However, a summons from Brookes could not be ignored.

'Take a seat, Iain. Cigarette?' offered Brookes.

'Eh; no thank you sir. Been off them for over four months now.'

'Really? Don't know how you manage it. You must be made of stronger stuff than me.' Brookes lascivious look and wetting of his lips with the tip of his tongue, which kept darting in and out suggestively, made Wallace want to throw up.

'Oh, it wasn't too bad. I was never a heavy smoker anyway, Mr Brookes.' Wallace decided to drop 'sir' even though it went against twenty years of grain in security work of one sort or another.

'Never get the odd bit of temptation?' Brookes was fluttering his lashes now.

'No. Can't say I do,' replied Wallace curtly, looking Brookes square in the eye.

'That's a good sign, Iain. Young Booth can't be getting on your nerves then?'

'Definitely not, Mr Brookes,' said Wallace, who was the Security Officer responsible for Booth's probationary period of training. 'Young Booth is a bit dour at times, and takes himself far too seriously. But he is good at his work. Real flair for it, I would say. Seems determined to do well.'

'Yes. I'm not surprised you should say that, Iain.' Brookes sounded quite smug. 'That particular character trait had been noticed by us already. Nice to see our judgements aren't always wrong.' He grinned irrepressibly at Wallace.

135

'Tell me,' continued Brookes, glancing down at the pale pink manilla folder in front of him – trust him to choose pink ones, thought Wallace, who favoured buff coloured folders himself – 'how is he mixing with the rest of your people?'

'Bit of a loner by all accounts. Doesn't try to ingratiate himself, if you know what I mean.' Whoops, Iain, he checked himself. Don't go too far.

'Not insolent or offensive, I hope, Wallace.' Brookes was subtly telling Wallace not to step over the mark.

'Oh, no; takes instructions well. Has the knack of asking all the pertinent questions. He just doesn't seem all that interested in people.'

'No social activities, then?'

'The Rifle Club is all I can think of, if you'd call that a social activity. One of their aces, in fact, according to Campbell. Nothing else as far as I know.'

'Female acquaintances?'

Not that you'd be interested in these. Nothing like the real thing, eh Roger? as my old Chief Petty Officer used to say. The thought flashed through Wallace's mind.

'Not much opportunity in our department, Mr Brookes. Though what he gets up to at that old croft of his I wouldn't know,' added Wallace.

'Quite. Well, Iain, thank you for your time. Just like to know how our new boys are settling in, that's all. Keep your eye on the chap, and do let me know if there are any problems.'

'Of course, Mr Brookes.'

'Well, Michael, my son. Old Roger's taken quite a shine to you, it seems. I think he fancies you a bit. Better watch out the next time you bend over!' Wallace nudged Booth in the ribs as they went into the canteen together for lunch.

'Just let him bloody well try,' growled Booth, reaching for a plate of braised kidneys and liver. 'I'd give him what for.'

'Maybe he'd like that.'

'Get on with you, Iain.'

'Seriously, laddie, he does seem content with your progress to date.'

'So he should be. I work a bloody sight harder than him.'

'Who doesn't, Michael? Cushy number that Personnel. How come you didn't fancy it yourself?'

'With my accent?' Booth sneered. 'You've got to talk posh Oxbridge and wear the old school tie for that department. No Iain, I'm only good enough for Security. No offence, like.'

'None taken, laddie. I know only too damned well what you mean. Anyway, I guess we'd better get back on the job now.'

Michael followed Wallace back over to the office which they shared, one of several en suite at the heart of the plant's security block.

Michael Booth was, in fact, doing well at his work. Remarkably well. After only four months in post he had a complete command of the routine aspects of his job. And he was impressed. With a total investment of billions of pounds to protect, successive governments had insisted that the UKAEA had been absolutely thorough. The best brains in the security business had torn each other's scenarios to shreds before coming up with what were now the standard procedures in every one of the Authority's atomic installations. Every known measure was in use to combat industrial espionage and sabotage. By 'adequate measures' – the standard, under-stated phrase recorded in Hansard whenever the matter was raised by some concerned member who was otherwise not making an impression in the House – the government meant ID cards to be shown on demand; remote control closed-circuit television in every strategic laboratory; electronic surveillance of phone calls, both business and, if warranted, personal; spot checks on key personnel's mail; a security force armed with revolvers and sub-machine guns; killer dogs and electrified fences. Not to mention personal dossiers on every worker above the level of auxiliary, compiled initially by Special Branch and kept up-to-date by the Authority's own snoopers. Booth was definitely impressed. Though as time went on and he observed the busloads of workers coming in and out of the plant each day; the constant comings and goings of local contractors and their crews who were growing fat on the maintenance of fabric; the way routine checks were carried out; he realised that there could never be complete security. Short, that is, of a total militarisation of the entire operation. He would not be surprised if the rumour that a small SAS squad had easily breached the defences in 1981 was true – although no-one in security ever spoke about it. He did know that the SAS often tested out supposedly secure establishments in this way. So maybe they had removed, then returned, some classified files just to prove the point.

As a graduate, Booth's job was not to monitor the banks of television screens, nor to patrol perimeter fences, armed to the teeth. His particular forte was administration, although he did not put more than a fraction of his degree work into practice. Still, it was good, regular employment which gave him satisfaction, job security and the prospect of slow, steady promotion. And it more than financed his leisure. In fact, his account with the Alliance Building Society was in quite a healthy state, despite having paid out £200 for his gundog, Charlie. And there was only one thing the average Yorkshire bloke preferred to see rising more than his bank balance.

'Going home for a few days at Christmas, Mike?'

Booth, by nature, was not looking forward to the festive season with all its enforced cameraderie.

'Where's that, Gerry? If you mean soddin' Stepney you can forget it.'

'But you could go for nowt, lad,' Gerald Campbell mimicked. 'Thought all you Yorkies would take every bit of brass that was going your way.' Gerry grinned cheekily as the next set of targets were being replaced, twenty-five yards down the range from them.

'Nah. That's your bloody Teuchters – Campbells o' the glen and that ilk,' Michael laughed. 'Now shut up, will you Gerry, till I concentrate on these targets. I feel a good score coming up.' Booth got himself into a comfortable prone position, making sure the pad on his elbow was in firm contact with the floor to avoid slipping.

'What do you mean coming up? You've been scoring great all

night, man. You should be entering next year's County Championships with averages like 98 and 99.'

'No way, Gerry. At least not till I've had a good bit more practice at this distance. In London all we ever had were fifteen yarders, with the occasional one at twenty.' Booth tightened the sling round the back of his hand and biceps by a notch then proceeded to pepper the tiny half-inch diameter bullseyes with the .22 calibre shot. He made nine clear and just smudged the edge of the tenth for a score of 99, which hadn't been bettered all evening. The flanged measuring plug indicated he had only been .05 of an inch short of a possible.

'Great shooting, Mike. Hell, you'd win the damned championship with a score like that. Must be that old BSA Martini you've got,' Campbell laughed.

'No, it's not all that great. Now, if I had an Anschütz maybe I could really start shooting, if you'll excuse the pun, Gerry. And anyway I'd have to complete half-a-dozen cards like that to even be in with a chance.'

'Well, it's four months away, Mike. You'll be making these scores regularly by then.'

'Wish I was so confident. We'll see, Gerry.'

'Hey! Look at the time! Only twenty minutes to closing.'

'Right on. Better get going, then.'

Five minutes later they were in the social club bar. At 62p a pint this was one perk neither man disclaimed.

'Pint of Beamish, and what'll it be for you, Gerry, Seventy Shilling? ...... yeh, and a pint o' Seventy Shilling, please. Ta, love.' Michael thought the Beamish had a bit too much of a head on it, but at these prices he wasn't prepared to argue.

'Thanks, mate,' said Gerry. 'Seriously, Mike,' he continued, returning to his earlier theme, 'does this place not get on your nerves a bit at times? Does mine. I couldn't survive without the odd break away.'

'Not really. Though maybe I've just not been here long enough. Mind you, I was always used to a bit of isolation as a lad.'

'Well, I suppose it's a bit different for you right enough. But this place will be dead over the holiday period. That old crofthouse of yours will probably be snowed up in any case.'

'Good point there, Gerry. Hadn't thought of that. But there's no way I'm going back to London after less than six months away. And I've lost contact with all my mates in Yorkshire. There's really nowhere else to go.'

'Nonsense. Tell you what. The way you were scoring tonight we could fair do with you in the team.'

'Team? Didn't know you had one.'

'That's not suprising. Our last match was a shoulder-to-shoulder way back before the summer when we got hammered by Pentland 'A'. We don't usually get organised till after the New Year. But there's a big open competition held each year down at Aviemore round about the second or third of January. We've been talking for years about putting a team in, but we've never quite got round to it. Too many blokes with family commitments at that time of the year.'

'Well I certainly don't have any of those.'

'Exactly. Me neither. What about having a word with a few of the lads next week? Maybe we could get a team together this time. All we need is four for this competition, unlike the usual six or eight.'

'Oh, heck. That means all our scores would have to count?' Usually it was the best four out of six, or six out of eight.

'Yep. But that shouldn't worry you, Mike. What about it then?'

'Aviemore, you said?'

'Uhuh. It's quite a place. Come on, man!'

'Right, Gerry. You're on. Aviemore.'

The November issue of the Authority's Newsletter, which was distributed to all of the UK's plants, listed Michael Booth and Gerald Campbell as members of the Dounreay team entered for the Younger's Small-Bore Trophy to be contested at the Aviemore Centre on 3rd and 4th January, 1986.

The recently appointed young secretary at the Dhubat Consulate in London did not question his orders, no matter how trivial they seemed to be. The snippet, which he had almost missed, was duly ringed, dated, photocopied and catalogued for onward transmission.

The team of Young Farmers from Strath Halladale had just been announced as the winners of the 1986 Younger's Trophy. They had won a tense shoot-off with their great rivals from Carrbridge by the tiniest of margins. One smudged bull by the Carrbridge number four had decided the issue after a re-gauge. The Dounreay lads had achieved a very creditable fourth place, but overall just could not match the consistency of the top marksmen, who were all in contention for Scottish places in the Commonwealth Games to be held in Edinburgh later in the year. They genuinely and enthusiastically applauded the winners.

Not in the least dispirited – who could be at this season of the year in Aviemore, with all its attendant delights? – the foursome made their way from the shooting range towards the bar in the Freedom Inn. They were very much looking forward to the grand ceilidh to be held in the ballroom later that evening. Well, three of them were. Booth had never been to a ceilidh, and was looking for a way out. He could not think up an excuse meantime, but he would before eight o'clock. His three companions were in high spirits, however.

'Whee-hee! Fourth place! Not bad, eh lads?' Gerry Campbell was delighted.

'Especially for our first crack at it,' said Robin Fraser.

'Yeh. And we were just pipped for third,' added Bob Simpson, the fourth member of the team.

'We-ll. I don't know, Bob. Three points of a difference is quite a margin at this level.' Michael was much more realistic in his appraisal of their performance.

'Ach, who cares, Mike. If we can stay together as a team there's no reason why we couldn't do better next year.'

'True, Gerry, true.' Booth did not sound too convinced.

'Anyway, what about this ceilidh? Should be some shindig. Have you noticed all the spare birds going about?'

'Who hasn't, Robin? There's some crackers all right,' Gerry continued. 'Most of them are up here with their companies and bosses, though. If they know which side their bread's buttered on they won't be spreading it around too much,' he grinned.

'But wait till they see us in action, Gerry. Most of these ponces look as if they wouldn't know what to do with a bird, if you ask me. We'll show them a thing or two, eh Mike?' Robin nudged his drinking elbow.

'You what?' Booth had been plotting his escape.

'The birds, Michael! Just wait till we get in amongst them tonight.'

'Oh, that's not my scene, fellas.'

'Not your scene? Missing old Brookesy, are we then?'

'You know better than that, Gerry.' Booth sounded quite aggrieved.

'Sorry, old son. No offence meant. Just a bit of crack, that's all.'

'Bloody better be,' growled Booth. 'Anyway, if you lads don't mind, I think I'll get a breath of fresh air before dinner. We've been cooped up inside all day long. Feel a bit of a headache coming on.'

'Breath of fresh air, did you say, Mike? You'd get blown down to Perth if you stepped out there. Best stay and have a couple more pints instead.'

'No. You lot go ahead. I'm going out for a walk. I'll catch you up at dinner.'

Aviemore can be one of the coldest places in Britain. At five o'clock in the afternoon of this fourth of January it most definitely was. A raw north-easterly was sweeping the long, narrow main street clear of all but the bravest souls. Booth toiled into it for about quarter of a mile before giving up the hopelessly unequal struggle. As he turned abruptly back in his tracks towards the hotel he almost bowled over the fur-swaddled woman battling along behind him.

'Thank goodness you did not decide to stay out in this for long, Mr Booth!'

Shamin el-Fazzah was gasping for breath. She was used to winter sports in Chamonix and Aspen, not in the wilds of the

Scottish Highlands.

'Shall we go in here, Mr Booth?' she added, indicating the cosy chalet-style tearoom they had stopped outside.

Booth was too stunned to refuse. His lungs had been coping admirably with the icy hurricane but he lost his breath instantly as he followed obediently in the warm fragrant breeze of her wake. Shamin shook her hair free from the hood of her musquash and wolverine Eskimo parka, unzipping it fully as she did so to reveal a beautifully shaped cashmere sweater the exact shade of her camel skin boots.

Michael Booth had never been picked up like this before. He was at a loss for words. Still a virgin at twenty-three, he was totally discomfited by this vision inviting him to sit down at a table beside her. Booth was shy of women in general; but he was shit-scared of this mature, self-assured female who, at around twenty-eight or twenty-nine, was at her peak of perfection. Shamin, however, was well prepared.

'Congratulations, Mr Booth, on doing so well in the competition.'

Booth was not the first, nor would he be the last, to be mesmerised by Shamin's eyes, smile and gentle touch.

'But ...... but we only came fourth,' he spluttered, without thinking about any of the obvious introductory questions.

'Aha! Modesty in a man appeals to me, Mr Booth. It is a rare quality. But you omit to mention that you personally scored more points than any other member of your team, is that not so?'

'Well .... yes.' Michael, who had in fact averaged a personal best of 99.25 over the two days, began to grow in confidence. 'However, you did not follow me just to congratulate me on my score.'

'No. But we must begin somewhere, eh, Michael, if I may? My name is Iffat Bolkiah. You do not know who or what I am, and you will never see me again after today. But we have important matters to discuss.'

Booth was well and truly hooked by now, as the tea and toasted muffins finally arrived. He allowed Shamin to continue, not knowing in which direction to go himself.

'As I said, Michael, we have important matters to discuss. You are settling in well at your new job, I believe? That is good. You enjoy your work?'

Visions of the small print in the Official Secrets Act which he had been obliged to sign, though he had never read it, floated mistily in front of him as Booth assented that he was happy at Dounreay.

But how the hell does she .....? Before he could complete the thought, Shamin continued.

'To come to the point, Michael, my Government .....'

Oh Christ, he thought. What on earth's going on here?

'..... believes that you can be of considerable assistance to us.'

The Secrets Act snapped into sharp focus now.

'How? Eh? What do you mean?' He was stuttering now, having lost whatever confidence Shamin might have encouraged in him with her initial flattery.

'Simple, Mr Booth.' Shamin had decided to stop playing games with him. 'Certain pieces of information which you can easily gain access to, would be .....'

'But I'd get twenty-five years for anything like that!'

'Not at all. You are being melodramatic. We are not talking about highly classified information, Mr Booth. Just a number of points of routine detail which would be most helpful to us. We have no wish, nor any need, to turn you into anything like a traitor. Just a bit of low-level industrial espionage, you might say.'

'And if I refuse?'

'We do not think you will, Mr Booth. In fact, to quote *The Godfather*, we are going to make you an offer you cannot refuse. You are familiar with the content of the Special Branch vetting report to the UKAEA on yourself? No? I am not surprised.'

She slid a photostat copy of it across the chequered tablecloth to him.

'We have our sources, Mr Booth, as you can see. The Official Secrets Act has been circumvented more times than you would care to believe.' Shamin had answered his next question before his confused brain had properly formulated it. 'Go on! Read it!'

It was all there. Primary and secondary school reports, including confidential comments and statements from his teachers; university records and interviews with lecturers;

personal and social habits backed up with photographs, most of which he had never seen before; subscriptions to periodicals; bank statements and medical records; political views and affiliations, including associations with known dissidents. More thorough than he had thought it would be. So this is what the Prime Minister had meant in her recent Newsnight interview when she had been defending Special Branch's extensive surveillance of picketing and demonstrations as being in the interests of the preservation of public order.

'Interesting, Mr Booth? But there is a very serious omission, is there not?'

She paused for his reply.

'An omission which would cost you your present job and all the benefits it has been giving you.'

She waited in vain as Booth scanned the report again.

'Come, come. You have surely not forgotten the name Will Taylor?'

He now saw one of the reasons why he would not be able to refuse her offer. His fleeting association with those students in Friends of the Earth. And the fact that his photograph was most likely lying unidentified in some Special Branch file of that demo he had marched on. Christ Almighty! He would most certainly lose his job. And with no signs of the recession diminishing, heaven knew when he would get another one. For the second time in his life the prospect loomed of having to forfeit everything he enjoyed. Back to Stepney's dole queues? Join his father in a wharfside warehouse?

'I am sure I do not have to spell out the consequences for you if someone in Special Branch were to do a little more careful research, Mr Booth.' There was an edge in her voice now. 'They might even come across this,' she added, handing over a 7 x 5 print which showed a group of students in an angry demonstration. 'You are quite clear in the enlargement.'

Booth went white.

'Where did you get this?'

'Hardly relevant, Mr Booth. But, since you have asked, Special Branch do not have this photograph. Rather, they have not spotted it. Yet. But my contact within C11 ....'

'C what?'

'C11, Mr Booth. Britain's secret police. Oh, yes; they exist. However, let us look on the positive side, shall we?' Shamin smiled reassuringly at Booth.

'Is there one?'

'Oh, most assuredly, Mr Booth. There always is. If you agree to cooperate with us, £20,000 will be deposited tomorrow in a Luxembourg bank on your behalf. As soon as your assignment has been completed the account number will be phoned to you. In the meantime this envelope contains £5,000 in cash as a sign of our good faith. A permanent job overseas as a security officer in one of our oil holdings will also be yours for the asking if you should so desire.'

Booth quickly compared these benefits to unemployment ones. 'What do I have to do?' he asked weakly, handing back the photograph.

'That is better, Mr Booth,' said Shamin, giving him the brown envelope. 'It also contains full details of what we want to know, and how and when you will communicate it to us. Oh, you may keep the photograph for your album,' she smiled beatifically. 'The negative is all we need. And now, Mr Booth, goodbye!'

Booth did not go to the ceilidh that night.
The blinding headache was very real indeed.

10

With Riotous Living

GEORGE Taylor was having a bad run of luck in the Black Velvet, one of several modern casinos in Newcastle. He was a regular visitor to the club, about two or three times a month on average, and was on slightly more than nodding terms with the management. He always felt a bit out of his class amongst the flash young types who seemed to make up most of the clientele. Like many a Geordie he had come to accept the insidious doctrine of the social inferiority of anyone who lived north of the Home Counties and who had their origins in the lower working classes; a viewpoint which successive Tory governments had reinforced in their policies of neglect and deprivation for the far north of England and for the whole of Scotland. Fortunately the up-and-coming generation of northerners knew better. Knew, in fact, that generations of hardship had endowed them with a fierce determination to survive and to succeed and had instilled in them a grittiness, resourcefulness and indomitable spirit which was a match for any group of people anywhere. George's fears were absolutely groundless, as most of the well-heeled folk there were also Geordies like himself, and one Geordie will never look down on another no matter how much they might disdain those who had the misfortune to have been born outside the Newcastle area. George, as he was more than slightly aware, was well tolerated in the club, and not just because he paid his way. His brawn and uncouth mannerisms made him something of a character, not to say novelty, to some of the younger female set.

'Hi, George.' It was Beth. She was always putting him on. 'Going to win enough to ask me along on your next trip?' she teased.

'Not bloody likely,' George scowled. Though he didn't half fancy the idea. Beth's rounded face, large breasts and ample thighs were close to his idea of perfection. She'd be a helluva good ride, he had often thought. 'Way things are going tonight I'll be lucky to get back myself in time for the next trip.'

'If the cards are all that bad why not come over here and buy us a drink?' Beth said, indicating her dark, slender girlfriend with a sideways nod.

'I'll take one more shot, lass, then I'll be right on over.'

George's luck remained the same.

'What'll it be, then, girls? None of your Blue Lagoons either. I've lost too much tonight to be able to afford those.'

'Too bad your poker's not up to much,' Beth grinned at him. 'Surprising in a big fellow like you!'

'Cheeky sod,' he scowled. 'I'd let you see it if I thought you weren't too young,' he added hopefully, surprised at his own bravado.

'I'll settle for a gin and tonic for the present, thanks,' said Beth feigning a bashful look, 'and a Bacardi and coke, Raqia?'

Raqia smiled her acceptance.

'Maybe one of these days I'll pluck up the courage to call you at cards, George.' She wasn't just humouring him either. Being a fairly big girl herself it wasn't just George's build that attracted her. There was something immensely lovable about the man. Maybe it was his unusual face. She had once laughed at a Glasgow girlfriend's description of someone having a face like a half-chewed caramel. Now she knew what she meant. George's was more like a partially-worked piece of clay abandoned before the sculptor had got round to putting in the fine detail.

Funny name that, thought George as he came back with the little round tray, the two dainty glasses flanking his own towering pint of Newcastle Brown.

'Here you are, ladies,' he said, reaching for his own pint first. 'Fair makes a person thirsty all that work,' he nodded over towards the croupiers who had a steady stream of customers.

'Don't think you've met Raqia before, George, have you?'

Beth introduced them without once taking her eyes off George. Maybe it's his eyes, she thought. One dark green, one dark brown. They could be kindly, mischievous, menacing in turn. That is when not fudged by alcohol.

'Raqia is at the university studying marine biology. We share a flat in Leazes Crescent, near the park.'

'I don't know about the park,' said George, 'but it's rare and handy for United's home games.'

'Don't mention them to us, George. Nothing but trouble most Saturdays there.'

'I've heard all about you from Beth,' said Raqia.

'Don't take her word for it, love. Try me out for youself,' George laughed coarsely. Tonight his eyes were definitely in mischievous mode. 'How come I've never met you before, then, Raqia?'

'Oh, I have only been over here since September. This is just my second visit to the casino.'

'Where you from then?'

'I don't suppose you will have heard of Dhubat?' teased Raqia.

'D'you what?' echoed George.

'D'you baht,' Raqia spelled out for him with a mock Yorkshire accent.

'As in Ilkley Moor, you great pillock! It's on the Persian Gulf, George,' Beth informed him. Raqia allowed the slight geographic inaccuracy to pass uncorrected.

'Ah well, you learn something new every day. Another round, girls?'

'Come on, George, let me buy this one,' said Beth. 'You must have lost a small fortune tonight already.'

'''Bout sixty quid, I reckon.' George was almost boastful, though he could ill afford to be.

'That's nothing for someone coining it in like you over at Windscale,' Beth tried to console him.

'Don't you believe it, lass. I'm not one of them bloody

scientists, you know.'

'What do you do, then?' asked Raqia.

'Feel these,' Beth told her, grabbing one of George's thick forearms as he made an exaggerated attempt to cover his balls.

'Not those,' she grinned as George's eyes registered their disappointment. 'These, Raqia. He's a driver. One of those big juggernauts. And don't believe him about how poor he is. Last time he was in here he was boasting about all his special payments and allowances up at the plant,' she added.

Boasting had been the word. In fact, the job wasn't all it had appeared to George in the advert in *The Sun* when he had noticed it a few years previously. Plenty of perks, sure – hostel accommodation, travel allowances, holidays, good pension – but for actual cash in hand he was better off working for his old private haulage contractor. They had never been too fussy about logging hours or paying taxes, and there was always a bob or two to be made on the side with a lot of the firms he delivered to who didn't have their own fleet of vans. He was seriously considering giving it up – security and all – and returning to Newcastle for good. Trouble was he owed a hell of a lot of money to some of the lads in the hostel; and he was becoming much less welcome at the Jack of Spades, a Newcastle den which specialised in poker, poker and more poker, and to which, as a result of the longest bad spell in his life, he now owed several thousand pounds.

Despite this, George, who couldn't quite get used to the idea of women buying him a drink, insisted on another round.

'Same again, girls?'

'Only if you insist,' Raqia gave in, half reaching for her purse.

As George shambled over to the bar, Raqia turned to Beth.

'You were right, Beth. He is a character, as you say.' She laughed. 'And quite attractive in his way.'

'Here, Raqia, what are you suggesting?' grinned Beth.

'Oh, nothing. He does seem to have taken a beating tonight, though, despite his apparent good humour.'

'Hey, you really like him?' Beth wasn't as surprised as she sounded.

'Well, it might be rather interesting,' confessed Raqia.

'You mean we should ask him to ....'

'Would you mind?' interrupted Raqia.

'Mind? You must be joking! I've always fancied him. We'd certainly give him something to boast about back at the plant.'

'And he might give us something to boast about back at the university, if that bulge in his trousers isn't a lunchbox,' Raqia giggled.

'You really on then?' asked Beth.

Before she could answer, George was back.

'Right you are, girls. Hope you can both hold your drink,' as a fleeting thought flashed through his head of what might happen if they could not.

'And what if we can't, George?' Beth aimed a playful jab at his ribs.

'Get away with you, Beth. Those things only ever happen in films.' George sounded downright envious.

'Do you think so?' asked Raqia.

'Mind you, some of the young college lads in the hostel spin a few yarns about wild student parties. Most likely all talk, though. Not that you two would know otherwise,' he added.

'Fancy coming over to our flat for a few more drinks then, George? Maybe you'll find out differently,' Beth laughed.

But the allure in her voice was unmistakable.

George looked first at Raqia, then back at Beth.

'You shouldn't lead a bloke on like that,' he huffed.

'Who's leading anyone on?' Raqia asked him. 'We had better go now while I'm still fit to drive.'

Beth nodded to George.

'That's right, George. Nobody's having you on.'

She laid both hands on his arm for emphasis.

Well I'll be fucked, George thought to himself. And I'll not be the only one, he added, gulping down the half-pint of dark brown sludge remaining in his glass.

Though perfectly sober after only four or five pints, George sat in the back of Raqia's Peugeot 205 GTi in a stupor.

Christ, he thought, am I really going to get it into a couple of college birds? The surging pressure against his fly confirmed his thoughts. Je-sus. He couldn't believe it.

As the car squealed to a stop, Beth looked round reassuringly.

'Here we are. Looks like some of our neighbours are having a rave.' They could hear the Sex Pistols' obscenities as soon as the car had stopped. She jumped out and pulled her seat forwards. George squeezed through the tiny opening, with Beth hauling on his left arm.

'Not my type of music that,' George grimaced.

'Nor mine,' Raqia agreed. 'We'll try not to get invited in if we can help it.' She smiled.

George almost melted.

God, they mean it, he thought. The little cunts really mean it.

Raqia's eyes fell appreciatively to George's twitching crotch.

Once over the threshold things happened quickly. The girls' flat was harshly lit at first till Beth plugged in the smaller lamps. She clicked on The Eagles cassette which was already sitting in the small player, and poured three large drinks – Scotch for George, vodka for herself and Raqia – as *Hotel California* turned her even further on. George's eyes were flickering all over the room – scatter cushions and pile rugs on the floor, pop art and motto posters covering the walls. After two very large whiskies in quick succession, his eyes weren't wandering about so much. They were too busy trying to focus on the two attractive girls lounging beside him.

Conversation had been stilted since they came in. George wasn't quite sure what was expected of him. Then he felt Beth's fingers working along his thigh and loosening his belt. Raqia brushed her lips over his eyes and face and caressed the back of his neck.

George's response was instant. He developed the biggest hard-on either of the girls had ever seen.

Beth could not resist it. She eased it out from the constraining trousers and Y-fronts, and ran her tongue from base of the shaft to the moist tip several times, nibbling gently as she went. Slowly, and with not a little effort, she took the giant head into her mouth. George had never felt any sensation like the one Beth was now giving him. Up till now he had thought this kind of thing only happened in Harold

Robbins' books. Now, as he sprawled on the cushions with a woman going down on him for the first time in his life, he realised that Robbins must have had a hell of a ball researching his novels.

Raqia continued undressing herself and George at the same time, offering George only her breasts and lips to kiss. Which was probably just as well, as George had only been liberated in the past few seconds, and wouldn't have known what to do otherwise. Even Harold Robbins hadn't gone into that much detail as far as he could remember. And anyway, he would probably have bitten something off, such was his ecstasy at that point.

Beth slithered out of her top and slacks as she continued working on George, then returned one hand to his balls while using the other on herself. She had something of a reputation among her boyfriends as an exponent of deep throat, but there was no way she was going to risk George coming in her mouth – God, he might choke her. As she eased her teeth and lips free from the massive prick, George hauled her up and onto him. She almost came with the strength of his grip on her shoulders.

George tried to turn her onto her back.

'Hell no, George, you'll kill me with that. Stay where you are.'

Raqia mixed some more drinks and put on Vivaldi's Four Seasons, which, after the BBC series on Casanova which she had seen on video, seemed absolutely appropriate to her.

Beth lowered herself gently onto George. She gasped as much with pain as pleasure as she took in his throbbing tip. She climaxed right there and then, and her complete descent onto him came in a spasm of delight. George tried to press her buttocks down further onto him, but she tore his hands away, convinced that another centimetre would put her into hospital for major surgery. All she was aware of was her entire insides filled with searing, pulsating fire. Gradually she began moving again at George's insistence. As she did so she was able to accommodate him with greater ease, until she was thrashing about on top of him, and made no protest when he rolled her over and began ramming in and out of her.

'Christ!' she moaned. 'Fucking mother of God! Aaahhhh!'

Beth came again like none other she was ever to experience. George's sperm gushed into her like the lager in the famous advert. It reached parts of her that none other ever had. She could almost feel it crashing against her womb, like surf on some Irish beach in Ryan's Daughter.

Raqia knew that George would be out of action for some time now, so she just snuggled in to his other side and drew an acrylic fur throw over them. She was a bit apprehensive anyway after witnessing what had seemed to her like Beth's tortured climax at such close quarters, and was quite relieved when George dozed off immediately after downing the other large Scotch and dry ginger ale she had poured for him.

Beth could not sleep. After about half an hour she began gently kneading George's limp penis with both hands.

Within seconds she was back on top of him and George became drowsily aware that the fantastic dream he was having was not really a dream at all.

It was only around five in the morning that sheer exhaustion claimed Beth and George for a few hours of deep and well-earned sleep.

Raqia, meanwhile, had gone into her bed, not daring to take George on. She was up first in the morning at around 09.30 and brought large quantities of fresh orange juice, black coffee and toast into the scene of last night's orgy. George wolfed down the food amidst hearty grins as the girls' naked bodies lounged in contrast to his massive hairy bulk, their hands occasionally caressing him playfully.

'Where did you get to last night?' Beth asked Raqia.

'You must be joking, Beth. There was no way you were going to let me in on the action. I just went to bed.'

'Jesus, George, you were fantastic.' Both she and George were getting excited again, George visibly so as Beth began stroking his stomach and teasing her fingers downwards through the thick mass of hair on his belly.

'Surely you have both had more than enough already!'

Raqia was becoming genuinely concerned for her friend's gynaecological welfare.

'Mind your own business, Ms Nadir,' said Beth with an outsize grin as she placed her coffee mug on the floor beside the cushions.

'Well, I've got work to do,' said Raqia. 'There's a meeting at the Students' Union at 11.00. I'd better get along.'

'You've got work to do?' replied Beth. 'And what do you call this, then?' she asked as she made a grab for George.

'A meeting on a Saturday morning?' George sounded a bit peeved that he wasn't going to get to sample Raqia. 'What the hell for?'

'Oh. She's into this Ban The Bomb thing just now,' Beth told him with more than a hint of cynicism. 'Nothing better to do with her time.'

'Come, Beth, it's not that childish. We know The Bomb is here to stay. We are just trying to prevent it from ever being used, and trying to slow down the proliferation of nuclear armaments.'

'You've lost me there,' confessed George, who was by now wishing she'd get the hell out of it to her damned meeting if he wasn't getting to screw her.

'I'll give you more details some other time, George,' Raqia was in no way putting him down. 'Perhaps the next time you're in Newcastle?'

'You mean I can come back here again?' George couldn't believe his luck.

'I'd be most disappointed if you didn't,' Raqia told him sincerely. 'Anyway, I'd better fly,' as she moved away from George's arms. 'Maybe next month it will be my turn to get to know you better?'

'Be my guest,' laughed George, as Beth took him firmly in her hands.

Raqia used the month before George's second visit to good effect. Information is easy to come by in Newcastle, as it is in any town if one approaches the right people; and at the end of one week of low-key enquiry she had a complete rundown on George. She was looking forward to his next visit.

Beth was also looking forward to it, but for a different reason. For the first week after George had returned to Sellafield she had felt like she could never be satisfied by another man again. Half-way into the second week it dawned on her that a month was a long time, so she decided to try anyway. She was relieved to discover that she had been wrong; although she still had to admit that George was something special.

It was with great difficulty that Raqia persuaded Beth to give her the first night with George on her own.

'Don't worry, Beth. There will be plenty of him left for you,' she promised, as Beth left to spend the night with a geology student in the halls of residence at the university. As it turned out, Raqia didn't leave quite as much of George as she had intended to; but there was still no shortage for her friend the following evening.

George did not arrive at the Black Velvet until almost 11 p.m., two hours late for his date with the girls. Had the meeting not been so important, Raqia would have left shortly after 9 p.m. She was not the type who had to stand that kind of treatment from any man.

She had not been wasting her time in the club, however. Backgammon, an old favourite of hers, had just been discovered in Newcastle and introduced to the club. Several sessions had made her about £125 better off; so she was in fairly good humour when George eventually showed up.

In fact, George did not enter the club. He was barred at the door by Mark and Sam, the two ex-wrestlers who worked as 'commissionaires' at the casino. Raqia heard the argument going on and rushed over.

George was in a bit of a mess. He had been in a fight, and had taken more than he had given by the looks of him. He was also drunker than he should have been – Raqia recalled his sudden capitulation to the whisky the previous month. Like many a big man, George could not hold his spirits all that well. Little wonder he was being refused entry.

'Look, mate, you've already had one pasting tonight. If you try to push in here, me and Mark will make you a hospital case,' Sam was patiently explaining.

'But I've a date inside,' George said unconvincingly.

'Not in your state, pal,' Mark told him. 'The management are quite strict about that. You've been here often enough to know that.'

George was not all that drunk. He eyed up the two bouncers.

'Will you take a message inside for me, then? Uhh?'

'That won't be necessary, George,' Raqia's voice cut through. 'Just you wait there and I'll be out in a minute when I collect my coat.'

'D'ya see? Bloody told you I had a date in there,' said George to Sam, who was busy ogling the lovely young woman in disbelief.

George attempted to push through to Raqia. Big though he was, Sam had an arm lock on him in a split second, with Mark ready to move in, in the unlikely event of his mate needing assistance.

'George!' shouted Raqia. 'Don't make a fool of yourself, please.'

The sight of her near to tears sobered George up.

'All right. Yeah, you're right. OK lads, I'll wait here while the lady gets her things.'

'Attaboy,' Sam told him, although he held the lock on for enough seconds after George's submission to ensure no further tricks from the big fellow.

Raqia was out in a few seconds and steering George round to the 205. With difficulty she got his bulk inside, and wasted no time in driving home. George was in a bit of pain climbing the couple of flights of stairs to the flat. He sank gratefully onto the pile of cushions on the floor.

'Well, well, George. You are in a sorry mess,' Raqia baby-talked him. 'Just as well Beth is not here to see you.'

'Beth? Oh yeah, Beth.' The one he had read about in *The Lonely Lady*. 'Where is she, then?'

'Oh, don't worry. You will see her tomorrow. She had to visit her mother tonight down in Whitley Bay.'

'Whitley Bay? Used to go there for my holidays when I was a kid.' George slurred his way through the sentence with difficulty.

No, thought Raqia. I'm not going to get any sense out of him tonight.

'What have you been up to, then, George?' she asked.

'Fight. Got in a fight with two blokes at the Jack of Spades. Bastards. Oops, sorry. Took me by surprise. Ouch!' he exclaimed as two of the cushions moved apart, depositing a tender part of his anatomy on the hard parquet floor. 'That was bloody sore,' he told Raqia, rubbing the base of his spine. 'Bastards put the boot in too.'

'Poor George. Look, why don't you just take this,' she said, handing him a large whisky, 'and let's sleep it off till morning. Hopefully you'll be in better shape then,' she winked at him.

The whisky took its usual toll on George, and he hardly protested as he was led into Beth's bedroom, undressed and tucked in for the night.

Several hours later in her own bed Raqia gradually gained consciousness of her state of arousal. Strong muscular fingers were probing deep inside her, curling in and outward against the remainder of the hand which was pressing firmly against every contour of her mound. At the same time, something hard and hot was pushing open her thighs from behind and trying to join the fingers already inside. Moaning gently she hooked her right leg backwards and up over the thick limbs pressed alongside hers.

George's three fingers withdrew from her now streaming passage and reached round and under her left side, lifting her with ease backwards onto his stomach. Raqia lay on her back on top of him and guided his marvellous cock deep inside. George's hands caressed her face, neck, breasts, belly, pussy, thighs, everywhere at once, as she spread her legs wide over his and pushed herself rhythmically up and down, her hands resting on her lover's hairy thighs.

'Never, never, never,' she moaned, had she been made love to like this. Never had she experienced so many different sensations at the one time, as George's hands ceaselessly traced patterns over her naked glistening body; now her neck being quite firmly massaged, now her clit being lightly tapped, now her flat hard stomach being gently stroked and tickled by the fuzzy backs of George's fingers. And all the while that marvellous mass thrusting deeply inside her.

George could feel the tightening in his balls and the build up of pressure inside his tubes as they prepared to explode. He rolled over, still holding Raqia in position, until she was lying face down clenching the pillows with both hands and gasping her way through one orgasm after the other, until she almost fainted. George was only just aware of the pleasant sensation of her delightful buttocks curving against his stomach when he came. The first enormous spurt thrust him even deeper into his unprotesting partner from this position, and he held himself there until he was spent.

They lay together like that for a long time after, Raqia loving the feeling of being crushed under George's bulk, until even his powerful forearms began tingling with the strain of supporting all that weight. Raqia reluctantly eased off her tight grip on George's now limp sticky organ and allowed him to roll off. Often after intercourse she would make her partner lie over on his stomach then sit herself astride his back and bring herself off to orgasm by rubbing her clitoris up and down on the bone at the base of his spine. This time with George there was no need to, as she was thoroughly satisfied — which was just as well considering the state of George's back after the fight!

She laughed to herself at last month's naive concerns over Beth's female bits; and was delighted at her own ability to stretch and accommodate George so easily. Had Raqia known more about western history or contemporary European society she would never have been apprehensive in the first place. The Roman predilection for inviting donkeys to their orgies to couple with eager empresses and whores has been faithfully recorded. And many a farmhand has lost half a week's wages on the village tart's ability to absorb far more of the bestial appendage than he thought possible. George boasted that he was hung like a stallion; but, with no disrespect, he could not even compete with a Shetland pony.

As it was, Raqia couldn't even be bothered wiping herself with the Kleenex tissues she always kept at the bedside. She just nestled into George's huge frame from behind. They both slept soundly till morning.

Raqia was first to wake. George's face was now showing vivid bruise marks from the night before, but otherwise he was curled up contented as a baby. She slipped on a long Thai silk housecoat and made up a tray of ham, eggs, toast and tea.

'Waken up now, George,' she whispered into his ear as she rumpled the soft stubble that passed for hair all over his huge head. He kept it closely cropped so that no one could get hold of it in a pub brawl, he had told her the night before.

'Uh?' George turned towards her, reaching out for her shoulders to pull her down.

'Come on, you great lump, sit up. I don't want to waste this good food.'

The smell of the ham and eggs was too much for George.

'What I've got for you can keep hot for a while yet,' he grinned, taking the tray Raqia handed him before she slipped under the covers beside him.

They both concentrated on the food for a few minutes. Raqia had seldom eaten breakfast with such gusto.

'Well, George, you seem to have recovered quickly after your escapades last night,' she leered at him, brushing away some crumbs which had fallen onto her breast.

'I wasn't all that bad, was I?' George mumbled through a mouthful of toast.

'I'm not talking about that, you great mutt,' she grinned, stroking his flaccid member. 'I'm talking about your fight. You were in a pretty bad shape. What was it all about anyway?' Raqia really sounded as if she had not the faintest idea.

'I sort of overstayed my welcome at the club, you might say.'

'The club?'

'Yeah; the Jack of Spades over on Aelred Street. I go there quite often when I'm in town. Lot of the lads I used to work with are regulars there. Good bunch of lads, too.'

'Good? After they beat you up?'

'Hell no. It wasn't my mates did this. It was those bloody bouncers.'

'But couldn't they just have put you out if you were drunk?'

'Jeez, Raqia, don't you know anything? You could be pissed as a newt in there and nobody would bother. I was worked over on purpose.'

'But is that not a matter for the police then?' she asked, putting the tray down on the floor.

'Now you really are being daft. Listen, these geezers don't do it just for fun. You might say it was a reminder I was getting.'

'Are you in some sort of trouble with this club, then? Is that it, George?' Raqia turned and nuzzled into his side.

'No other word for it. £2,800 worth of trouble in fact.' George played absently with her fine jet black hair. 'The management want me to settle up fast. Some hopes,' he added.

'And if you don't? What will they do to you then?'

'Oh, nothing much. Not for three grand. Probably just a few ribs put in – couple of days in hospital.'

'But that's terrible, George.' She had a genuine horror of violence, even when it wasn't this close.

'Perhaps I could help you in some way. My parents are quite well off. I could ....'

'Dammit, girl, I couldn't take any money from you.'

George meant what he said. Geordies are fiercely independent when it comes to money matters. The idea of a handout, especially from a woman, was not on.

'But suppose you were to earn it?'

'I've never charged for my services before,' laughed George, making a quick dive for Raqia's fuzz.

'You'd make a fortune if you did, George,' she said seriously, making no effort to protect herself from his marauding hands. 'Although I don't have to pay for it just yet either.'

Too true, my nut brown maiden, thought George.

'No. I had more of a business deal in mind.'

'Go on, then.' George had made a few unofficial deals in the past, and was prepared to listen to any reasonable proposition.

'I have some friends at the university. Remember I rushed away the last Saturday morning you were here to go to a meeting? Well, they would pay rather a lot for certain pieces of information.'

'Information? Me?' George sounded incredulous. 'I don't know a thing that would be of any use to anyone, let alone your lot of intellectuals. I'm only a driver. Right waste of time me signing the Secrets Act.'

'Oh, we wouldn't want anything like that,' Raqia protested. 'We are not spies or anything. Every university in Britain has a group like us. We write letters to the newspapers and to MPs and people like that; go on protest marches, demos and sit-ins. It's all quite open and above board. We are simply trying to make the general public aware that there is a problem and that it will not go away by simply ignoring it.'

'So how could I help you then?' George was slightly puzzled.

'Well, this summer we are planning to draw attention to the hazards of transporting plutonium, especially by road, inside the United Kingdom.'

'Hazards?' George interrupted. 'It's safe as bloody houses. I should know.'

'That may be; but we want to get people asking questions anyway. If there is the slightest risk at all we want to emphasise it.'

'But I tell you, Raqia, there is no risk. The stuff is completely safe. It's packed inside hell knows how thick a container; there's an armed police guard and convoy which travels every inch of the way with us; our routes and timings are kept secret right up to the last moment. There's no way anything could go wrong.'

'I know all that. That's what every MP in the country is told to say whenever he is asked about this. But suppose we were to get advance warning of a shipment and organised a small protest – say a dozen or so students with placards, etc.? If we could show that even that was possible, it would give a lot of people something to think about, don't you see, George?'

'Yeah. If they had nothing else to think about. But even the driver isn't told in advance where he's going. We get a set of route cards just before we leave the plant.'

'But someone must know in advance. There must be dozens of people with access to that kind of information.'

'Sure; but I'm not one of them,' George reminded her.

'Not even for £5000?'

'For what?' George was sure he had heard right, but wanted it said again.

'£5000,' Raqia spelled it out. 'We would pay £5000 to embarrass your employers and the government. It would be a great victory for us. And it wouldn't be doing any real harm,' she added.

'Right enough. £5000? It 'ud take me a year to earn that kind of cash with this old fellow,' he said, placing Raqia's willing hand on to the rapidly awakening member in question.

George Taylor thought a lot about that £5000 over the next few weeks and about what he could do with it. But he couldn't for the life of him think of a way to get the information Raqia wanted. Every idea that occurred to him had at least one fatal flaw.

He was due a fortnight's holiday sometime in July or August. The drill was to put in for two or three choices, one of which would be agreed by Personnel. Obviously they would not let him go if there was a shipment due. But that, at the very best, would only pin it down to a particular fortnight – and even then the chances would be about four to one of finding out. Such favourable odds were appealing to George, who was still piling up the gambling debts, but even if they came off would not give the result he needed.

Suppose he asked Jack Munro? Jack lived in the hostel and, like himself, enjoyed a flutter. In fact he enjoyed it far more than George, as his luck was considerably better. George owed him about £250. Jack worked as a clerk in Administration; he prepared all the documentation which accompanied each consignment. He was sure to have access to advance delivery schedules. But how to approach him? Directly was out: he'd overreact and report George to Security, nothing surer. Holiday arrangements? But he would tell George to go through channels. What if George offered to square his debts by doing an outside job during a few days 'illness' when no consignment was due? That would not work either. Jack would not risk anything like that for a lousy £250. Cut him in for a couple of thousand? George would be in maximum security within hours of such a proposition.

What was that girl's name at the Chapelcross plant? Jean ..... Jean Muir. Could she find out from her end? But even if she was willing to try – and she had only known him for a couple of months since his last trip up there – what excuse could he give for wanting the information? And what exactly did she do there anyway? A telephonist, he thought. Anyway, the excuse of planning their next meeting was too lame for anyone to believe. He could have driven the ninety miles any free weekend.

Then George had his first stroke of luck for some time. One

afternoon in the middle of a game of billiards he just failed to make a break of sixteen points with an in-off the white, which just caught the corner of the pocket and left his opponent with an extremely easy shot next.

'Not a bad break, George,' Brian Gorman told him. 'But you'll improve with all the extra practice you'll be getting over the summer.'

'Cheeky bugger. When did you last score fourteen? Anyway what's this about extra practice? I thought we played enough of this as it is.'

'You haven't heard yet? It was in The Observer yesterday.'

'Come on, Brian, you know I don't read that snob paper,' said George, sinking another red. He followed up by potting Brian's cue ball then playing his own and the red to opposite sides of the baulk cushion.

'True. Anyone who pots his partner's ball and then does that wouldn't have the class to read a decent paper,' Brian retorted.

'Sorry, mate,' George grinned. 'There wasn't anything else on though.' He then played a lousy shot after Brian's foul, leaving the red hanging over the top pocket. 'Shit. Go on, then. What was the paper saying?'

'Seems like you drivers are going to be out of a job soon.'

'What?' George interrupted him with a bellow. 'What about our security and pensions?'

'Oh, not literally out of a job. But you'll certainly have lots less work to do and more time to spend in here. They are going to start sending plutonium by air to Dounreay from Carlisle airport at Crosby-on-Eden. Via Wick airport, instead of by road all the way,' he added.

'Get away, man. Why the fuck'd they do a daft thing like that?'

'Who knows? The paper didn't give much detail; but it seems that so many people have been complaining about the dangers of road transportation that the Authority has come up with this plan instead.'

'But that's crazy. You know as well as I do that they're as safe as houses on the road. Did it say when this was going to start?'

'Sometime in the summer. Anybody's guess really. But it's really going to screw up you drivers' jobs.'

'Too true. We'll be glorified taxi-boys. Here to the airport and back again. Hell. That's not for me, Brian.'

'Can't say I blame you, George. Though at least you'd still be getting out of this place every so often.' Brian was thinking of his own job driving a security jeep around the plant's perimeter.

'Nah. Depends what a person's been used to. Reckon I'll get out of this place for good if that happens. Come on then, old son, let's see you beat that,' as he completed three beautiful in-offs in a row.

George won his game of billiards that afternoon, together with £1 from Brian. But more than that he now saw clearly, for the first time in weeks, how he was going to get his hands on the £5000 – in addition to whatever redundancy payments he would get out of British Nuclear Fuels.

George had been a lifelong member of the Transport and General Workers Union. That is, until he had taken on his present job. In its early days the British nuclear industry had been even more successful than the oil companies in keeping out the unions. Not that they had an official policy – that would have been illegal – but there were all sorts of off-the-record ways of discouraging union infiltration. Old habits, like old soldiers, have a reputation for dying hard. George had never been a union activist – otherwise he might never have been employed by the Authority – but he knew enough of union tactics to realise what he now had to do.

First, a request in writing to Personnel for a meeting with all drivers and 'mates' connected with deliveries. This would involve bringing in some men from other nuclear stations, and would obviously take a few weeks to set up. Meantime, George got to work on the drivers in Sellafield, not that there were all that many. The issues were quite clear-cut: loss of hours for overtime; overnight allowances; and, a fact which no modern management team would ignore, job satisfaction. Before a week was out George had formed a caucus of men who were prepared to take a fairly hard line with Personnel, although a few expressed doubts as to just how far this particular set of bosses would allow themselves to be pushed. In the event, the men were to be pleasantly surprised.

Three weeks later the thirty-or-so drivers and co-drivers assembled in one of the plush conference rooms in the Admin Block at the plant. It was 10.30, and tables were generously laden with tea, coffee, sandwiches and fancies. The atmosphere was quite informal as James Sotherby, Deputy Director of Personnel, welcomed the men to the meeting and announced that discussions would start at 11.00 after everyone had enjoyed the coffee break.

'Coffee break?' muttered George to his mate. 'We ain't bloody well started yet and these management wallas are stopping for coffee and fancies. Pity they haven't laid on a tankard of Newcastle Brown,' he grinned.

'Well, gentlemen, I would like to thank you all for coming here this morning to express your concerns about recent developments unfortunately announced in the press. We had hoped to discuss the matter fully with you before any kind of statement was made to the media; but there seems to have been some sort of leak – not, I must hasten to add, of a radioactive nature!'

There were few chuckles of appreciation at this feeble attempt at humour.

'First, allow me to fill you in on the background to the recent decision. Over the past two or three years there has been a growing lobby of environmentalists pressing Parliament and the Authority to introduce ever more stringent safety controls on the transportation of radioactive materials, plutonium in particular. You know, and I know, that our present arrangements are entirely satisfactory; but, unfortunately, the Authority has found it impossible to convince the Parliamentary Select Committee set up last year that this is so. There is a very determined, highly vocal, and well-connected group centred on the universities and the media, who seem intent on imposing as many restrictions as they can dream up on our conduct of the nuclear energy programme to which successive governments have committed this country. Indeed, many would like to see us out of business entirely, and placed at the mercy of the even less stable elements of wind, wave and sunshine. This, I can assure you, will never happen.

'In order to somewhat allay the fears of these misguided persons, we have decided to introduce some changes in our tranportation procedures. In future, all deliveries of nuclear fuel elements will take place by air. They will be taken by road under armed guard from the plants to the nearest civilian or military airfield, then taken by specially designed Argosy planes to the airfield closest to their destination. There will obviously be significant changes in working conditions for many of you, including, I am afraid, the prospect of relocation for several crews around the country at provincial centres to meet the air deliveries. But this, gentlemen, is where you come in; and I now invite your comments or questions.'

There were a few moments of silence before the first speaker got up, a thin-faced, serious looking chap who worked in the south-east region.

'First thing I'd like to ask is whether or not this decision is capable of being reversed. It seems to me that, apart from the effect it is going to have on our working conditions, the whole idea is crazy. How on earth can this method possibly be safer than the present one?'

'Two points there,' observed Sotherby. 'First, I'm afraid the decision is irreversible. We have given a guarantee to this effect to Parliament. Second, while appreciating your comments about safety, I can assure you that there will be no increased risks associated with our new proposals. We have spent the past two years perfecting the design of special containers, which have been tested to a standard agreed to by all western nations with a civil nuclear programme. These containers will withstand any credible accident. Of that you can be certain.'

No-one there doubted Sotherby's assertion.

'That's all very well,' continued Herbert Lang. 'I didn't for a minute doubt the ability of the design engineers. But won't this new system increase the security risks? I mean, with the present system the fuel is delivered direct from here to the plant. You are now adding two changeover points to the existing simple routine.'

'Good point, Mr ......?'

'Lang.'

'Mr Lang. As you know security precautions are about as stringent as we can make them just now. In addition to those already in effect there will be special transfer arrangements made at each airport. Local and Authority police will be assisted by members of the Armed Services at all points of transfer where plutonium is involved. The security chaps, like our design engineers, Mr Lang, have done their homework.'

George Taylor was beginning to wonder how many of his colleagues had ever been on a trade union negotiating committee. Wasn't anyone going to get to the point?

'Mr Sotherby, it's obvious that the matters raised so far pose problems for the Authority only, and don't really touch on the matters of concern which have led to today's meeting.'

George glanced round at the talker, a balding middle-aged man with a heavy Lancashire accent.

'Our positions as drivers are seriously threatened by the new arrangements. Most of us were long-distance drivers before coming to BNF. Few of us came here for more money. We were attracted by the better job security and pension prospects. But what we are now faced with is a drop in income – for those of us who are not made redundant – and the status of glorified delivery van drivers.'

That's better, thought George.

There was a spontaneous burst of 'yesses' and 'that's rights' from the rest of the men.

'Yes; well, I can appreciate the depths of your feelings, gentlemen,' Sotherby replied. 'I can only repeat that I am sorry we did not have the opportunity of holding a series of discussions before the news got out. We might have been able to avoid some of the fears and disquiets which you now have. If I can start with the last point first. You men are amongst the cream of the country's Heavy Goods Vehicle drivers.'

Wily bastard, George was thinking.

'For many of you, the lack of long distance runs will be the toughest part of the changes to bear. You won't exactly be 'delivery men'; but the Directors take the point. We have decided that any driver over the age of fifty who so wishes may retire with full enhancement of pension rights. Anyone below that age who chooses voluntary redundancy will receive a pro-rata pension plus an extra ten years' reckonable service for purposes of severance pay calculations.'

This was the moment George Taylor had been waiting for. He was on his feet quickly.

'Some of us might be very interested in accepting this offer, Mr Sotherby. Could you give us some idea as to when it will come into effect?'

'I can do better than that; I can tell you exactly when it will come into effect.'

Jesus, he's fallen for it. George couldn't believe it.

'The first Argosy delivery will be made on 25 July from Carlisle to Dounreay. Our scheme will come into effect then, and all calculations based on service to that date. That should give those of you who wish to do so plenty of time to find alternative employment. Of course, you may leave sooner, but you would lose one year's reckonable service that way.' Sotherby was blissfully unaware of the fact that he had just increased George Taylor's redundancy payment by the sum of £5,000.

George could hardly wait for the meeting to end; but there was still a lot of business to get through.

The main issue still to be resolved was on the potential loss of earnings from overtime and allowances on the long hauls. There was a lot of hard talking done by the majority of men who wanted to stay on. An hour later they were more than happy to leave after Sotherby had agreed that existing additional payments would be conserved in future wages where the men were not required to undertake the journey themselves. In other words, a consignment from Sellafield to Dounreay would continue to net the drivers the same wages as at present, although they would only have to drive to Carlisle and back.

The Company was being as generous with the taxpayer's money as the most hopeful man had wished for.

Brian Gorman had been right: there were going to be a lot of improved players in next year's billiards league.

Shamin el-Fazzah was delighted to receive the next weekly

report from her cousin. For two years now Raqia had been groomed as Shamin's assistant in the intricate affairs of their family. Her enrolment in Newcastle University had been purely fortuitous; but now that Sellafield was featuring largely in the family fortunes her location in the north of England was proving to be invaluable. This latest piece of information was worth far more than its weight in gold.

11

Be Ye All Ready

ADNAN Ben Hadef al-Mahjub, Personal Secretary to Emir Hanif el-Fazzah, studied with interest the contents of the courier bag he had just been handed. One item in particular caught the Mullah's attention. Yes. His young protegé in the London Consulate was doing his work well. This was what he had been waiting for.

The document in question was a cutting from the property section of the The Times of 19 March 1986:

CASTLE OF DUNGOE, CAITHNESS

Prestigious 19th century baronial castle situated on secluded bay in north-east corner of Scotland. Magnificently appointed public rooms (6), bedrooms (12) and servants' quarters. Extensively modernised with full central heating, triple-glazing and insulation. Designer decorated throughout. Usual lodge, garages and outbuildings. Estate extends to 1250 acres, of which 200 are arable.

Dungoe is situated 17 miles south of Wick airport. Full particulars from, and expected offers over £320,000 to:

Macpherson, Robb and Sinclair,
10 Charles Edward Drive,
Inverness,
Scotland.

Al-Mahjub was relieved. Outside the Emir's immediate family he was the only man in Dhubat entrusted with full details of el-Fazzah's plans. Indeed, as Personal Secretary to the head of state, he, along with Taherali, had been given responsibility for the logistics of the entire operation. For months now he had been on the lookout for a suitable base in Scotland from which to launch the final stages of the scheme. Ideally, he would have preferred a location in Central Scotland, roughly equidistant from the twin foci of the plot. But, on reflection, if the base was to be closer to one than the other, the north was to be preferred. It was less accessible, but more secluded; and ideal surroundings for what they had in mind.

They must have this place – and fast. Time, though not yet running out, was precious. His telexed instructions to London were being decoded within the hour.

Since the discovery and exploitation of oil in the Middle East, Arab sheikhs had been very rich indeed. When they quadrupled the price the petroleum-parched West had to pay in 1974, they became mega-rich. They also became the scapegoat of British politicians for the disastrous performance of their economy in the '70s. In truth, the malaise in Britain's economy was much more deeply rooted than in the sands of the desert. It went down to the clay sub-soil of the British way of life, as was proven by the continued economic doldrums even after Britain itself became a major oil producer in the 1980s. But, at the time, it was more convenient to direct popular discontent away from the basic issues of mismanagement, union intransigency, under-investment, and a deplorable record of stop-go misdirection of the economy by both major political parties, and to focus instead on avaricious

Arabs intent on dominating the stock exchanges of the world. Thus all classes of British society could exonerate themselves from any share of the blame for their once-great country's steady slide towards oblivion, and Margaret Thatcher could get away with squandering tens of billions of pounds of oil revenue on propping up the dole queues which she had created.

One of the immediate results of this policy was an open hostility towards Arab investment in the UK. Like any shrewd operators, however, the sheikhs were undeterred. Their solution lay in the jungle that is British company law which allows investors to operate under intermediate guises and makes it very difficult for all but the most dedicated professionals to cut through the morass of holding companies and subsidiaries to arrive at the true identies of the owners. Even major British heart and cancer charities were found to have invested unwittingly in tobacco which kills 100,000 people a year. Not that there is any direct parallel with the Mafia and its legitimate up-front outlets in the USA, but the British system can achieve the same degree of anonymity for anyone who wants it, and is open to every bit as much fraud.

Hanex Consolidated Holdings had been set up by Hanif el-Fazzah in 1975 to handle all of his UK property, commodity and unit trust investments. It had been enormously successful even before the collapse of sterling to virtual parity with the dollar which made Britain the bargain basement of the world in late 1984 and early '85. Then, with el-Fazzah and countless Arab and American speculators flooding the London Exchange with dollars, the value of his company had multiplied by a truly remarkable twenty-seven times in just over a decade. El-Fazzah was delighted with its performance.

The instructions to buy Dungoe Castle and Estate still came as some suprise to Sir Lionel Williston, Chairman of the Board and Managing Director, however. At the asking price he thought it decidedly over-valued, even allowing for the weak pound. He would not personally have recommended its purchase; but orders were orders. He could only put it down to the whim of the Emir. And those whims had to be obeyed.

Williston put the usual channels into effect.

Lorna Gilmour answered the phone promptly on its second ring. '332956,' she grumped. Miss Gilmour was not a happy person. Who could be, working in such decrepit surroundings? The office, like that of many a perniciously purse-proud solicitor's, was in a dreadful state of peeling paintwork, tawdry furnishings and ancient electrical fitments. Its Dickensian disdain for the comfort of its occupants was in marked contrast to the two plush, stodgy, Volvos parked outside belonging to the firm's two surviving partners.

'Good day. Do I have Macpherson, Robb and Sinclair?'

'Yes.'

'Be so kind as to connect me to your senior partner, please.'

The Englishman's manners were impeccable even in the face of such rudeness.

'That'll be Mr Macpherson.'

There was a twenty second delay as she rang through.

'Who's calling?' Miss Gilmour came back on the line.

'Colonel Rae-Bramwell.'

Another twenty second delay.

'You're through now.'

The following morning full details of the property were delivered by first-class post to Colonel Rae-Bramwell. He passed them on unopened to his brother-in-law, Sir Lionel Williston, at his Knightsbridge office.

Exactly forty-eight hours later Hugh Macpherson was stunned to receive a firm offer of £350,000 from the Colonel's solicitors, Marsden and Williston.

'Roderick! Will you look at this?' he called to his partner, Sinclair, in the adjoining office. 'You'll not credit it!'

'Don't say you've had an offer for the Bonnie Lassie!' The rusting ancient hulk had been impounded by the Caledonian Canal Trust ten years previously for failing to pay wharf dues, and had been up for sale ever since.

'Be reasonable, Roddy, now. No. But we do have an offer for Dungoe.'

'Dungoe. Already? But that's impossible. We've only sent out one set of particulars and that was only two days ago.'

174

'I know. They won't even have inspected it, let alone arranged for a valuation.'

'And what are they offering?'

'Three-and-a-half.'

'Three-and-a-half? But that's thirty thousand over the asking price!'

'Aye. And about eighty thousand more than it's worth.'

'Who would pay that kind of money, Hugh?'

'A Colonel Rae-Bramwell.'

'Is he listed?'

'Not in last year's edition.'

'He would be if he had that kind of money to throw away.'

'I was thinking that myself, Roddy.'

'He must be a front for some Arab, Hugh.'

'Aye, I was thinking that, too, Roddy. So what do we do?'

'What do we do? Accept it and register the transfer at the House of Sassines right away. "Caveat emptor," laddie, "caveat emptor"!'

'That sounds a good idea.'

It was. Macpherson, Robb and Sinclair had just netted £18,000 in conveyancing fees as solicitors and commission as estate agents to Captain Ruaraidh Macdonald, the vendor. And if Colonel Rae-Bramwell, or whoever he represented, had bought a pig-in-a-poke that was his affair, thought Macpherson, who was having the afternoon off to go along to Grampian Television to record his latest Reflections homily. No self-respecting Calvinist would ever let his religion interfere with a good business deal.

Colonel Rae-Bramwell sold Dungoe Castle to Capital Developments, a totally owned subsidiary of Hanex Consolidated Holdings, for £365,000 the following week.

He repaid his £350,000 interest-free loan to Elfaz Trust, another subsidiary, the same day.

The Sunday Times and The Observer of 6 April both carried similar adverts from estate agents Bonds of Edinburgh that a wealthy overseas client of theirs required to lease a medium-sized Scottish estate with good shooting and fishing from mid-June to mid-September. Replies were requested within ten days.

Of the seven offers which Bonds received from the combined adverts, that of Capital Developments was deemed to be the most suitable, and was accepted by return.

Ben Hadef al-Mahjub was well content with that month's progress.

His next problem was how to place sixteen crack commandos into the Scottish Highlands by early July. Fortunately, he reflected, matters were well in hand on this front also.

With many a country in the world this would have been one of the trickiest parts of the operation. Fortunately, he mused, he was dealing with the British. Since the final death-throes of their four hundred year old empire in the 1950s and '60s, and the growing public awareness, especially amongst the young intelligentsia, of the ill-gotten gains of colonialism, the British had adopted preferential policies towards their new Commonwealth partners. Although mainly fiscal and trading, these benefits also extended to immigration – until the flood had to be clamped down on in the late '70s – and to education. Nowhere was this tendency more evident than in admissions to centres of higher learning in the UK. Despite substantial reductions from their peak around 1978-79, the Universities Central Council on Admissions was still handling about 12,000 applications a year from prospective overseas candidates, of whom some 6-7000 would gain entry to recognised universities alone. This number more than trebles when polytechnics, nursing and teacher-training courses are taken into account.

These applications are not, of course, confined to Commonwealth countries. Two years previously there had been nineteen aspirants from Dhubat, of whom eleven had been accepted. A year later, no eyebrows had been raised at UCCA when they had received twenty-eight forms by the closing date of 15 December 1985 for the following session; especially as the majority had been for courses in geology, computing, civil engineering and business management studies, all of which were experiencing a substantial increase in popularity. It had been noted that the new government of Dhubat had placed a number of endowments with worthy research projects at various institutions in the north and midlands of England, but this in no way influenced the universities' decisions – or so South Yemen had been assured when all but three of their hopefuls had been turned down. Al-Mahjub had also taken advantage of the fact that four of the Scottish universities did not process their admissions through UCCA, but handled them entirely independently, even of each other.

In all, by the end of April, a total of twenty-one Dhubatis had received offers of places, six of them unconditional, from nine English and Scottish universities. All were accepted; although only five actually intended to commence their studies the following October.

There was always the chance that Special Branch would investigate one or other of the 'students', but this was unlikely. So many aliens came into Britain each year that the SB usually confined its activities to known or potential subversives when they were not monitoring the behaviour of the IRA, picketing miners, or left-wing demonstrators. Providing his students did nothing to arouse suspicion they would be safe enough for the last crucial month's preparations.

And if any were picked up .... al-Mahjub allowed himself an uncustomary smile. Pity help the unfortunate curs from Special Branch. The sixteen men on whose shoulders rested the final outcome of the most audacious mission ever undertaken anywhere in the world were not likely to be deterred from their purpose by some glorified traffic wardens.

The harbour at Helmsdale, where the river of the same name thankfully mingles with the relative calm of the cold, silver-grey North Sea after its hazardous journey through the wild Strath of Kildonan, had seen better days. Originally built by the well-meaning, but totally misguided, Countess of Sutherland in the early 19th century to provide a livelihood for the miserable peasants she had forced from their crofts in the interior to make way for much more profitable sheep, it had experienced an extremely short-lived boom around the year 1819. Thereafter, apart from a relatively prosperous period as a base for herring fishing in the late 19th century, its decline as a port had been steady. Like many a down-at-heel harbour in the north-east of Scotland there had been hopes of a new lease of life as an oil supply base in the 1970s and '80s, especially when three or four rigs began drilling just twelve miles off-shore in the Beatrice field. These hopes had not materialised; and the harbour, deserted of all but a couple of intrepid lobster boats, and badly in need of renovation, was a rather forlorn sight.

A steady stream of visitors, mainly English, Dutch and German, passed through Helmsdale each year. Most carried straight on through, having filled their petrol tanks in Inverness for fear of not finding a garage any further north, heading up the A9 to John O'Groats. A small number who had taken the trouble to study the excellent brochures prepared by the Caithness and Sutherland Tourist Boards stopped for some refreshments before turning inland to visit the scene of Scotland's most famous gold rush at Kildonan in 1869. The handful who, on this 27th day of June, followed the well-worn cobblestone path down to the old harbour were more than amply rewarded for their troubles. Few, if any, had ever seen such a spectacular motor yacht outside a James Bond movie. It would have been the main attraction in Acapulco or Sausalito; but alongside three little peeling lobster boats in Helmsdale it was quite out of this world.

Fearghas Cahill should have been concentrating more on the abrupt descent from the heights of the Ord of Caithness. Hairpin bends, single-track bridges, roadside ditches on one side and sheer drops of hundreds of feet on the passenger side made the approach to Helmsdale from the north one of the most dangerous stretches of road in Scotland. Serious accidents in driving rain or coastal fog were all too common, and it was one of the first roads to have the snow-gates locked across it in winter, after three drivers had perished in twenty to thirty feet drifts in January 1978. Today, however, the weather was perfect; but the road still demanded the utmost respect. Cahill was lucky to get off with merely grazing the crash-barrier as he let his eyes wander from the road once more in the direction of the sea. He could not take his eyes off the Elvira as it majestically approached the harbour.

'Steady on, Fearghas,' he spoke aloud to himself.

An easy-going ex-patriot Irishman who had found happiness and contentment with Customs and Excise in Wick, Cahill was on his way to clear the Elvira for landing in the UK. By rights the yacht should have made Wick, the nearest Customs and Excise base, its first port of call; but the radio request asking special permission to put in to Helmsdale had been readily agreed by Cahill. He fancied a wee drive on such a fine day. It would add nicely to his expenses for that month; and the yacht's Radio Officer had clearly hinted that the owner would show her appreciation in kind for his consideration in saving them the trouble of having to by-pass, then double back to their destination, Dungoe. It was pure routine as far as Cahill was concerned; although as soon as he got his first glimpse of the sleek, white Elvira he had to admit that this one was vastly different from the run-of-the-mill Scandinavian and Polish trawlers which took up most of his time. Not that he objected to trawlers, the Scandinavians in particular: they supplied most of his and his mates' reading and viewing materials, beating anything they could get by mail from London. And they brought a roaring trade to Wick's three full-time prostitutes. Come to think of it, Fearghas chuckled to himself, the enthusiastic amateurs don't do so badly out of them either!

Having just narrowly missed one of the many vicious raised stones which were supposed to mark the edge of the road, but which could so easily somersault a lightweight van, Fearghas got into Helmsdale in one piece at last. He parked his rapidly rusting Lada just off Main Street and glanced at his digital watch. Once again he cursed the fact that he had bought an early, expensive model and had to press an awkward little button with his other hand before the thick purple face deigned to flash the time for him. It was maddening.

'For what I paid for this ten years ago I could buy a multi-dialled, multi-time zoned, multi-functioned, multi-fuckin-fantastic chronograph today,' he muttered; gratified, however, to find that he could manage a quick pint at The Laggan before boarding the Elvira at 12.30.

'Afternoon, Hamish.' Fearghas rubbed his hands in anticipation. 'Not a bad day.'

'Well, well, now. If it ain't me old fren, Mr Cahill,' the landlord did an excellent Irish accent, betraying his north-eastern Caithness origins. Fearghas had been amazed on coming to Wick seventeen years previously to discover how close the natives sounded to his homeland. 'What'll it be, Mr Cahill?'

'Pint of Special if you please, Hamish.'

'Still trying to bust our little drugs network, eh, 'Gus?'

'We're not interested in small fry, Hamish. We've got you under constant surveillance. Waitin' for Mr Big to show up one of these days.' Cahill's American accent wasn't a match for his host's Irish. 'Anyway I hope you can pull the birds quicker than you can pull pints,' he added, nodding at the glass of froth which Sinclair was pouring off beneath the counter. 'Otherwise you must be helluva frustrated.'

'Nothing wrong with my sex-life, Fearghas. Nothing that a few of your specialist publications wouldn't put right anyway,' Hamish confided from the side of his mouth as he slid the pint over to Cahill.

'Now, now, Mr Sinclair. And what makes you be thinkin' I'd be carryin' that sort of stuff around with me, now?' Cahill's brogue was thick and couthy. 'Might get searched at the customs when I leave this shit-hole of a place and cross the border back into Caithness, now, mightn't I?'

Cahill downed his pint smartly, decided after much thought not to have another, and left for the harbour.

'Hope you didn't have the plug in the sink there,' he flung at the landlord for his parting shot, 'and sell the slops to some rich unsuspecting German tourist. That's not what your spillage allowance is for.'

He was out of the door in a flash, failing to hear Hamish Sinclair telling him that just because you bastards did it in Dublin pubs didn't mean to say it was done in his establishment.

'Definitely not run-of-the-mill,' Cahill reiterated on approaching the Elvira. The two tourists who were firing away excitedly with their Kodak Disc cameras obviously thought so too.

They looked on enviously as the customs officer was welcomed aboard the shining vessel with the Grand Cayman registration.

'It was very good of you to accede to our request, Mr ....' Shamin charmed him in her usual fashion.

'Cahill, ma'am. Fearghas Cahill.' Any time, he thought to himself.

'Mr Cahill,' she beamed at her latest captive. 'We have had a long journey already; and your kindness means that we shall now be able to make Dungoe at a reasonable hour. It was really most considerate of you.'

'Not at all, ma'am. Glad to be of service.' The slight tremor betrayed his insecurity at being confronted by such an obviously superior beauty. He immediately began fumbling with the straps on his briefcase.

'Well, we do appreciate it, Mr Cahill. But it's much too soon to get down to formalities.' She gently tugged his sleeve away from the briefcase. 'I'm sure you would like to see round our little pleasure craft first?'

'If it's not too much bother, ma'am.' Although he did not need an invite to get a good nosey round.

'Of course it isn't. You're not in a great hurry, are you?'

No way, thought Cahill. 'No. There isn't exactly a queue of ships like this lined up in Wick bay!'

'I dare say,' said Shamin unassumingly. 'So, if you would care to follow me ...'

Anywhere, my darlin'; anywhere! His feverish mind was

181

working overtime again. He followed her. In fact, he followed every delightful move she made as she led him up onto the bridge. Cheesus, he sighed inwardly, what a figure.

'Captain Youmah, Mr Cahill.'

'Eh, pleased to meet you, Captain.' Cahill had not been concentrating on his name.

'My pleasure,' replied Youmah, lying through his sparkling white teeth.

'Yes,' said Shamin. 'The Master of the Elvira.'

And of all who sail on her? Cahill thought her smile to Youmah was a little too meaningful.

'It must be a joy to manage such a craft, Captain.' Cahill looked appreciatively around the mariner's nirvana of gleaming brass and rosewood, with its array of sophisticated electronic navigational and communications systems.

'It is indeed a privilege, Mr Cahill.'

Was it his imagination, or did the skipper really wink at the doll?

The engine room and galleys below deck were no less impressive; though nothing compared with the view of Shamin's veloured bottom ascending the stairs in front of Cahill as he was being taken up to the living quarters.

'Talk about oriental splendour?' he would recount to the lads in Mackays that night. 'Wall-to-wall goatskins; velvet sofas; cocktail bar; sunken marble double bath; and the biggest fuckin' sheikh-sized water bed you ever saw in your life! Complete with mirrored ceiling above it,' he added lasciviously to the sceptical, streetwise regulars. 'You name it.' He shook his head in disbelief.

'Ach, it sounds almost as good as Room 11 upstairs,' indicated Murray, the host, with a tilt of his head.

'So that's why that sonofabitch Jim was always in there,' grinned Fish, downing his Stolichnaya in traditional fashion.

'All the regular reps get it,' said Murray.

'Aye, if you're not using it yourself, ya rascal!' Tom raised his Stoli with a wink to Iain. 'Nasdahrovyeh ee droozhboo!' and over the smooth, oily, ice-cold nectar went, courtesy of Murray.

After the tour, the generous measure of Hine XL, and the casual conversation, Cahill methodically went through the necessary documents which the ship's captain had completed.

182

Gone were the days when foreign ships had to heave-to offshore and fly the yellow flag pending clearance by the health authorities. Now the Customs and Excise carried out several agency functions on behalf of the health people. De-ratting certificate, Infectious Diseases, Prohibited Items; all were in order.

His token check for contraband confirmed Shamin's 'nothing to declare'. It is doubtful if even the most thorough search imaginable would have located the cache of Heckler and Koch MP5 and G8s, AK47s, Rugers, grenades, plastic explosives, two-way transmitters and hand-held anti-tank gun concealed in water-tight containers inside the fabulous bed which had been the object of much of Cahill's speculation. It was enough to equip a small regiment. It was going to have to be.

As Cahill was coming up and out of Helmsdale later that afternoon each left-hand bend revealed the Elvira nosing further out beyond the breakwater in his rear-view mirror. He was muttering unintelligibly about some lucky sods having all the luck.

Mind you, Fearghas me boy, he told himself, you didn't do so badly yourself, now, did you? The bottles of VSOP Remy clinked against each other on the back seat as the car hit yet another damned pot-hole.

By the first of July all sixteen of al-Mahjub's task force were safely resident within the UK. To avoid any hint of suspicion they had arrived individually, at different times, from various points of origin in Europe and the Middle East. They had all gone through immigration and customs at the international airport nearest to their respective university towns.

On the following Friday, 4 July, sixteen unsuspecting landladies from Southampton to Aberdeen wished their new lodgers an enjoyable trip hitch-hiking around Britain before term time. They were all assured that there would be no need of forwarding addresses, as the students would be in regular contact by phone with their families back home from wherever they happened to be on their travels. None of the women questioned such satisfactory arrangements, especially as the young gentlemen had insisted on paying two month's rental in advance. They were all too preoccupied with working out how many short-term lets they could make on the side during the busy tourist season when their lodgers were away.

The eight from London, Kent, Southampton and East Anglia met up at platform one in Euston Station at 08.00 on Saturday 5 July. They bought one-way second class tickets to Glasgow, and boarded the 08.40 in pairs, several carriages apart. Their light rucksacks fitted inconspicuously in the overhead racks.

At Preston three hours later, four others who had registered at 'red brick' universities joined, having hitched across country from Leeds and Sheffield.

Yousuf Hurion had only been seven years old when his father had decided to break with centuries of Bedouin tradition and take up his Emir's offer of free housing, medical services and schooling for his sons in a modern village being put up just five miles outside the new town of Dhubat. Steady, well-paid employment from the massive amount of construction work going on nearby guaranteed a secure and vastly improved standard of living for old Tariq, his three wives and fourteen children, six of whom were old enough to work.

By and large the family adapted well to their new environment; but Yousuf, the youngest of his mother's children, was possessed by a wild, restless, nomadic spirit which refused to succumb to a sedentary existence. He constantly truanted from school, and played havoc with the other pupils and teachers when he was there. Deprivation of privileges, punishment assignments, enforced detention and frequent severe beatings made not one whit of difference. At home, his hyperactivity found release in tantrums, bad language and vandalism. All attempts at reason failed. His parents despaired. An evil future was forecast for him by the religious elders. At the age of ten he had stolen some bread, salt, goat cheese, dates and water and disappeared into the desert. He had been found twelve days later in a dried up wadi, parched, blistered and delirious, with vultures scrabbling around in the sand waiting for the certain smell of death.

His saviours were not, as he had prayed for, a team of Bedouin goatherds or caravan merchants with whom he could have spent the rest of his days wandering between watering-holes. He had, in fact, became disorientated in the featureless arid interior within three days, as can easily happen to all but the most seasoned desert dwellers, and had ended up close to the border with Qasar, a no-man's-land shunned by local tribesfolk of both nationalities for fear of marauding forays from the opposite side of the frontier. Fortune had favoured the boy's bravery: instead of his brutalised remains being fought over by hyenas, he was spotted by one of his own country's desert patrols returning from a raid into Qasar.

In the boy's delirium he experienced a sort of heightened awareness of sight and sound, something akin to that felt by users of lysergic acid. The shimmering heatwaves and swirling dust of the approaching vehicles; the shifting, dazzling reflections of the high sun; the stillness shattered by roaring engines; the scrunching of stone and sand by heavy-duty tyres; the squeal of metallic disc brakes being hydraulically locked together. All were surrealistically and indelibly emblazoned into Yousuf's mind. The rescue was cathartic. The old heroes passed away, and new ones took their places. The camel-driver was replaced by the commando, the goatherd by the guerilla.

The idolisation of these devils of mercy, as he was to call them in later years, continued long after he had been returned safely home. These hardened desert rangers had really been taken with the lad's pluckiness. They visited him during his convalescence, encouraged him with his schooling, showed him ways of profitably using his leisure time. No longer were his considerable energies frittered away in a frenzy of anti-social behaviour: they were channelled, dammed, harnessed and released in a disciplined, controlled flow of aggression which would sweep him towards his new goal in life.

Now, at twenty-eight years of age, Major Yousuf Hurion had been the obvious choice to lead the assault team into the UK. Not the oldest of the group, but by far the most capable, Hurion was in many ways the perfect soldier. Intelligent, decisive, resourceful, nerveless and with an unshakable loyalty to his regiment and commanding officer, Abdu Chakir, Hurion had distinguished himself on several occasions along the borders with Qasar and Omali. His capacities for endurance and survival were remarkable, his skills with explosives and hand weapons legendary. The fact that he had won his decorations in one of the smallest armies on earth was of no significance. It was also one of the toughest. Hurion would have made his mark anywhere.

But he was worried now on this Saturday morning. He had studied Glasgow's one-way system until he knew it as well as he knew the streets of his own village, Qum-al-fayah. He could handle the second-hand Ford Transit minibus he had bought five days earlier from a rather dubious outlet in the city's east end with ease. But he had never driven in conditions like these in his life. Pedestrians stepped in front of him with total disregard for their own safety. Taxis zig-zagged with abandon and a perpetual thumbs-up sign from the drivers across the four-lane roadway. Double-decker buses stopped, started and overtook each other at approaching bus-stops with never a signal. For the first time in his life the nerveless, programmed killer was on edge. He wished fervently that he had left the van at his lodgings and taken the bus in from Hillhead.

He turned in off Cambridge Street to the multi-storey car park with relief, which instantly turned to rage as he read the sign over the entrance banning landrovers, caravans and minibuses. He remembered that the nearest parking lot was just around the corner at the top of Hope Street, but the wretched one-way system forced him to by-pass it on Cowcaddens Road, then down Renfield Street, along Renfrew Street and back up Hope Street. Having cut across a No. 54 bus to get into the left-hand lane he discovered that the open-air site was no longer in use as a car park as construction work had started on it. Cursing furiously in his native tongue

Hurion again made the slow circuit round into Renfield Street, heading straight on down this time to Clydeside and the old St. Enoch's Station car park. The three-quarters of a mile journey took him twenty-five minutes thanks to the congestion caused by traffic from a thirty-mile radius descending on to the third largest shopping area in Britain. St. Enoch's was full; as was the massive space in behind Argyle Street's redevelopment zone. By the time Hurion had been forced to the south side of the River Clyde by the traffic flow and found a derelict lot near Gorbals Cross, a full hour had elapsed since he had hit the city centre.

He silently thanked the intuition that had prompted him not to meet his compatriots directly off the train that coming afternoon at Central Station. They were to rendezvous with him and the other three who were already in Scotland at the main entrance to the Kelvingrove Park just off Sauchiehall Street to lessen the risk of a hold-up in the rush-hour traffic. From there it was an easy matter to head onto the urban motorway via Charing Cross and north-east onto the A80 for Stirling and the M90 for Perth.

Meantime the commando Major had some shopping to do. He would rather have been alone in the desert than fighting through these crowds heading for the summer sales.

The cramped interior of the small shop in Nelson Mandela Square belied the fact that it could supply the cartographical needs for an expedition to just about anywhere in the known world direct from stock. The section on the British Isles was crammed from floor to ceiling with the complete range of maps published by the Ordnance Survey. Hurion knew exactly what he was looking for, but before he could begin helping himself, a cheerful assistant intent on displaying her spatial awareness skills established his co-ordinates and quickly zeroed in.

'Good morning, sir,' she breezed, 'can I help you?'

'No, really. I think I know where everything is,' Hurion put her down kindly.

'Oh, that's fine. Not many people do in here. Which area are you interested in?' she persisted.

Hurion was not going to shake her off easily.

'The north of Scotland and north-west England.'

'Oh well you will need some assistance, then.' She was triumphant. 'These little steps we have are quite difficult to balance on. We'd rather the customers didn't use them. You'll need them to reach up to Caithness and Sutherland. Now, what exactly are we looking for, sir?'

'Actually I need a set of 1:50 000 OS sheets, and a corresponding set of geological maps.'

'They are over there, sir.' She indicated the Institute of Geological Sciences maps a couple of shelves to the right. 'They are also published by the Ordnance Survey.'

'Yes. I know that.' Hurion was trying to be patient.

'So you are interested in geology, then?'

'Yes. In fact I've just got a post as a research student at Strathclyde University.'

'That's marvellous. So you'll know Dr Lyall,' she surprised him. 'He was my tutor last year.'

'Your tutor? So this is only a vacation job for you?' Hurion was playing for time. 'I was only introduced to him briefly yesterday afternoon. He seems very pleasant.'

'Yes. He is, rather,' she smiled. 'It will be the inch to the mile geological surveys you'll be wanting then?'

'Yes, thank you.'

She was rapidly extracting the necessary sheets from the rows in front of her and passing them down to Hurion. 'I'll get you a wee box for these in a minute.'

'That would be most kind of you.'

'Oh, not at all.' She really was being helpful.

'One other thing,' said Hurion. 'Could you recommend a good up-to-date road atlas for me?'

'No problem, sir. The Reader's Digest, the AA, the Sunday Times ......'

'I was actually looking for something a bit more mobile. You know, something that would fit easily into the car's glove compartment.'

'What about the latest edition of the Shell Motorists Atlas, then? It really is quite comprehensive, and very accurate.' She passed one over for him to browse through.

'Yes. This is excellent,' he said.

Twenty minutes later Hurion emerged from the geographer's Aladdin's cave carrying a medium-sized cardboard box which contained all the maps necessary for his PhD thesis.

The skills of the OS cartographers were renowned the world over; but Hurion still made a mental note to double check the accuracy of the maps at the earliest opportunity. He recalled from his orienteering training that the Chinese had deliberately falsified all of their official maps in the mid-1960s to hopefully lessen the effects of a pin-point accurate offensive nuclear strike by either the USA or the USSR. The ploy had been revealed by an American spy satellite engaged in the Pentagon's own topographical survey of mainland China. Hurion doubted if the British would be so unsubtle as to build in any margin of error approaching the ten miles or so in the Chinese examples; but he would carry out his own reconnaissance to make sure. After all, the Atomic Weapons Establishment at Aldermaston, which occupies two square miles of Berkshire, does not even appear on most maps of the area.

In the event Hurion need not have worried, although he was right to be thorough. A few compass readings and several careful measurements were to confirm that the combination of British map-making pride and the open nature of British society had produced results on which he could stake his life if necessary.

He might have to.

Hurion had been assured that the one British Rail train which always ran on time was the London to Glasgow. It by no means did, but this 5th of July it was spot-on. At precisely 13.58 the most deadly hit-squad ever to enter Glasgow apart from the Aberdeen Football Club made its disjointed way along the platform and out onto Gordon Street.

Half-an-hour later the four taxis had deposited the students within quarter-of-a-mile of each other around Claremont Street, Royal Terrace and Clifton Street. From there it was a short five minute stroll to the two waiting minibuses.

The sixty mile journey to Perth took just over an hour, thanks to the new ring road system round Glasgow and the

Stirling by-pass. The Dhubatis spent overnight in bed and breakfasts scattered across the town. They were thoroughly refreshed for the remaining two hundred and ten mile drive to Dungoe on the Sunday.

That same Saturday night Ann Pettigrew and Bill Lyall, who was considerably more than her tutor, were taking in a Swingle II concert in the Apollo Centre.

'Got a super sale from one of your new research students today, Bill. Worth about £4 commission to me.' Ann was saving hard for a trip to Greenland in September with Bill and a group of his other under graduate students.

'Good for you,' replied Bill, 'but he must have got me mixed up with someone else. My department's budget has been frozen for yet another year. Anyway, love, let's not talk shop tonight, eh? Fancy a quick slice of pizza and a glass of red in Dino's before the show?'

'Great! Have we got the time?' She glanced at the Mickey Mouse watch she wore upside down on her right wrist. 'Yep. But maybe I shouldn't, Bill. Too many calories for my liking,' though the idea was appealing.

'Nonsense, lass. There's not a picking on you. And I should know.' He squeezed her affectionately. 'Anyway, a few extra pounds of blubber will help to keep out Greenland's icy blasts in the autumn.' He began whistling the old children's hymn *From Greenland's Icy Mountains* to emphasise his point, but it was lost on Ann who hadn't been in church since her parents had had her christened.

'Oh well; if you say so, Bill. A Four Seasons?'

For the time being she forgot all about her sale of that morning. It would only assume enormous significance for her later on that summer.

Hurion's men assembled in the main car park just in front of the Regal cinema at 09.30. With their college scarves and rucksacks they looked like any of dozens of student groups currently in the Highlands on fieldwork exercises. No-one, and there were only a few dog-walkers about at this early hour on the sabbath day, gave them a second moment's thought. Within minutes the two vans, driven by Hurion and Sallal, had passed the roundabout at the Dewar's whisky plant just outside Perth and were on to the new A9 heading north for Inverness.

This killer road of only a few years previously had been vastly improved in the decade since the early '70s. Up until then it had claimed hundreds of casualties, especially in the summer when caravan convoys had caused innumerable bottlenecks and tail-backs on its narrow, twisting, steeply-graded sections and in the score of small towns and villages it passed through. All protests to have the road up-graded had been consistently ignored until just after the General Election in 1974 when the Scottish National Party had gained over 30 per cent of Scottish votes and eleven seats in the House of Commons. Part of their election campaign had been to build a dual-carriageway road from Inverness to Perth; so, to pre-empt a further resurgence of nationalist fortunes, the Government had immediately started their own modernisation of the dreaded A9. Cynics had not been slow to point out the parallel with Walpole sending General Wade into the Highlands on a similar mission after the Jacobite Rebellion of 1715. That had not prevented the 'Forty-five' and Bonnie Prince Charlie. The SNP were still hopeful for their future.

Careful not to break any speed limits, the two minibuses were still by-passing Inverness on the new Kessock Bridge at 12.00, having passed through some of the finest scenery in Europe without a glance. Not even the magnificent view from the roadside high on the Struie Hill overlooking the Dornoch Firth distracted the men from their cards and stories. At Ardgay, Hurion was tempted to signal in to the Lady Ross Hotel on the left when he spotted two trucks of the Territorial Army allegedly out on combat manoeuvres. For the first time on the journey his men were eagerly looking out of the windows. But it would have been no contest. His sixteen would have annihilated the forty-or-so overweight, out-of-condition mature boy scouts inside swilling beer and wolfing cheeseburgers. Anyway, his lads didn't need the practice; and they had to keep a low profile from here on in.

Six miles further on, just north of Bonar Bridge, Hurion's party did stop in a large empty lay-by. They parked just enough apart from each other and from the entrances to discourage any other traffic from trying to pull in. The hill-walking schoolteacher and his young mistress who were blissfully screwing away on the soft, springy heather high above the sea-loch had chosen their spot well. The high, impenetrable tangle of vivid yellow gorse and broom between them and the road below guaranteed their privacy as the commandos relieved themselves into the ditch before carrying on the last hour to Dungoe.

At 2.30 in the afternoon the concealed entrance to Dungoe Castle was reached. The driveway was effectively barricaded by stout wrought-iron gates. They were quickly opened as Hurion's leading Transit sounded the agreed sequence from its horn.

The crew of the Elvira, which made a stirring sight reflected in its mooring just offshore from the white-walled castle, had been busy over the past week. The sturdy baronial residence had been converted into a small-scale operational headquarters. Everything necessary for the success of their mission was already there.

The next two or three weeks were going to be very busy ones for Hurion and his squad. The overall plan had already been formulated, but much still remained to be done. Each man's role had to be very clearly defined; every minute detail of the operation had to be specified; contingency plans for each major phase had to be drawn up; detailed reconnaissances had to be carried out; and, in addition, normal military training in fitness, hand-to-hand combat and weapons handling had to be maintained. It was to be no relaxing holiday for the Dhubatis on their newly-acquired Highland estate.

The day after Hurion's men's arrival, Monday 7 July, the Elvira set sail from Dungoe. Her presence in the small anchorage was really too conspicuous an attraction for locals and holidaymakers alike. Someone was bound to be tempted to trespass onto the estate for a closer look. The fact that there is no such thing as trespass under Scottish law is generally unknown amongst the public at large, so the notices which Captain Youmah had had erected around the estate had been effective up till now. But Hurion wasn't taking any chances. He ordered the Elvira out to sea.

Not even Shamin questioned these orders. She knew who was in command at this front-line phase of the operation. And, anyway, she could do with a break, especially away from these coarse louts of soldiers who were swarming all over the place. She had certainly earned a rest now that her contribution to the exercise was over. Her only dilemma was whether to head for a couple of weeks lazing about on her houseboat in Kashmir, or to have a fun-filled activity fortnight at the luxurious millionaires' Santa Lucia Club in the Caribbean, whose owner had been begging her to be his guest for over three years now since its opening. She would make her mind up on the two day boat trip to the south of England.

By Sunday 20 July Hurion's men were ready. Every· detail from Booth's and Raqia's reports and their own observations and trials had been sifted and analysed into a plan which seized, like all good plans, on the simple and obvious, although it would require precision and boldness to execute.

At 04.00 on Monday the 21st, Nahaz Khan and his five companions left Dungoe in one of the Transits for the long drive to the Lake District town of Keswick. By six o'clock in the evening their four-man tent was pitched on the municipal campsite which would be their base until the Friday. The team would take turns to keep a twenty-four hour guard on the contents of the van, from the inside.

At 09.30 on the same Monday morning Hurion cursed with the animal venom which makes the Arab unparalleled at this form of expression.

He had just finished deciphering the call from the London consulate which had been collecting and passing on Booth's reports from the post office box number they were using. Shamin was not going to be pleased; she was going to have to fly back to the UK immediately from her tropical island.

The only thing which displeased Shamin was the unholy hour in the middle of the night when she was awakened to receive the urgent telex which had been forwarded, without delay or respect for the four hour time lag, from London. She had been bored out of her mind surrounded by loud-mouthed Australian and American industrialists and their dreadful wives shrieking and splashing in the pools. The minor members of European aristocratic families who repaired there in the in-season of January and February had been replaced now by brash, uncultured young bullion dealers from Holland and England, drawn to the sumptious Club and the Trade Winds surfing.

She had found John Laverock, the Club's multi-millionaire owner and yachting friend of her uncle, inordinately dreary and pompous. No. Hurion was wrong. She was delighted to receive this summons; especially as she savoured her last fleeting encounter with Alister Graham in Venice.

Had they really made love in the upstairs gallery of the delightful rococo Scoletta dei Battioro? Yes; they had. And, just as she was climaxing he had teased her into thinking that the smoke-detectors in the ceiling were security cameras which had captured their whole table-top performance for the young student at the front desk downstairs! Now there was a man for you, she sighed, as she caressed herself under the shower.

She would turn Alister's unscheduled visit to the Winfrith Research and Development Establishment to both their advantages.

12

Into The City

ALISTER Graham, Master of Science and Doctor of Philosophy, chuckled with glee as he strolled through the Castle Gardens in the capital city of his beloved Scotland. He had only one thought on his mind – and it was not the boring buggers he had left behind at Winfrith the previous afternoon.

'A'm gonnae git ma hole the nite, a'm gonnae git ma hole,' he kept reminding himself in the broad Scots dialect he often lapsed into when he got excited, rubbing his hands together in anticipation. It had been over two weeks since 'Mr Nasty', as he called his favourite appendage, had been in action with someone else.

Actually, participating in an act of sexual intercourse with a female of an evening was not all that rare an occurrence for Dr. Graham. He was, not to put too fine a point on it, as randy a bastard as had ever come off the Island of Lewis in his native Hebrides – and that is saying something. On that hard-living island, where the infants are weaned on whisky, and where the alcoholism and illegitimacy rates are amongst the worst on the planet, the young lads have a simple motto: if it moves, screw it; if it doesn't, kick it. Alister wasn't much into violence these days, although he had been a wild man in his late teens and early twenties; but anything that moved still had to be on the lookout! What was going to make this evening so special, however, was the fact that he was going to renew acquaintance much sooner than he had hoped with the most exotic woman he had ever come across.

He had met Shamin just over a year earlier in Teheran at a conference where she had been representing her country as its Scientific Adviser. It had been a memorable experience. She had disappeared from his life after Iran until the following March when he had received a cryptic telegram from her in Geneva. She had gone there to an international fuel cycle conference organised by the US Atomic Industrial Forum, only to find that the conference had been boycotted by the British in a fit of pique at the Greenpeace-inspired international criticisms they were receiving over their waste disposal programme. She had beckoned Alister to Venice for two days, signing the telegram 'Shhh... you know who!' He did; and was off to the Adriatic like a shot.

When a similar telegram had been delivered to him at Winfrith the previous day he had not hesitated. He had got to Edinburgh the same evening, determined to splash out and repay Shamin for her lavish hospitality.

To balance the impression of the Hebridean Islands given in the statistics already quoted it must be said in their defence that they top the league in other aspects too; most notably in education. No-one has as yet come up with an entirely satisfactory explanation, but the Islands produce a significantly higher number of university graduates per capita than any other area of Scotland. And many of them, despite excellent job opportunities elsewhere, return to the Islands to live. There are crofters, fishermen, drivers, postmen and UB 40 holders galore with some of the most impressive academic credentials it is possible to obtain anywhere in the world.

The young Alister Graham had been no exception. He had taken – stolen would be a better description of it for all the effort he had put in – a brilliant first class honours degree in nuclear physics at Glasgow University when he was still just twenty years of age. This had been followed with a highly distinguished DPhil at Oxford, after which he had been snapped up immediately by the Ministry of Defence and set to work with a group of equally bright theorists at the

Aldermaston Atomic Weapons Research Establishment on the problems of tactical fission weapons. Six years later he had been transferred to the Royal Ordnance Factory at nearby Burghfield, Britain's nuclear bomb factory, to oversee the manufacturing of the system he had been theoretically working on.

Fission bombs are the basis of any nuclear arsenal. The fundamental concept behind them is quite simple. If the nuclides of very heavy elements like uranium-235 or plutonium-239 are bombarded by neutrons they break up, releasing massive amounts of energy and radioactivity. They also release further neutrons which in their turn collide with other nuclides of heavy elements starting a divergent chain reaction resulting in an explosion of very high intensity.

The engineering required to realise the concept is a complex affair. The fissile materials used must be of high purity and sufficient in quantity to achieve a critical mass – the smallest amount in which a self-sustaining chain reaction can take place. They must be placed in a reflective container which prevents neutrons escaping and which holds the materials together long enough to attain the maximum explosive yield. There is less than a hundred-millionth of a second between each of these collisions; so that the entire chain reaction takes place in less than a microsecond. As 99 per cent of the energy is released in the last 0.05 microseconds of the chain reaction, the timing of the bomb mechanism is absolutely crucial.

Alister Graham's work was centred initially on neutron reflectors, working mainly with beryllium and natural uranium. Later, at the Royal Ordnance Factory, he combined this with work on the intricacies of the implosion technique of bomb manufacture. Eventually, ways had been found to produce small atomic bombs in the form of artillery shells which could be used as tactical nuclear weapons – a compromise between the limited explosive power of conventional weapons and the almost limitless energy pent up in atoms of uranium and plutonium.

This work had absorbed Alister for a decade. By the early 1980s he was without doubt one of the nation's leading experts on nuclear weapons.

Then disillusion had set in. Suddenly, quickly and

irrevocably. His had not been a gradual conversion to pacifism, but more of a Damascus road experience. Throughout his time at Aldermaston and Burghfield he had never once questioned the morality of what he was doing, so caught up was he in the pursuit of science and its technology. The issues were not ethical; they were experimental – mere practical problems for his mind to solve. He had neither the time nor the inclination to read Hermann Hesse. He was not the slightest bit interested in the politics of Reagan or Thatcher. He didn't give a fig about the plight of the Poles or the anguish of the Afghans. The failure of Strategic Arms Limitations Talks between the East and West due to the continued and undiminished belligerence of both sides simply meant more job security for himself. He was, in short, apolitical.

Then, one night in the local pub, all this had changed. He had gone in on his own, purely on spec., as he would say, for a few pints. He chose a table alongside one at which four women were seated. His friendly nod went unheeded as he started sipping his Theakston's Best Bitter, which was far and away the best pint he had ever come across anywhere in the world. At first Alister had been more interested in listening to Meat Loaf, Bonnie Tyler and Elkie Brooks whom he had activated with his 50p in the juke-box in the corner; but as these classics gave way to Kajagoogoo, Boy George and Culture Club when a group of leather-jacketed motor cyclists commandeered the corner, he found himself picking up snippets of the conversation at the table next to him in an effort to blot out the lunatic lispings of the latest fads to hit the pop scene.

It turned out that two of the females were from the Women For Peace campsite at nearby Greenham Common and the other two were interviewing them for a local paper. Only once before had Alister listened to a debate involving the peace women. He had been up in Scotland on holiday and had watched a television programme which had brought together three caricatures of the peace movement with long hair, ankle-length skirts and no bras, and three archetypal, highly lacquered ladies of the high Tory establishment. 'Brought together' is the wrong phrase. They had been set loose on each other with a totally bewildered and bemused chairman who hadn't a clue how to control them. It had been the funniest show Alister had seen in many a year.

On this occasion, however, the discussion was low-key, highly articulate and rational. There was no attempt to polarise issues or score cheap debating points. What emerged, as far as Graham could hear, was a picture of caring, concerned women who were willing to endure discomfort, squalor, ridicule and police harassment in order to make their points about the fate of the earth and, hopefully, mobilise sufficient public pressure to rescue their doomed planet in time.

Alister's conscience was pricked; although his prick would never be conscienced. He actually bought a copy of *The Fate of the Earth* by Jonathan Schell the following day and read it at a sitting. The basic thesis was sound: that mankind, indeed the entire planetary ecosystem, was doomed if the holocaust came. However, while agreeing with the author about the dangers inherent in the horizontal proliferation of nuclear technology, Alister felt that Schell had made some unwarranted assumptions about the inevitability of the coming holocaust and had glossed over the problems of control and disarmament in a facile manner. But the book did get him thinking seriously about matters he had disparagingly dismissed or wilfully ignored for years.

There was no way he could turn his back on the world of nuclear physics and engineering; not only because it was all he knew, but because he passionately believed it had a useful peaceful role to play in the betterment of mankind. But he could, and did, re-assess his values and reorder his priorities. Within two months he had made his decision to give up his work with weapons and turn to the peaceful applications of the science he was steeped in and loved.

It was this new career which had taken Graham on assignments around the world, and had brought him to Edinburgh now. To date he had been in San Francisco, Seattle, Ottawa, Teheran, Tokyo and Brasilia in addition to most of the European capitals, thanks to the discovery by the personnel pyschologists of the UKAEA of his latent talent as a public speaker, and to his wide-ranging experience in all branches of the nuclear industry. He carried out his public relations role with enthusiasm and considerable skill, though, as often as not, with tongue in cheek. He, more than most, knew how relatively easy it would be to subvert a peaceful programme into a military one. When he was not on the conference circuit — or circus, as some of his colleagues called it — he was engaged as a member of the Authority's unofficial and highly confidential 'think tank', with a roving commission which gave him entry to every nuclear establishment in the United Kingdom.

Alister left the sunken Gardens and meandered past the Usher Hall, scene of the first ever full-frontal nude on the British theatrical stage, he remembered, out onto Lothian Road which runs at right angles to the famous Princes Street. He could see the gleaming white Mercedes 450 SEL which Shamin had asked him to pick up for her, standing proudly outside Caledonia Executive Car Hire.

A few minutes later driving out past the Zoo towards the airport Alister reflected on how he had come up in the world. His first encounter with a woman had been in the back of her dark blue Mini van when he was fourteen. He had gone with some of his mates to a dance in Stornoway where he had been picked up by a rather grubby primary school teacher in her mid-twenties who made a hobby of stealing the virginity from high school boys. He had run back to his mates to announce his triumphal coming of age.

'Smell these, boys! Smell these!' he had grinned, thrusting the offending and highly offensive fingers up under their noses.

Now, twenty years on, another car was connecting him with another woman. But what a car! And what a woman!

'Yep, Ally boy,' he winked at himself in the mirror, taking a break from singing Sandie Shaw's *Puppet On A String,* 'you've come a long way, you handsome bastard.'

So had Shamin. And she didn't look a bit put out by the journey either, as she elegantly floated across the floor of the domestic arrivals lounge towards him with all of the assurance, but none of the arrogance, of the successful woman. This supreme and rare confidence was the product of her grace, beauty, wealth and intelligence; she had been favoured by the gods and abundantly blessed. It was not born, as some less fortunate creatures would have us believe, entirely of her inner self. There was no way that a clumsy, plain, impoverished and moronic female, or, for that matter, any in the broad category in between these extremes, could have exuded a similar air, no matter how high an awareness of the true worth of herself as a person she possessed. And that, as they say, is just too bad. Mala fortuna!

Their reunion was not an effusive, gushing, overtly affectionate affair, thanks as much to Alister's Scottish reticence over public displays as to Shamin's Islamic sense of decorum.

'Hello, Shamin. Welcome to Scotland.' Alister smiled, held both her hands, and kissed her lightly on the forehead. 'It's grand to see you again.' His almost black eyes shone with pleasure.

'Alister.' The smile was absolutely genuine. 'I have been looking forward to seeing you again also. It has been a long four months.' Shamin's oval brown eyes glistened appreciatively as they took in Alister's broad frame and his cheery ever-smiling face topped by a mass of curly black hair, already greying at the edges.

They drove straight into the heart of the city. Edinburgh, with its magnificent 18th and 19th century architecture, and its splendid castle which dominates the town centre from atop its stupendous volcanic block, is one of the most beautiful, yet under-rated cities in the world. Alister recounted its attractions to Shamin on the way in from the airport, but, to his relief, she was more than content to leave off sightseeing until the following day.

Alister had booked them into the Hanoverian, a resplendent Georgian hotel overlooking a tree-lined circus in a quiet part of the city, yet still only a couple of hundred yards off Princes Street. Renowned internationally for its cuisine, and sumptuously appointed in traditional style, it was the first and automatic choice of the wealthy cognoscenti who demanded the very best in accommodation and knew where to find it. Alister's return treat for the Cipriani was much appreciated by Shamin.

Their evening dinner was superb. Traditional Scottish fare at its peak of excellence. Parcels of full cream cheese wrapped in delicately smoked Perthshire salmon was followed by a Chateaubriand of prime Aberdeen Angus steak, which had been marinated, teriyaki-style, in fine malt whisky and wild native herbs, then medium grilled to perfection. Had Shamin arrived three weeks later she would have been treated to that rarest of Scottish delicacies, red grouse; but the season did not open until 12 August. Ripe raspberries from the Carse of Gowrie, smothered in double cream from the heart of Ayrshire, completed a simple, but sumptuous meal which Alister had chosen at Shamin's request from the vast menu of gourmet dishes available. They barely had room for the delicious Caboc double cream cheese rolled in oatmeal which was brought to them with the coffee.

After a couple of Drambuies, which Shamin had never tasted before, in the oak-beamed lounge they went upstairs to their suite of rooms on the third floor.

'Give me ten minutes to shower and freshen up, Alister,' said Shamin at the door of her room. 'I must get the smell of this smoke out of my hair.'

They had been sharing the lounge with a group of cigar-smoking American computer manufacturers who were over from Silicon Valley in California to view and consider a potential factory site in Dundee. The purity of the Scottish air and water, together with the availability of a highly skilled workforce, made Scotland an ideal location for their type of industry. Indeed, several such firms had already set up in business in Central Scotland, and were doing very well for themselves. These factors did not seem to be the main concerns of this particular group of entrepreneurs, however. They had been loudly discussing the best ways of screwing the British taxpayer out of even more grants and concessions than had already been hinted at by the Scottish Development Agency, and when best to transfer the business back overseas in order to maximise the rip-off. Some of them had obviously been having talks with colleagues in other like-minded corporations, who had already taken the long-suffering British taxpayers for millions.

'I don't know if I can wait that long,' grinned Alister, faking a lunge at her.

She pretended to sigh and scowl at him, although she would have had him right there and then in the corridor if they could have got away with it.

Six minutes later Alister opened the adjoining door between their rooms and walked in as Shamin was coming naked towards his. All of the restraint of meeting and dining in public vapourised instantly.

'O....o...ohhhh; I've been longing for you, Dr. Graham.'

Shamin's breath was coming in tiny spasmodic ripples as she whispered into Alister's ear.

Alister lowered his head and brushed his lips over her neck and round until they met hers. Their kiss was long and deep and hungry. As Alister hardened uncomfortably into Shamin's abdomen he loosened the embrace a little, stepped slightly sideways and let himself spring free alongside her waist; then instantly tightened his hold on her, pressing his right leg in between hers and rapidly flexing his thigh muscles across her already moist opening. Shamin gasped with the intensity of his fervour. She took hold of his penis and began squeezing it gently. Alister replaced his thigh with his hand and probed his index finger in and up as far as it would go, lifting Shamin onto her tiptoes and driving her to a rapid orgasm as he took her weight on his right hand and arm. She came with a soft suffusing sigh as Alister lifted her clean off the ground, her arms wrapped around his neck, and lowered her gently by the buttocks onto his inflamed organ. He relaxed his support of her sufficiently to make her tighten her own grip with her arms and cling even closer to him with her legs up and over his waist. She slid further down onto him until he was completely home.

Alister gently rocked Shamin back and forwards in this position, caressing her back and neck with one hand and using the other to take some of her weight along the top of her thigh, moving his fingers in to fondle her lower lips beside his penis as he did so.

'Careful, darling. You are so deep it hurts a bit!'

Suddenly he spun her round a couple of times in a series of short, sharp movements, making her head swim giddily, then walked with her across the room and crushed her against a wall, still using his height advantage to keep her feet off the ground. He held her in position with the force of his own weight and the rigid hardness of his organ, and moved microscopically in and out of her with extreme rapidity. They both came within seconds, Shamin with a high-pitched gasp and Alister with a long, deep groan.

With the first twinges of cramp in his calf and thigh muscles, Alister gratefully lowered his lover to the floor. Both their bodies were quivering with excitement as Alister, all power gone from his legs, slumped his weight down onto Shamin's shoulders.

They had little breath left to waste on speech.

'Ohhh. Alister. That was incredible!'

'Aye. It wasn't bad, was it?' Alister panted in reply, nuzzling his nose into her ear and filling her head with the gentle sounds and heat waves of his exhalations.

They collapsed onto the large bed and snuggled in to each other.

'Would it hurt if I kissed him?' Shamin asked after about ten minutes.

'Nah. I'd love that, darling.' Alister was too weak to move.

Shamin nuzzled her way down over his hairy chest and stomach and picked up his tired tool with her lips and tongue until it had disappeared completely into her mouth. As she licked and nibbled and sucked, the life came surging back into him and he swelled enormously. He caressed the back of her neck and ran his fingers over her soft well-defined face. It was a strange sensation for him to touch the cheek which was bulging outwards with his erection, and to feel himself throbbing through the velvety thickness of his lover's flesh. He wondered if it was anything like the thrill a heavily pregnant woman would get tracing the outline of her unborn baby's head beneath the drumskin tension of her tummy. He pulled Shamin up to kiss her.

But she couldn't stay away from his organ and went back

down immediately to play with it.

'He's enormous, Alister!'

'No he's not. It's only half an inch longer than average!'

'Maybe. I have seen longer ones! But you're so thick. The head on him is gigantic!'

'Get away with you woman.'

'No, really. I've never seen anything like it. I can hardly get my lips round him. Look,' she demonstrated the problem to her partner's delight.

'No kidding?' Alister was beginning to swell elsewhere, but with pride this time.

'No kidding. Since you obviously know the average length, what's the average thickness, Dr. Graham?'

When Alister had read the relevant article in Forum magazine a decade earlier he had been more concerned with penile length than girth, not appreciating then that breadth was much more important than depth of penetration to most women. He could not recall that 9.6 cms was the norm for the circumference of the adult male organ.

'I can't for the life of me remember, Shamin. And even if I could it wouldn't help, as I've never taken my own measurement before.'

'Well, I'm going to measure you now, and we'll see how you compare with the national average later on!'

'You can't do that!'

But she was off the bed in a flash and rummaging about in the hotel's courtesy pack of goodies in the bedside cabinet.

'Come here, woman!'

Shamin could not find what she was looking for. There was a Bible, courtesy of the Scottish Society for the Propagation of Christian Knowledge; soap, bath salts and shampoo; matches, writing materials and shoe shine; an ample supply of packs of coffee, cream and sugar; and a little wallet of needles and thread. But not a sign of the required tape measure.

'Don't be daft, Shamin. Come here!'

'Hello. Room Service?' she said, picking up the phone beside the colour TV. 'Could you please send a tape measure up to room 323, please? No, no. I've found the sewing materials, thank you; but I do need a measure. Yes; room 323. Thank you very much.'

She was back on top of Alister in two leaps.

'Now then,' she re-addressed the fat sausage which lay twitching across his hairy abdomen, 'you are not thinking of going back to sleep, are you?'

Any such thoughts it had were quickly dispelled in the heat of her mouth.

'Mmmm. Stay there,' Shamin warned Alister's proud pillar as she darted to answer the door.

'Oh, thank you very much. That was quick,' she said, flashing a naked shoulder round the narrowly opened door to take the tape measure from the bemused bellboy in exchange for two pound coins.

'Let me see how you measure up then, my fine fellow.'

Shamin again ignored Alister and spoke directly to his muscular member as she advanced on it with tape looped loosely between her fingers.

Five or six long shaft-searing sucks later Shamin applied the tape to the pulsing purple protuberance which stretched Alister's foreskin almost to bursting, and which was probably responsible for the occasional minuscule lacerations he suffered at the point where the foreskin is attached to the head on the underside of the penis, and which invariably took several applications of Tea Tree to heal over and allow him to resume normal sexual activity.

'So that's why you use French condoms!' The king-size pack now made sense. '13.5 centimetres at the head!' Shamin announced triumphantly. 'And; Good God! Fourteen and a half at the root! Well ...... almost. We don't want to exaggerate, now, do we? I'll bet that is pretty near a record.'

'I don't know about that, you crazy woman,' laughed Alister. 'We can look it up in the central library tomorrow if you like!'

'Yes; we shall.'

' Come here now till I see you, Shamin.'

Alister took her by the shoulders and half lifted her up the bed towards him. She came willingly.

'Now it's your turn, my beauty,' said Alister, kissing and nibbling her breasts until the nipples were hard and erect. He continued caressing them with his hands as he snuffled downwards across the fine downy covering on her stomach, breathing in her delicate, warm, herbal fragrance in long satisfying draughts, until he reached the soft black forest which protected and cosseted the largest labia he had ever encountered. He worked his tongue into them, pursing them outwards with his lips, as Shamin spread her legs wide to give him access.

Alister buried his face into her, rubbing her clitoris with his nose and pressing his forehead down onto her pubic bone. As her back arched in rapture her hands pressed his head harder against the heaving mound, almost preventing him from breathing. She had already come before Alister's tongue entered her as far as it could go and began darting in and out.

Christ! I hope she doesn't knock my crown out, thought Alister, as her grinding pussy crashed into his teeth. I'd have a hell of a job finding it in there!

As much to avoid damaging his dentition as anything, Alister slid himself up and onto Shamin, entering her suddenly and forcefully as she came again in tremors of ecstasy.

'Oh! God! I'm so happy,' she whispered in his ear. 'I've never been happier in my life!'

'Me neither, Shamin. You're gorgeous.'

As they lay together afterwards Shamin fantasised as she came down slowly and lingeringly from her peaks of pleasure, still enjoying their mutual caresses.

'Wouldn't it be great if you had two, Alister?'

'I had the last time I counted,' said Alister, groping for his balls in mock panic.

'No, no. Two of these,' laughed Shamin, lightly squeezing his tired member.

'Two? What ever for?' he asked incredulously.

'I'd just love you in my mouth at the same time as you were in here,' she said, taking his hand and gripping it between her legs.

'Jesus! Some folk are never happy!' Alister affected an angry tone of voice. 'You might have told me beforehand and I could have brought one of my mates along!' Several willing accomplices sprang to his mind.

'Oh, there's no way they could compare to you, Alister. Anyway,' she added, just in case her joke had misfired, 'I was only teasing.'

'Cock-teasing,' chuckled Alister as he lifted her chin to kiss her.

It was around 3.30 in the morning before they drifted off to sleep.

After a late morning brunch Alister and Shamin left the hotel and wandered through the spacious streets between the airy buildings of the 18th century New Town, the brain-child of Lord Provost George Drummond and the planner, James Craig. In the chronic overcrowding of 17th century Edinburgh forty thousand people were crammed, often in twelve storey tenements, into the area around the Royal Mile between the Castle and Holyrood Palace. The New Town, with its splendid examples of the work of Robert Adam the architect, had attracted the middle and upper classes from this medieval quarter at a time when Edinburgh was becoming a major centre of the arts and learning under the leadership of the philosopher and historian David Hume. Its street names – George, Frederick, Hanover, Charlotte, Queen, King, Princes – proclaimed Edinburgh a loyal supporter of the Union with England. The rest of Scotland has never forgiven it.

An hour later Alister was pointing out the main landmarks of the city to Shamin from atop the towering battlements of the Castle. To their right lay the magnificently restored 'lands', or tenements, of the old High Street and Canongate, which were now amongst the most expensive and sought-after pieces of real estate in Scotland. Beneath them, running the entire length of Princes Street to Calton Hill and its famous Victorian monuments, the marshland and Nor' Loch had been long since drained and tranformed into the exquisite Castle Gardens. This haven is as equally appreciated and frequented by locals as by the tens of thousands of tourists who flock into the city each year. In the far distance beyond the suburbs, majestically straddled by the rail and road bridge engineering marvels of the 19th and 20th centuries, were the glistening waters of the Firth of Forth shimmering in the heat haze.

'It really is a unique and beautiful city you have for your capital, Alister. It compares to any I have ever seen.'

And Shamin had seen nearly all of them. She was quite sincerely delighted with Edinburgh on this, her first visit. She also knew that it would never be possible to come again in the future, and so determined to make the most of this short stay. She dragged Alister, who would gladly have spent more time indoors with her, but who was enough of a gentleman to let her have her way, on a seemingly endless tour of museums and other places of architectural and historical interest, of which Edinburgh is full, as Alister found out to his dismay. Shamin revelled in the round, but more than made up for it to Alister in their suite at night.

On the Friday morning of 25 July Shamin had booked an appointment for herself at Remarks, the city's top beauty salon. Alister was going to pick up a couple of items for her to take back home – some Edinburgh Crystal goblets and a couple of books on the city's past and present – as Shamin hated shopping herself. Not that Alister was all that keen on it either! They were to meet at the Athenæum for lunch before Shamin's afternoon flight to Amsterdam.

Alister was tailed from the minute he left the Hanoverian. He got the crystal at Jenners and asked for it to be delivered to the hotel. He then wandered up The Mound and nipped in to Rafferty's for a haircut. By this time the pubs were open. Alister sank a couple of pints of real ale in Greyfriars Bobby's Bar at the top of Candlemaker Row before heading over to James Thin's on South Bridge.

As he left Greyfriars Bobby's and crossed to Chambers Street his brain registered the electrical impulse triggered off by the hypodermic needle entering his left thigh a fraction of a second before the hundred milligrams of Scoline began to take effect, reducing him to a shaking wreck before total paralysis and loss of consciousness set in. He was amply supported on either side by the two deceptively soft looking young men in T-shirts and denims who had overtaken him, and bundled into the hired Ford Sierra Cosworth which pulled up alongside. Such is the indifference of big city centres that they did not have to use their well-rehearsed line about their mate having an epileptic fit.

By the time the Cosworth had negotiated the centre of Edinburgh and was heading out Corstorphine Road towards the M8, Shamin was on the airport bus from Gatwick to Heathrow for her Concorde connection to Bahrain.

13

Into The Hand of Spoilers

WHEN Alan Cameron had first arrived in the far north of Scotland in November 1974 he had been appalled by its bleak desolation and remoteness, a feeling which was reinforced by the ghostly greyness of the few buildings he was able to see in the area round about Wick airport. An intensely cold wind was driving clouds of mist in from the North Sea. He was chilled to the bone in the short walk from the plane to the airport Portakabins which passed as a terminal. Had it not been for the excitement and challenge of the work which had brought him here, there was little doubt that he would have taken the next flight out to the comparative warmth of a south of England winter. Even the Dumfries of his childhood was infinitely preferable to this.

Now, on this glorious July morning some twelve years later, he was glad he had resisted his first impulse to flee what had seemed to be a barren sub-Arctic wasteland. He now knew and loved almost every inch of this north coast of Scotland. And he had never seen it better than this morning as he urged his powerful Audi multi-valved, four-wheel drive coupé along the spectacular single-track road between Farr and Tongue. What more could one ask for? Stupendous cliffs and rock formations, teeming with dozens of varieties of seabirds to the right. Gently rising moorland, the home of deer, wildcat and the infamous Beast of Skerray drew the eye towards the hills of Naver inland. Ahead lay the incredible sands of the Kyle of Tongue, a haven for the few sun-worshippers who were fortunate enough to know of their existence. But their treachery just below the surface of the waters had caused the Jacobite ship Le Prince Charles Stuart to founder in 1746, and required the most skilful navigation from skippers of even shallow-draught boats of the present. In the far distance, the majestic mountains of north-west Sutherland.

What more, indeed, could a man ask for? Unless, of course, it was to have such a delightful passenger as Karyn, who had arrived in Scotland for the first time only two days earlier. Her first twenty-four hours had been spent in bed and had not been much of a rest for either of them – not that anyone was complaining.

Now it was time for Alan to show her something of his adopted homeland.

He slid a cassette of Karyn's favourite Brandenburg Concerto, the Fourth, into the tape player. As its lyrical woodwinds conjured up the sylvan delights of her homeland, Alan's left hand began to tap out the continuo part on her naked thigh. Karyn parted her legs and slid down the seat until her silky pubis conducted her lover's fingers in a frantic fugue of their own composition which soon outstripped the Bach. As Karyn came, juices spurting from her now tender pussy and bathing her engorged lips, a wicked Anglo-Saxon spoonerism on the word 'contrapuntal' crossed Alan's mind.

As his fingers slowed down to the andante of the middle movement, he had to forcefully retrieve them from between Karyn's locked legs in order to help steer the car through a particularly tricky section of the road.

'Oh, stay, my love,' moaned Karyn. 'Stay,' as she reached out to replace her composer's hand.

Fortunately for both of them Alan's grip on the wheel was too strong for Karyn to break. Her arm slid off his and slapped against his groin.

'Aagh!' he screamed in mock anger as her hand grazed over the erection which threatened to burst through the pair of sawn-off Wranglers he wore as shorts.

'He'll fall off if you touch him again,' warned Alan, whose priapic organ had developed an arthritic ache after the excesses of the previous two nights' prolonged and impassioned lovemaking.

'I'll bet he doesn't,' sang Karyn, as she eased Alan's zip over the bulge.

Try as she might, however, she was unable to get his 'old man', as he called it, out into the open.

'Damn these seat belts,' she muttered. 'You'll have to take your shorts off.'

'God, woman, I can't do that. We'd get arrested. And what about my insurance if we had a crash?'

'True. They'd probably say you were inadequately covered,' joked Karyn. 'But what are you worried about? There hasn't been a policeman in sight all day.'

'But what if we meet another car in a passing place?'

'Oh, they could only see the top half of your body. Although this little fellow might well reach above your waist by the feel of him! Anyway, we could just cover him up with a towel. No-one would ever know.'

Dr Cameron had never remotely conceived of such a situation, but now he found himself lifting his backside off the seat as Karyn wriggled his shorts down to his ankles then leaned over to take his throbbing cock into her mouth. He reduced speed immediately, still holding the car in top gear, and moved his hands round to the twenty-to-two position so that his left forearm could rest on Karyn's head, and he could give her neck the occasional caress whenever the winding road permitted it.

As she exquisitely sucked him off — what idiot had called it a blow job? he thought — he did well to keep the car on the road.

'You'd better stop, Karyn. I'm going to come!' he yelled, using third gear to brake the car.

Her only response was to accelerate. She felt his semen coursing upwards through his wildly pulsing prick, then surging against the roof of her mouth, before burning its way down her eager throat. Alan fought to keep the Audi on the road as Karyn lovingly licked the last glistening drops from him, sending frissons of almost unbearable ecstasy throughout his body and making him roar with delight.

'Stop it! You'll kill me!' he cried, as Karyn's bobbing head slowed down. 'You're crazy!' He marvelled at her expertise.

'Mmmm. That was gorgeous. I love your taste,' she said as she sat upright again.

'God,' gasped Alan. 'I wonder how many guys have come at sixty miles an hour on this road? You Scandinavian sex-maniacs aren't real,' he grinned at Karyn. 'You'll be telling me next that it's part of the driving test over there.'

'Now there's a thought,' smiled Karyn, as she stroked the velvety softness of his exhausted organ which had collapsed helplessly and heavily into her hand. 'And if all the learner drivers were as nice as you I might even apply for a job as an examiner,' she laughed.

Now that Alan could concentrate on his driving again he really put the Audi through its paces. He still had only one hand on the wheel, but now his other was on the gear stick. He had regretted a few purchases in his life, but never this magnificent, thoroughbred roadster which never failed to thrill him with its outstanding performance. It gobbled up the few remaining miles between Torrisdale and Tongue.

The view as they approached the Kyle was marvellous. Endless yellow sands, being pounded still finer by a blue and white foamed surf which the relentless tides swept in even on such a calm day as this, were framed in the foreground by magnificent trees and a wide carpet of luscious greeny-yellow rape, while the mauve heathers in the background gradually blended to sepia in the mountains in the far north-west.

'What glorious trees.' Karyn sounded surprised. 'I thought you told me that this part of the country had been swept bare thousands of years ago by the ice and wind?'

'Most of it was,' reaffirmed Alan. 'But this is such a sheltered spot. And we're now far enough away from the North Sea tides that the last remaining traces of the Gulf Stream which flows along the north-west coast can still have a warming effect on the soil. There's even the odd palm tree in the village. I'll show you later.'

'Lovely. And maybe another day we could go up into those gorgeous hills in the distance? They look so inviting.'

'No way.' Alan gave a nervous bray. 'They might look OK from the distance, but I wouldn't go up into them for anything.'

'But why not?' Karyn couldn't for the life of her understand his strange attitude. 'I thought you enjoyed hillwalking?'

'Oh. Yes. I do,' he stuttered. 'But .... I wouldn't go up into those hills. Not ever again.'

'So you have been before?'

'Once.' He nodded. 'On a walking and fishing trip with two of my colleagues at Dounreay.'

Even now in the vivid brightness of a summer's day Alan's spine started to shiver and the hair on the back of his neck to bristle with waves of fear at the first mention of that experience over four years earlier. He had consciously fought the memories to the back of his mind, and had confided the story to no-one lest they thought he and his friends were crazy. But it had happened. It really had happened. He found himself now telling Karyn what he hadn't dared tell anyone else.

'I can't explain what took place on that trip, Karyn. But it took place alright. We had walked through a high pass and come on to a vast plateau at about 2000 feet. It was early evening. The only noise was the wind – a low steady grumble not unlike the sensation you get holding a conch shell to your ear. We walked for about a mile to the southeast and pitched the tent twenty yards or so from the shore of a 'dubh lochan' – a water-filled hollow in the peat – which wasn't even on the Ordnance Survey map. David and myself blew up our small dinghy while Fergus set up the primus stove a few paces from the tent. We unpacked the rest of our gear to let it dry out – I had fallen into a swollen stream in the morning and we had all got a soaking in the effort to rescue me – and laid it on the ground.

'After a quick snack – we didn't want to spoil our appetites for the barbecued trout later in the evening! – we got into the dinghy and rowed out. The loch shelved abruptly into inky black a few yards from the shore. We stopped about thirty yards out. Ian cast out into the middle of the loch while Fergus and myself faced the shore and our campsite. The wind had dropped. It was utterly still. Uncannily so. None of us noticed at the time, but there wasn't even a midge or a cleg in the air. About twenty minutes passed. We caught nothing.

There wasn't even a ripple on the surface of the water. The loch was unutterably dead. Without any visible sign of agreement we headed for the shore. Our tent was still standing – but our gear had been strewn around the moor for hundreds of yards in all directions away from the loch. No-one spoke. We had seen and heard nothing. There wasn't another living soul for miles around. Not daring to break the unearthly silence we gathered in our belongings and got the hell out of the place down to Achnaharra, with many a glance over our shoulders. None of us has been back since.'

By now the icy electrical shock waves had reached Alan's sideburns and were glaciating over his cheekbones. He was glad of Karyn's hand gripping his own.

'God, Alan. I'm glad you never told me that story in the middle of the night.'

'It's not a story, my lovely.' The chill in Alan's voice gave her goosebumps. 'And anyway we have much better things to concern ourselves with in the middle of the night.' He squeezed her knee and turned the car down a rough track which led to a totally deserted stretch of beach.

Before the car had come to a halt Karyn had pulled her short, Egyptian cotton sheath dress up over her head and was off, her naked bronze body flashing across the warm sands. Alan took his few remaining clothes off at a more leisurely pace before tracing Karyn's wispy footprints over the soft sands. By the time he caught up with her and laid out all they needed for the day ahead – towels, suntan lotion for himself, some fruit and Karyn's favourite Apfelsaft – Karyn had been in and out of the cool waters of the Atlantic. Her skin glistened with moisture and was refreshingly cool to his touch. It did not feel that way for long.

'You must come in,' she pleaded with him. 'It really is quite warm.'

Alan, who was strictly a heated-indoor-pool man, did not believe her for a second.

'You're joking! I've tried to get in before and have never managed over my knees. That water is freezing!'

'It's not, you big softy! Its fine once you're in. Much milder than our fjords. Come on!'

'Oh! I suppose there's no way out without losing too much

face,' grumbled Alan as he tiptoed in after the bronze arrow which had just dived through a massive wave.

As the water surged over him he was pleasantly surprised, even though his balls recoiled in shock and almost disappeared up his long-forgotten inguinal canals. The shallow bay, the last lukewarm traces of the Mexican current, and the warm summer sun combined to make the waters bearable. At any rate, his tool was grateful for the chance to get the steam taken out of it.

Karyn, remembering his discomfort in the Paris pool, and sensing that he would be even more nonplussed in the open sea, came near to him. The water was amazingly translucent on this part of the coast and enabled them to see each other clearly. As they splashed and played with each other Alan felt himself stirring. He couldn't help it. A touch of her hand was enough to get him started, let alone her naked body cavorting with him like this.

Karyn wasn't slow to notice.

'We couldn't, could we?' she asked hopefully.

'It's worth a try! Come here and we'll see.'

Karyn stood with her back to Alan, facing out to sea, and floated forward on the water as he supported her stomach and edged himself slowly into her. It felt a bit dry and uncomfortable at first – salt is not the ideal lubricant, nor was sand as he was to find out later – but once he was in fully it was magic just to stand there with a sensation of weightlessness letting the swelling of the surf do all the work.

'Love you Karyn!' he yelled at her through the roaring spray.

Two hours later they made love for the last time. Loosely draped in a large towel apiece, they slowly returned to the car.

Karyn had just stepped into her dress when Alan noticed the greasy finger prints on the Quattro's highly polished bonnet. As he bent down to wipe them off he was only just aware of the two figures running towards them down the track, waving horribly efficient looking Heckler and Koch sub-machine guns and looking mean enough to use them.

Within five minutes Alan and Karyn were experiencing a much less comfortable ride homewards, trussed together on the cold metal floor in the back of an ancient Landrover, wondering what the devil was happening to them.

They didn't have to wait long to find out.

Round about the year 1850 BC a new tribe of Early Bronze Age settlers had arrived in Caithness and, using the most advanced technology available to them, had proceeded to construct a cathedral – or was it a calendar or a computer? – consisting of about a hundred standing stones in thirteen rows on a hillside overlooking the waters of the Pentland Firth. Almost four thousand years later a similar tribe of 'white settlers', as the locals called them, came north to construct their megalithic monument to modern technology on virtually the self-same site. The juxtaposition of and causality between the two cultures were an endless source of reflection, fascination and inspiration to Roddy Macdonald, a pensive, idealistic young artist who had come to Caithness in an attempt to find himself and some life in meaning, as he occasionally joked.

This past year he had been working on a set of photographs in which he was trying to make a statement about the relationship between the two monuments so far apart on the time plane, yet so close together on the spatial. Slowly and painstakingly, and after much experimentation with different lenses, angles, exposures and darkroom effects, he had arrived at a lofty conception which, unless he was meticulously careful, could easily look like cheap pornography.

At a disco in the local hotel in Wick which he often visited after teaching a nightschool class, he had met a long-haired local beauty whose wide-eyed innocence and fragility would have captivated Zeffirelli, if not Botticelli himself. She had, after much persuasion, and with many reservations, agreed to model for him.

Roddy had met Mhairi at the bus station at 9.15 that morning. After many a detour criss-crossing the main road a dozen times to deliver newspapers, parcels and even toilet rolls, Roddy had remarked, the bus got them to Thurso just after 10.45. A quick cuppa there and they set out hitching a ride along the road to Reay. Traffic was fairly brisk that morning with golfers and tourists heading west, and Mhairi's long hair, legs and lithe figure got them a lift in next to no time.

By 12.00 they were seated amidst the standing stones of Upper Dounreay. Mhairi took the tumbler of Californian Rosé Roddy offered her, then lay back on the heather to sunbathe as he busied himself setting up the tripod and camera in exactly the right spot. As he did so, he mused, with no small amount of self-satisfaction, on the canvas he was creating. An uncompromising artist, he sought kudos from no-one, but he knew that his two great idols, the late nineteenth century Norwegian expressionist, Edvard Munch, and the twentieth century Spanish surrealist, Salvador Dali, would have approved. Dali, of the metamorphosis of square stones to spherical steel through the medium of the girl's curvacious body; Munch, of the angst and terror in the eyes, which he was going to burn out later in the darkroom; both, of the perfection of nature as she was brutally raped by primitive technology and forced to witness the horrendous birth of a totally unwanted and unnecessary bastard monstrosity after a gestation period of four millenia.

'OK, Mhairi. Sorry to take so long.'

'Oh, that's alright. I was enjoying it lying here in the sun. It's lovely up here with that wee breeze – keeps the midges away.'

'Yeah, they're a curse on a calm day. Do they affect you badly?'

'Not really. Just annoy me, that's all. Not like my sister who comes up in great big lumps every time she gets bit.'

'It's amazing, isn't it? They're so small you can hardly see the wee buggers – yet they can give you a helluva sore bite. Anyway, I'm glad you don't have any unwanted lumps to spoil my pictures.'

'Huh! Is that all you'd be worried about, your pictures?'

'No, no, no. I was only joking. Come on, now,' he added, taking her hand and pulling her to her feet.

He started taking shots of her right away on the little Ricoh FFI compact he always took on assignments, just to get her relaxed and used to the idea of being photographed. It's no easy thing to stand in front of a camera, even for professionals, and Roddy well knew the importance of putting his model at her ease. He made her talk to him all the time and constantly praised her to reassure the flagging self-confidence which is always present at the start of a session, especially with a girl who has never done it before.

'That's marvellous, Mhairi. Now, could you go over to that stone there? The one that's almost fallen over near the end of the row.'

'This one here?'

'Yeah. Fine. OK. Could you angle yourself round towards it a bit more? Hold it. Good.'

He took half-a-dozen Polaroids to check the composition, and called her over to see them.

'It's going to work!' he announced gleefully. 'I knew it!'

'What's going to work?' she asked, as Roddy handed over one of the prints to her.

'The whole idea. Look. Perfect.'

'But that's horrible! You've got the reactor dome sticking out in front of me. What's nice about that? Should you not move around a bit to cut it out?'

'It's not meant to be nice, Mhairi. I want you standing there, naked next time, being raped by the stone. The dome is to make you look pregnant. I'm trying to show the . . . '

'What?' The shriek of horror cut him short. 'No way, boyo! That's obscene. Raped by a stone? You're sick!'

'Oh, come on, Mhairi. This is serious. I'm not like that,' he trailed off half-heartedly and shrugged his shoulders in despair.

'Maybe so, Roddy. But I'm sorry. I . . . . I just couldn't do it. I'm sorry.'

'Oh, fuck off then!' Roddy was instantly remorseful. It was not so much that he was annoyed with the girl, her prudishness and lack of feel for what he was doing; rather that he was exasperated that his artistic concept was not going to be realised. Not with Mhairi anyhow.

'Thank you, mister high-minded artist!' Mhairi was close to tears.

'I didn't mean that.' Roddy vainly tried to make amends by putting his arm round the girl's shoulder to comfort her. 'Really; I didn't.'

'Don't touch me you sex maniac!' She recoiled away from him

and started off towards the narrow lane leading down to the main road.

'Wait a minute, lassie! At least let me take you home,' Roddy pleaded.

'No way! I can manage on my own, thank you very much.'

And she was gone, leaving the bewildered photographer behind trying to analyse where he had gone wrong.

'Bitch! bitch! bitch!' he muttered for a long time afterwards.

Halled and Yahya had been parked just off the A836 for about an hour and a half in their tiny Fiat camper.

'Why the fucking hell does Muhsin not call in?' Halled enquired civilly of his partner. 'Doesn't the goat-fucker know the fucking drill?'

'He should,' agreed Yahya. 'It's been well enough rehearsed. Maybe he's run into some problems.'

'That's possible,' agreed Halled grudgingly.

'Or they might even be having trouble transmitting.'

'No. If anything, we might have difficulty receiving them with all the interference that fucking US base must be generating,' he said, pointing towards the complex of masts and antennae which announced the existence of the subterranean spy station at nearby Forss.

'That's a point. Maybe we should head inland a bit and get some higher ground.'

'Yeah. That hill over there must have a road going into it. It'll also be a good vantage point to signal to Kaldi and Mata from. We should have thought of this last week.'

They stopped in the entrance to a field of barley, about half-way up the hill, and waited impatiently for the call sign.

'Hurry up, man! For fuck's sake hurry up!' Halled grunted through clenched teeth.

A few minutes later, their attention was distracted from the radio set by the sight of Mhairi loping past, with Roddy a few paces behind under the weight of all his gear, on their way up to the ancient monument.

Within half an hour the call came in. They didn't use any

code, as they figured no-one overhearing would understand a syllable of the rare desert dialect they used in everyday conversation.

They were right. One radio ham in Wick who had erected a monstrous mast in his back garden, much to his neighbour's chagrin, and who had just come off the night shift at the local Caithness Glass factory, did pick them up by accident as he twiddled his way across the shortwave band range they were using. He didn't dwell long on the gibberish, assuming it came from a couple of Turkish or Lebanese merchant ships off the coast, and continued his search for someone to have a meaningful conversation with, as his wife screamed at him to do something useful around the house for a change.

'Got you loud and clear, you mothers! Go ahead.' The relief in Halled's voice was unmistakable.

'We're on our way back east now. We've got Cameron and his girlfriend.'

'What in hell's name took you so long? You had us worried as fuck.'

'Long story. Cameron and the girl weren't in the house when we got there. A neighbour said she had met them and they were heading into Reay for some supplies before going sunbathing. Fortunately, the woman in the general store knows everyone's business. The couple had headed west towards Tongue. It took us two hours searching every side road to the beach there. We got them eventually at our ninth or tenth attempt.'

'You lucky bastards!'

'Don't need you to tell us that. He's the key man.'

'They're all key men,' Halled reminded Muhsin and Sallal. 'Thank fuck you got him.'

'What about the girl? Do we dump her or what?'

'Eh? No. Wait a minute. Couldn't you get her to make the phone call?'

'That wouldn't work. She's German or something. It's got to be a local.'

'Yeah. I'm just thinking out loud. Hell, you'd better hold on to her just now. You never know, she might just get found and all hell could break loose before we get into the place. She might come in useful later on,' he grinned at Yahya. 'Right. Get on with the next phase. We're heading back along the coast to rendezvous now.'

Halled switched off the transmitter and told Yahya to signal out to Kaldi and Mata in the bay.

Their acknowledgment came flashing back instantly, as if they too had been passing the few hours impatiently.

'Let's get on with it, now,' Halled said, eager for action.

They were just reversing the little Fiat onto the road, to go down into Reay where they intended to kidnap the middle-aged lady in the general store and force her to make the phonecall to Brocklehurst, when Mhairi came running down the slope.

'Look at that!'

'I am, my friend, I am. That's the girl who went up with the bearded goat an hour ago.'

'Are you thinking what I'm thinking, Halled?'

'One broad's as good as another broad,' grinned Halled.

'Like hell they are. Have you forgotten what the old bag in the village looks like?'

'How could I?' groaned Halled. 'She's just like my fucking mother-in-law.'

Yahya was just about to ask which one, when Mhairi reached the van.

Halled was out in a flash and had her pinned from behind, his forearm pressed across her windpipe making it impossible for her to breathe, let alone cry out for help. Yahya gagged her expertly, then tied her hands and feet with the rope they had brought for Mrs McIver in the village. They placed her gently in the back of the little camper. Halled, having lost the toss of the coin which he had pulled out of his trouser pocket, returned to the driving seat, while Yahya jumped into the back beside the girl.

The sight of her thrashing about helplessly on the floor, the smell of her sweat which made her dress cling to her and define every inch of her body, and the sound of her muffled squeaks through the scarf, were too much for Yahya.

He drew out the knife which had already disemboweled a dozen desert tribesfolk, including three women, and slit the cord round her ankles, forcing her legs apart with his knees as he did so. He ripped off her briefs with one hand, and began tearing at his belt with the other.

'Not now, you stupid bastard!' snarled Halled, jamming on the brakes. 'She's got to be in a fit state to make the call. Perhaps later, if we've time . . . who knows?' he winked at his companion in the mirror.

'Sorry, Halled. I just got carried away. I've never had a European woman before.'

'Nor I, my friend. So, let's hurry up and get this phonecall out of the way, huh? Then we'll toss the coin again. Best of three,' he added in case he lost a second time.

The nearest phonebox was just off the main road at a tiny hamlet called Buldoo. Halled turned in past it for about fifty yards, then reversed down a wild hawthorn-edged path towards a deserted crofthouse.

Mhairi lay huddled on the floor on her side, knees drawn up, afraid to move a muscle.

Halled rolled her onto her back as Yahya took out his knife again.

'All we want you to do is make a phonecall for us,' he told the girl in as pleasant and soft a voice as he could muster.

'After that you will be free to go. Unharmed,' he added in a gruffer tone which made it unnecessary for him to state the corollary.

'Nunh! Nunh!' She shook her head, not believing a word of what he was saying.

Halled nodded to Yahya. He grabbed about a foot of Mhairi's hair and sliced it effortlessly. He then pushed her dress up slowly, savouring every instant, and grabbed her fuzz out from her body. As he laid the cold knife blade flat on her lower abdomen and began inching it down menacingly towards her mound she nodded her head as vigorously as she could, tears streaming down her cheeks.

'That's better. It's been fifteen months since my friend last took that kind of a scalp. Now, this is what you do.'

Twenty minutes later Mhairi said into the phone, 'That's alright, sir.'

Halled pressed down the receiver cradle.

Then he tossed the coin, winning the right to go first on the third throw.

When they had finished with her, Mhairi, wishing that she

had stayed on the hillside and given herself symbolically to the standing stone, lost consciousness as Yahya's knife sliced into her.

Walter Brocklehurst was in many ways an extremely fortunate man. As one of the top group of administrators at Dounreay he enjoyed prestige, power and an enormous salary and benefits package in return for a working week which was the envy of many. Not that he was just employed as a temporary consultant when his services were required. No; as Director of Projects his was a permanent full-time position. However, like many employees of the UKAEA from the lowliest process worker upwards he appeared at times to be seriously underemployed, as far as the native population was concerned. In his case, however, it was not so much that there was very little to do; it was more a matter of how he interpreted his job. In his earlier days in middle management he had cursed the way in which his superiors had delegated most of their duties down the ladder to minions. Now, having got to the top of that self-same ladder, he had, in his own turn, made an art, indeed a science, of delegation. His speciality was flow charts illustrating how everything got done. One wall of his office was covered in them. As the number one co-ordinator of the various pieces of research which were undertaken in the plant he had no intentions whatsoever of becoming involved in the nitty-gritty of work planning. He had more than earned these particular spurs earlier in his career masterminding intricate projects. Nowadays he was more concerned with general aims than specific objectives; with broad timescales than detailed goal attainments; with global sums than departmental requisitions. He was, above all the other roles which could be assigned to his post, a facilitator, as he liked to philosophise with his peers at Board of Directors meetings. An 'ethos emanator', as he had once christened himself, whose prime function was to provide the proper environment to enable others to get on with their work. Brocklehurst, it must be said, was good at his job.

At 2.15 on the afternoon of 25 July he was buzzed on his personal communications receiver which, for him, was an absolute necessity of life as he was one of the most elusive men in the establishment to pin down to any one place as he 'facilitated' through the day. Central Administration had just received an urgent phone call for him. The telephonist had explained that Dr. Brocklehurst was in conference, and asked the caller to phone back in ninety minutes from then – a standard procedure which Brocklehurst himself had laid down for all external calls to nurture the notion that he was always gainfully employed – but, on being told that it was an emergency, she had reluctantly put the call through.

The telecom pager caught Brocklehurst as he was halfway from his own office to that of Henry Tomassen, Director of Finance, to discuss the following year's budget. It was to be an important session. In the wee small hours, both men knew better than anyone else exactly how the public and the politicians had been conned over the years about the myth of cheap and abundant electricity from nuclear sources, although neither would ever admit it publicly. The truth was that production targets expressed as percentages of the national output of electricity from all sources of generating power had never been met by the nuclear establishment, and that costs had soared higher than Concorde itself due as much to overmanning, non-productive overtime and general inefficiency as to the construction and building delays so often cited by the apologists for the nuclear industry. Add the costs of research and development, reprocessing of nuclear waste and decontamination and containment – 'decommissioning' as the industry labels it. Take away the number you first thought of. And the answer is still the greatest scientific and economic lie of the century.

Now, however, that the very existence of the Fast Reactor development was being seriously questioned by the public, let alone its advancement on a commercial basis, the work of people like Brocklehurst and Tomassen to justify their existence and perpetuate the myth took on a new sense of urgency. The complacency of the '50s, '60s and '70s would not ensure the viability of the industry into the '90s and beyond. Brocklehurst stopped at the first telephone he passed and was put through to the caller without delay.

'Hello. Dr Brocklehurst?' queried the nervous and harassed voice on the other end. 'This is Mrs Mackenzie from the shop. I'm afraid Mrs Brocklehurst has taken another bad turn and gone home in a taxi. I've just phoned Dr Brodie and he's on his way to your house just now.'

'Good heavens! She must be quite bad this time?'

'Well . . .' The caller hesitated. 'She must be. The doctor went straight away.'

'I see. Best get along home myself in that case. Thank you for phoning, Mrs Mackenzie.'

'That's alright, sir.'

'Oh, Mrs Mackenzie? Best just close the shop for the rest of the day.'

But the receiver had already been put down at the other end.

Brocklehurst rang through to Tomassen.

'Henry? Walter here. Henry, I've just had an urgent summons home.'

'Margaret?'

'Yes, I'm afraid so. Seems she has taken another bad bout. George is on his way to see her at the moment. Think I'll just pop over myself for an hour and make sure everything is tickety-boo. Can I see you later this afternoon?'

'Nonsense, Walter. There's nothing that can't wait until tomorrow. Come in about 10.30 – or, if that's not convenient, anytime over the next couple of days.'

'Right, Henry. Will do. Cheers for now.'

'Cheers, Walter. And I trust Margaret's not too bad.'

Margaret, in fact, was not too bad at all.

Like many an 'atomic wifie', as the locals referred to the spouses of incoming nuclear scientists, she had taken a long time to overcome the culture shock of being uprooted from the civilised delights of southern England and transplanted into the totally alien environment of the barbaric north of Scotland. Thurso and its surroundings had been as bad as she had anticipated. Things had, however, gradually improved over the twenty-three years since she and Walter had moved there. The town had grown, in size and amenities. The Arts Society, Live Music Association, Film Society and Field Club had collectively been her salvation from utter boredom. She had developed a keen interest in yoga and had achieved her lifelong ambition to become a vegan.

Three years earlier she had persuaded Walter that, with the onset of the depressive menopausal years, she needed a full-time interest. They had opened what had become a thriving and highly lucrative organic produce shop in Thurso where she pottered about whenever the notion took her, leaving the day-to-day running of the business, at Walter's suggestion, to a very capable local lady who had been promised a partnership if it all went well.

Of late, however, Margaret's health, despite years of dedicated pampering and the elimination of all known and suspected carcinogens from her diet, had begun to deteriorate.

She had concealed the growing uneasiness that something serious was amiss with her from her husband for as long as she was able. The progressive degeneracy of multiple sclerosis, diagnosed a few months previously by Dr Brodie, a valued family friend and connoisseur of the arts, had now reached the stage where she was unable to hide the symptoms from Walter. No-one knows why – or if they do they have been prevented from saying – but Caithness has the highest recorded incidence of MS in the world. Fortunately, a disease which has struck down many a person instantly had been kind to Mrs Brocklehurst. After a series of initial falls and temporary loss of muscle power, it appeared that she had entered a period of remission. In many cases, such relief from the symptoms could last for decades. Margaret and Walter were keeping their fingers crossed.

This afternoon, however, she was in the pink. At that very moment she was in Marishka's, an upmarket craftshop run by a sister atomic, looking for a gift for her mother's 80th birthday.

Brocklehurst jogged across to the Admin block car park where he had a reserved bay whose ample dimensions allowed even him to bring his little car to rest within the allotted space, and set off for home in the hamlet of Stoorie four miles to the east and about a mile to the south off the main A836. As he crested the ancient, hump-backed bridge three-quarters of a mile from the village on the single track road, he was forced to brake furiously and pull into the passing place on his left to avoid crashing into the old Landrover coming towards him.

The driver of the Landrover appeared to panic, and also pulled into the passing place at the last moment, nudging into the front of Brocklehurst's Ford Fiesta, as he did so.

The passenger was out of the Landrover immediately. But instead of apologising, he dragged Brocklehurst from his seat, coshed him insensible in one blow, and bundled him into the back of the landrover alongside Alan Cameron and Karyn, both of whom were still as securely tied as when they had been dumped in half an hour previously.

Sallal checked his watch and cursed loudly.

'Ten minutes to rendezvous,' he snarled to Muhsin. 'What the hell took him so long to get here? As if we hadn't lost enough time already tracking down those two lovebirds in the back.'

Muhsin didn't answer. He shot the old Landrover over the bridge and gunned its modified, uprated six cylinder power unit towards the white dome clearly visible a few miles to their left.

'Passenchers for Wick, Aberdeen and Edinburgh should proceed to the departure gate now,' sang the tannoy in a strong island lilt.

That's a laugh, thought Willie Gunn. There's only six of us here, only one plane in sight, and only one door in the wall – that must be the departure gate.

'For passenchers continuing to Edinburgh,' the Orcadian lass continued, 'there will be a short stopoffer in Aberdeen to allow the Shetland flight to choin you.'

The trusty old Viscount turbo-prop lay shrouded in the haar of Kirkwall airport as the handful of passengers approached it.

'Is Scotch mist the only weather you guys ever get up here?' Gustav Schultz, Chief Sales Executive of Standard Texan Oils Inc., directed his question at Gunn, whom he assumed to be Scottish, rather than at the two swarthy student-types with their bulky backpacks.

'If it doesn't clear soon this old kite will never make Edinburgh in time for my conference.'

'Ah wouldnae worry, Tex, if ah wis you. It'll clear before we leave the Mainland.'

'Before we get to the mainland, you mean, Jocky?'

'Nah. Before we leave the Mainland of Orkney, man. Just you wait and see,' added Willie with the absolute certainty of one who had travelled this route many a time before.

Willie was not an Orcadian, despite his local knowledge. He came from Ulbster, a cluster of small cottages and derelict crofts about seven miles south of Wick in Caithness. It had seen semi-prosperous times in the late eighteenth and early nineteenth centuries under the improving landlord Sir John Sinclair, whose main claim to fame was that he had started the Statistical Account in Scotland. Hard times had set in midway through the nineteenth century. The local fisherfolk, despite carving out a stupendous staircase down three hundred feet of solid rock at Whaligoe, and walking the seven miles daily into Wick to the market with their catches, had failed to earn enough cash to supplement their meagre income from the land. They had fallen deeper into arrears of rent like thousands of crofters throughout the Highlands of Scotland. Only government legislation and the setting up of the Crofters Commission had enabled a residue of them to survive on the land into the welcome subsidies of the twentieth century.

Willie Gunn was one of the more fortunate inhabitants of the tiny community in recent times. He had landed a job as an apprentice mechanic in a local garage as a result of a placement on Wick High School's work experience scheme, and from there, after his time was out, had got a job with a large firm of agricultural engineers servicing farm machinery throughout Caithness, Sutherland and the Orkney Islands.

'Sure hope you're right, fella,' said Schultz. 'I sure as hell wouldn't want to be fogbound in this shit-hole of a place for any length of time.'

Willie couldn't agree, but wasn't prepared to argue the point. Had the plane not left he would have headed straight back to the caravan outside Kirkwall where he had spent the previous night in the arms of not one, but two, local lassies – not that any of the lads in the Caithness Club were going to believe him! – who each had been drowning the woes of a broken love affair in the hotel in which Willie always stayed when he was over. He had bought them a drink, and an hour or so after closing time they had invited him back for a nightcap. Willie collected the 40oz bottle of Johnnie Walker Black Label which the landlord always managed to include in his bill for accommodation and board as he was a regular customer on a company expense account, and set off into the darkness of the road heading up the hill towards the golf course with his new-found friends, not knowing what the night would bring. It had, in the event, brought a damn sight more than he had hoped for. His only worry now was that he had left a good third of a bottle of whisky behind in the caravan, and that he might have picked up another dose of the clap. You never know with all those fuckin' oilmen around, he thought.

At any rate, the plane took off on schedule, much to the relief of the Texan and the two youth hostellers, and to the regret of Willie who would now have to return to the constant refusals and naggings of his wife without delay. At least he would not have to pretend to have won yet another bottle in the club weekly raffle to account for his vast store of booze. He would feign fatigue for a few days and keep his fingers crossed about the clap, though.

The flight across to the Scottish mainland was at very low altitude.

'Good to see you fellas taking the energy crisis so seriously,' the Texan approved of the fuel economies of such a trajectory. 'I must work you into my address this afternoon,' he said patronisingly.

'Say, Jocky.' Willie was getting no peace from this persistent prattler. 'Would that be your fast breeder reactor we can see in the distance along the north coast there?'

'Sure is, Tex.' Willie affected a Southern drawl. 'Pride and joy of Caithness. These boys'll be taking over when all your oil dries up.'

'Yep. That's what the bastards will be crowing about at our symposium. Still, it won't put me out of a job. All that crap about oil running out was put out by the nuclear industry using false statistics based on the known oil reserves of the 1960s. Admittedly,' he grinned, 'it was connived at by the oilmen in the '70s, who used the petroleum phobia to good effect in wringing giveaway concessions from your Labour and Tory governments to develop the North Sea. No, sir; the black gold's gonna last for a long time yet.'

As the plane came low over Duncansby Head lighthouse at John O'Groats, the massive rock stacks which millions of years of erosion had carved out from the land were clearly visible.

Wick airport was only a few minutes away in a straight line due south between there and Noss Head lighthouse at the other end of the grand sweep of Sinclair's Bay.

Up ahead in the cockpit Captain Harold Greene glanced at his Rolex.

'Couple of minutes in hand, David.' His First Officer nodded instantly in agreement, having already made the calculation taking account of the following wind. 'Might as well have a little detour.'

With that, he banked the plane to the right and began following the line of the smaller Freswick Bay towards Buchollie Castle, which dated from the twelfth century and which had been the base of the Norse pirate, Sweyn Asliefson, who had terrorised the seas for miles around. Greene had been wanting to make this pass for a few weeks now ever since he had heard the public lecture in Thurso by the young archaeologist who had led the team from Durham University which had excavated the Viking remains at Freswick a couple of years previously. They had uncovered much which was new, including evidence about the dwellings and the extent of the Norse fishing industry; and had then gone on to carry out an extremely laborious coastal survey by criss-crossing the area between the A9 road and the coast on foot. Why the dickens they had disdained the use of aerial photography to assist them he couldn't figure out. In actual fact, the team didn't disdain the use of photographic reconnaissance: they quite simply could not afford the expense of an aerial survey on their tight research grant. But Greene was right. The view from the air, which was well off the usual flightpath, was most enlightening. From this height – he had gone down even further to the five hundred feet legal minimum – every detail of the relief, shape and layout of the settlement was crystal clear. He marvelled at the size of the main longhouse, which had turned out to be the earliest complete example of its kind found on the Scottish mainland, thanks to the radio-isotope dating techniques which had been used on the fibrous pottery remains which were contemporaneous with the earliest phase of the building.

'Quite something, eh, David?'

David Grant was not really turned on with archaeological remains.

'I suppose so – if you're interested in that sort of a thing.'

Greene headed back on course over Auckengill and across Sinclair's Bay, whose coastline was dotted with Iron Age brochs, ruined castles and the resplendent Ackergill Tower luxury hotel. He was taxiing down the main runway bang on schedule a few minutes later.

The two students, who had been talking anxiously to each other during the brief detour, relaxed as they checked their watches. As the plane came to a halt at the terminal buildings, Kirsty Falconer, the female stewardess – well, she makes a welcome change from the male stewardess they normally put on this run, thought Willie Gunn – thanked those passengers about to get off for having travelled British Air.

'You're welcome,' Willie grinned at her as he got up from his seat and made for the exit.

He was stopped in his tracks by the muzzle of an AK 47, an old-fashioned weapon, but one whose trustworthiness and utter reliability had been proven time and time again by the veteran desert fighter, Yousuf Hurion, in whose hands it easily sat.

'What the fu. . . .'

Willie was stopped in mid-expletive by the clipped and heavily accented voice of Hurion, who had discarded his camping gear.

'Stop. Everyone off.' He motioned to the Texan and the two middle-aged ladies. 'Hurry, and no-one will get hurt.'

The stewardess swung the exit door open and stood aside to let Gunn out first. As he came towards the gunman at the top of the steps Willie faked a stumble and threw himself at the Arab. Hurion calmly side-stepped, felled the Scot with a karate chop which almost broke the base of his spine with its force, and released a short burst from his favourite weapon.

Particles of Willie's skull spattered the tarmac a split second before his body landed with a dull thud.

It was the first sign for Captain Greene that anything was amiss.

'Now; the rest of you leave the plane as quickly as possible.'

Hurion was not asking them.

'You bastards!' Schultz spat out. 'Roll on the day when you and your friggin' wells shrivel up.'

Hurion ignored him.

The two women passengers followed the American down the steps, trying unsuccessfully not to look at Gunn, for whom there was nothing anyone could do.

Hurion ordered Kirsty Falconer to close the exit door, then motioned her into the cockpit beside Harold Greene and Grant.

Captain Greene's receiver was demanding to know what the bloody hell was going on. The excited air traffic controller could easily be seen in the small control tower sixty yards away.

'Right,' barked Hurion. 'You will do exactly as I say. Cease radio contact now.'

Greene did so.

'You will now take off and fly due west to land at Dounreay.'

Instantly, and with chilling certainty, Greene grasped the gravity of the situation. The possibility of this had haunted him for years. Indeed, the thought had often occurred to him that there was a novel waiting to be written on this very theme, and that he could be the man to write it. But, such had been his commitments that he had never got past the vaguest outline of the theme in his mind.

'Impossible,' said Greene. 'The landing strip there is meant only for light planes and the smaller executive jets. We could never put down there.'

Greene was, of course, bluffing. As a former second-round loser in the BBC Mastermind competition, who had given British airports as one of his specialist subjects, he well knew that the runway at Dounreay had its origins in World War Two as a strategic airbase for the defence of the British fleet in Scapa Flow, pre-dating the atomic site. Although now shorter, it could easily accommodate a Viscount.

'Captain, I admire your sentiments. But you are running out of time, and I of patience. I have been assured a landing is possible. You will do as I say immediately, or . . . .'

Hurion waved his AK47 towards Kirsty and David Grant and let his voice trail off menacingly.

Greene taxied out and took off into the gentle breeze which was coming in from the prevailing south-westerly direction.

Duncan Jamieson had come up to Wick from Haddington, a sleepy little market town near Edinburgh, only the previous month. He enjoyed his first appointment controlling the small amount of traffic which went through this little provincial airport. Today, however, he could hardly control himself as he looked out of the window at the events unfolding before his eyes at the speed of light. No sooner had the shots been fired, and Willie Gunn's body had landed on the tarmac, than radio contact was broken by the Viscount.

'A hijack! It's a fucking hijack! Right here in fucking Wick!'

The startled Wick wifie who had just brought Jamieson his afternoon cuppa had never heard the notorious Anglo-Saxon adjective pronounced with such a pucka accent. It really amused her, as if a little three-year-old had suddenly, and for the first time, come out with the baddest word in the world.

As the plane taxied and took off Jamieson kept it in visual sight, but lost it quickly in the sudden haar which blew in over Reiss golf course, to the annoyance of the handful of players who were out on it and who were having yet another lovely summer's day spoiled by the vicissitudes in temperature of the air being sucked in from the cold North Sea by the warm land.

His radar showed it to be flying due west, then the blips vanished from the screen as the aircraft went below the scanner's range.

In the seconds during which this was happening Jamieson sent out a general radio alert which was simultaneously picked up by the local Wick Radio Station and the United States Air Force communications centre at Forss, which lay halfway between Thurso and Dounreay. He also assumed, correctly, that the pilot would be unable to send out the special signal code 7500 via his secondary surveillance radar, a transponder signal which alerts all searching radar systems of the airliner's name, number, height and speed, and which activates the lights and klaxons which warn of a hijack. There was nothing Jamieson could do about that.

As the message came into the Wick Radio operations room Norman Hill cursed the interruption to his concentration. His old schoolmate who was a radio officer at Cullercoats, had just launched a menacing Morse move sending his queen into a strong attacking position against Norman's castled king.

'Hold on, Nathaniel. Something's just coming in. Jesus! It's not quite the Titanic all over again' – the Wick boys never let the others forget that their station, which the Admiralty had set up in 1910, had been the first to pick up those fateful signals – 'but there's been a hijack from Wick aerodrome!' Charlie Stronach switched the alert through the loudspeaker so that everyone could join in the excitement, as they usually joined in a particularly juicy ship-to-shore lovesick call.

The bishop to bishop three move which would release Norman's fianchettoed clergyman to counter the audacious queen would have to wait till later.

Captain Greene considered throwing the Viscount into a sudden sweeping climb to throw the terrorists off balance. But what then? Both he and his First Officer were securely strapped in. Only the stewardess had any freedom of movement, and what chance would she have of disarming such an assailant? Whatever happened, he could not risk his lovely Kirsty in any way. As it was, all of his attention was needed to fly the craft in accordance with Hurion's instructions. As a regular pilot on the Orkney-Wick-Edinburgh route, Greene had often bemoaned the lack of topographical interest in the east and extreme north of Scotland. Now, being forced to hedge-hop a cumbersome Vickers Viscount at gunpoint beneath the radar screen operated by the USAF at Forss and by the personnel of Dounreay's own small radar station at Saint Margaret's Chapel, Greene thanked the gods for having had the prescience to make Caithness flat.

'You realise that we can't put down there?' Greene repeated his earlier bluff, as the little concrete ribbon appeared after about eight minutes flying time.

'Well, Captain, you'd damn well better try your hardest,' Hurion told him grimly. He fleetingly recalled some hairy moments in the air before parachuting into Omali, and knew that this part of the operation was going to be touch and go. Not because of anything Greene had said – he knew that to be lies – but because, unlike the pilot, he knew that major construction work was under way at the landing strip. The runway was being strengthened and lengthened to take the new heavy shipments by air which were scheduled to have started the following day, but which had been disrupted due to the union disputes which had caused delays in construction on the runway. The shipment leaving Sellafield that day was to be flown into Wick airfield under cover of darkness later that night.

There were not as many visitors as usual that afternoon at the Dounreay Exhibition Centre. The heat had taken most of the locals onto the golf courses and rivers, and most of the tourists onto the beaches. Sir James Gartshore reflected that he too should have gone fishing. Admiral Duff's little well-stocked loch a few miles inland at Lieurary would have been excellent on such a day. And, if the little blighters weren't biting, there was always the superb vintage port with which the Admiral was so liberal.

Twenty minutes into his well-rehearsed routine and he knew for sure he should have gone fishing. After all, as the Director who had steered Dounreay through the trying times of the 1970s when detractors had been everywhere, and with achievements like his under his belt, not to mention his more than adequate pension, he had no need to lecture throughout the summer to bus loads of elderly tourists who could only think about their next cream tea, and who didn't give a fig about the differences between slow neutron bombardment and fast neutron bombardment. Still, it gave him an interest beyond fly-tying, and meant that he could virtually leave his massive index-linked pension intact with Munn and Dunning, the merchant bankers in Edinburgh of which he was also a part-time director.

As he was breaking down the intricacies of particle acceleration to his uninformed and uninterested audience of West Country Women's Institute members, one of whom was tittering to the others that it was a new form of radioactive laxative, he was rudely interrupted as Halled checked his watch with the roar of the Viscount overhead. The two Dhubatis, having disposed of Mhairi, had simply followed the 'Visitors' signs into Dounreay and joined the tour without a question having been asked. All of the assault team had taken advantage of this bonus over the previous three weeks. They had laughed at the irony: men who were 100 per cent capable of garrotting their way past armed guards or silencing Rottweilers with two fingers had simply to walk in like the dozens of other tourists who visited the plant every day in the summer months. The plans at Dungoe had come alive after these visits.

There were shrieks of horror from some of the women at the sight of the two dark-skinned armed men.

'Over there.' Yahya pointed them towards the far wall, away from the entrance, with his Ruger.

'But gentlemen, this is plainly ridiculous,' Sir James spluttered. 'There must be a mistake. What possible use could I be to you?'

Halled did not want to tell the old boy in case he had a heart attack and rendered himself useless as a top, but expendable, bargaining pawn when the going got rough later on.

The barrel of Yahya's revolver pressing into his lower back at the spot where his kidneys had been playing up the previous week edged Sir James forwards.

None of the now strangely calm group of women dared make a move as Halled covered them with a steady sweep of his right arm. The security officers at the entrance were unarmed. Their sole tasks were to relieve visitors of their cameras, and to indicate to visitors where they could relieve themselves.

In fact they had been so absorbed in a careful analysis of the advantages of the Olympus OM-2SP which Halled had handed in over the older OM-IN that they had not even seen the initial encounter.

Now, as Sir James was propelled towards them, they were powerless to interfere. Unlike Sir James, who appeared to regard the gunmen with genuine disdain, they recognised the Rugers for what they were – the most fearsome hand guns in the world: Magnum force manstoppers, which were capable of dismembering any part of the body at such close range.

Outside the building the three figures began the four hundred yard walk past the Central Administration Block and the staff social facilities area in the direction of the landing strip. With the simultaneous alarm from the Fuel Reprocessing Plant and the unscheduled arrival of the hi-jacked airliner, Dounreay was in the grip of its biggest ever security exercise. Only this time it was for real.

When the alarm went, Michael Booth, who was having a coffee with Gerry Campbell in the staff canteen, leapt off his seat and rushed to the exit followed by his friend. As he came out into the open he all but ran into Sir James and the two Dhubatis. Only the pointed Ruger stopped him.

Yahya recognised Booth instantly from the dossier of photographs they had spent weeks studying.

As he opened his mouth to shout, 'Not me! I'm Boo . . . ' his entire throat was blown away in mid-vowel by the force of the blast. His head was barely held in place by a few remaining shreds of sinew and spinal column as his body crashed backwards into the arms of Campbell.

Sir James quickened his pace without being told as he saw the damage done to the young man and realised the very real predicament he himself was in.

Dr Peter Hargreaves was one of the few remaining workaholics at Dounreay. In the pioneering days of the '50s they had been the norm rather than the exception, but since then they had became a rare breed indeed.

Not a few had passed away, as the common euphemism had it; mainly of stress-induced diseases brought on by the rigours and awesome responsibilities of their work. But not always. The British nuclear industry has had some radiation casualties, not that they often admit to them. In this, of course, they are simply following the lead given to them by the British government. In February 1983 Mrs Thatcher, the then Prime Minister, had categorically denied in Parliament that any British naval craft had suffered residual contamination hazards after the British nuclear atmospheric contamination test at Monte Bello in Western Australia on 3 October 1952. The Ministry of Defence to this day insists that safety precautions in this and similar tests which took place between 1952 and 1958 in the South Pacific and Western Australia were beyond reproach. This is in stark contradiction to the testimony of people who had taken part in the operations at the time, and who had been ordered to stand in the open to witness the explosions and suffer the effects of atomic rain. It is also at odds with independent research conducted by a group in the Department of Social Medicine at Birmingham University which has assembled clear and irrefutable evidence of blood and lymphatic cancers amongst British servicemen who were on active duty in the test areas significantly in excess of the norm for the numerical group in question.

Admittedly, nothing like the criminal disregard for the safety of its workers that took place in some Soviet establishments ever occurred in Britain. In the Kurnakov Institute in Moscow workers were blatantly exposed to the full damaging effects of highly radioactive materials at close quarters without protective clothing, safety screens or glove-boxes; and liquid radioactive wastes were discharged into the normal sewage system. And in the Radium Institute in Leningrad many of the directors died at relatively young ages of reported lingering illnesses which were obviously radiation-induced.

A far more significant number of Hargreaves' former colleagues had emigrated in the famous 'Brain Drain' of the '60s and '70s; tempted overseas by astronomical salaries, almost unlimited research facilities and budgets, and freedom from public accountability. Hargreaves himself had received numerous such offers, one of which early in his married life had actually, to his perpetual embarrassment, got him into the Sunday papers. He had spent a six month sabbatical in California at one point in his deliberations, but could not tolerate the brash, pushy, dollar mentality of all around him, nor the lack of effective regulatory controls over an industry totally subservient to the profit motive. He returned home with his young wife utterly convinced that his future lay with Britain.

Of those fast breeder pioneers remaining after the spate of early retirements and golden handshakes following the first of the cutbacks of the Thatcher administration, Peter Hargreaves was the undisputed doyen. Not only was every minute of his normal working day totally consumed in frenetic activity; much of his leisure time was also spent in the same laboratory he worked in during the day.

His work was of a complex and fascinating nature in the Fuel Reprocessing Plant at Dounreay, researching and refining the intricacies of the solvent extraction process. Dounreay was unique, not only in the UK but in Europe, in that it had been designed to be as self sufficient as possible, and was the only nuclear plant which could accomplish virtually its own entire fuel cycle on site. Only the final separation and manufacture of the actual fuel rods was beyond their capacity to handle.

The seventy-eight fuel assemblies used at the core of the fast breeder reactor each contain three hundred and twenty-five individually sealed pins of plutonium and uranium oxide in a highly stable ceramic form. These pins, or rods, undergo extensive changes during the fission process and as a result of the effects of neutron bombardment. The volume of the fuel alters and distortions in the geometry of the stainless steel cladding appear in the fuel pins. As a result of this, each assembly has to be removed after only 10 per cent of the available fuel has been consumed. Reprocessing then takes place.

The first stage is to reduce the enormous amount of fission heat built up. The rods are allowed to stand for a month under sodium in a fuel store in the reactor.

Further reductions in heat take place in sodium-cooled post-irradiation caves. These are heavily shielded compartments where the highly radioactive materials can be safely stored and worked on by sophisticated remote control methods. After six months of this secondary cooling stage, the ends of each assembly are cut off remotely by laser, and the main assembly is cleansed of sodium deposits.

Only then can they be safely transferred, in large, heavily shielded flasks, to the reprocessing plant. There they are put into fuel disassembly caves, where the outer casing is cut away by laser and the exposed rods are individually extracted and cropped into little pieces ready for dissolving in highly concentrated nitric acid. All operations within the orange-bathed containers are carried out by remote controls, which are partially operated by highly skilled process workers and partially by programmed microcomputers. After the acid has done its work the solutions go through an incredibly complex process of separation by filtration and centrifuge to remove the insolubles and the highly active liquid wastes, and to produce the final concentrate of plutonium nitrate for shipment to Sellafield, to complete the back-end of the fuel cycle.

Hargreaves' life's work was passed amidst the complexities of this latter chemical separation process, constantly striving for improvements, checking, analysing, putting hypotheses to the test. His work was largely based on practical experimentation, but he often made use of his local computer terminal which gave him direct access to the mainframe machine in the central computer installation. Over the years he had been responsible for many an innovation, often in collaboration with his colleagues at the Winfrith research site, which had increased efficiency and saved time and money. His laboratory notes and computer data were worth their weight in gold, if not plutonium, to any country developing a nuclear capacity.

Because of the sensitivity and importance of his work, Hargreaves had his lab situated in an area of the complex well-nigh inaccessible for anyone without the necessary identification and positive vetting clearances. In common with the handful of other top security labs, there were certain specific and secret procedures operative in addition to those in general use throughout the site.

As Mata and Kaldi sat in their small rubber dinghy gently rolling in the swell which reached right into Sandside Bay they cursed the ill luck which had condemned them to this purgatory. Neither man was used to the sea, but Kaldi in particular was beginning to get really upset with the motion.

'You alright, Kaldi?' Mata, a surly withdrawn individual, was not normally so solicitous about his companion's health. Today, however, was different. Today his life was going to depend on his partner's reactions and efficiency as much as on his own. He wanted reassuring that his mate was fit enough. 'You alright, I said?' He glowered at his fellow fisherman.

'I would have been, had this damned delay not occurred. Why the fuck did Muhsin's target have to take a sudden unscheduled holiday and throw our whole timescale out of joint?'

Had he ever seen Karyn he would not have asked such a silly question.

'Ha! You tell me, my friend. But he'd better have a very good reason for making us sit here pretending to fish for three or four hours,' he added with a wicked grin as he drew his fearsome knife across his throat.

Alan Cameron's sudden leave had, indeed, caused problems. The original plan had centred on his normal working routine.

Now, because of the uncertainty surrounding the exact timing of his interception, a few hours leeway had had to be built in. Hence Kaldi's bout of sea-sickness.

Sallal and Mushin had dropped Mata and Kaldi off at Reay at 10.00 that morning as they had made for Cameron's house. They had inflated the small assault craft, which had been painted yellow to disguise its purposeful appearance, using the Landrover's footpump. After transferring the gear on board the foursome had split up.

To begin with, the two in the boat were in quite good spirits. As neither man was comfortable on the water they had stayed in close to the shore, although their clumsy pretence at fishing would not have fooled any local who had noticed them.

'Funny kind of rock that,' remarked Kaldi.

'Whereabouts? There's rocks all around us,' Mata wasn't really all that interested.

'There. On each side of the village. The dark ones with the white speckles and the pink lines in them. They're not at all like the rocks in the pictures I took last week.'

'No? I'll take your word for it,' grunted Mata.

Kaldi had, in fact, spotted a remarkable feature of the geology of that part of the coast of Caithness. Almost uniformly the same flagstones laid down in the Old and Middle Red Sandstone or Devonian period some 350 million years ago, the coastline was interrupted for about a mile around Reay by an outcrop, known to specialists as the Appinite Suite intrusion, of older igneous rock. This Reay diorite, which in earlier days had been quarried because of its hardness for use as road metal, had been pushed to the surface during the last great mountain building era in Scotland, forcing apart the weaker layers of porous sedimentary rock above. The diorite was granite hard, having a similar mineral composition, with the quartz and felspar imparting the white speckles and pink veins in it; and its intrusion into the sandstone had probably caused the bay, in which they were, to be formed.

Had Kaldi been aware of this he would have heaved a sigh of relief as they moved further round the bay towards Dounreay and its, for their purposes, more amenable geology, a couple of hours later.

On their reconnaissance trip the previous week the Dhubatis had encountered fairly stiff currents as they had left the shelter of the main Sandside Bay and rounded the low headland to Dounreay – or, Downreay, as the older locals preferred to call it. They had allowed for this in their finalised schedule; but today, of course, they had plenty of time on their hands. It was just as well, as the current was even more contrary than usual, despite the calm day above the surface. Their sturdy little seven horse power Volvo outboard motor had to work hard. They took up position a quarter of a mile offshore.

As they went through their fishing charade again, they were spotted by John Mackay, one of the two armed security guards on duty at the back entrance to the Fuel Reprocessing Plant which was the part of the atomic complex situated closest to the perimeter fence along the foreshore.

'Would ye look at that, Graham,' he nudged his partner, and pointed out to sea.

'Headbangers!' Cunningham shook his head in disgust. 'Must be bloody foreigners.'

'You're no kidding,' chuckled Mackay. 'None of the locals would fish in these waters with all the swill this place pumps out.'

'Aye. At least they wouldn'a fish like that,' laughed Cunningham. 'They're feckless,' he added, as he saw the two men trying to disentangle their crossed lines.

'Too true, Graham. Mind you, there's nothing wrong with putting out some creels for the lobsters and crabs. I made a good few hundred out of them last season myself.'

'No doubt, John. But I'll bet you didna eat many yourself.'

'D'you think I'm daft, man? No fears. Sold them all to Neil Sinclair in Scrabster. He ships them all south.'

'Neil Sinclair? He's doing all right for himself these days. See his latest big Volvo? He must be getting a damn sight more for the lobsters down south than he's paying you for them.'

'Oh, aye, he will be, Graham. They fetch about £6 each in the season. But I heard he got the limousine for next to nothing as a backhander for investing in that new fleet of trucks of his.'

'Investing? Investing, did you say? That was all Highlands and Islands Development Board money he bought the trucks with.'

'Makes you sick, doesn't it? Because he boozes, sings the Gaelic songs and whores around with that son-of-a-bitch of a Development Officer . . . .'

'Aye; while screwing the arse off his wife behind his back,' interrupted Cunningham.

'Ach, man, you're just jealous 'cos you haven't had a go at her yourself.' Mackay allowed himself to digress.

'Too true. She's a bit of a cracker all right. Worn well for her age. Though from what I hear half the blokes in the Round Table have already had a shot at her, and there's quite a little waiting list amongst the other half.'

'Yeah. She is a bit of all right. All the good living on that fat cat's salary and expenses,' Mackay explained.

'Anyway, where was I before you so crudely interrupted me? Oh, yeah. So he wangles a massive grant of taxpayers' money for his crony and sets him up for life. Makes you sick, man.'

'And the HIDB mannie won't have done so badly out of it, either. Just wait and see. A year from now his wife will be driving around in Sinclair's Volvo, which they'll 'buy' from him for £100 just to keep it legal.'

Neither man recognised the irony of their own position. As lifelong stalwarts of the masonic order, the two retired Northern Constabulary policemen would have recoiled in self-righteous indignation at any insinuation of graft in their landing plum sinecures at Dounreay ahead of dozens of more needy local people without fat pensions to cushion them against hard times.

While the two guards were philosophising on the prevalent local view of the microeconomics of the rural north of Scotland, their attention swung away from the dinghy. They did not see Kaldi vomit his breakfast and previous night's dinner over the side. Nor did they see the flash of sunlight off Mata's mirror as he acknowledged the signal from the prehistoric standing stones on the hillside above Dounreay.

'You'll feel better after that, my friend,' Mata reassured Kaldi. 'We'll get some action now,' he added as the signal flashed over the steel sphere of the original fast breeder reactor's dome.

'Thank God for that,' said Kaldi, as he swilled some seawater round his mouth to take away the vile taste.

The two men went efficiently into the routine they had perfected off the coast of Dungoe over the past three days. They secured the rods firmly in place over the ends of the dinghy. While Kaldi lay down and wriggled into his rubber suit Mata blew up the first of the two life-size dolls, dressed it in Mata's discarded clothing and tied it down beside a rod. Then the two men changed places and repeated the performance. Once the dummies were in place, and they had thoroughly checked the gear they had taken on the dinghy in the guise of fishing baskets, they took it in turns to slip over the side into the cold waters of the Pentland Firth.

While neither of the men was fond of small boats, they were both excellent swimmers. Even so, it took just over fifteen minutes for them to arrive at the bottom of the twenty foot high rock shelf which ran along this part of the coast, and another few minutes to locate the exact point at which to start their short climb.

They stopped halfway up to stow their wetsuits in the large crevice which had been their marker, then carried on till they were at the top.

The enlargements of Kaldi's telephoto shots had revealed a number of small fissures in the otherwise solid rock and flagstone into which the electrified fence had been driven. These narrow irregular crevices, which extended under and beyond the perimeter fence into the main compound, were the results of millennia of erosion working on stress weaknesses in the rock or on joint weaknesses in the mica cementing materials which held the porous sediments together. The last great ice age was present in Caithness up to about 10,000 years ago, and its effects on the landscape were profound. It had shaped the hills and valleys, the lochs and river beds, the goes and caves of the spectacular coastline. In the period after the main effects of the predominant Scandinavian ice sheet, which pushed in from the dry ground of the North Sea area, there was a less intensive phase of local glaciation. On the fringes of this area an Arctic climate produced, amongst many other effects, frost-shattering of the fissile flagstone. It was mainly this latter phenomenon, together with the subsequent effects of high winds and seas which had produced the cracks visible through Kaldi's 400 mm lens.

Once on eye-level with the bottom of the fence the two took it in turns to slowly chip and prise away with hammer and chisel the stone bordering the crevice they had previously decided to work on. They were thankful that the fence was not patrolled in daylight, but were mindful of the fact that twenty thousand volts were on permanent guard duty.

Within half an hour, thanks to their many training sessions on the rocks of the east coast at Dungoe, the original nine inch wide crevice, which ran to a depth of about eighteen inches under the fence, was sufficently wide and deep to allow them a safe passage under the impregnable netting. From that point onwards they would be relying on suprise, speed and sheer bravado for their part of the mission to be a success.

'Helluva sultry today, John.'

'Aye; its not bad, Graham. Damn sight better than last week's night shift anyway.'

'That's for sure. Nothing worse than yon fog creepin' in from the Firth. Even gets through the old thermal underwear!'

'Hope it didn't do you any permanent damage,' chuckled Graham.

'No way,' said John boastfully. 'Take a surgeon's knife to do that,' he added, as he broke regulations by taking his cap off to wipe his bald head.

Graham Cunningham was going to add a further dubious reference to the pale scalp, when he remembered how touchy Mackay could be about this supposedly obvious manifestation of his virility.

'Better here than round there,' Cunningham nodded in the direction of the front entrance to the fuel plant, where another two guards were on duty. 'At least we've a bit of shade.'

'Yeah. Should be thankful for small mercies,' Mackay agreed.

John Mackay was to get no more small mercies that day. Before he or Cunningham could free their Webleys from their black hide waist holsters they were looking down the muzzles of the twin Heckler and Koch P5A3 sub-machine guns so favoured by Britain's own SAS and capable of firing six hundred and fifty rounds per minute. Their arms froze over their now freely perspiring heads as the two swarthy terrorists, who had suddenly materialised from under the ground, ran towards them.

'We will have no hesitation in killing you if necessary.'

Kaldi's carefully learned English phrase had a tone which left no room for doubt about its sincerity.

'Inside. Now,' he commanded.

As the four figures passed through the rear entrance door they were clearly seen by George Williams on monitor three of the bank of closed-circuit TV screens which covered the fuel reprocessing plant. The intentions of the two armed men in combat gear could only be guessed at. Williams' duty, however, was clear, and had been rehearsed often enough in simulation sessions, though never for real. He simultaneously activated the alarm system within the building and the signal which alerted Iain Wallace, Head of Security, at the central security block.

When the lights from the FRP flashed in an irregular pattern and the klaxon sounded on Wallace's console he had two jeeps roaring towards the Plant within forty seconds. Their screaming engines and gears were swallowed in the reverberations of the Viscount as it made its first low pass over the complex.

The insistent pulsing of the electronic bleep transformed the workforce within the fuel reprocessing plant. Each area of the block was sealed off by specially trained personnel who had a security function in addition to their normal work. Critical operations and experiments continued; all routine work ceased and personnel retired to emergency quarters. Had the electronic sound signal been a continuous one, the process of evacuation would already have been under way. As it was, everyone knew that the plant was functioning normally. Security Officers dispersed themselves rapidly and purposefully about the building, each with pistol drawn and ready for use.

'Over there,' barked Kaldi, indicating the corridor that would take them to Dr. Hargreaves' lab.

Their hostages moved obediently, hands still in the air.

'Hurry!' Kaldi moved them into a fast jog.

They reached the first barrier before it had been sealed off. Mata's weapon told the young assistant scientific officer who was in the process of locking the corridor doors that he should move to the side. He did.

Two armed guards suddenly appeared coming towards them. In the narrow confines of the corridor there was no way they could get in clear shots without endangering their colleagues.

They froze in position as the terrorists approached, and threw down their weapons as Mata raised his menacingly.

'This doorway is locked. You are trapped here,' one of the guards told them, a few yards further on.

'Open it.' Kaldi's coldness cut into the guard.

'We can't,' he was told. 'It's been locked from the other side.'

Mata released a stream of high caliber bullets which had no difficulty in coping with the ludicrously simple double mortice lock. The two guards had their keys taken from them and were locked into a small side room by John Mackay.

As they hurried towards the entrance to Hargreaves' laboratory they were just in time to hear the sucking swish as the airlock on the massive lead and steel door was operated. Mata realised that an anti-tank mortar would have had no effect, let alone the toy he held in his hands at the moment. Kaldi noticed the closed circuit camera covering the area they were in. He pushed John Mackay within range of it and directed some unmistakable sign language into it.

Nothing happened.

He sent a 9mm bullet searing through Mackay's left thigh. Mackay lay writhing in agony, praying for the door to open. Then he lost consciousness as his right knee-cap was pulverised by the impact of Kaldi's second shot at point-blank range.

Kaldi waited twenty seconds. Then he splattered Mackay's skull all over the floor and door. As Mata hauled Cunningham before the blood-speckled camera lens the air rushing into the vacuum was easily audible in the tense silence following the shooting. Cunningham was prodded through the door as it swung open slowly.

Hargreaves was seated in front of a glass window set into a five foot thick concrete and lead wall, operating a remote controlled pair of PVC-encased tentacles which dangled overhead and disappeared into the shielded chamber. Through the aquarium-like window, which contained a five inch thick solution of zinc bromide giving the same level of radiation protection as the surrounding walls, he was utterly absorbed in the delicate operation. The plutonium-239 he was experimenting with had been taken straight from an irradiated fuel pin, and, at that stage, was the most highly dangerous substance known to man. One millionth of a gram would result in death by cancer, according to the usually conservative guidelines issued by the International Commission on Radiological Protection which sets the safety limits for workers in the world's nuclear industries. Some independent researchers claim the dangers to be ten times that admitted by the ICRP.

Hargreaves ignored the intruders, as he had the alarm which had signalled their presence some ninety seconds earlier.

'But Dr. Hargreaves!' pleaded Aline Macleod, the young scientific officer who worked closely with him. Her large brown eyes were wide open with horror at the sight of the armed terrorists and at the thought of what might happen to the lovely old man beside her. As if to reinforce her worst fears Kaldi prodded his gun into the base of Hargreaves' spine. He turned round reluctantly to see Mata pointing his weapon at Aline. Slowly and carefully he edged out of his seat, handing the delicate controls over to his trembling assistant as if all their lives depended on the successful transfer.

Only when he saw John Mackay's shattered remains outside the still-open air lock did Hargreaves begin to comprehend the gravity of the situation.

The security officers in position between the lab and the exit knew that they could not get involved in a shoot-out with the terrorists. Even to delay them further would probably cause the death of at least one more of the hostages.

The front exit from the fuel reprocessing plant was ringed by guards. Using their human shields, Kaldi and Mata emerged into the bright sunlight and headed straight for the two security jeeps. One of the guards, in an effort to break up the small group and offer clear targets, released his two straining Doberman Pinschers. They only got a little more than halfway before one of them was dropped on the spot, while the headless carcass of the other tottered on a few extra yards. Dogs are excellent against weekend CND or Friends of the Earth protestors, but their snarlings come to nothing against the venomous wall of lead spat out by German assault weapons at the speed of sound.

Within seconds the group was at the vehicles. Kaldi shot up one of them and climbed behind the wheel of the other.

Mata forced Hargreaves into the back, then joined him, keeping Cunningham as a buffer between himself and the guards. As the jeep lurched forward in the direction of the runway, the colour slowly returned to the ashen-faced Cunningham as he realised his part in the ordeal was over.

Greene lowered the undercarriage and reduced thrust, rechecking his instruments for three greens. As he came in to land he could see the JCBs and dumper-trucks on the eastern approach. He broke into a cold sweat for the first time when he realised the amount of usable runway still in operation. He might well have been telling the truth earlier on.

As Kirsty and Hurion braced themselves for the touchdown the plane's nose lifted abruptly as the runway ran past underneath.

'What the hell,' Hurion exploded. 'I warned you not to try anything on.'

'Didn't you see the vehicles at the top of the slope?' Greene yelled back at him. 'I could never have stopped her going down that incline. I'll try in the opposite direction.'

Hurion cursed the informant who omitted the details of the slope in the runway and the position of the construction vehicles vis-à-vis the approach. He also cursed himself for not noticing it on his reconnaissance visit. The entire plan might have aborted there and then due to such an oversight.

Greene took the Viscount on a low looping circuit around the nuclear plant. As he approached the runway for the second time he dropped his airspeed to the point of stalling and got the wheels down on the first available foot of concrete. The slight slope worked with his perfect timing, and, as the collection of jeeps and Landrovers rushing to the scene flashed by, Greene knew he was going to make it comfortably. The cumbersome construction vehicles began lumbering off the section under repair like so many dinosaurs startled in their grazing by one of Von Daniken's fanciful flying saucers.

Without being told, Greene turned the plane to face back down the slope for takeoff.

As the Landrover carrying Cameron, Karyn and Brocklehurst barrelled along the main road and came in sight of Dounreay the Viscount roared past just over their heads. It had veered inland and come round the low hill behind the USAF base to avoid not only the radar but a visual sighting from the small station at Saint Margaret's.

'There she goes!' yelled Sallal, as if the driver had failed to notice the noise and turbulence which had almost swept him off the road.

'I didn't think it was a golden eagle, you jackass!' Muhsin actually grinned at Sallal. 'We're not too far behind schedule, thank fuck.'

He accelerated rapidly out of the last bend before the nuclear station.

'What the . . . . ' Muhsin shouted as the plane, which had almost touched down, suddenly overflew the landing strip.

'It's OK,' roared Sallal, as they came into view of the construction vehicles and saw the plane bank into a tight turn to come in from the other direction.

'Is he going to get down at all, Sallal?'

'He'd fucking better! I don't fancy driving all the way home in this.'

By now the security forces at Dounreay were coming alive after the initial warning they had got from Wick Air Traffic Control. They were in the very act of closing the main gates as Muhsin threw the vehicle across the road into the wide sweeping entrance. Fortunately the gates were of a very light, flimsy construction. The Landrover scraped through with only the loss of the front nearside wing, which was a fibreglass replacement one and not the original steel, as the guards belatedly went for their weapons.

Muhsin gunned the souped-up engine to its limits and raced towards the top of the slope, overtaking the fire tender and ambulance on the runway as he did so. An organised pandemonium had broken out in the plant. In addition to the emergency vehicles, three other security jeeps were converging on the runway. They were just beaten there by the Viscount, which began braking almost before all the wheels were down.

Muhsin, with his greater initial momentum, roared past them all, almost catching up on the plane itself. As he slewed to a halt and spun a uey on the handbrake, he and Sallal were out of their seats in an instant and had their hostages lined up in front of the Landrover. This part of the exercise had been, like the rest, scrupulously rehearsed during the weeks at Dungoe. Sallal covered the hostages. Muhsin stood to the side of them, gun cradled in one arm while the loudhailer was held in his free hand. As it was, with the Viscount negotiating a well-nigh impossible 180 degree turn on the narrow tarmac, the seven watt electronic megaphone was lost in the plane's sound waves.

The security guards, however, did not have to be told what was happening. They contented themselves for the time being with encircling the Viscount and the small group clustered beside the Landrover.

The Viscount had just completed its turn at the top of the runway, with the Landrover containing the hostages drawing up beside it, as Halled and Yahya approached. One of the security jeeps came at them and four armed officers jumped out; but, on seeing Sir James covered by both terrorists, they hesitated. That moment's hesitation was fatal. It gave the stolen jeep, driven by Kaldi, time to mow into the small group of guards, killing one of them outright and maiming the others. Before Mata could even sight on the two squirming on the ground from the back of the jeep, Yahya had leapt forward and shot them both.

'Run, you old dog!' Halled screamed at Sir James, as Kaldi began reversing towards them, burning rubber all the way. He squeezed the wheezing elder statesman into the front, wedging him between Kaldi and himself. Yahya jumped into the back beside Mata and Hargreaves.

Having witnessed this carnage in a few split seconds, there was no further attempt by any of the other security officers to prevent Kaldi roaring over to join Sallal and Muhsin who had, by this time, assembled their group of hostages out in the open, awaiting transfer to the plane.

The rear passenger exit in the Viscount opened to reveal a nervous looking Kirsty Falconer. Behind her, Kalil, Hurion's sidekick, was busy fastening one end of the rope ladder, which had accounted for the bulk in his rucksack, to the metal frame of one of the seats. He finished in seconds and passed the ladder to the stewardess who let it drop to the tarmac.

Sallal was up the swaying steps in a flash. Muhsin passed up the box of handcuffs from the back of the Landrover which would be used to secure each hostage to a different row of seats within the plane, followed by the boxes of explosives and paraphernalia, then quickly joined Sallal, who was covering the group on the ground. Muhsin moved further into the plane and watched the stewardess and First Officer in turn as Kalil strapped them in their seats.

Next, Cameron and Brocklehurst slowly made their way up as Mata held the bottom of the ladder as taut as possible. Cameron and Brocklehurst refused the outstretched hand of Sallal at the top; but Hargreaves was only too glad of the proffered assistance. He was hauled aboard, badly scraping his shin in the process, and passed inside.

Kaldi and Mata were up next, leaving only four to come. It was obvious that Sir James Gartshore who by now was suffering badly from exertion and excitement, was going to need quite a bit of assistance to cope with the small, but very awkward, ascent. Mata and Kaldi knelt in the opening and leaned over to take an arm as Halled braced his shoulders beneath Sir James's ample posterior. They inched him up a rung at a time, and, with considerable effort, took him aboard.

The surrounding guards were itching to have a go as the group on the ground dwindled to just Yahya and Karyn; but the sight of the Arab's knife posed over the girl's left breast to carry out a radical mastectomy without anaesthetic, and his Ruger pointing at Sir James's unmissable back, restrained them. Karyn, who was beginning to shiver in the shade of the plane, assumed she would be last up after all the terrorists were aboard. She contemplated darting beneath the fuselage out of range of the gunmen and running to the safety of the nearest security vehicle. With Sir James held in the doorway with a gun at his head, however, Yahya was safe on the ground on his own; and Karyn was ordered up the ropeway as the leering gunman enjoyed the view of her naked body up her dress. As soon as Yahya had climbed up and was safely on, Sir James was pulled away from the exit and the door was slammed shut and locked.

Up front in the cockpit Hurion settled himself into the seat vacated by David Grant, the First Officer.

'I think you know what you have to do, Captain,' he told Greene, who had enjoyed a grandstand view of the last two minutes' carefully choreographed mayhem.

Five hundred metres down the slope, with the air-speed indicator coming up nicely, he was forced to brake furiously as the two Buccaneer strike jets, which had been scrambled from RAF Lossiemouth on the east coast the second the alarm was given and it had appeared that Dounreay was a likely target, screamed into his vision and came in to land towards them.

'Keep going!' Hurion shouted at the Captain. 'They'll not risk a collision!'

But it was too late. Greene had already, by his initial braking, aborted the take-off. Being short of runway, there was no way he could regain sufficient speed for take-off.

'You fool!' Hurion turned on Greene as the Buccaneers, who

had practised this overshoot manoeuvre hundreds of times at Lossiemouth and at Wick civil aerodrome – to the supreme annoyance of the local inhabitants – swooped up and over them as their wheels were within inches of the ground.

'I told you to do exactly as I said.' The snarl was accompanied by a wave of the AK.

'I'm sorry. But your voice registered a millisecond after the Buccaneers. I reacted instinctively.'

Hurion knew that the Captain was speaking the truth, and that he was not being deliberately provocative.

'I'll just try again.'

'Right. And this time, no matter what, keep going.'

'Roger.' Greene acknowledged sarcastically.

He disarmed the anti-skid facility on the braking system and accelerated the right-side engines. Keeping the left side at idling speed, and using the toe-operated section at the top of the rudder pedal to brake the left mainwheel, he rotated the tiller-steered nosewheel to execute the left-hand turn which would take him back up the runway. He had just completed the same procedure at the top of the thirty-one metre wide runway when the Buccaneers returned. One of them repeated the earlier manoeuvre, only this time it did touch down, forced by its greater speed to use part of the starter extension to the runway, and screamed to a halt right in front of the Viscount. The other fighter maintained a tight orbit overhead.

'What now?' Greene asked.

'Raise him on the radio.'

Greene, who had flown the corridor into Berlin on numerous occasions, was well-versed in the procedures for making radio contact with fighters. He had always assumed that it would be a MiG 23 or Sukhoi 15 belonging to the Soviet bloc, however, and not one of his own country's strike planes that he would be involved with. At any rate the procedure, which was laid down identically in every manual of every international airline company in the world, was the same.

He switched to 121.5 megahertz, the VHF distress frequency which the RAF pilot read on its first harmonic, 243 MHz. The response from Wing Commander Bert McAdie in the grounded Buccaneer was instant; though, of course, the civilian pilot cound not hear the UHF reply. This was of no concern to

Hurion, who delivered one terse message.

'We have seven civilian hostages on board apart from the pilot. If you do not clear our path and airspace for take-off in thirty seconds you will observe one of them lying dead on the runway. The rest will follow at further intervals of thirty seconds. The responsibility is yours,' Hurion added just before he switched off, fully aware that the Buccaneer pilot would know that their conversation was being picked up by the American spy satellite hovering one hundred miles overhead and recorded at the nearby Forss base. It would be produced at any subsequent enquiry or court martial into the RAF pilot's conduct, and would help to clear him. Hurion checked his watch.

Forty seconds elapsed with the Buccaneer still in place. He shouted some instructions in Arabic to Muhsin.

Karyn was released and dragged to the front exit hatch which Halled opened. He had been right earlier on that day. Karyn was going to come in useful; though not in the way he had hoped.

'Don't do it, you motherfuckers!' yelled Cameron hysterically as he launched himself from his seat. Even before the handcuff jerked him to a halt, Yahya had him pinned in a head-chancery and forced his face up against the window to witness the scene.

Karyn looked pleadingly at Muhsin. He hesitated for a fraction of a second as Hurion gave him a curt nod; then sent a bullet searing through the back of her neck up into her cranium, pushing her forward with his free hand as he did so. As the first woman he had ever loved thudded onto the ground and lay there spreadeagled in a pool of blood, Alan threw up all over himself. Yahya released him with a curse and he slumped back into his seat sobbing uncontrollably.

Wing Commander McAdie's first instinct, as he watched in suspended nightmarish horror, was to blow the Viscount into the other side of oblivion with a blast of 68mm rockets from his 18-tube launchers and to hell with the consequences. His years of highly disciplined training, however, took over as Kirsty Falconer's head appeared through the hatchway a few seconds later; and he turned his fearsome fighting machine round to make way for the ungainly Viscount which straddled over the girl's corpse like a gigantic vulture.

Hurion prodded a stunned and seething Captain Greene into action.

'Glasgow,' barked Hurion, as Greene hauled the Viscount into the air.

Greene, still climbing, banked to the left and headed almost due south. Visibility was truly excellent. There was no need to request the assistance of his First Officer.

The Buccaneers were instantly alongside, slightly above and behind the cockpit of the Viscount. They gave Lossiemouth an update, then began routine communications with Inverness, Rannoch, Glasgow Approach and Glasgow Tower at the regular reporting points on the straight route south.

Within minutes Glasgow, Prestwick and Edinburgh airports were on full alert as the three most likely destinations within the Viscount's remaining fuel range.

14

Consider Your Ways

GEORGE Taylor eased on the massive air brakes of the thirty ton Volvo articulated lorry and operated the electric window on his mate's side of the luxurious cab. Dan Stimson handed over his documentation – ID cards and security clearances, vehicle particulars and documents, details and timings of cargo, route and destination – to the approaching security officers, whose guns were clearly displayed at their sides. They had all gone through this process with one another many times before, yet each stage was closely scrutinised. Finally, Ted Smith gave his partner a nod, the massive gates opened noiselessly, and Stimson got his documents back. Taylor chose second gear on the big semi-automatic ten speed selector, and moved slowly in behind the waiting police escort of six armed officers on their powerful BMW 1000cc motorbikes.

'Great way to travel that,' said Stimson, nodding at the big two wheelers. 'Bet these ones can go, eh, George?'

'Don't know that I'd be too comfortable on one of them, Dan.'

'Right enough,' agreed his mate, who knew George's weight to be around seventeen stones. 'Never try one when you were younger?'

'Nah. Could never afford anything like that when I was a youngster. Not like those bloody yuppies who tear up and down the motorways these days. Anyway, you get a better view from up here.'

'Not to mention a bigger seat,' added Dan, ducking the feinted forearm smash.

Two of the bikes took up the rear and the small convoy started off.

George had driven over this road dozens of times. Normally he enjoyed this narrow, twisting, fifty mile stretch to Carlisle with its unexpected blind spots and sudden steep gradients. This was what professional driving was all about. Anyone could steer it along in top gear at 55 mph on a motorway; but here, George was in his element.

Normally. Today, he was, not unnaturally, quite tense. He had risked not only his job, but a spell in jail for having given details of the journey to the students. Still, it would be quite harmless, as Raqia had promised him. Probably a handful of pimply youths, with college scarves around their necks so that everyone would know they were at university, waving placards at them as they inched through the tiny streets of Keswick or some other place. And the authorities would never trace it back to George anyway. He would never be suspected of mixing with student types. They would probably zone in on some of the young scientists fresh out of college if there was going to be any kind of an enquiry.

Shit, he thought. I shouldn't have blabbed so much about Beth and Raqia to the lads — not that any of them believed me anyway.

But he had not been able to resist it. Anyway there would be no reason for a post-mortem at all. Just a few kids with banners. Probably would not even hit the Cumberland News let alone the national dailies if the Establishment had its way.

About ten miles short of Wigton on the A596 George's already disjointed thoughts were shattered completely.

The four leading motorcycles had disappeared round a double S-bend on a fairly steep up-gradient when he and Dan heard a burst of what were unmistakably shots. George came out of the second part of the bend at about 15 mph and was just able to stop before crushing the two rear machines which lay on their sides, spinning rear wheels blowing dust from the rough road surface.

'Fuckin' hell,' shouted Dan, as George instinctively operated the cab's electronic locks as he jammed on the brakes, stalling the engine in the process.

Neither could believe what they saw. Twenty yards ahead a Ford Transit minibus was side-on blocking the entire road. One of the policemen was lying screaming on the steeply sloping grass verge with blood pouring from a gaping leg wound. The other three were already being disarmed by a couple of young men in combat gear, while a third was covering them with a sub-machine gun.

As the two police in the rear tried to squeeze past the huge trailer on the right hand side to assist their colleagues, two more men appeared from behind the dry-stone dyke about two yards off the road. One of the escort scrambled to get his Smith and Wesson .38 hand-gun and was instantly sent spinning into the shallow ditch with a 9mm bullet lodged in his right shoulder. The other one was quickly disarmed and taken to join the group at the front.

In the space of these few seconds George Taylor could do nothing apart from sit tight. Dan Stimson had activated the emergency radio transmitter which was monitored thirty miles back along the road at Sellafield. Within seconds every police unit between there and Carlisle would be alerted, and reinforcements would be on the way. Inside the purpose built cab they were quite safe, surrounded by bullet proof glass and lightly armoured steel plating.

'Fucking bastarding students,' George muttered.

'You what?' Stimson exclaimed. 'Some bloody students, with sub-machine guns and automatic pistols!'

'Forget it,' growled George. 'For God's sake forget I ever said that, Dan, d'you hear?'

'What now then, mate? Any chance of reversing?'

'You've got to be joking. We'd be off the road within a few yards.'

'Maybe that would be a good idea, considering what we're carrying.'

'Christ, Dan, you're right! Its the fucking plutonium they're after!'

Before George could even press the electronic ignition button one of the terrorists ran to the front of the truck pointing a

30mm anti-tank mortar through the windscreen at him.

'Jesus, George! He's got a bloody bazooka!' yelled Stimson. 'Don't move!'

George had no thoughts of a hero's death. He removed his hand from the starter button.

The sideways movement of the mortar and the guerrilla's head told George and Dan to come out of the cab.

'Nothing else for it, Daniel. I always said we should have a helicopter escort as well for this fucking stuff. Not our fault if those yobbos in security don't know their jobs.'

Once on the ground beside the four able-bodied policemen, the small group of prisoners were left in no doubts as to what was happening. Two of the terrorists stood guard over them. The other four raced into the Transit and came out with two large kit-bags.

They proceeded at tremendous speed to place large quantities of plastic explosives and detonators all around the enormous metal container marked 'RADIOACTIVE' on top of the Volvo's trailer, ignoring the steel superstructure surrounding it and keeping it in place. The seams and lock on the container were given special attention. The leads were taken into the driver's cab.

The six policemen and Dan Stimson were bundled into the rear of the minibus after having hoods placed over their heads and hands handcuffed behind their backs. The two wounded officers were allowed to keep their hands free. Two of the terrorists occupied the front of the minibus, with two in the rear keeping their guns on automatic, ready for instant action.

Kassim, the swarthy muscular one who had been doing most of the wiring, climbed into the cab holding the trigger mechanism which would blow everything sky-high. He held it in one hand with the nonchalance of the psychopath as he invited George Taylor to join him in the cab with a wave of the assault rifle he clutched in the other.

The oldest of the group righted the leading motorbike and switched on the two-way radio.

'Get this and get it straight,' Khan said in heavily accented and deliberate English. 'We have taken over the plutonium consignment headed for Carlisle. We have eight hostages, two of them already badly wounded. The cargo has been thoroughly and expertly booby-trapped. We demand safe and speedy conduct North. Do not attempt to stop us. Our lives are valueless – those of your citizens are not. If we go, the plutonium goes, together with half a million of your people.'

Without bothering to switch off the transmitter he trundled the motorbike over to the grass verge and cleared the other bikes off the road. As he sprang up into the cab and took the window seat the reformed convoy set off.

In the few seconds during which the action had taken place, not one word of command had been given or taken by anyone. A well rehearsed drill had obviously been taking place.

Woman Police Constable Jane Ashley was about to take her mid-afternoon coffee break when the communications room in which she worked crackled with an intensity she had never before witnessed. In the space of ninety seconds the alert from Sellafield was followed by the shattering news from the terrorists. Her switchboard, like that of every police station from there to the central belt of Scotland would remain in a state of crisis for the next five or six hours.

'What's on the night, then, Sam?'

'Aw, nuthin' special, Spike. Me an' the burd are jeest goin' tae the pitchers fur a wee change.'

'What's up? Fed up wi' the dancin', like? Gawd, son, when ah wus your age me and the wife – well, she wisnae the wife then, like – we wis niver away fae the jiggin'.' Bill Robertson got up from his packing case and did a wee twist to emphasise the point.

'Away wi' ye, grampa!' Drew McColl howled in laughter.

Spike Robertson was a bit put out at this.

'What the hell ur ye laffin' at, Sam? Ye're jeest jealous that you cannae move like this.'

'Jealous, Twinkle-Toes? Of what? Anyway, ya daft ol' bugger, they don't dance like that nowadays any more.'

'Naw. More's the pity. Aw this shooder shruggin' and heid boppin'. Youse huvnae a clue you youngsters,' mocked Robertson, shuffling round a couple of boxed freight containers.

'Aw ah don't know about that, Spike. It's a different fashion noo, that's all. Anyway, as ah said, ah'm jeest goin' tae the pitchers the night.'

'Nae imagination. Christ son, ye should be dumpin' that lassie — whit's that, two years ye've been goin' oot wi hur noo? — and goin' oot oan the randan yersel'. Ah'm tellin' ye; wi' your pecker an' ma personality ah'd show ye how tae hit Glesca on a Friday night.'

'Doan't feel sorry fur me, Spike,' Drew grinned contentedly. 'Ah'm doin' all right fur mahself. Ye doan't go short wi' a burd like Michelle.'

'Probably not, ya' young rascal. Anyway, ah wis only jokin'. Ye've got good taste, son, ah'll tell ye that. She's a bit of all right, your Michelle. By the way, does she call ye' "Sam" as well?'

'Naw.' McColl switched to his poshest west-end Glasgow. 'I get my full title from her. Andrew.'

'Get away! Andrew?' Robertson had a good belly laugh. 'How did ye get a nickname like "Sam" anyway, son. Ah mean, there's nuthin' wrong wi' Drew.'

'You should talk, Spike. It's becos ah hit the ball so hard at fitbaw. You know, surface-to-air-missile. S.A.M. Sam. Ah got it in the third year at John Street in the Modern Studies class. Sorto' stuck wi' it noo. Anyway, what about "Spike". How'd you get lumbered wi' . . . .'

The emergency bleepers in their breast pockets ended their conversation abruptly.

They flicked on.

'All security personnel to my office immediately. I repeat. All security personnel to my office immediately.' The voice was Jim Anderson's, Head of Security at Glasgow Airport. The tone was unmistakably urgent, if not a bit panicky.

Sam and Spike were not used to such interruptions. Like many security officers at provincial airports their jobs were intensely demanding on paper but invariably boring in practice. The constant vigilance which they were supposed to maintain against thieves, smugglers, hijackers and terrorists never usually amounted to more than escorting the odd football drunk out of the terminal buildings after a Rangers or Celtic supporters' charter had returned from Europe. Most of their day and night shifts consisted of a series of cursory checks around the passenger and freight buildings at regular intervals. They had long since reduced this to a routine designed to interfere as little as possible with their chats, tea-breaks, papers, darts and pool. They were a couple of skivers.

'Must be a Civil Defence exercise or something, Sam.'

'Yeh, Spike. Better look smart anyway.'

Two minutes later the duo assembled with the other fourteen officers on duty in the central security suite.

'What the hell took you buggers so long? Don't you know we've got an emergency on here?' There was no way they could have known. Anderson was obviously rattled.

Yep. He's definitely on edge, thought Drew McColl. Wonder what's up?

'I'll put you into the picture right away, lads. The Manager's just had all Section Heads into his office. Five minutes ago he was contacted personally by Group Captain Forrester from RAF Lossiemouth. A Viscount has just been hi-jacked on the Kirkwall-Wick run. There's been some sort of a terrorist raid on Dounreay, and the plane is now flying south with a number of hostages on board. Two of his Buccaneers are escorting the Viscount. They're headed in this direction, and it's a reasonable bet that they'll put down here, if only to re-fuel.'

There was a chorus of mutterings from the security officers. So something was happening at last.

'This could be the big one, lads. We're the first major airport on its flightpath. Anyway, we have to act as if the damned thing is going to come down here. It's cruising at 240 knots, 8000 feet. It left Dounreay at 12.45, so it'll be in our vicinity within forty, forty-five minutes from now. We'll have to get cracking.'

'The Old Man,' he referred to Clive Richards the Airport Manager, 'has already set the ball rolling. Air Traffic has been alerted to reschedule or divert all arrivals and departures over the next two hours. He wants all runways cleared. Passenger and Information are taking care of the necessary announcements and bus transport arrangements for travellers affected. We'll have to evacuate all passengers from the terminal building in case things get nasty, and all non-essential office and catering staff. That'll be you and your squad's responsibility, McLaren.'

'Right, sir.'

'Freight. Nothing new gets in through the gates. Robertson, you and your sub-section can deal with that. Anything already loaded onto vans or lorries can leave. But make it snappy. Otherwise, have all staff and outside personnel evacuated from the freight terminal and warehouses in twenty minutes from now. Understood?'

'Yes, sir. But won't it take longer to organise the movement of vehicles? These artics . . . . .'

'Damn it, man. Who cares about lorries. Get the bloody people out.'

'OK, sir.'

'Now you all know the drills, lads. I'm depending on you for the smooth running of this operation. Any questions?'

'Just one, chief,' Ron Weir piped up. 'Presumably these hijackers are armed?'

'Of course they're bloody well armed. How the fuck do you get hold of a plane and a dozen top scientists otherwise?'

Anderson really was wound up. It was the first time any of the men had heard him use the Anglo-Saxon expletive.

'And, what's more, they're prepared to use them. Five security boys and two civilians dead at Dounreay and Wick already. The bastards. Get this straight, Weir, and the rest of you.' He glowered round the room. 'This isn't a civil defence exercise. They're not playing games. This is for real.'

'What are they using, then, sir,' Alex Jordan asked.

'How the hell should I know? Mls, AK47s, Hecklers? What's the difference?'

'Well, with all due respect, sir,' Jordan continued, 'our Webleys aren't going to be much good against that sort of fire-power.'

'Of course, you're correct, Alex.' Anderson was beginning to level off. 'A detachment of infantry is being mustered right now at Dreghorn Barracks. Should be here within the hour.

Let's be clear, lads,' Anderson could see that some of his men, like young McColl, were looking a bit anxious, 'our job is just to contain things till the big boys get here. The regular army will supply whatever fire-power proves necessary. We won't be mixing it with these Arabs unless there's absolutely no alternative.'

McColl wasn't reassured. And Michelle wasn't going to like getting stood up.

'OK, then, lads. Let's get on with it.'

'Just where they should be, sir.' The excitement in Douglas Bremner's voice in the Glasgow ATC Tower was barely controlled. Under normal circumstances and weather the Viscount would have been flying above cloud on IFR, instrument flight rules, and would have to be regulated by ATC Glasgow backed up by approach radar. On this unusually fine day, however, the hi-jacked aircraft was flying under VFR, visual flight rules, and was keeping ground-control guessing as to its intentions by maintaining radio silence. The Buccaneers, of course, were communicating navigational data routinely, but lacked civilian radio for direct contact.

'240 knots, level at eight zero,' Bremner continued. 'Distance to run, 40 nautical miles.'

'Fine,' replied John Ritchie, the Chief Controller on duty. 'Let me know the instant their flight level alters, Dougie.'

Richie turned to the other ATCs at their computerised screens.

'What else do we have on the go?'

'Two flights cleared for take-off,' Rognvald Brown told him.

'Surface wind?'

'Northerly at one five knots.'

'OK. Proceed. But don't hang about. The last thing we want is traffic on the runway if our visitors do decide to drop in.'

'Right, sir.' Brown issued rapid instructions to the two pilots at their holding points.

'Incoming traffic?' Ritchie wanted to know.

'Quite a lot on the go, John,' his second-in-command, Senior

Controller Andrew Grieve, told him calmly. Glancing round the monitors, he read off the essential coded details which signified direction automatically to the ATCs.

'NW 035; Boston; level at four one zero; distance to run 120 nautical miles; commencing descent.'

'UAL 938; La Guardia; level at three three zero; distance to run 80 nautical miles.'

'SN 691; Brussels; level at one eight zero; distance to run 60 nautical miles.'

'UK 825; Amsterdam; level at nine zero; distance to run 35 nautical miles.'

'BA 4902; Heathrow; level at four five; distance to run 15 nautical miles.'

'BD 006 . . . . .'

'Right. Thanks, Drew.' Ritchie thought of bringing the last one in as it was less than four minutes from final approach, but decided against.

'Sir!' It was young Bremner. 'Viscount and escorts down to level six zero. They're definitely coming in!'

'Better divert them all. Prestwick and Edinburgh? I'll leave the details to you, Drew.'

Ritchie glanced at Bremner's screen. 30 nautical miles to run. Nine minutes to touch-down.

'It would be nice to keep them as far out on the runway area as possible. Give the army boys a better chance to go into action. Try to raise them again on the radio, Dougie.'

It was a forlorn hope. Hurion was obstinately refusing even to acknowledge, let alone reply.

'Glasgow Approach to tango four three. Glasgow Approach to tango four three.' Bremner momentarily forgot that the RAF aircraft could not be reached directly.

'No use trying to raise the Buccaneers, son,' the Chief reminded the lad.

At this very moment Wing Commander McAdie's fighter buzzed low over Glasgow Tower on his own recce to check his instincts once he knew the Viscount was going in. He was still livid at the image of Karyn lying like a limp rag doll on the tarmac at Dounreay. He knew where he wanted to put the bastards down. Any fucking where.

He noted with approval that Glasgow's active runway and its

holding areas were clear, and that security vehicles were already on their way out to block off the approaches to the terminal buildings. Guessing that the Viscount was still flying in silence, he returned alongside and gave Greene the thumbs-up to indicate all was well for his approach.

Captain Greene was familiar enough with Glasgow's simple layout not to need more specific instructions. He came down low over Kirkintilloch and Bearsden, and touched down without incident. After Dounreay, he would never again worry about a landing.

The Buccaneers shadowed the Viscount all the way down and along to the end of the runway, keeping it in their sights all the time. Two dark blue airport security Landrovers were already in position.

'Rather obvious of them, Captain?' Hurion asked rhetorically. 'Isolating us out here until the army arrives, hoping we make some elementary mistake.' Hurion was under no illusions as to the way things were going to develop. 'I think until our little surprise package arrives we shall be in a stronger bargaining position over beside the terminal.'

Greene took the Viscount through 180 degrees and slowly moved forwards, only to find the Landrovers blocking his path.

'Not more silly heroes.' Hurion shook his head. 'Get me the control tower, Captain.'

'We have them now, sir,' Bremner announced his triumphant breakthrough in communications to Ritchie.

Ritchie grabbed the microphone, but before he could utter a word, Hurion was giving his usual crisp orders after his uncharacteristic asides to Greene.

'Order your security vehicles to clear our path to the terminal buildings.'

'Would it not be easier and safer for you to carry out whatever negotiations you have in mind in the open, as you are?' asked Ritchie.

'Control, my patience is being sorely tried. You will do as I say. Captain Greene's life is now expendable. I have sufficient experience to carry out the necessary manoeuvres myself.'

Ritchie did not doubt this for one second. Jim Anderson got his orders instantly.

'As you say. You will be able to proceed in a few seconds.'

Greene took the Viscount slowly across.

'Thank you, Captain. You will now join the others.' Hurion personally ushered Greene through. 'All hostages will remain strapped in. I do not expect us to be here too long, so you should not be too uncomfortable.'

Just over an hour later the 1st Bn.Queen's Own Highlanders (Seaforth and Camerons) arrived in convoy from their Edinburgh barracks where they were serving as the current public duties regiment. They took up position in a semi-circle around the Viscount, as the Buccaneers went off to refuel and await further orders.

Hurion, however, took hardly any notice. He had broken off all radio contact with the control tower, and was playing a waiting game of nerves with the authorities.

The 22nd Special Air Services headquarters at Bradbury Lines in Hereford had been alerted as soon as the incident at Wick Airport had taken place.

Major Jeremy K A Winthrop was proud of his little group in this quiet rural part of southern England. And so he should have been. The SAS, as it was known, was *the* crack commando group in the British armed forces. In fact, even its rivals in other national armies secretly acknowledged it as the best such force anywhere in the world. His men were the elite of several branches of Her Majesty's Service.

Originally formed in 1942 in North Africa and disbanded at the end of WW2, the SAS was restarted in Malaya in 1950. It evolved into its modern format in 1952 when the British were involved in an acrid, no-holds-barred struggle with guerrillas in Aden; and since then has seen action in many parts of the world. They had fought in Cyprus, Kenya, Malaysia, and in numerous small conflicts remote from the headlines in areas like Borneo and the Arabian sub-continent where British interests were involved.

On occasion, individual members of the SAS had been seconded to foreign governments when their very special expertise had been needed. They had been into Entebbe in Uganda with Israeli commandos in 1976. They had assisted the Dutch in freeing a trainload of hostages from South Moluccan terrorists in 1977; and later that same year two of their number had helped out GSG-9, West Germany's new elite stormtroopers, when they flew into Mogadishu in Somalia to recapture a hijacked airliner with top German government hostages on board. In 1978 Major Winthrop himself had led the French Groupe Speciale when they had freed the President's wife from her kidnappers in Chad; and not, as some French cartoonists at the time had said, freed the kidnappers from the President's wife.

Once the shadowy, top-secret, undercover elite of the British army, they had hit the headlines in London in 1980 when they had stormed the Iranian Embassy and freed the twenty-six hostages on live television news coverage. They were a household name from that night on, and became legendary during the Falklands War in 1982 when they had penetrated behind Argentinian lines along with colleagues in the Special Boat Service to operate pin-point accurate laser-beam guidance systems for incoming Vulcan and Harrier bombers.

When word had come through of the hijack from Wick, Winthrop put a dozen of his men on standby. Twelve minutes later the news from Dounreay had mobilised the entire group of twenty-eight under his immediate command, awaiting news only of the Viscount's destination before proceeding there in their own RAF Argosy.

Only ten minutes after The Highlanders had gone into battle formation, the RAF airplane carrying the world's finest anti-terrorist fighters swooped in to land at Glasgow airport.

Major Winthrop was not the most senior officer present at the airport. But no-one in the emergency operations room which the airport manager had put at the military's disposal doubted his right to lead the exercise. This was nothing new to Winthrop. He was used to command in difficult situations, though this one looked quite straightforward.

First, though, he had to get these amateurs out of the way. He could not suppress a grin at the sight of the civil aviation security officers with their old-fashioned hand weapons. And, admirable though the Seaforth and Camerons were, this was not their cup of tea either.

'Mr Anderson, I'd like your men to concentrate on the airport buildings, if you would. This damned thing is too close to the passenger and cargo facilities. I want a total evacuation now of all personnel from the main block here. The building could be badly damaged if this gets out of hand. What about the nearby cargo bays?'

'Well, when we evacuated all non-essential workers from this block,' Anderson wanted to show that he had not been entirely overwhelmed by events, 'we also cleared the warehouse of workers and some vehicles.'

'Good. Could you now arrange for all incendiary materials to be removed from the two flanking buildings? The fire boys will have enough to do here if this little lot actually does go up. Mind you, I very much doubt if it will,' he added for reassurance and with quiet confidence.

'Yes, sir.'

'Oh! And Anderson?'

'Sir?'

'No media men beyond the check-in points. They will get their information and pictures when we are ready to give it to them.'

'No problem, Major.' Although both men knew that no enterprising newsman would be deterred by this.

Jim Anderson had no quarrel with this obvious division of labour. Like the average man-in-the-street he stood in absolute awe of the SAS and their lethal 'Hockler' and Browning weapons, and was quite happy to let them get on with the dirty work.

'Colonel Thomson, sir.'

Winthrop's salute was crisp if not completely convincing, as the overweight commanding officer of the infantry detachment came in.

'Major.' Thomson's return was exemplary. 'Well then, Winthrop, what do you suggest.'

Better to have it this way, thought the Colonel, than to have the expert take over only after it was obvious that he was out of his depth.

'Thank you, sir.' Winthrop looked out askance at the squad's semi-circular convoy around the plane. There were eighty men assembled beside their trucks, with a motley selection of machine guns, two-inch and 81mm mortars, 84mm Carl Gustavs, and Wombat anti-tank gun all trained on the silent Viscount. He did not say what he was thinking.

'I don't think we'll be seeing too much action just yet, Colonel, if this situation follows anything like a normal pattern — if any such thing exists, that is. If you could spare twenty men to assist the airport police in evacuating the passenger and freight areas that would be extremely useful and should speed things up nicely. I can't think why they brought the Viscount in so close — normally they like to be out clear in the open to lessen the chance of a surprise attack. They can only be wanting to threaten the terminal in the event of a blast and hoping we've decided not to alarm passengers and staff by a premature evacuation. At any rate, I'd like your trucks to take up position between the plane and the terminal, rather than hemming it in as now. Drivers only to carry out the manoeuvre. I don't think they will be stopped. Apart from that we'll play it pretty low-key to begin with. We'll dispense with the artillery in the meantime, and have your men move off about fifty yards. My chaps may well need some supporting or distractionary fire as we move in. It might be an idea to bring a couple of dozen men into the observation lounge. They'll know when to join in the action, if there is going to be any.'

Winthrop's own 'chaps' needed no such instructions. They used old Viscounts for practice down in Hereford.

Nor had Hurion's men needed any instructions. They, too, had practised on a Viscount in Dhubat, and had rehearsed thoroughly at Dungoe for each stage of the operation. As soon as the plane was at a halt near the terminal each man went smoothly and automatically about his pre-arranged tasks.

Halled returned to the cockpit with Hurion and crouched down out of the line of fire over the controls of the portable radio transmitter and receiver they had brought on board. He was interested in the short waveband around 91.1 MHz, and would remain so over the next five hours to monitor the progress of the other part of their team.

Muhsin and Sallal had been busy on the flight down from Dounreay transforming the Viscount into a prototype V3. All they had to do now that the plane was stationary was to install the detonators and make the final connections between the plastic explosives, wires and fuses which had been placed in the most vulnerable stress points at the wing joints, fuel storage tanks, cargo hold and tail sections.

Mata and Kaldi remained in the lower section of the plane, respirator masks in position, prepared to blow the heads off anyone who tried to force an entry through the hatches in the cargo hold.

The others stayed in the passenger compartment to guard the seven hostages and keep a lookout for any movement against the plane.

Hurion greeted the roar of the descending Argosy with a smile of satisfaction and anticipation, though with a degree of puzzlement. He would have been disappointed had the British not sent their Special Air Service to deal with him. From his studies he knew to expect their presence, but did not expect to be made so publicly aware of it. Obviously the perceived gravity and urgency of the situation had called for more overt, direct tactics on this occasion, rather than the more circuitious and predictable flight into nearby Prestwick and clandestine transfer by road.

It was a source of amusement to the Dhubati leader just how speedily the SAS Major commandeered the main field of action for himself and his squad. Hurion nodded appreciatively as Winthrop's orders were carried out. He also knew what was coming next. The rush of the SAS men to the shelter of the wings and fuselage of the Viscount. The loudhailer exchanges to attempt a negotiated settlement. The two mortar explosions to blast open the hatches in the plane's under-belly, followed immediately by the blinding flash, smoke and acrid gas of the stun grenades. The murderous exchange of high caliber bullets until each of the hijackers lay dead. The SAS had no secrets from Hurion, who had studied their earlier exploits with the delight of a fellow professional.

'But not this time,' Hurion startled his companion by thinking out loud.

Yahya and Muhsin saw Captain Peters at the same time. He stepped out from behind one of the Landrovers, making no attempt to seek cover. His powerful loudhailer boomed across and into the hijacked plane.

Hurion knew this was the moment when a dozen of the SAS would be approaching the Viscount from the tail section on a direct axis with the nose – one of the several totally blind spots to those inside. He made no effort to counter this move.

'We have your plane completely surrounded.' Peters' cultured voice sounded strangely coarse as it was amplifed many times. 'You do not have sufficient fuel to leave the United Kingdom. If you surrender now, many lives will be saved, including your own.' Hurion's men knew not to expect a reply from their leader at this juncture.

Five minutes later the Captain's disjointed syllables bombarded the Viscount for a second time.

'I repeat. You are surrounded. There is no hope for escape. We can guarantee your lives if you surrender now.'

There was no sign of movement within the plane; and still no response.

'Very well. You leave us no alternative. We can wait here for days until you are too weak to resist. Then we shall take you with ease. Or we may decide to take you now, the hard way.'

Peters was going through the standard initial bluff, and he guessed that the hijackers knew it. Still, it had to be done. Peters allowed another ten minutes to drag by.

'First hijack? Our seventh,' he lied. 'We could have you out of that old sardine can in forty seconds flat.' He was only slightly exaggerating. 'Want us to try? Come now, chaps. Let's be sensible and start talking.'

Hurion knew he could safely maintain silence for several hours more without any danger of an attack. But he did not want that kind of delay. In fact, he wanted to take the psychological advantage from now on in. He took the loudhailer which Halled handed him and shattered a window in the cockpit with the butt of his AK47.

'I congratulate you and the Major on the thoroughness of your actions so far. You seem to be following your usual operational procedures in such situations. If I am correct your men are already in position beneath our cargo hatches and wing sections?' That startled a few of the SAS boys.

'Clever fucking smartass,' muttered Winthrop. He now had more than a suggestion that this was not going to be so easy after all.

'You see, gentlemen, we are not a naive group of Japanese students, nor a volatile bunch of Palestinian Liberators. We, like yourselves, are dedicated professionals. Consequently, one offensive move by any of your men and this 'sardine can' goes skyhigh and everyone in the vicinity with it. You do not have to answer to your government for my men, as you were not held to account for the needless deaths of the freedom fighters from Khuzestan who tried to surrender to you in the Iranian Embassy. But you will be asked some very searching questions about the loss of the lives of so many others, including the eminent scientists we have on board. That is,' chuckled Hurion, 'in the unlikely event that any of you survive the blast.'

'Bastards,' said Winthrop, as he too came out into the open and stood beside Peters. 'Give me the speaker, Marcus. He probably means every word of it. But at least we've got them talking now. Better get on with the charade.'

'OK. So you have decided to take the hard option. I can only repeat what the Captain has told you. In the long run you have no chance of success, as you will find out. But, as you wish.'

'Major; I have seven hostages on board. All are expendable, starting with the stewardess, until our demands are met in full.' Inside the plane Alan Cameron began an anguished wailing, much to the disgust of the terrorists. But then none of them had ever lost someone they loved more than life itself.

'First;' Hurion continued after the implications had sunk in, 'your men will retreat from their positions under the plane in full view of us. Do not worry, Major, they will not be fired on. There is too much at stake.'

'Second; we need food and drink for my men and the hostages. It will be raised to the front entrance on a forklift.'

'Third; an RAF Hercules Transporter, fully crewed, fueled and fitted with reserve tanks will be placed at my disposal within five hours for our return to Dhubat.'

'These are impossible demands, and you know it,' Winthrop bawled. 'I do not have the necessary authority to meet your third condition.'

'Do not worry, Major. You soon will have. In about ten minutes you are in for a little surprise. In the meantime, however, please comply with my first two requests.'

'What the hell is he on about?' Winthrop quizzed Peters.

'Search me, Jeremy,' his second-in-command shrugged.

'No doubt we shall soon find out. All right,' he shouted. 'You men regroup over here.'

Six SAS men came out from under the Viscount, leaving two in place beneath the cargo hold.

'All of them, Major,' Hurion played a hunch based on what he would have done in the SAS's shoes.

Winthrop signalled the other two out.

What the hell, he thought, I can easily get them in again later on.

'I suppose we had better get the cunts some eats now,' Winthrop said grudgingly to Peters in his best Berkshire accent.

Colonel Thomson himself came across the tarmac at a brisk trot. He was considerably out of breath by the time he reached Winthrop.

'Report just come in from Cumbria, Major. Might not have any bearing on our situation, but I thought you should be kept informed in any case.'

Winthrop glanced at his Rolex. It was nine minutes since his last exchange with Hurion.

'A consignment of nuclear fuel left Sellafield an hour ago. Seems it was en route to Carlisle airport for transfer to Dounreay. Anyway, the escort failed to check in ten minutes ago. Cumbria police force are investigating right now.'

Hurion's cryptic comment of ten minutes earlier now became crystal clear to Winthrop.

'I'm afraid there is a tie-in with our situation, sir.'

Winthrop filled in the Colonel on Hurion's comments.

'Good God Almighty!' Thomson exploded. 'What next?'

'Their request for a Herky Bird had better be relayed right to the top without delay, Colonel.'

'Certainly. I'll see to that personally.'

Thomson rather liked the idea of being on the other end of a direct line to the War Office, as he referred to it, and the Defence Secretary. His contacts to date through his wife's family connections were only good enough up to the rank of Colonel. He was sufficiently pragmatic to realise that for a man of his limited ability to rise further, his circle of names would have to improve. Thomson felt no qualms about contemplating his own advancement in this way in the midst of such a crisis. Some opened doors, and some had doors opened for them. It was that simple. And there were plenty of precedents to quote in either category.

'Meanwhile,' Winthrop continued, 'we shall look for any opportunity to seize the initiative out here.'

279

'Righty-ho, Major. I'll keep you informed as news comes in. I'd best stay at the centre of things myself in the terminal. I shall send my adjutant out with any developments.'

'Thank you, sir.'

Winthrop was tempted to add, 'And don't forget to get yourself on The Six O'Clock News.'

Part Three

15

The Trumpets Shall Sound

DOWNING Street, for all its apparent vulnerability and air of bungling amateurism, is one of the best organised and swiftest reacting seats of Government anywhere in the world. Tightly-knit, with clear chains of command throughout the UK and within the highly professional permanent civil service, it is capable of coordinating and commanding in any crisis. This was a crisis. Its responses throughout would be appropriate, timeous and decisive, much to the relief of those further down the line.

Within minutes of the alerts from Dounreay and Sellafield being relayed to the Home Secretary he was in conference with his Prime Minister. They would be joined within the hour by the Secretaries of State for Defence and Foreign Affairs, and by the Joint Chiefs of Staff of the Armed Services.

Troops were ordered to the three most likely airports, and safe conduct was immediately sanctioned for the plutonium consignment from Cumbria to Glasgow.

Colonel Thomson's request for a Hercules C-130 Transporter was sanctioned thirty minutes thereafter.

Later that afternoon the full Cabinet would meet to discuss and decide on the options put to them by the inner cabinet.

The Prime Minister, Eleanor Savage, gazed adoringly into

the eyes only six inches away from her own. She adjusted a few wisps of hair that had somehow managed to escape the attentions of the aerosol lacquer and moved away from the mirror. She made her way downstairs to the Cabinet Room, knowing full well that the next two hours would be a waste of time. The decisions had already been taken at the council of war, as she thought of it. Still, one had to go through the motions of collective cabinet responsibility no matter how tedious.

Outside No. 10, the entrance to Downing Street at Whitehall was still swamped by a mass of media personnel and by the usual curious throng which gathers from nowhere when anything out of the ordinary seems to be happening. This was one occasion when no-one was to be disappointed.

The Rovers, Daimlers and odd London taxis had arrived at regular intervals from the nearby Ministries. Ever-patient 'bobbies' had ushered them through the crowds to deposit their pampered passengers at the hallowed steps. And what an assortment they were. Concerned, grim-faced saviours of the nation. Ever-alert vote-winners beaming at the cameras and crowds. Smug leaders of men who disdained to recognise any but their own presence. The feigned boredom of those who had been summoned too many times to care.

The onlookers, many of whom were foreign tourists who could not believe their good fortune at witnessing so much high-powered activity during their round of the sights, clapped politely as each notable acknowledged their presence.

When the Secretary for Trade and Industry was helped out of his car and onto his crutches the crowd cheered wildly at the pluck of the man who had lost so much in the IRA bombing outrage at the 1984 Tory Conference in Brighton. Even some of the hard-bitten media people briefly joined in.

Security, as always, seemed lax, but appearances can be deceptive. It was noticeable that no time was wasted in getting Ministers inside the safety of No. 10. Armed and watchful though they were from roof, window and street level, the security men could never rule out the possibility of some sort of kamikaze attack erupting from nowhere. Since the resurgence of IRA activities in November 1984, and the Americans' continued reluctance to condemn Noraid despite passionate pleas from the British, the security forces had doubled their efforts to provide adequate protection to leading politicians. There would be no more hoax bombs placed on the steps of No. 10 by phoney photographers. But they could never be 100 per cent sure. No-one knows better than a security officer just how difficult it is to defend against all eventualities.

They could breathe a sigh of relief once their charges had crossed the threshold of the PM's residence. Over £1m had recently been spent on improving its defences. Four layers of thickened reinforced glass on every window could stop a mortar attack. Electronic sensors and video scanners guaranteed safety from intrusion from any angle on, above or below the ground. Apart from the Royal Family's nuclear shelter at Bath, it was one of the safest places in Britain to be. Unless one was at the receiving end of an explosion from the redoubtable lady herself. There was no protection at ground zero for anyone when she blasted off, as the bungling ministers for education, finance and social services had recently found out.

Unlike some of the newcomers in her newly reshuffled Cabinet who were nervously tasting their first major crisis in politics, Eleanor Savage had a pronounced orgasmic glow about her when she entered the room. One fawning junior minister would dwell on this in his memoirs to come. She got a thrill out of power politics which she had never experienced in any other area of her life. Her beloved Archie did try his best; but then he never had a cruise missile down his Y-fronts, as the leader of the Opposition wryly commented off-camera on one occasion. To his eternal embarrassment – not to mention the hapless Archie's – the BBC had inadvertently (so they later protested) left the recorders running. The transcripts were quickly leaked to the gutter press by an enterprising technician. The cartoonists had had a field day. Sales of boxer shorts rocketed as smart advertisers saw the potential.

At any rate Mrs Savage was revelling in this God-given opportunity to direct popular discontent away from herself and her morally bankrupt Party. Four million people – a larger number than in the Great Depression of the 1930s – were languishing in unemployment and all its attendant miseries. Callously written off in the PM's over-simplistic approach to macro-economics, a pattern of ever-increasing social unrest was sweeping the country. Boredom allied to a sense of hopelessness and failure had led tens of thousands into physical and mental depression. An even greater number had vented their frustration in soccer riots, street fights and racial clashes. The year-long miners' strike had left a bitter taste throughout the nation, and old class prejudices had been clearly evident in the case of some miners convicted of more serious crimes than they had committed. The Chancellor had been unable to deliver on his promises to keep inflation down and output up. Major misjudgements had been made over the demise of the Greater London Council, and there had been unwarranted interference in the affairs of just about every other council in Britain. The country was in one hell of a state. With this plethora of evidence that their policies were not working over a wide spectrum, Savage's Tory government was at an all-time low. Great politicians of the past, like Sir Robert Peel, had had the grace to totally reverse policies in the national interest. This lady was on a collision course with destiny. And God help destiny if it did not step aside. She was now the least popular of all Party leaders in the opinion polls, and the Tories a clear third in the ratings. That was saying something given the death-throe struggles to reform the Labour Party and preserve the factious Liberal/SDP Alliance.

This would all change now, the PM rightly sensed.

She called the meeting to order with her customary throat-clearing and shuffling of papers.

'We are all aware of the enormity of the problem confronting us,' she began tersely and rather predictably.

'The Home Secretary and I sent the Army into position at Glasgow airport and authorised compliance with the immediate demands of the terrorists shortly after lunchtime. At this very moment an RAF Transporter is being prepared and could arrive at Glasgow around 8pm this evening. We have until then to decide what action to take.'

At this point the PM turned towards the Army general sitting to her right.

'We shall now review the military aspects of the situation.'

General Willowby knew the icy smile directed his way was all the introduction he was going to get. Not that he needed any, he reflected smugly. At fifty-one years of age his reputation was clearly established as a key player in the upper echelons of the armed forces. In the 1983 election campaign, which returned the Tories with an increased majority in the afterglow of the one-sided Argentinian armed adventure, there had been vicious rioting between Socialist and National Front factions. Willowby's decisiveness, tactical and strategic skills had been a major factor in the prevention of wider national disruption. So, too, had been his illegal use of regular soldiers disguised as police officers.

His neat, near-feminine frame sprang with feline grace from his seat at the bottom end of the table to materialise beside the large map of the Mediterranean and Near East which had been temporarily suspended to the left of the marble fire surround.

'Prime Minister, Ministers,' he nodded curtly in turn. Damned if he was going to appear overawed or deferential.

'For the past three hours the Joint Chiefs have been considering the options open to us. As you will see, none is without its drawbacks.' He wisely repressed the strong temptation to grin at this gross understatement.

'First, and most obviously, we could go straight in at Glasgow. The SAS and The Queen's Own have both the plane and the plutonium surrounded. There is no doubt in our minds that we could seize both, albeit with some loss of life.'

'Some loss of life?' Mrs Savage was incredulous. 'Some? Do the Joint Chiefs have any realisation of the casualties that would result if the terrorists carry out their threat of detonating the plutonium?'

'It is our considered opinion that this would not happen. We know these men are ruthless; but it is doubtful that they would resort to such an extremity.'

'Doubtful?' The Secretary for Northern Ireland joined in the discussion. 'Have you any evidence that these men are any more responsible than the IRA? It has been one of our strongest recurring nightmares that our friends across the water would get hold of a similar consignment. We have absolutely no doubts whatever that, in similar circumstances, they would gladly remove Glasgow – Maryhill and all,' he referred to the immigrant Irish stronghold, 'from the map to gain some major political advantage.'

The Secretary of State for Scotland, a pillar of the Edinburgh establishment, chuckled inwardly with satisfaction at such a scenario. Needless to say he did not venture the opinion. Not at the Cabinet meeting at any rate. He would wait until the security of the Scottish Tory Party conference in Perth the following month before sharing that one with a few grandees.

'Point taken, Minister,' Willowby continued unflustered. 'However we have every reason to believe that, in the event, the plutonium could not be exploded. The consignment is carried in casks, or flasks, designed to the most demanding international transport standards. In German tests to simulate a Phantom jet crashing into them the casks were only superficially damaged. The jet engines weighing one tonne each were compressed from three metres long to only 500mm on impact. It appears that the terrorists have wired up some 100lbs of plastic explosives. We doubt whether this could possibly create more damage than having the containers dropped from 30,000 feet, another test which they have easily withstood.'

'Sir Charles?' The PM invited her Chief Scientific Adviser to interject. Now in his seventy-third year, Sir Charles Waters was ready and more than able to enter the lists against the General, whose attitude he did not in the least like. As versatile as the PM herself, but infinitely more distinguished, he had led the Atomic Energy Authority throughout the pioneering days from 1953 to 1964 when Britain led the world. A Nobel scientist in the late '40s, he had only recently retired from a twenty year spell as Master of his old college. And he had still found the time to pen an award-winning series of novels.

'30,000 feet; 2000 feet: makes no difference, my boy.'

Willowby had not been so addressed since leaving Charterhouse over thirty years ago.

'Terminal velocity is what counts. 200mph on impact

regardless of height over 2000 feet. Not that Sir Isaac was in a position to verify that one, though.' Sir Charles did allow himself a grin.

'However, that is hardly relevant. What is relevant is that the casks General Willowby has referred to are not the same as the ones the terrorists have their hands on.'

This revelation stunned the entire Cabinet – Willowby included.

'Normally,' Sir Charles continued, obviously enjoying the drama of the occasion, 'fully-enriched plutonium-239 is formed into ceramic pellets, wrapped in several layers of steel, placed in stainless steel drums, then finally packed into the special casks the General has been telling us about. However, Arthur confirmed on the phone half-an-hour ago that this particular shipment is in containers which have not undergone such rigorous testing.'

Feeling threatened, the new Energy Minister resorted to the habitual refuge of the politician. He launched into an effusive assault on the critical faculties of Sir Arthur Norman, Chairman of British Nuclear Fuels Limited. Before he had a chance to go very far, Sir Charles jumped to his friend's defence.

'Come now, Minister,' he chided the forty-eight year old schoolboy. 'BNFL are a competent lot. They know what they are on about. And none more so than Sir Arthur. The containers in use have been tested to endure phenomenally high temperatures, and, although only ever dropped from around forty feet, the Company are confident they could withstand an air crash.'

'But why not use proven containers?' The Energy Minister would regret asking.

'Basically because there is no need to,' Sir Charles lectured him. 'This consignment consists of a plutonium and oxide fuel. It is much more stable than the fully enriched plutonium these special containers were designed for.'

'In other words, Sir Charles,' General Willowby thought a small opening had just presented itself, 'this consignment, even if subjected to a strong explosion, could not go critical and create a thermonuclear blast? In that case our first option is still on.'

'Not so.' Sir Charles now directed himself at the Prime Minister whom he knew was easily the most able person in the room.

'You see, the danger facing us is not that there might be a nuclear explosion. That is impossible with plutonium oxide in its present form. Rather, the danger is twofold. First, if these containers were to be split, and the pellets crushed in the open air, there would be massive damage from inhalation of plutonium dust. Microscopic fragments are fatal. Second, the shipment also contains about a score of deadly radioactive isotopes for use in checking equipment at Dounreay. These isotopes give off gamma radiation and must be handled with the utmost caution.'

'What you are saying, Sir Charles, is that there would not just be some loss of life, as General Willowby put it, if this lot goes up?' Mrs Savage put on her most concerned simper.

'My dear.' Sir Charles sent a sad smile across to his favourite politician. 'In an area as densely populated as Glasgow and Strathclyde there could be at least 200,000 dead within three days. Even without a thermonuclear blast,' this last comment fired broadside at Willowby. 'Moreover, the prolonged dangers from contamination to food and water supplies are almost incalculable.' He shook his snowy head.

'Thank you, Sir Charles. I take it we do not wish to explore this scenario any further?' The PM's question to the rest of the Cabinet was purely rhetorical.

'Please continue, General.'

'Thank you, Prime Minister.' Willowby, now that his first scheme had been so profoundly thrashed, had adopted a slightly more deferential tone.

'As we seem to have no option but to accede to the terrorists' demands for transport out of Britain, two courses of action are available to us. We either take out the Hercules en route to the Middle East; or we allow them to return to Dhubat and arrange a counter-strike of our own.'

He paused to allow the awesome implications of both to sink in. Turning to the map behind him he continued.

'As you can see, the most direct route to the Gulf – unlike that followed by Concorde which has to keep its supersonic boom over sea and desert as far as possible – is this one here.'

He traced the most likely airways across south-east Europe and Asia Minor. 'The Hercules, equipped with auxiliary tanks, can do this quite easily in one hop. In order to minimise the dangers of radio-active fallout, a groundstrike would be preferable to an airstrike. We could easily rig the fuel gauges to force them down in, say, central Turkey or Syria and hit them there, or we simply take them out over the least populated area along the route – in southern Iraq over the Al Widian or Al Hajara deserts.'

'Good God, man,' exploded Richard Blacklaw, the Foreign Secretary. In his excitement he momentarily forgot that not only expletives but even minor blasphemies were anathema to Mrs Savage.

'This is unthinkable! Not only would we be laying ourselves open to the charge of placing lives of UK citizens above those of, er, less fortunate areas, but the global repercussions would be disastrous. Turkey is a fellow member of NATO and CENTO. We would wreck both alliances,' he added, forgetting that the latter had been disbanded in 1979. 'Syria and Iraq are both Arab League countries – I do not have to spell out to this assembly the effects which any such unilateral action on our behalf would have on the delicate position in the Middle East. And if we were to upset that particular applecart our transatlantic friends would not be too favourably disposed towards us after the billions they have poured in since the Carter Agreement. Quite preposterous!'

'Precisely, Richard. Nor would the Soviet Union sit back during any of this.' Teddy Forrest, the young Scottish Secretary fawningly anticipated the only woman in his life apart from Mummy. Once described by a Trotskyist opponent in an Edinburgh University debate as being several goose-steps to the right of Attila the Hun, Forrest was, like Mrs Savage, one of the few surviving Russophobes in space-age Britain. 'The fall-out on Russian soil would provide them with sufficient excuse for retaliation against Britain.'

'Hardly likely, Teddy.' Virginia Elsham, Minister for the Environment, corrected him. 'As I recall, the dominant direction of the winds at this time of year over the Middle East and the Arabian Peninsula is towards the south and south-west. Away from the USSR.' With her First in

Geography and Meteorological Studies – hardly 'Greats', as some of the more traditional academics within the Party had muttered on her appointment to the Cabinet – Forrest was not going to take her on on this insignificant point of detail. He only backed certainties.

However, before Forrest could warm to his theme, this youngest member of the Cabinet (promoted far beyond his years and abilities by a PM seduced by his flatteries) was forced, with the rest of his colleagues, to listen further to the ever-garrulous Foreign Secretary who thought himself the only one entitled to exhibit more than a superficial grasp of international affairs. He wittered on about China's role in the ensuing crisis, making a great deal of Chinese aid to Iraq, before the PM cut him off quite brusquely.

'Quite, Richard. Which would seem to rule out the Joint Chiefs' second option.'

The icy smile with which she had introduced Willowby had now hardened into a frozen scowl as she invited him to become Aunt Sally for the last time.

Not that Willowby was surprised to see option two fall so summarily. The military had been fully aware of the international ramifications and the all too real danger of sparking off a thermonuclear World War Three. They had felt obliged, however, to put forward all of the alternatives regardless of the credence they themselves attached to each one. Option three was different, and the one favoured by all the top brass; which was why it was presented last.

'We seem to be left with only one viable scenario.' Willowby was back to his calm, totally self-assured best. 'And that is to allow the terrorists to return to Dhubat.

'It would not be easy, Prime Minister; but we could organise some sort of action to neutralise the threat of the Dhubatis turning the plutonium ploughshares into swords.' He had taken a lead from Sir Charles and ignored the rest of the Cabinet at this crucial juncture in his presentation.

'But, General, thanks to our Labour predecessors we have no troops at our disposal in the Arabian Peninsula or the Indian Ocean. And a Task Force would take such a long time to organise.'

She shuddered with delight at the memory of the Falklands

and at the prospect of little Dhubat allowing her to write another glorious saga in the annals of English history as the only other female Prime Minister had done before her.

'With respect, Prime Minister. We had envisaged a small commando-type force going in and out as quickly as possible. We have some experience of this sort of thing.' General Willowby modestly understated the unique achievements and skills of the SAS and SBS to date.

Eleanor Savage could have bitten her tongue off for making this polemical blunder. She was no longer in Opposition and could well afford to let some opportunities for scoring cheap political points pass. Old habits die hard. She made a mental note to doctor the Cabinet minute to make no mention of her gaffe.

'But surely many of the objections we have rehearsed against the first two options apply equally here? There could be massive contamination, widespread loss of life, and all the dangers of a more general conflagration.' Virginia Elsham would not go far in politics.

'I think not, Minister.' Willowby was determined not to have this option turned down.

'We shall be dealing with the terrorists on their own soil. There is no way they are going to detonate the plutonium in their own backyard. They will have their ultimate bargaining ploy removed, which would give us every chance of bringing out the hostages.'

It was strange, thought Sir Charles, but up to this moment, in almost two hours of debate, no-one had even mentioned saving the hostages. Important though they were, they would have been sacrificed without a moment's thought if need be.

Now that the matter had come up, Mrs Savage was quick to see the public relations advantages.

'Yes, General.' The icy smile had returned, much to Willowby's relief.

'Of course, Prime Minister.' General Willowby decided to be deferential at last. Mrs Savage beamed at him. She had known he would eventually.

'We would propose to limit ourselves to the rescue of the hostage scientists and to neutralising the capacity of the nuclear plant in Dhubat. It would be a bonus if we could bring out the plutonium too.'

'And how soon could your, er, commandos be ready to move out, General?'

'We are in a constant state of readiness, Ma'am.'

Willowby knew instantly from her eyes that this regal reference had clinched the day.

'We could be in Dhubat waiting for our friends to arrive, if need be. However, a few weeks planning would not only significantly increase our chances of success, but would also lull the Dhubatis into a false sense of security.'

'In that case we look forward to meeting you again, General.'

Mrs Savage was not speaking on behalf of her colleagues.

The Cabinet meeting was over.

16

There Came Chariots

GEORGE Taylor knew the route well, but he had always hated the highly dangerous, antiquated dual carriageway A74 which was Glasgow's, and therefore Scotland's, main link to the south. Like most Scots drivers and a few English he had never failed to notice the anomaly of Britain's splendid motorway system suddenly stopping at the border with Scotland. No wonder so many Jocks wanted independence (though he could never figure out why so few voted for it when they got the chance). And not a few Geordies would be averse to joining them.

Today the only difference George could notice as he moved steadily northwards was the larger than usual number of police outriders attached to his little convoy. That, and the helicopter scouting the road ahead. Otherwise things looked quite normal.

They were not.

The authorities had decided against the near-impossibility of closing the A74 to other traffic as soon as it was clear that Glasgow was the likely destination. That apart, a full-scale civil defence exercise was under way from Cumbria to Strathclyde. Medical and fire services; police and regular army detachments; local government emergency planning teams. All were on red alert and ready to swing into well-rehearsed action the second a disaster situation seemed inevitable. Meantime there was no point in spreading panic throughout the civilian population by alarmist precautionary measures. There would be panic enough when the afternoon and early evening news reports were broadcast, despite the government's attempts to impose a news blackout.

At the Hamilton intersection on the token piece of M74 motorway just outside Glasgow a brief stop was ordered by Nahaz Khan, the terrorist leader, at the service station. The Sierra Cosworth carrying Alister Graham hostage was allowed to join the procession in return for the freedom of the two wounded policemen who desperately needed medical attention.

They continued on the A776 to East Kilbride, thence on the A726 through Paisley, by-passing central Glasgow, to the airport.

'Who Dares Wins' is the motto of Britain's proudest specialist regiment. No-one knew better than SAS Major Jeremy Winthrop that this was not always the case. Because of its largely covert nature, few of the SAS's failures make national news. But the members of the fighting elite know. They are taught to learn by their mistakes; and they do.

So it was with a sense of relief deep within himself that Winthrop acknowledged the order, conveyed via Colonel Thomson, to stand down and co-operate with Hurion's demands for safe passage out of the UK. The odds against in this instance really did seem insuperable, even for his crack team. And no SAS unit took kindly to being used as a training exemplar of how not to do it. Sometimes, just sometimes, it was comforting to be subservient to the politicians.

'Pussyfooting, spineless bastards,' Winthrop spat at his number two as The Queen's Own Colonel's adjutant went back to join his CO in the relative safety of the terminal building.

'We could have taken them out, Marcus. No sweat.'

Captain Peters said nothing.

He knew that his boss knew that he knew too.

The Lockheed C-130 Hercules is the Trojan workhorse of the world's airforces from Abu Dhabi to Zaire. As XV305 taxied in close to the passenger terminal at Glasgow airport it dwarfed the Viscount, the plutonium shipment and the nearby army trucks.

Even in the full and certain knowledge that Downing Street must have authorised compliance with Hurion's orders, the Dhubatis were taking no chances.

The plutonium transfer was made first. It took all of ninety minutes to achieve, due mainly to the Glasgow staff's inexperience with this type of load. The prominent display of plastic explosives which remained in place around the deadly cargo throughout the manoeuvre might also have had something to do with the more-than-usual care given to the freight package.

Hurion's men were well aware that their most vulnerable moments would be during the changeover from the Viscount to the Hercules. Unlike the hijacks at Wick and Dounreay, the Dhubatis would now be surrounded by a score of the finest marksmen in the British Army. To counter any temptation, Major Winthrop was reminded that the Viscount and the plutonium were wired, and that the Viscount crew of three would remain trapped in their seats throughout the passenger compartment until a safe exchange had been made. These precautions were unnecessary. Winthrop was no mad major from the African bush. He had received his orders. He would carry them out.

There would be another day.

For such a massive plane – it is almost one hundred feet long, forty feet high, with a wingspan of over one hundred and thirty feet – the cockpit of a Hercules is rather cramped. The four main seats are for the pilot, co-pilot, navigator and systems engineer. The designers at Lockheed-Georgia Co had allowed for a fifth occupant – say a mission supervisor or trainer. At the point of take-off this jump seat was occupied by Hurion.

He would be spelled at two-hour intervals by his colleagues during the twelve hour flight at the plane's best economical cruising rate of 295 knots.

The moment the Hercules began to taxi for take-off, the four-man bomb disposal team from the Queen's Own Highlanders rushed on board the Viscount. It took only a few moments to cut the hostage crew free and send them to safety before the risky work of de-fusing began.

As the big plane gathered speed down the runway Captain Greene, Kirsty Falconer and David Grant, freed from their bonds, ran down the narrow aisle of their aeroplane.

At this precise instant Kassim activated the transmitter which demolished the old Viscount and a good part of the terminal building.

17

Behold A Pale Horse

THE use of slave labour was not exclusive to the Egyptians, Assyrians and Romans of old. British, European and American fortunes, as seen in many a resplendent house lovingly shown by national heritage groups, were built on slavery and the iniquitous slave trade in the seventeenth and eighteenth centuries. But, like many a historical evil, it has been refined to perfection by twentieth century mankind. No-one who has visited the war graves at Kanchanaburi or the death camp museum on the banks of the River Kwai can ever forget the horrors of Japanese brutality on the Burma Railroad. The present-day prosperity of many a German burgher, whether they are aware of it or are prepared to acknowledge it, has its foundation in the Hitler era of wartime conscripted labour of subjugated peoples.

But for the most systematic and brutal exploitation of forced labour Stalin's Soviet Union will hopefully never be surpassed. Roads, canals, dams, mines, factories, farms, even the much-vaunted Moscow underground so beloved of Intourist guides, all share the same foundations: the bones of millions of 'zeks'. How many will never be ascertained, but estimates range from six to twenty million lost souls. Conditions for all but a tiny minority were appalling. The lucky few were the scientists, engineers and mathematicians who were incarcerated in the relatively luxurious 'sharashkas' – up-market slave camps where the prisoners ate and slept reasonably well, and were given a tolerable environment in which to carry out their experimental and development work tasks. Peter Hargreaves was not unfamiliar with all this. But little had he dreamt back in 1968 when he read Alexander Solzhenitsyn's exposé that he himself would one day become a member of such a privileged 'First Circle'. Albeit in surroundings of comfort undreamt of by Dante or the Russian dissident.

Of all those press-ganged into service in Dhubat, Hargreaves was the most philosophic. A kindly man in his early 60s, he had long since been widowed after his young wife's premature death of bowel cancer at the age of thirty-two. They had had no children, and Peter had never entertained any thoughts of remarriage. Some bereaved find solace in religion, some in family, some in alcohol, some in debauchery, some never. Hargreaves found his within himself. And within his work.

With only distant relatives in the UK, and with few local ties in the north of Scotland, he was almost happy to get on with the job in hand in his new surroundings. Especially as fascinating new scientific ground lay before him.

Hargreaves' kidnapped colleagues had required varying degrees of persuasion to co-operate. From the moment the plutonium consignment had trundled through the gates of Glasgow airport, each of the scientists had known exactly what was going to be required of them. Their initial briefing by Feisal al Alfi, Director of the Dhubati nuclear programme, had merely acted as confirmation of what these not unintelligent men had perfectly well deduced.

Dhubat already had the basic plant facilities through a

mixture of legitimate purchases from licensed suppliers, and clandestine dealings with the shady and highly dangerous international nuclear mafia. They already had the people with most of the theoretical skills to carry out the conversion work. Nuclear science knows few national or linguistic boundaries. The symbolic formulae are a sort of pictographic Esperanto accessible to all with the eyes to see. Almost any junior honours student could produce an explosive device of sorts given the proper materials and facilities. What the British scientists would provide in a crash programme where there was no room for error or blind research alleys was essentially practical experience, leadership and quality management.

That is if they chose to co-operate.

They chose to co-operate.

Within a week of arrival in Dhubat the scientists, normally isolated from each other on the site, were brought together for an animated slide sequence of Margaret Brocklehurst's shop in Thurso being blown to smithereens minutes before Mrs Mackenzie, the manageress, arrived to open it for the day.

A dossier on both women's day-to-day routines was shown.

The implications did not have to be stated.

Three days later, with Brocklehurst now hard at work with Hargreaves, Alan Cameron and Alister Graham sullenly began to get on with things.

At 05.00 that morning they had been taken down to a basement and forced to witness the garrotting of a terrified Sir James Gartshore by one of Hurion's thugs.

With the last dispensable hostage now gone they did not want the two Thurso ladies on their conscience.

The physician attending Alan Cameron had been genuinely puzzled. The dozens of tests she had run on her patient had all proved negative. Yet the symptoms could not be denied. He had lost twenty pounds in the three weeks since coming to Dhubat. Not surprising given his loss of appetite, despite the dietician's flair and concern. His gut and bowels were in turmoil. Eyes bloodshot; face gaunt; mouth and gums ulcerated. Constant headaches and insomnia. Listless to the point of barely functioning during the working day; socially withdrawn at leisure. He was like a man haunted.

Just as puzzling to the eminently well-qualified doctor was the way in which the distraught engineer suddenly returned to normality. Had Alan Cameron been more communicative and Dr Taslima Rahman more perceptive, the diagnosis would have been straightforward – acute grief reaction.

Cameron had been haunted – by the memory of his beloved Karyn and her mindless, brutal death.

And then he had found a new sense of purpose.

Alister Graham had no such problems. Possessed of a cast-iron constitution and the ability to doze off in a tumble drier, he was thriving in the cossetted luxury of the sheikhdom. Once he had been coerced into co-operation he saw no need to deny himself the occasional delights of Shamin when she made herself available. Why the hell not? She had only been doing her job. And now he would do his. But in his own way and at his own pace.

There were more ways than one to throw a few tools in the works.

Brocklehurst was delighted with the progress of the project under his oversight. The team were cracking on with things. And none more so than Alan Cameron's sector. Brocklehurst had long been aware of Cameron's brilliance and ingenuity; but the sheer pace and insatiable appetite for work of the man astounded him now. It was reminiscent of his relentless drive back in 1972 to overcome the leak at the Dounreay reactor. And, in an inverse way, it was.

Pressurised water reactors present a mesmerising sight to the lay person. Their complexity overwhelms the casual visitor who senses something almost magical at work. Nuclear engineers, however, are not being diffident when they reduce the mystical wonders to basics – pumps, cooling pipes, waste conduits, pressure gauges, temperature gauges, fuel rods. To the informed that is all they are. No-one had to tell Alan Cameron what was what. Although this particular plant was new to him, it was simply a variation on a basic theme he knew well from both a practical and theoretical viewpoint.

The Franco-German consortium which had built the Dhubati facility had basically used the Westinghouse PWR design favoured in France over the Babcock and Wilcox design which had gone awry at Three Mile Island in March 1979. It was still not foolproof. French officials at the time of the Pennsylvania disaster freely admitted that their reactors had developed similar faults, but with much less serious consequences. The greatest advantage in the Westinghouse design is that the steam generators have a much higher water capacity than those in the Babcock and Wilcox system. In an emergency this gives the operators over seven times as long to bring the situation under control before a fatal reaction sets in.

To this inherently safer design the Germans had added a few refinements. Their input came from the Kraftwerk–Union people. As was common in German atomic power plants, not one but two additional cooling systems were built in. With extra automation and electronics it was impossible to manually shut down a cooling system, as had been done in America. This joint design, together with a far higher degree of operator training, rendered accidental damage of the kind which had driven the Harrisburg reactor to a critical state impossible.

No. If the Dhubati plant was going to malfunction in a spectacular fashion it would have to be deliberately engineered. And no-one was better qualified or more motivated than Alan Cameron.

International pressures on Dhubat and on the British government had been as intense as predicted in Cabinet. The United Nations Security Council had characteristically talked of imposing wide-ranging economic and political sanctions on Dhubat. These would never materialise due to the self-interest of member states. The Americans, ever mindful of their friends in Israel and of the need to preserve whatever fragile semblance of peace existed in the Middle East, urged caution and conciliation. The Soviet Union warned of the dire consequences of unilateral action for world peace. The British press, apart from urging the seizure of all Dhubati assets in Britain, was as utterly divided as ever.

The British Prime Minister's mind was correctly read by the xenophobic jingoism of The Sun newspaper which declared:

WE'RE GONNA GETCHA

echoing their joy over what many considered to have been the cold-blooded murder of the crew of the Belgrano in the Falklands War as it was in the course of complying with British orders.

The only person in the world better qualified or more motivated than Alan Cameron was about to go into action.

The radar operators at the Dhubati military airbase near the border with Qasar were good. They had been tracking the RAF Hercules Transporter at its 33,000 feet service ceiling for the last twenty-five minutes as it approached Dhubati airspace. Ninety seconds before they scrambled a couple of

Super Etendard fighter interceptors the Hercules turned back, just ten miles from the border.

No operator in the world – indeed no radar system in the world – could have identified the eight SAS men gliding silently down through the desert darkness across the border and deep into Dhubat. No photosensitive satellite or terrestrial monitor was capable of recording the insistent infra-red signals which linked the direction-finders built into each paratrooper's helmet to keep the men together as they manoeuvred the specialist parachutes.

They landed thirty-five miles inside Dhubat at 01.00 hours. Just before dawn, at 05.00, they had penetrated a further twenty-four miles. Four nights later, the fluent Arabic-speaking squad, unhampered now by their flowing Bedouin robes, were dug in within sight of the reactor complex.

Unlike Hurion's men at Dounreay they were denied a guided tour courtesy of their hosts. They supplemented their detailed briefings on the Westinghouse–Kraftwerk blueprints with visual observations of security routines. They did not like what they could see. They could only guess at what they could not.

On the third night, at 03.00, they donned respirator masks and went into battle.

The plan was quite simple.

Unlike the Americans in the Teheran desert in April 1980 they would not call up six AC-130 Hercules, eight Sikorsky RH-53D helicopters, and an assault force of ninety US marines to rescue the hostages and retrieve the plutonium.

The British, in time-honoured fashion, would go for the groin. Knock out the factory and the materials become redundant. Save the hostage labour force if you can. But if you cannot, knock out the factory. Everyone in Britain had seen The Heroes of Telemark at least twice. Forty years on, eight SAS warriors would do nicely. And one Hawk helicopter screaming in to get them the hell out of it when it was over.

The operational nerve centre of any nuclear plant is the

reactor itself. Such is the intensity of radiation produced that the surrounding environment must be protected by a biological shield of reinforced concrete several metres thick. These walls, floor and roof are together known as the containment vessel. Every reactor has one. It has to, or no operator could survive within five miles of it. Like a Russian matryoshka doll this protective vessel conceals another – the pressure vessel. This surrounds the inner core of fuel elements. Its primary function is to resist the intense pressure of the water used to cool the highly fissile reactor core.

To breach such defences by conventional methods would require many tons of TNT. Eight commandos cannot cover six miles every hour of the night with this sort of backpack. And camels cannot be trained to operate Four Sail parachutes with precision in total darkness.

Fortunately, there is a much simpler solution. Knock out the coolant system by cutting off its supply of water and you have a catastrophic core melt-down in less than sixty seconds. At 3300 degrees Fahrenheit the China Syndrome develops. The reactor core begins to collapse. At 3600 degrees it triggers melt-down. The fuel elements melt and the resultant super-hot molten mass – about twice as hot as lava from an erupting volcano – burns through the containment vessel into the earth and 'all the way to China' – or wherever the antipodes is located from the reactor site. Massive amounts of long-lived radioactivity are released.

Alan Cameron and Alister Graham had failed to bring about this scenario, stymied as much by strict surveillance as by the sophisticated automation of the Franco-German design.

The SAS team were confident of success. Their offensive chemical weapons, sanctioned by Margaret Thatcher in 1980 along with Cruise missiles and Trident, would deal with whatever opposition they met. 0.4 milligrams were fatal if inhaled. Once at the reactor core plastic explosives would do the rest.

The eight brave soldiers died to a man long before they could breach the inner security of the reactor vessel.

The Dhubati guards inside the building did not inhale the requisite amounts of VX nerve gas.

They wore respirator masks too.

And they had far more firepower than their assailants.

18

A Sign In Heaven

NO visitors are allowed on the island of Diego Garcia.

In 1965 it would have been a pleasure to go there. A tiny, sand-fringed coral atoll, undisturbed by the cyclonic storms which ravage many an Indian Ocean island. Eighteen hundred inhabitants who subsisted happily on coconut palms, guano and turtles in a year-round temperature of twenty-five to twenty-nine degrees Celsius.

But in 1965 'Great' Britain stole Diego Garcia from Mauritius. In 1966 the UK leased it to the USA as a re-fueling base for the US Air Force and the US Navy.

By the early '70s the last of the natives had been deported; and by the '80s nearly every square inch of this once idyllic island was covered in concrete – harbour facilities, runways for B52 nuclear bombers, satellite communications, fuel dumps, living quarters for the five thousand US servicemen and British Royal Marines stationed there.

Such an annexation and militarisation was an affront in a United Nations designated zone of peace. It was bitterly contested, to no avail, by every country bordering the Indian Ocean.

No-one would want to go there now. Unless you were the crew of the British nuclear submarine breaking your return journey to Faslane in Scotland from your mission to the Gulf of Oman. Diego Garcia was no Pattaya; but its rest and recreation facilities would be most welcome before another twenty-two days and nine-and-a-half thousand miles beneath the surface.

The lightly-armed Polaris missile launched from HMS Repellent had unerringly sought out its target in Dhubat. It did not just knock out the coolant system and trigger the dreaded China Syndrome. It vapourised the reactor, the hijacked plutonium and everyone within one thousand metres of ground zero.

Back in London, the Prime Minister gently hummed her favourite old Sinatra melody as she tried in vain to complete The Sunday Telegraph enigmatic variations crossword. She would never write her memoirs with that elusive, and highly-prized, fountain pen, even if her rightful frame of mind were to return.